Acclaim for
The Realms Thereunder

"*The Realms Thereunder* is a fantastically compelling novel mixing the best of fantasy, adventure, and intrigue. It's one of those can't-put-down tales you'll be thinking about long after turning the last page. Fans of C. S. Lewis, the Inkheart Trilogy, and of course Stephen Lawhead will find much to enjoy in this well-crafted read."

—C.J. DARLINGTON, TITLETRAKK.COM;
AUTHOR OF *BOUND BY GUILT*

"With beautiful imagery, thoughtful imagination, and a touch of humor, *The Realms Thereunder* is an excellent beginning to an insightful and exciting new fantasy series."

—MELISSA WILLIS, THECHRISTIANMANIFESTO.COM

"For lovers of Stephen Lawhead, his influence shines through in this story of fantasy, reality and everything in between!"

—LORI TWICHELL, RADIANTLIT.COM

THE ANCIENT EARTH TRILOGY
BOOK TWO:

A HERO'S THRONE

ROSS LAWHEAD

THOMAS NELSON
Since 1798

NASHVILLE DALLAS MEXICO CITY RIO DE JANEIRO

Published in Nashville, Tennessee, by Thomas Nelson. Thomas Nelson is a registered trademark of Thomas Nelson, Inc.

Thomas Nelson, Inc., titles may be purchased in bulk for educational, business, fund-raising, or sales promotional use. For information, please e-mail SpecialMarkets@ThomasNelson.com.

Publisher's Note: This novel is a work of fiction. Names, characters, places, and incidents are either products of the author's imagination or used fictitiously. All characters are fictional, and any similarity to people living or dead is purely coincidental.

Library of Congress Cataloging-in-Publication Data

Lawhead, Ross.
  A hero's throne / Ross Lawhead.
    p. cm. — (The ancient earth trilogy ; bk. 2)
  ISBN 978-1-59554-910-5 (trade paper)
  1. Fantasy fiction. 2. Christian fiction. I. Title.
  PS3562.A864H47 2013
  813'.54—dc23   2012036812

Printed in the United States of America

12 13 14 15 16 17 QG 6 5 4 3 2 1

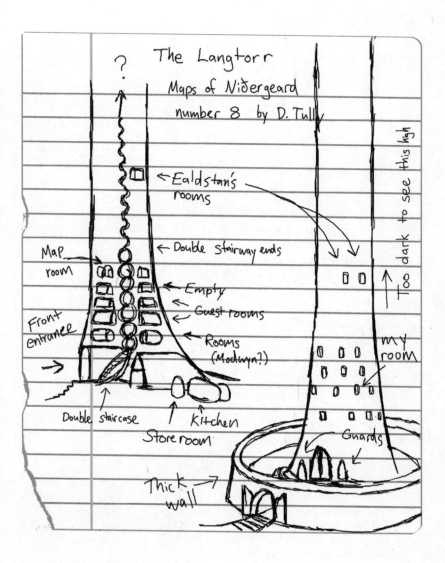

The Langtorr

Maps of Niðergeard

number 8   by D. Tull

?

← Ealdstan's rooms

Map room

← Double stairway ends

Front entrance →

← Empty

← Guest rooms

← Rooms (Modwyn?)

Too dark to see this high

my room

Double staircase

Kitchen

Storeroom

Thick wall →

Guards

What have the strong gods given?
Where have the glad gods led?
When Guthrum sits on a hero's throne
And asks if he is dead?

— G. K. CHESTERTON, THE BALLAD OF
   THE WHITE HORSE

For Mom—An inspiration to
adventuring heroines everywhere

A Tale of a Western Isle

So, this is my tale, and it happened a long time ago. A long, long time ago, before there were Christians in the Hebrides. And it's about this here monk, see, and this here boy.

The monk was from the low country, and he was travelling to Broadford in Skye in order to spread the word of God among the inhabitants of that island, for there were even then folk living on Skye, although they were from an old and strange people. This monk's name was Coel, and he was not native to those lands, but his name is remembered there still. He had a boat that was so small he had to sit in it cross-legged. This type of boat was called a coracle and was common in the time I am telling you about.

It was a damp, grey day on the sea—the type where a man didn't know if there was more water beneath the boat or in the air around it. The island of Skye ahead of him could not be seen at all, and the first he knew of it was when he heard the whisper of sand underneath the bottom of the boat. The monk was glad for this and gave thanks to God for not forgetting him in the fog.

Stepping out of the boat, water squished into his leather shoes as he made his way up the beach.

He drew his bark up behind him, toiling along the wet shore, and set it against a cluster of rocks and boulders in order to shelter himself from the wind and mist.

He had just made his camp when he heard the sound of voices raised in wails of lament, loud shrieks and shouts, awful they were.

He followed the sound of these tormented cries to the forest that lined the beach. There before him, walking through the trees and the mist, he saw a shifting line of figures dressed in clothes of fantastic colours and design. They were marching in procession behind a column of jet-black horses that hauled a silver skiff, upon which was a glass coffin, containing the body of a very old woman. She was very beautiful, even for being dead, and although the fantastic bier dragged on the ground, it never hit a bump or fell into a rut.

The monk was canny—canny enough to realise that it was a Færie funeral he was observing. Planting his walking stick into the ground, he knelt and, to protect himself, began to read to himself from the Gospels, keeping his eyes trained fast on his book. He read out loud so as to keep the holy words in his ears, so as to seal them, in a way, from the cries of the damned.

As he read, one of the members of the funeral train—a boy dressed all in green—left it and came and crouched in front of him. Coel did not raise his eyes to look at him, he merely kept reading.

The procession disappeared and the wailing diminished, eventually vanishing altogether. But the boy did not leave Coel's side, and so he continued reading, not wanting to allow himself to be tempted into follies.

He read on, straight through Matthew and, when he finished that, continued on to Mark. And from Mark he went to Luke, and

Luke on to John. And then he was finished; he had no more scriptures to read.

So he decided to pray—a long-winded and exhaustive prayer it was. He bowed his head low—very low, so as to shut out vision of the boy who might work enchantments on him to entice him away to destruction.

When he finished his prayer, he opened his eyes and looked around.

The boy was still there.

"I have marked all that you have read," the boy said. "Tell me, is there any hope of forgiveness in those words for my people?"

Coel spoke kindly but cautiously to him, fearing to be drawn into an enchantment. He said that there wasn't mention of salvation for any but the sinful sons of Adam.

Hearing this, the boy became disconsolate, and he picked up the wailing that he had laid down earlier and plunged himself into the sea.

CHAPTER ONE

"The Dragon Changed Everything . . ."

— I —

It is a golf hotel in Galashiels, just over the border. Gentle green slopes of the Scottish lowlands stretched into the distance, the pale, patchy greens only interrupted by an occasional blob of yellow.

They had driven through the day in the police cruiser, arriving at about six in the evening. Alex and Ecgbryt took turns driving. Freya drifted in and out of sleep, still exhausted from her ordeal. Daniel, next to her, gripped the door handle next to him so tightly it was as if he were the only thing holding it in place. Freya would look across to him in the moments when she awoke, and although his eyes were closed, he didn't seem to be sleeping.

They had taken two twin rooms—Daniel and Freya shared one and promptly fell asleep again. And now, on the restaurant's terrace after a hearty meal of meat, potatoes, and gravy, they were listening to Alex talk about dragons.

"It really did. I mean it—the dragon changed *everything*." Alex paused to let this sink in. "Before then, it was just simple creatures that we were dealing with—the low or single 'elementals' as they're called; trolls, sprites, wisps, that sort of thing. Those sorts wander through our borders all the time, causing trouble, and often wander back out again without anybody taking notice. They're not what you'd call complex creatures, so they can drop through the gates quite easily. When the gates are open, that is—there's sort of a season for it.

"Anyway. We'd noticed an increase in activity lately, but it was very gradual, and nothing we couldn't handle. Ecgbryt and I were monitoring it, and we thought we had more time.

"But dragons are a different kettle of fish all together. Talk about your complex elementals . . . They're actually many types of elements all layered together, wrapped up in one. And smart. So smart." He sat back, shaking his head. "Something like that doesn't just drop in from one world to another. It was brought here, possibly pulled here—*summoned*, maybe—or it was raised here, which is even more upsetting. So this was a new development. Its arrival was no accident or chance circumstance—it was pretty much a declaration of war."

"By who?" Daniel asked.

"That's a good question."

Alex took a long sip of his pint, then cradled it against his chest.

"Was it big?" Freya asked.

"The dragon? Big enough," Alex said, lifting his eyebrows. "I was lucky it was only a hatchling. Ecgbryt said it couldn't have been more than a few weeks old. And it near finished me, even at that."

"How do you know all this?" Daniel asked, leaning forward on the table.

"My family descends from a very small clan in the high-lands—one of the secret clans. We own a distinct tartan, which we never wear. We've been called, through the ages, the 'Nethergrund Cannies,' that is, those that have knowledge of the lands beneath. But really we only use that to refer to ourselves, since we are a very secret clan, and few on this earth have knowledge of the knowl-edgeable people. It has always been such, and it is best as such.

"Our current appointment goes back through the Forty-Five and the Fifteen, to the fourteenth century. Our purpose was to defend the hidden land in three ways: to protect, to procure, and to uphaud. Protect the portals to the nethergrund, procure provi-sions for whatever was needful—be it metal or tools for smithing and carving—and to uphaud, to repair whatever tunnels have been felled by time and disuse. When I was a boy, I would be taken underground with my father and my grand-da to walk the tunnels, and I gained the ken. I learned them just as they learnt them, by sight and by memory. We had maps, but they are old and inaccurate. The best way is to walk them yourself. I many times walked the area where you popped up. And killed yfelgópes too."

"Tell them about Ealdstan," Ecgbryt said, placing another empty pint glass in front of him. That made three.

"I met him once, just the once. Grim and uncommon mean, he seemed, although, mind you, I was only eight."

"Why? What'd he do?" Freya asked.

"He argued with my grand-da about something, while my father stood by. None would speak of it to me afterward, but I gathered he wanted me to perform some task—a journey and *then* a task—but my grand-da refused. Said I was too young and the thing was needless. Aye, I believe it was the same task he sent you both on that he was wishing for me."

"Killing Gád?" Daniel asked.

"Aye, mebbe, mebbe. I don't recall Gád being discussed, but as

I said, I was young. My family had many conflicts with Ealdstan over the years."

"Why?"

"They didn't like the direction he was taking. And Ealdstan called them traitors to his cause, although my father attempted to be conciliatory. And for myself? Well, I don't really know what we've found ourselves in the middle of at the moment. If it was just a crazy old wizard, that'd be one thing. But like I said, the dragon changed everything."

"How?" Freya asked. "I mean, I understand that dragons might be a big deal, but how exactly does that change things?"

"Dragons cause all manner of mischief."

"That's a truth, and putting it mildly," Ecgbryt said, signalling for another dark ale.

"Aye, putting it mildly," Alex assented. "You see, it's not just the trouble that they cause in themselves—stealing sheep and livestock, people, pets—it's also the effect they have on the area around them, in what you might say a spiritual sense. They literally depress the entire region they inhabit."

"Depress it?" Daniel repeated.

"Aye," he said with a nod. "I've felt it many times; it's a thick, heavy, dark emotion that sticks to you like tar. Makes you tired, makes you sluggish. Not everyone associates moods with places, and so it takes most off guard. You don't wake up when you want to, you don't go out as often, you retreat into your cave. And when you do go out, you're peevish and fashed, as are the people you meet. Everyone is at one another's throats, knives out—suicides, theft . . . it brings out all that is worst in human nature."

He shook his head. "It used to be that we were prepared—the whole *country* was prepared—against these sorts of attacks. I'm talking about the old days—the golden olden times. The old poems talk more about a knight's virtues than his weapons; read *Gawain and the Green Knight*, see if I'm wrong. Read *Pearl*. Think about the knights of the round table; leaders with integrity. The common folk were neither here nor there, and there was an extremely high percentage of enchanters and evil princes per capita, it's true, but society was, on the whole, well-provisioned for means of correction against such mystical incursions. That is not true today. Most don't even acknowledge any sort of spiritual threat—any sort of spirit, even—and those that do have been lulled into an opiate daze by cushy lives, quiet cars, easy jobs, fast food . . . a hypnotic dance of colours and social interactions on your computer screen. People fight for their lives, but we've forgotten how to fight for our souls."

"Okay, but what does the dragon *mean*?" Freya asked, trying to get him back to the topic at hand. "You think the mythical world came into our world?"

"The *mystical worlds*, yes. There are more than one of them, and with Ealdstan missing and Niðergeard destroyed, our world is vulnerable to invasion."

"Niðergeard has fallen?" Daniel said.

Ecgbryt shifted in his seat. "Niðergeard has fallen," he said. "It is overrun. I blundered in unwittingly and was lucky to escape with my skin when I found yfelgópes roaming the streets, pillaging the smiths and stores."

"How did the yfelgópes organise and mobilise without Gád?" Daniel said. "Was it Kelm?"

"We believe so," Ecgbryt said.

"Who is Kelm?" Freya asked.

"Kelm Kafhand," said Ecgbryt. "Your paths have not crossed with his—even I would not know him to see him. He is the general of the yfelgóp army and moves at Gád's will as if he were his master's own hand. Since Ecgbryt came to me, we've been going over the library top to tail and found no mention of anyone by that name. Not in our library, at least. There were other libraries kept by cannies all over the isles, but over the years they have diminished and lost touch with each other. There once were cannies in Wales, Ireland, and all over England—the West Country, Kent, Winchester—but relations between them wore down over the years, and Ealdstan did not keep them up."

"Okay, so he's invaded Niðergeard," Daniel said. "What are you going to do?"

"*Do*, young Daniel?" Ecgbryt answered. "What do you think we are going to do? We are going to take it back!" He pounded the table with his fist, making their glasses and cutlery jump.

"Yes!" Daniel shouted. He pounded the table too. "Yes, yes! That's exactly what I wanted you to say!"

Freya, unsettled, looked to Alex. He was more subdued but smiling eagerly.

"What do we do? What do we do first?" Daniel asked, leaning in, his voice a harsh, excited whisper.

"It is no easy task planning to retake the underground realm with just a handful of faithfuls," Ecgbryt said, raising his palms. "Even with the stout party that is gathered here. No, we will need to marshal our resources, build an army."

"What about the sleeping knights?" Daniel asked. "Can we use them? Storm the city in force?"

"Patience, young Daniel, patience! First we would have to locate the knights and the tunnels used to access them. It is not a case of just wandering through the many thousands of tunnels— the old and inaccurate maps and texts would have to be studied and compared to modern ones. Then a route would have to be plotted—not as easy as it sounds—in order to pick up as many knights as quickly as possible."

"That couldn't take that long to do, surely?"

Ecgbryt stroked his trimmed beard and eyed him. "Such an undertaking may require years. Several years at least."

"Years? Really?" Daniel asked, shrinking back in disappointment.

"Years, certainly. Which is why you are lucky"—Ecgbryt's eyelids drooped teasingly—"that we have already done all that."

"Really?" Daniel was as giddy as a child at Christmas. "Freya, that's—" He became aware of the volume of his exclamations and lowered his voice. "This is what I've been waiting for ever since I left—the chance to go back and settle things once and for all. I've been seeing yfelgópes, you know, hunting and killing them. I knew this battle wasn't finished, I *knew it*! When do we start? When do we invade?"

"Calm down, Daniel," Alex said seriously. "It's not as easy as all of that. We need to do more than just round up the knights. That's just one aspect of the plan, and . . . actually, maybe this is a good time to introduce the fifth member of our party."

"The fifth?" Daniel asked.

Alex made a vigorous waving motion into the dark bar area of the hotel. A woman emerged from the shadows; she looked to be about fifty, sturdily built, but trim and fit. She wore pea green slacks, walking boots, a wide tartan scarf, and a beige travelling jacket that appeared as old, hard-worn, and tough as she. Her hair, silver-grey, was pulled back in a short ponytail.

"Daniel, Freya, this is my Aunt Vivienne," Alex said, introducing them.

"'Aunt Vivienne?'" Daniel said, echoing him. "Seriously?" He made an unattractive sideways smirk at Alex.

"Vivienne Simpson—my dad's sister," he explained.

"His baby sister. Call me Viv," Alex's aunt added emphatically. "I'll be joining you"—she lowered her voice—"*down under.*"

"I don't think we can be bringing people's *aunts* to Niðergeard," Daniel scoffed. "I've been there. Not everyone makes it out alive. I can't be responsible for dragging peoples' *aunts* through one of the most dangerous places in the country." Vivienne's eyes sparkled as she leaned forward, placing her knuckles on the picnic table.

"Young man," she said in a very lightly accented yet musical voice—was it an Edinburgh accent? "I'll have you know that I can walk thirty miles a day for weeks, if need be. I've hiked up K2 and over twenty Alpine peaks."

"When? Thirty years ago?" Daniel asked.

She didn't bat an eye. "I have made countless trips underground; not just in this country, but all over the world. Have *you* traversed"— Freya loved the way Viv rolled out the word *tra-ver-r-rsed*—"the hidden tunnels of the Tibetan mountains? Have *you* mapped the London subterranean passageways, the forgotten undergrounds, the Fleet River? Do you know where the seventeen sunken churches of Britain are located? Have you taken dives to Llyonesse?"

"Well, no, but—"

"Can you not only read but *speak* seven dead languages? *Young man*, if you are to have a hope of returning from the underground realms in one piece, then you will do best to heed my experienced voice." She now straightened to her full height. "And not scoff at assistance freely given. I have already visited the Langtorr, I'll have you know."

"Really?" Daniel asked. "How did you get in and out when Ecgbryt only barely escaped from it?"

"How indeed?" Vivienne said coyly.

"Okay, okay, I'm sold," Daniel said, grinning and holding up his hands.

Vivienne pursed her lips and glared at Daniel, getting the measure of him.

"So that's settled, then. Aunt Viv, please, take a seat. The plan is this: Daniel, you and Freya will accompany Aunt Viv down to Niðergeard—as a special task force."

"A task force to accomplish what, exactly?" Freya asked.

"Fact finding, primarily," Vivienne said. "But we shall also function as agents of opportunity."

"What does that mean?"

"There are additional tasks—missions, if you like—that we shall endeavour to complete, should circumstances present themselves."

"Such as?" Freya asked.

"Such as the Great Carnyx," Vivienne said. "It is a large horn—"

"They remember," Ecgbryt said. "They were there; they have seen it.'"

"I do remember," Daniel said. "The horn. It's a bronze sort of thing, long, curved at the top and bottom—made to look like some sort of an animal shouting. You mean that?"

"That's the one," Alex said.

"Hey, I remember—if you blow it, then it wakes up all the knights in the country. Why don't we just get that instead of rounding them up individually?"

"We could if we knew where it was, which is the point of going to look for it. In any case," Vivienne continued, "we're not exactly certain what it does. Do either of you know what the inscription says on it?" They shook their heads. "It's printed up one side and it reads: '*Bláwst þes horn and se æftera here laðiast.*'"

The enchantment that Daniel and Freya received on passing through the first arch to Niðergeard still worked, for their minds already understood the words and their meaning.

"'Blow you this horn and summon the next army?'" Freya said. "Is that right?"

"Yes, you have it," Ecgbryt said.

"Why wouldn't that inscription refer to the sleeping knights?" Freya asked.

"It may," Alex allowed, "but it doesn't expressly refer to them. It could be talking about something else. And without Ealdstan to confirm, we just don't know."

"So how do you find out for sure?" Daniel asked. "I mean, if it could be anything . . ." Visions of otherworldly armies crossing through fields of mist at the horn's call flooded his imagination.

"It's going to be your job to find out," Alex said.

"You mean find the horn and blow it? Sounds simple enough—if it's there to blow."

"A war is not fought with just might of arms," Ecgbryt said. "It is also won by wit and cunning. Especially when numbers are few or uncertain, a small amount of knowledge can be key. Why, I remember—" He caught himself and frowned, his gaze seeming to turn inward for a moment and then back to them. "I remember times when just a little information has turned the tide of an entire war. That is the sort of information we will need. We not only need to know if this horn can be found and made use of, we need to know what happened to Ealdstan, Modwyn, Godmund, Frithfroth—anything you can find."

"Mostly we want information," Alex continued. "If the worst has come to the worst—and we now have every reason to suspect that it has—then Ealdstan has been imprisoned, incapacitated, or even killed. He would not have allowed Niðergeard to fall otherwise."

"Are you sure?" Freya said, clearing her throat. "I mean, when we met him, all those years back, he didn't exactly seem on top of things. He stopped you from blowing the horn then, if I recall. What's to say that he didn't turn traitor?"

Ecgbryt gave a vigorous shake of his head. "Niðergeard has been Ealdstan's labour of love for near a score of centuries. To let it fall into disgrace—he would quicker slit his own throat."

Freya bit her lip. They weren't factoring Gád into the equation. Should she tell them? It would be admitting to guilt, admitting to being a silent witness to Swiðgar's death—of hiding what really happened to him. She opened her mouth to say something.

And then closed it.

"So he's dead or being held captive," Daniel said. "We need to free the city and, therefore, free him. I'm ready now. When do we get going?"

"Wait," Freya heard herself say. "Just wait a moment. I'm uncomfortable with the idea of . . . charging back into the city and starting a war by summoning the sleeping knights. Is this really the best plan?"

"The city is occupied," Daniel said, smacking his palm on the table. "We must liberate it. Stop the dragons, save the world. Right?"

"Okay, but is this the best way? Do we even know what's going on in—"

"What exactly do we need to know, Freya?" Daniel broke in. "They wouldn't hesitate to kill us. That's all *I* need to know."

"But we don't even know what's going on down there. Maybe it's *best* that Niðergeard has fallen. I mean, what good has it been doing anyone?"

Daniel nearly exploded. "It's . . . Freya! It's been—"

Alex held his hand up. "It's not about what good it's been—although it's been plenty over the centuries, that's certain—it's about the future, about protecting this country from future invasion—about stopping the one that's already in progress."

"Right. Exactly," Freya said. "It sounds like—with the dragon and everything—as if there's a larger problem beyond Niðergeard. Shouldn't we address *that*, instead of a dusty old city that everyone has forgotten about?"

"Young Freya," Ecgbryt said after consideration, "you may be right. But the situation is as you stated—we simply do not know enough yet. We need answers from Niðergeard and her people. And you three are the best for the job."

"Three?" Freya asked.

"You, Daniel, and Vivienne," Ecgbryt said.

"But . . . the army. Shouldn't you go around and gather them before we know what the deal is?"

"Freya," Ecgbryt said in a stern voice. "Kelm and the yfelgópes will need to be defeated, whatever the situation. Trust me on that. Their progress will only harm us."

Freya shook her head. "Count me out," she said.

"What do you mean?" Daniel asked.

"I mean, I'm not going. You don't need me."

"Oh, what? You're losing the argument so you're going to sulk?"

"Not at all. I'm no good at fighting, I'll just get in the way. More likely killed. It's dangerous and I'm not prepared for that, so I'm not going."

Daniel's mouth hung open, a half smile of disbelief across it.

"Let's all take a moment and find some space to have a bit of a think," Vivienne said, rising. "It's a lot to take in all at once."

"Freya," Alex said, when she eagerly rose too, "don't go too far. Stay on the grounds and try to avoid others—you're a celebrity now. Your picture has been plastered all over the news. The 'twice abducted girl' story has rather sparked the public imagination."

Freya nodded.

"If someone does recognise you, just say that you are already in the escort of two police officers and find a way to contact Ecgbryt or myself. I'm Constable Simpson, he's Constable Cuthbert.'"

She nodded and struck out toward the golf course to stretch her legs.

II

Freya skirted the edge of well-cultivated woodland. It wasn't the messy, organic sort of woods that you got in actual forests; it was the thinned out, well-tended woodland where anything rotten or dead was quickly carted off.

"They tricked you. They blindfolded you with their lies, told you all sorts of fantastic tales until your head started spinning, and when you were all mixed up, they took off the blindfold and pushed you where they wanted you to go."

Gád's words came back to her easily. It had been so hard to repress them, to push them away into any dark closet of her mind, but now they were coming back to her freely, in complete snatches. They'd obviously left more of an impression on her than she knew.

"They want to control us, make us live in the past with them, give up our identities, our hopes and dreams—make us something less than human."

She had expected a villain but instead found someone who made a lot of sense. And he'd given her what she most wanted: an escape from their underground prison—which was considerably more than anyone else did for her. Even for all the hype about his power and wisdom, Ealdstan did not do that.

However, Gád had told her to lie, and he had killed Swiðgar. Those two things could not be forgotten.

But his words kept coming back, as if she were hearing them for the first time. It was like digging for a skeleton in the ground; every so often a bone unearthed, and she would fit it together with what she already had. Given time, she felt she could piece together the entire conversation.

"They told you I was an oppressor, but what if I'm a freedom fighter? A revolutionary?"

Rationally, she knew that there was little reason to take what Gád told her on trust, any more than Ealdstan. But even if Gád was not completely right, he couldn't be as wrong as Ealdstan and Modwyn and the rest of them, with their secret battles, stockpiled soldiers, and weapons and enchantments for some supposed future mystical battle. With a creeping realization, she found that she sided more with Gád that with any of the Niðergearders. Ecgbryt and poor Swiðgar included.

She suddenly noticed she was walking faster now—her hands, arms, and shoulders were clenched, and she was sweating. Anxiety was taking over; it almost had control of her.

She wished she had her pills, but her pills were long gone. She hadn't escaped Stowe with them, and right now it would be next to impossible to pick up a new prescription. Her heart was going as fast as an alarm clock bell. Without the pills, life was like a death-metal soundtrack with the volume kicked up to eleven. It was hard to think and hard to feel anything except the Fear. She ran through some exercises that a therapist once tried to teach her—she built up the mind-wall and tossed every fear that she came across over it, but that was only of limited help. She could still hear her fears behind it—scrabbling, skittering, climbing . . .

"You're right, you know."

Freya whirled and found Aunt Vivienne looking into the trees.

"Sorry to interrupt your solitude, but I wanted you to know: you're right. I know it, you know it—and that's why we all need you to go down there with us."

Freya looked away. "I don't know what I'm doing," she said. "I don't really want to go back. For years I've been terrified—literally terrified, often almost paralysed with terror—of being sucked back into that world, of what would happen to me if it did." She looked about at the trees, then back to Vivienne. "It's ruining my life—it's ruining me. I've thought of killing myself lots of times. Regularly, I would say. I probably never had a chance of a normal life after getting sucked into Niðergeard, but I think I could have a life without fear if I could go back there and deal with it."

Vivienne came closer to her. "Well, don't go off and do anything foolish. You're a good thinker, and I feel that we need thinkers more than we do fighters in a situation like this."

"I'm worried about Daniel, that he'll mess things up. He's too eager to run in and start chopping people's heads off."

"I believe I can keep him in line. I know his type, but I need you with me."

"And Ecgbryt. We don't need the knights yet. It's stupid to send him off to get them. Wouldn't we be better off taking him with us?"

Vivienne shook her head. "We not only must find out if we can find and wake the knights; we need to try and save them. They're already being tracked down and killed. The dragon Alex discovered had killed all the knights and made their chamber its lair. We have to get to the others before they're discovered too, and Ecgbryt and Alex are the best qualified and able to do that."

Freya chewed her lip. This was the time to tell Vivienne about Gád if she was going to, but she still wasn't sure.

"They told you I was an oppressor, but what if I'm a freedom fighter? A revolutionary?"

Freya looked out over the green landscape of Scotland. A light rain was moving in on the hills ahead of them, misting the horizon in a grey blur. *If I'm really going to wade into a war,* she thought, *then I want to make sure I'm on the right side before I start sharing information.*

"Dreary weather, eh?" Vivienne said.

"We'll miss the view when we go underground."

"Does that mean you're coming?"

"I don't think I have much choice."

"Wonderful."

"How do we get there?"

"Through the Langtorr tunnel," Vivienne said matter-of-factly.

"The what?"

"The Langtorr tunnel. You must know the Langtorr, correct? Ecgbryt said that's where you all stayed. If you go to the top of it, it connects here—well, to the midlands at least. We've been keeping a very close eye on it. It seems to be still open and unguarded by the yfelgópes."

Freya felt like she was plunging downward already. "The Langtorr . . . It's been there all this time?"

"Indeed. I even did a quick scout of it myself."

"You've been to the Langtorr? Recently?"

"Just to see if I could or if we had to arrange something else. There are scads of entrances if you know how to look for them. The Langtorr is the most direct one."

"Would Ecgbryt have known about it? Even years ago?"

"Certainly. It's one of the oldest gates."

Freya turned her back to Vivienne. She could feel her face flushing with rage. There *had* been a direct exit from Niðergeard. They could have been sent home at any time at all. The only reason she'd agreed to go on that ridiculous quest was to get back home—something Ealdstan told her was impossible to do unless they destroyed Gád. She had known they were being used but had consoled herself by knowing that there was no other way through the terrible situation they were in. But it was another of Ealdstan's lies—and one that all the other Niðergearders—Modwyn, Godmund, and Ecgbryt and Swiðgar included—were complicit in.

That settled it. She may not wholly be on Gád's side, but she certainly wasn't on the side of those who would manipulate small, helpless children into going on missions of assassination. Was he a revolutionary? Then she was too.

III

Kelm Kafhand sat on the hero's throne. It was a chair made of rough-hewn stone and sat atop an irregular pile of rubble in the largest courtyard of Niðergeard. Coal fires burned in braziers at the base of the pile. It was difficult for him to heave his powerful but unwieldy form up the heap, but the view gave an appropriate perspective for his thoughts.

Kelm huffed in large, ragged breaths as his enormous chest moved up and down with a slow, inevitable regularity. His body may be still, but his mind was racing—running through exercises and evil thoughts to help while away monotony. His scowl was deep—he had been frowning for decades.

Occasionally he would sneer in pleasure at a particularly ugly thought, but even then the large jowls that anchored his face to his shoulders and chest would remain unstirred. His eyes were buried beneath a flabby brow that pressed down on his cheeks and created a series of folds that masked his eyes. His face, grotesque as it was, was not one without emotion. Long, shaggy eyebrows moved and twitched almost constantly, and his wide mouth had found nuance and subtlety in conveying fifty shades of displeasure unobtained by younger, more inexperienced faces.

He was doing what he always did, whether he was eating, drinking, dreaming, or just sitting: he was plotting. Plotting was as natural to him as breathing. Every minute of every day was filled with cooking up plots—small acts of meanness or large acts of cruelty, it didn't matter. Most of his plots never went further than the grin on his own slimy lips, but that didn't matter. Each plot kept his mind in shape for the next one.

Kelm's lieutenant, a wretched little yfelgóp with a large head and weak arms, slouched into view from around one of the buildings and began his address with a bored drone. "Your honour, my general, most exalted among all military leaders, illustrious master of the underground races and magnificent commander of the five unseen armies"—the lieutenant drew in a deep breath before finally getting to the point—"a messenger has arrived."

Kelm glared at the miserable creature for almost a minute before nodding. During that time the lieutenant merely stood gazing vacantly at his esteemed general, breathing heavily through his mouth and drooling. Kelm decided that none of his soldiers could be as stupid as this man looked and therefore this one was trying to fool him, and therefore needed to be killed. He already had what must be a dozen plots to accomplish it, but he'd need to spend time selecting the most satisfying one.

For now, he signalled to the lieutenant, who turned away unceremoniously and shuffled back through the curtain. A moment later the messenger appeared.

He was dressed in white with a light, full-length travelling cloak made out of a thick, bleached hide. Kelm's lip curled with pleasure; his breathing shifted into something that, in him, perhaps passed for a type of slow laughter.

The messenger frowned.

Kelm's breathing slowed. "You look like him."

"But I am not him. I am his mannequin. His fetch."

Kelm wheezed. "And what message does Empty-Grinner send to me in your empty shell?" the enormous leader asked, contempt raw in his voice.

The messenger bristled at Kelm's tone. "A wise man would advise you to be more respectful of your superior."

The right side of Kelm's mouth jerked upward, showing a flash of black and orange teeth. "Show me a wise man and I'll consider his advice. Show me a superior and I'll show him respect."

The messenger gave a sly smile. "Wisdom and superiority are not mine to possess. I merely speak and listen for those who are greater than myself." He gave a bow but kept his eyes on Kelm's.

"Gád and I have an understanding," the massive general said with a belch. "There is none other who can control his troops with the skill that I can."

"No. You killed all those who might have."

"It is right that it was thus. Power is undeniable—in me it is irrepressible. He who is strongest must lead, and none have proven to be my strategic equal. It is I whose strength and prowess allowed us to conquer this city. I raised this hero's throne, and now, *I rule.*"

"None but Gád," the messenger said quietly.

"What?"

"None but Gád have proven to be your equal."

It may have been the fire that made Kelm's eyes gleam viciously for a moment, but it was only for a moment, and when the gleam left, Kelm's face had a fairly apathetic cast to it. "My ambition does not extend to Gád's . . ." His breathing caught and he let out a wheeze. ". . . responsibilities. What Gád has, Gád can keep. I shall remain here."

"That is very generous. I'm sure that Gád thanks you for such a consideration. But perhaps when Gád has more, then you will want more? I wonder, have you already numbered Gád's days in your mind?"

Kelm's face was expressionless for several seconds, and then he let out a loud, ugly snort. "Watch yourself, your words tread closely to outright sedition."

"I had better do what I came to do then, hadn't I? My master's message is this: events are even now in motion. The two lifiende heroes have been reengaged and will shortly be on their way here. You are to resist them but not defeat or collaborate with them. Keep them alive. You are to bait the bear—to within an inch of its life—but not to kill it."

"This is an inglorious assignment."

"I imagine it would be harder to keep these overworlders safe while they're running around down here rather than to just smite them outright. Consider it a test of skill—and one, despite your own convictions about your prowess, I personally doubt you'll manage.

"In any case, they must be allowed to blow the horn. It is all over for them when they blow the Carnyx. It shall be the honeyed hook that, when pulled, will bring steel jaws rushing in on them."

Kelm nodded. "I understand. It will be done."

The messenger turned and beamed at Kelm. "Very good. And now with your permission, I may depart?"

He lazily flicked his hand. The messenger bowed and turned to walk away.

Kelm's lieutenant appeared again, his face twisted into a question. Kelm narrowed his eyes and then nodded. The lieutenant lumbered off.

Kelm sat patiently for several moments, which turned into several minutes. His lieutenant did not return.

With a supreme effort, he lifted himself out of his chair and manoeuvred down the pile. The courtyard guards were missing.

One of the city's silver lamps lay askew in the path ahead. He went to it and picked it up and found that it illumined a scene of carnage. Bodies lay everywhere. All four guards lay on their backs, a thin cut at the base of each of their necks that poured blood out into a deep puddle. The lieutenant lay a small distance apart, his own knife in his chest. He was twitching slightly, painfully trying to breathe.

The general squinted into the darkness to try to see some trace of a pale figure dressed in white. Nothing was visible between the buildings.

Kelm went over to his lieutenant and peered down at his face.

Then he raised his foot and brought it down hard, ending the officer's misery. He turned to one of the yfelgópes who yet lived. "You are my new second officer," he informed him. "Draft a new guard immediately. Then bring me my dinner." The newly promoted lieutenant bowed.

Kelm climbed back up to the throne and continued to brood and plot.

IV

Two days later they walked along the grass verge beside a road that ran along the fields and farmlands of Warwickshire. Their trip to Scotland had only lasted as long as it took to get provisioned and kitted out in sturdy hiking and spelunking gear. They had stayed in Alex's parents' manse—on land where Freya and Daniel had emerged after completing their quest in the under realms. They met Alex's father and Vivienne's older brother; James was privy to more information than perhaps even Ecgbryt had about the underground realms, but his days of travelling below were far, far behind him, he said, gently tapping a knee with his cane.

"You'll be best off wi' Viv, I can tell ye' tha'." His accent was stronger than either of the other Simpsons, and with it he continually sang his sister's praises. "I'd take her as she stands now over myself in my prime, any day. Yes, you'll do well with Viv, if there's well to do! I'll gi'e you what support I can up here, but dinnae expect it'll be much. You'll stay in my prayers—count on that."

Freya found him a kind and affable man ready to help out but lonely in the years since his wife died.

During the stay in Scotland, Freya felt that she had finally managed to catch up on her sleep, and now, hitching her rucksack up her back and loosening her breathable waterproof coat, Freya felt considerably more prepared than she did eight years ago. All she'd had then was her school uniform and a jacket. Now she had several changes of hard-wearing clothes, military-grade food rations and utilities, and shoes that cost more than a month's rent.

They were getting close. Freya could see Ecgbryt checking his map more and more often—every dozen paces or so, in fact. He had a lot of maps. "Is this what you've been doing for the last eight years?" she had asked Ecgbryt after seeing the stacks of them on Alex's dining room table.

"Aye. I have been marking and charting the positions of the sleeping knights across the isles," Ecgbryt answered, running a palm over a map of the British Isles that was spread before him. It had crosses and annotations in red, blue, and black. Beneath his other palm was a stack of papers that he had been diligently copying details of the map onto. "I have been hunting out the ancient markers and indicators, tracking the legends and secret demarcations of the old land that I used to live in. I am sorry, both of you, for not contacting you before now," he said apologetically, thinking, mistakenly, that there was accusation in Freya's question. "But only I could do this task, and only Alex could assist me.

"Do know that of me, Freya," he said, raising sad eyes to her. "I am sorry."

Alex, just ahead of her, looked at his watch and then turned, pulling open a long, metal gate. "Shortcut," he explained. "But let's try to pick up the pace. The sun's about to set," Alex called out in his soft Scots accent. "Daniel, Ecgbryt?" The two behind them hefted their packs and lengthened their strides across the thickly grassed field.

Focusing primarily on keeping her footsteps measured and even, Freya tried to stifle the nervous energy that was coursing through her, which was making her hands and knees shake. She wanted to run away and collapse to the ground all at the same time. The Fear was now an ocean that was pressing against her wall, threatening at any second to push it over and sweep her away on waves of terror. So instead, she built a boat and put the Fear beneath her feet. As the sea raged around her, she only watched it roll and bob past the window. Soon it would be "The Evening," when horrible things could happen; the sort of things that sent her life careening beyond her control. There were traps and pitfalls in the half-light that were not there in the day or the night, and they were actively trying to search one of them out.

"Can I ask you a question?" Vivienne bustled up close to Freya. She was apparently as strong as a mule. Where Freya constantly flagged and felt crippled by her load, Vivienne bounded quickly and merrily beside her. "No, don't turn to me," Vivienne said in a quiet tone. "Don't stop. Keep your voice low. Your friend, Daniel."

"Yes?"

"Is he alright? I mean, is he well?"

"Well?"

"Aye, well. I only ask because he wanders around at nights, talking to himself."

"He does?"

"Aye. Now, I only need four hours of sleep a night—one of the few benefits of being as old as I am—but I'd guess that your friend there has had less than that—much less. If any at all, in fact."

"Really?"

"Really. You wouldn't know anything about that?"

"No. Honestly. I've been sleeping like crazy. I wouldn't have noticed if the building fell down around me."

"What happened to him? Was it really Elfland?"

"I suppose so—he says it was. I really don't know."

"Keep a sharp eye," Vivienne said, and then she shouted, "Are we nearly there yet?" in a jovial bellow.

"Almost, Aunt Viv," Alex said, calling over his shoulder. "Look, you can see it there."

Alex made a gesture, and Freya saw a fenced-off area to her right that seemed well looked after. It was tidy and neatly mown. Through gaps in the bordering hedge, she could see a curved line of grey stones.

They approached the stone circle, which Freya judged to be thirty meters in diameter and made of dark limestone. They entered at the small wooden gate, which bore a wooden sign that informed them, beneath the English Heritage symbol, these were the Rollright Stones. They began to walk the circumference, passing the stones inside, on the right. The smallest markers of the circle came up to about their knees while the largest were a couple feet taller than Ecgbryt.

Ecgbryt was counting stones, and this was apparently not as easy as it sounded. Alex and Daniel were doing a control count. Every five stones, Ecgbryt would turn and compare his number with Daniel and Alex.

"I count twenty, thus far," Ecgbryt called over his shoulder.

"Twenty also," Alex reported.

"Twenty," Vivienne said.

"What are you looking for?" Freya asked.

"The stone that does not fit," Vivienne told her. "It is said that no two countings of the stones in this ring are the same. The stones come and go. We are looking for one of the ones that is going."

Freya nodded her head as if to say that made perfect sense. She dismally fell into step behind them, contemplating the dark days ahead of her. She took one last, long look at the aboveground scenery.

It was then that she noticed the four of them were not alone. A man, large, and shouldering something bulky, was standing between two of the stones on the other side of the ring. At first Freya thought it was another hiker or a tourist, but he was wearing a dark, shaggy coat that hung from his shoulders and came to just above his knees. His legs and feet were bare and stocky, hairy. His face was black with bristles around the mouth, his head as shaggy as his coat, to the extent that the hair from one entwined with the other.

He was just standing, staring at them, and something in his aspect seemed menacing to Freya. The twilight shone into his eyes, making them large and bright, like cat's eyes in a dim room, giving him an added animalism.

"Come away, Freya," Vivienne said, coming alongside her and pulling her gently by the shoulders. "We see them. Keep to the task. Quickly now."

"Let us speed on," Ecgbryt said, continuing the circle, brushing the tips of his fingers against the dark stones. "Thirty-five. What have you?"

"Thirty-five."

Ecgbryt grumbled.

"There's another one," Daniel said to Alex in a low voice as a man, almost identical to the first, stepped out from behind the standing stone by the wooden gate.

Freya hurried to catch up to the others, Fear gaining on her. "I'm still not—ah!" She reeled as a third man stepped out just in front of her. Up close she could see the matted hair of his massive cloak quite clearly, as well as the features of his face, which were broad and rough, his mouth and nostrils protruding snout-like. She could also smell him. He stank of grease and wind and dead animal. He loomed over her, gazing intently but not moving. She hurried around him to stay with the others.

"Who are they?"

"They're . . . people we'd hoped not to run into," Alex said. "We should be fine if we hurry. As soon as you go through the portal, then you'll be safe. Mostly."

Freya looked across to Daniel. He was keeping his eyes on the men behind him, a hand under his coat where his sword was, an eager, sneering grin on his face; he was counting under his breath.

"Forty," Ecgbryt said.

"Forty," Alex said, coming to stand next to the knight.

"I've got forty-one," Vivienne said.

"Forty-one also," Daniel said, joining them.

There were more of the hairy men now—six in total—striding between the stones.

"It is one of these, then," Ecgbryt said, studying the stones behind him. He circled one that stood about five feet high. "Which one? Which one . . ."

Freya took two steps toward Ecgbryt and then froze in terror as the men—the six of them that they could see plainly—started howling at the top of their lungs. As each one stood, heads thrown back, they began to shudder and shake, their fur coats bristling. By degrees they leaned forward, spasming, arms extended, transforming. Their fur skins drew tighter around them, their arms and legs growing thick and bulky, and their skin darkened as fine fur grew everywhere, even on their faces—faces that lengthened, noses flattening into snouts, jaws widening, opening to show teeth that grew visibly. Their eyes turned black and sank back into deep, dark-furred brows.

Their arms—now forelegs—touched the ground and the transformations were complete. Where large men once stood, now there were large, black bears with slavering jaws and clawed limbs.

Freya gaped. "Oh, you're kidding me."

As one, the bears rushed them, tearing across the neatly trimmed lawn at a sprinting pace.

"Yes, yes. Here. Daniel, Freya—it is time, quick!" Ecgbryt yelled at them, but Freya was rooted to the spot. She felt Daniel tug at her arm and she stumbled forward, trying to pick her feet up far enough so as not to stumble.

Ecgbryt drew his axe from his rucksack and stepped forward to deal with the bears. He pulled a silver can from his belt and tossed it on the lawn. Freya watched as it rolled to a stop on the grass and then exploded in a flash of light and a head-rattling boom.

Of all of them, Freya was the only one who hadn't braced herself for the flashbang grenade. Woozy and blinded, she felt arms join around her waist and she was hoisted off the ground. She rubbed her palms into her eyes to try to clear them. The last she saw in the twilight of the overworld was Ecgbryt wading through white, smoky vapours, swinging his axe swiftly around him. A bear carcass already lay at his feet, but the others were rallying. She heard the sharp, tinny pops of Alex's firearm, Ecgbryt shouting, and then she was pulled down into darkness, as if into the grave—as if into the Fear.

She was released and stumbled down a short flight of steps, shouting and grabbing at the stone walls. She stopped her slow fall by pushing her weight against a wet stone wall, its texture and smell all too familiar.

The sounds dimmed, and the last suffused rays of light disappeared as the darkness around her became complete.

CHAPTER TWO

Echoes of the Fall

---- I ----

Hartlepoole

Sean Pitt walked Anna Powell home along the side path of the motorway that skirted their city. It wasn't a very scenic route to walk—it was littered, noisy, and polluted—but it was nicer because Sean liked Anna, and he thought that Anna liked him back, even though she ignored him at school. But on Wednesday evenings, when they both had orchestra, he was able to walk her home, just the two of them together, alone.

The route was well known to him, and he had long-standing fantasies of, at certain bends and turns, either taking her hand in his, or putting his arm around her, or maybe even leaning over and kissing her on the cheek. These fantasies were so tied to different parts in the route that they were virtually landmarks.

But they were still fantasies nonetheless. For some reason, he never got the courage up to do any of it. Part of the reason was that she was always rumoured to be going out with Mark Morris, but most of it was that he was paralysed by the idea that she would stop walking back with him on Wednesdays. Some time with her every week was better than no time with her at all. And so every week he did nothing, and every Wednesday evening he kicked himself for his cowardice.

But it couldn't last forever. School was ending in a few weeks, and he resolved to take some action. Today, he told himself, was different. The fact that he'd told himself that every Wednesday before this one was "different" was irrelevant and didn't detract from today's difference. Today his courage wouldn't fail.

"I can't stand Megan anymore," Anna was saying. "We used to be *really* close, but now she's just ignoring me."

"Yeah," Sean agreed. He couldn't recall who Megan was. He was pretty sure Anna had never mentioned her before.

"She's always been a moody cow, but we used to get on, at least. And Jenna told me what Megan told her about me, which was all lies, obviously, saying Mark and I got it on, when we never have. She's such a big liar."

"Yeah," Sean agreed again. The path was taking them beneath the overpass, which was always busy with traffic but was also the most secluded of all the spots on their winding way home.

"I like you, Sean," Anna said after an uncharacteristic moment of quiet. "I always feel like I can talk to you. I'll miss you when school ends."

"Well," Sean said, flushing, "you know . . . I . . ."

Anna stopped. "Who's that over there?"

"Where?"

Propped against one of the columns was a heap of something or other that, in the low light, gave a silhouette like a person, but it was a trick of the eye; it was far too big to actually be someone.

"It's nothing," said Sean. "Just some bin bags or something."

"No, it's moving," Anna said, moving up the concrete ramp toward the pillar.

"It's just the wind," Sean said, faltering. The news had been going on about some missing children lately, and he suddenly wanted to be away from here. Quickly.

"All right," said Anna, and she turned back toward him just as the silhouette leaned forward and stood up.

Anna caught the movement out of the corner of her eye, shrieked, and froze. Sean's legs convulsed beneath him. His instincts told him to run, but he couldn't leave Anna here alone.

"Anna, come away," he said, tugging her sleeve.

Anna shook her head.

"What's wrong with you? Move!" Sean growled.

"I—I can't. I'm too scared."

"Be scared of what will happen to you if you don't," Sean said as the inhuman thing straightened to its full height. It was not just tall but bulky, chunky. It was either made of dirt and rubbish, or that stuff was embedded in its skin. As it moved bits fell off.

It growled as it started to slide down the concrete escarpment. It stopped directly in front of Anna. Its face lowered; instead of skin it had black sludge, which oozed itself into a grin that revealed massive, yellow, pebble-like teeth. "Pretty," it said, lifting an arm and hand. "Tasty," it said, reaching out for her.

In a flash, Sean picked up a length of metal pipe that laid nearby—part of a mangled signpost. He hefted it above his head and ran forward, bringing it down heavily on the thing's shoulder, just above an orange traffic cone that appeared to be a part of its back.

It felt the blow—barely. It reacted as Sean would react if a three-year-old hit him with a cardboard tube. He got the monster's attention though.

"Run, Anna!"

Anna broke into a sprint, across the field toward home, not daring to look back.

Sean dropped the heavy bit of metal in his hands and made to follow her, but the monster took two large strides toward him and swiped with his arm. It was like being hit by a falling tree trunk, and the blow sent him flying through the air where he smacked into one of the concrete pillars of the overpass.

His head swam and his perception rippled, like jelly tossed into a swimming pool. He was dizzy and sick, and wondering why everything had become so dark.

He shook his head to clear it, and through a dim tunnel of fuzzy grey, he saw an enormous head with even more enormous teeth grinning at him, as though it was very far away, but he could feel and smell a breath that stank like rancid ditch water.

"Tasty," the face said, and Sean felt a massive hand wrap around his arm and he was lurched upright, which made the world spin horrifyingly. There was intense pain and a chomping noise and then nothing more.

II

Freya clutched at her chest and fought for control of her breathing. In the sea of terror, she found a brick and then another and set them together. Piece by piece, she rebuilt the wall until finally she and Fear were two separate entities again. But when, in her mind, she stood on solid ground, she found that Rage had made her higher, and drier. These were the two opposing forces inside her now: Fear and Rage. The Rage she felt she could control, and use it against the Fear.

She felt Vivienne's hand on her shoulder and her warm presence behind her. "Deep breaths, Freya darling. Deep breaths."

Stronger now, she pushed herself up, bracing herself against the wall of what seemed to be the end of a long passage. Stairs rose up behind her and terminated in dark stone. The portal had already shut. Daniel was exploring; he had flicked on a small flashlight and was inspecting the area.

"See anything?" Freya asked, her voice barely more than an inaudible whisper. She took a deep breath and asked again, "What do you see?"

Daniel shined the light back at her; its brilliance cut into her eyes. She was already getting used to the darkness.

"It's just a cave."

"Are you okay?" Vivienne asked.

"Yes."

"Anything broken?"

"No."

"Do you need—"

"I'm fine, I'm fine," Freya snapped testily. "I don't need to be coddled."

"Right, good." Vivienne shouldered her pack again. "Let's get moving; it's just a few miles."

Freya hoisted her pack up on her shoulder as well and then fell into step behind Vivienne and Daniel. The pace and sensation of walking in the dark was sickeningly familiar now.

They walked for about an hour in what felt like a fairly straight line. Freya dwelt on the anger inside of her, trying to stoke it by meditating on all that she had unfairly suffered, the last time she was here and ever since, but found that she couldn't hold on to the flames—it was just too exhausting. After a time she found that it had fallen away from her, leaving her alone with just the cold emptiness of the Fear.

The tunnel dipped and Vivienne stopped.

"What is it?" Daniel, behind Freya, asked.

"It's a door."

Freya took a deep breath. "So open it," Daniel said.

"Here we go," Vivienne said, and there was a metallic rattling and then a creak as an ancient metal door swung open. Stepping through it, they found themselves on a landing where a circular stairway continued downward.

She wasn't prepared for the smell. It wasn't overtly unpleasant, but it so instantly and so fully brought back the emotions of her first time here that she wanted to weep.

She sucked her breath in, inflating herself, doing her best to bury all the emotions within her. Not even a day into her new mission and she was nearly an emotional wreck. She stepped through the doorway and almost automatically took a step back in order to re-enter several more times, but then she thought, *Why bother? I'm already here.*

"I don't believe it," she muttered loudly. "All this time—there was a door at the top of the Langtorr. We could have gone back anytime we wanted."

"Yeah," Daniel said. "But you wouldn't have left, even if you knew about it. You would have gone on the quest anyway, just like me."

"Now come you two, no squabbling," Vivienne said. "We've got other things to—"

"No, actually, I think I would have just liked to have gone home," Freya cut in. "Having had a chance to think about and reflect on it at length over the past eight years . . . I think I would have just liked to have gone home."

"I don't think so. You would have done the right thing in the end."

"We've got other things to focus on," Vivienne said.

More Rage boiled up inside Freya. *That's good, I can use that,* she thought. "Really? The right thing? Trick two thirteen-year-old children into going on a dangerous, top-secret mission?"

"That's enough now," Vivienne said.

"Well, I'm *glad* I went," Daniel said. "And you are too, deep down. What we did made a difference. We killed Gád."

"I said *enough!*" Vivienne exclaimed in a hushed, urgent voice. "If you two weren't so busy scrapping just now, you'd have heard what I'm hearing."

Freya swallowed a breath. "What is it?"

"Listen."

Up from the twisting stone passage came the sound of leather-soled shoes on stone stairs. Standing very still, Freya watched as Daniel slowly shrugged open his coat. He quietly adjusted the leather strap that held his sword's scabbard so that it hung freely at his side and not hitched up to his chest. This action was not unnoticed by Vivienne, who turned slightly and placed a hand on Daniel's shoulder.

Freya blinked in the blackness but soon found that a light was growing from the stairwell beneath them. She stood her ground, tentatively, standing on the balls of her feet. She watched the far-thest corner of the wall below them to see what would appear.

The face was the first thing she saw—it was white, haggard, and surrounded by a black halo of frizzy, unkempt, and matted hair. It was illuminated from below by one of the silver lamps of Niðergeard.

"Frithfroth!" Daniel exclaimed.

"Frithfroth, it's us—it's Daniel and Freya. Do you remember? We were children—" He broke off.

Freya wondered if the old man might be blind. The way his lamp cast its light, it was hard to see his eyes; she could only spot two dim gleams of reflected light. When Daniel started speaking, Frithfroth stopped.

"Who is he?" asked Vivienne.

"He's the Langtorr's sort of . . . housekeeper person," Freya said a little uncertainly. "But when we knew him, he wasn't—" Freya didn't have to describe the unfortunate man in order to make her point clear. The long, gaunt face was definitely that of Niðergeard's ward and the Langtorr's protector, but he was wasted away, almost literally a shadow of the already slight and wiry man whom they had first met. His eyes were sunken and his cheeks collapsed in on themselves. He kept advancing, and now Freya could see his hunched shoulders and thin limbs. He held his arms up to his chest, but he had no hands—only two terrible-looking puckered scars at the end of his wrists. He wore a dusty, fraying tunic that had decayed through in places. Leather garments beneath his shirt were similarly deteriorating and, she believed, rotting.

Daniel and Freya both retreated back a step. Daniel found his voice first.

"I remember," Frithfroth said then, in a voice that came from a very long way away. "I remember . . . Daniel and Freya, the lifiendes. Have you come to destroy this place?"

Yes, thought Freya. *Perhaps.*

"No," said Daniel.

"Pity." Frithfroth looked down at his scarred wrists. "So what do you want?"

"We want to help," Daniel said, turning back to Frithfroth, whose face was impassive, showing no thought or emotion. "We're here to liberate you. We're here to run the yfelgópes right out of the city."

"First, however, we want answers," said Vivienne firmly.

"Answers," Frithfroth repeated, staring into nothing. "Answers depend on questions." He turned and started walking awkwardly down the stairs—a slow, unbalanced walk, halfway between a lurch and a limp. He led them down the corkscrewing stairs into the Langtorr, the last stronghold at the centre of Niðergeard.

They hadn't gone far before they passed a small hole in the

thick wall that afforded a view down to the city. Daniel was the first to pass by it, and he stood, looking wordlessly through it. Freya joined him and crowded her face near the window as well. Frithfroth, aware that they were no longer following, waited silently a few steps below.

"Let me have a look," Vivienne said, and Daniel stepped back to allow her room at the window to look through.

The plunging feeling in Freya's stomach wasn't caused just by the dizzying height, but by the familiar sight of the city. Far below them, Freya could make out the dim lights that illuminated the streets and what looked like a perfectly curved pile of rubble.

"The wall is gone," Daniel lamented. "Crumbled away into nothing."

"And there are other ruined buildings," Freya said, spotting irregular piles of stone in the square stone buildings below them.

"They attacked . . ." Frithfroth said, continuing his slow, awkward gait down the stairs. "They attacked . . . It is hardly what they . . ." Frithfroth paused and put the stumps of his wrists to the temples of his head.

"I see it all as if before me every moment: The girl—now, the girl I judge to have a good head on her. But the boy is too skinny by half—he looks sickly. A boy of that age should already be filling out and gaining strength. And his eyes are constantly wide and goggling—eager though they may be, he has not yet seen the sights that turns a boy into a man, much less a warrior.

"I hear Godmund giving final cautions and advices—they fall on inattentive ears, and I fancy even he does not mark fully what he is saying. That's of little matter. We are all just marking time until Ealdstan deigns to grace us with his presence.

"The watch bell tolls for change. Godmund makes an excuse to leave. I stay. The old man finally arrives and gives his bitter benediction. He no sooner lowers his hand before the alarm bells ring.

"Another attack!"

Frithfroth's face was horror-stricken as he stared sightlessly in front of him. Daniel, Freya, and Vivienne just followed, wide-eyed and bewildered. They were afraid of what might happen if they interrupted him, just as they were afraid of what might happen if he were to continue.

"I leave in the company of the twice-cursed Cnafa and Cnapa—to go back to the Langtorr, to secure the tower, to protect the ruler, and to provide for the citizenry.

"Arrangements made, I climb the walls of the inner courtyard in order to observe the attack. I find Breca there, standing also. It is he who holds the responsibility of defending the inner court and the Great Carnyx. He is the last defense for the citizenry of Niðergeard, but his first responsibility is to the Carnyx.

"'I do not see them. What are they doing?'

"'They are making feints,' Breca informs me. 'They are masking their true numbers and movements. All we can do now is fend them off where we can and wait for the main body. But it could come from any angle—or several.'

"'Where is Ealdstan?'

"Breca shakes his head. He does not know, but he is certain he will arrive. Ealdstan has always been our defender against the yfelgópes—he stood always on the first line against the attackers. He will not fail us.

"We stand there, gazing out at the sea of hostile besiegers, with one thought in my mind: *Where is Ealdstan?*

"I feel a hand at my shoulder. 'There,' Breca says, pointing.

"I watch as yfelgópes come bubbling up over the wall, mounting it on ladders and scaffolding. Heaven save me, I am relieved. Finally, the fight has come at last. I hear the order to arms and my heart rises within me. The lifiendes are on the move—Kelm and his army must be feeling the threat of it; that is the reason for their attack. It is desperation.

"We fight. Salt of sweat and tang of blood rich on our lips. For days our long argument rages, sometimes within the city, sometimes without. Often I held the wall with the other defenders, those of the townsfolk who suited up to force the enemy back.

"Time carries on. The enemy rarely flags. The only way to slay an yfelgóp permanently—as with the sleeping warriors—is to kill it by mortal hand, or to remove its head from its body and heart from its chest. But in the heat of battle there is not always time for these operations. Very rarely, in fact.

"There comes one of those eerie quiets that occasionally pass in battle—when warriors become fatigued in body and spirit, and, by what feels like mutual consent, withdraw from the field to regroup, recoup, and recover.

"Godmund decamps to the gap in the wall, which is still widening, crumbling away; it is a war council of sorts, come to meet. Those guards and citizens of Niðergeard who are still able to stand are doing so atop the outer walls and towers, but the battle is taking its toll.

"Modwyn is being summoned from the tower. She arrives, glorious in her silver and green enamel armour. She has brought a map of the city and spreads it onto a slab of stone.

"It is explained to us how the city stood, and plans are made for the next press of attack. For now the yfelgópes are unnaturally calm. We mean to press our advantage while there is power still in our limbs.

"It is just then that we hear the sound of digging—a harsh, grating, staccato of pickaxes and pounded chisels. In a city carved from the very stone that it rests upon, each strike of axe and tool reverberates through the whole and feels like a blow to the bones.

There is nowhere to escape the noise of it. The besiegers work ceaselessly, continuously. The noise is deafening, maddening, and terrifying. Sometimes, in the silence, I hear those noises again.

"We do not know why the digging has started just then, after so many years. Something must have changed, but we don't know what. We wonder if it could be the lifiendes—could they be so successful so quickly? Could this be the final, desperate lunge of our all-but-defeated attackers? Or have the lifiendes failed and this was to be the killing blow?"

Frithfroth stopped and turned toward them, his eyes at last seeing them again.

"I never did find out the answer to that question. Did you succeed?"

"Yes," said Daniel.

"Ah," he said.

The farther down the Langtorr they went, the wider the stairs and expanse of their descending circle. They passed a few iron doors set in dark alcoves but did not explore them. There were other viewing holes that looked down to the city below, which grew closer and closer. They were able to pick out more details each time, evidence of the truth of Frithfroth's tale—collapsed buildings, and then as they went farther, cracked walls; closer still, littered streets.

A rope handrail suddenly sprouted from the wall, which some basic spiral carvings ran above. Both Freya and Daniel recognised the pattern, and they knew to look for the door to Ealdstan's study. When they came upon it, however, they found the door warped—almost bent in two—and lying against the wall. Inside, they could see a large stone table had been upended.

"What happened here?" Vivienne asked.

Frithfroth came back up a few steps and looked at the ruined portal. "Godmund decides it is time for answers, and so he comes looking for the person he believes has them. Ealdstan has not shown a whisker of himself since the battle, and no one has been able to spare the time to search for him. Some of the tower guard, Modwyn, and I search the entire tower. Every room but this is searched—Ealdstan's metal door is shut tight. We pound and kick at it, but to no avail.

"Godmund brings smiths in to cut and pull the door apart from the wall. He thinks to dig the worm out of its lair, but it is too late. Ealdstan has departed. And still the digging continues. The grains of sand of Niðergeard's fall are continuing their trickle down.

"Our situation is most desperate. And is about to become worse."

III

The four of them reached the ground floor of the Langtorr and looked over the rail of one of the two wide staircases into the grand central foyer. Apart from being dusty and dark, it was much as they remembered it. It had been badly kept up—two tapestries were hanging on the wall at an odd angle—but otherwise it was not ruined or ransacked in any way.

"Incredible," Vivienne said, pressing a hand against her chest. "In all my days, I could never imagine . . ."

Frithfroth continued down the stairs below them. He stood in the centre of the reception room, where Daniel and Freya had once been welcomed by Modwyn.

"This is where we are overcome," he said. "This is where I am betrayed. While I collapse in exhaustion—I who should be most watchful—two guards are murdered and the gates of the inner keep unbarred. The doors of the Langtorr itself open in a wide and warm welcome to our enemy.

"Something has changed in the air. I can't think what until I realise that the bone-shivering sound of the tunnelling has ceased. I am still cursing Cnapa for not waking me when I see his body lying in the door of the Langtorr, bleeding his life blood out onto the ground.

"I run to him and kneel, but I know before I am within a pace of him that he is gone. I put a hand beneath my faithful servant's head and feel a knife at my neck." Frithfroth raised his hand and tilted his head upward.

"It is Cnafa. His dagger drips dark blood down my chest—not my own, but that of his brother. I demand to know the reason.

"'I serve the ruler of Niðergeard,' he tells me insolently. 'His wishes are my orders.'

"I spit on his orders. A swarm of yfelgópes envelop me and I am taken to Kelm, also called Kafhand, who stands beneath the arch of the inner wall. It is the first time I have seen him. He is massive and terrible, like the face of God's wrath. Behind him stands the yfelgóp forces, and before them, pushed into the ground, are the people of Niðergeard.

"Kelm the conqueror looks at me with killing eyes. 'Where is the woman Modwyn?' he demands.

"'By now she will be safely far away,' I answer.

"'Remove his left hand.'"

Vivienne gasped as Frithfroth stretched out his stump of a left arm. "A sword and a fire are brought; the one heats the other until it is red hot. The swordsman is skilful and strong, his cut swift and clean." His eyes poured tears as he retracted his arm.

"Through the fog of pain, Kelm speaks to me once again. 'Where is the woman, Modwyn? Where is the man, Godmund? Tell me.'

"For the second time, I spit on his wishes.

"'Remove his right hand.'"

Frithfroth raised his other arm. "It is strange. I can feel my fingers, feel my fists clench, but neither are there."

The door out of the Langtorr was open, just a crack, perhaps not even wide enough for one person to slip in. The patch of stone just inside of it where Breca and Cnapa had died was stained dark. They looked out to the deserted city. Silver lamps from building fixtures, half buried in rubble, threw light onto ruined streets and buildings.

"What happened then?" Vivienne asked.

Frithfroth swallowed, blinked, and then looked at them all. He had returned to them from the past. "There is a mighty shaking. All of those within the inner courtyard, all of those except for me, fall instantly dead. Those holding me drop to either side, just as my severed hands had, and as lifeless.

"Kelm, standing just feet away on the other side of the gate, is taken aback. As I rise to my feet and run back to the tower, I hear him give an order to pursue. I leap over the body of the traitorous Cnafa on my flight back to safety, straining for every inch.

"Only when I reach the tower's doors and hear no sound of pursuit do I risk a look back. Those who had followed Kelm's orders had fallen upon crossing the threshold. Kelm just stands, frozen, not sure if he himself should risk crossing. I come in, push the doors together with my shoulders, and fall senseless."

Frithfroth's head tilted downward. "I have been here in the years since. Ealdstan is departed now—this is the age of Gád Gristgrennar. The city is in ruin. They ravaged it after their victory. I could hear them . . . collapsing buildings, attacking the statues. The first thing they did was to raise a hero's throne—to elevate it higher than the buildings around it. And they cheered Kelm as he mounted it."

Frithfroth fell silent. After a time it became clear that he was finished.

"So what about Godmund?" Freya asked. "Where is he?"

Frithfroth shook his head. "Truly, I do not have any notion. He is not in the tower. I assumed he escaped and that he would return after rousing an army, but time passes and he remains unseen . . . Perhaps he was slain after all."

"What was it that killed everybody—that stopped them from entering the tower?" Daniel asked.

"That was Modwyn's power. Her last gift before she left."

"She's gone too?"

"Yes," said Frithfroth despondently. "She, too, is gone."

"You said 'the age of Gád' just now," Vivienne said. She had been inspecting the large tapestries that were hanging off the wall but turned to face Frithfroth. "What do you mean by that?"

"Is that not apparent? He rules here."

"No," Daniel said. "Frithfroth, I'm sorry for not returning earlier, but . . . Gád's dead. I killed his heart. Freya saw him die. Right, Freya? Tell him."

Frithfroth turned his lifeless eyes toward her. She nodded. "Yes, that's right," she said, meekly lying.

"Is Kelm still out there?" Daniel asked.

"Yes," Frithfroth said in a low tone.

"Who else commands the yfelgópes besides Kelm?"

"Where are you going with this, Daniel?" Vivienne asked.

"Information. We came here for information, right? What about it, Frithfroth?"

"Kelm is the only one who orders them. There are no captains or lieutenants, as far as I can make out."

Daniel was walking back and forth in the entryway, craning his neck to see more of what lay beyond the large doors. "Is there any chance that he would know that we're here?" he asked.

"If you entered by the upper door, I do not know of one."

Daniel turned, excited, his hands opening and closing at his side. "We can take him off guard!" he exclaimed in a hushed voice. "We can defeat the yfelgópes by cutting off their head—killing their leader!"

"I'm not sure, Daniel . . ." Vivienne said.

"No," said Freya, as firmly as she could, turning and coming back to the centre of the room. "We should stay here. There's more going on than we know; we should find out what it is."

"We know enough. We know how Niðergeard got taken; we know that Kelm's here. If we go fast, we can find him, kill him, and hole up back here and wait for Ecgbryt and Alex to arrive."

"But then what would the yfelgópes do?" Freya asked. "There's no telling how they'd react. They could completely flip out—run away, chase after us—it's not in the plan."

"The plan is to liberate Niðergeard, and this is a way to do it."

"No, we've got to wait here for help."

Daniel smirked at her. "I guess people don't really change," he said after a moment. "Viv, you agree with me, right?"

Vivienne looked from Daniel to Freya and then back. Her concerned, puzzled face was a rigid mask. "Actually, no," she said. "Daniel, there's no rush. We can look around here, and—"

"There's every reason to rush! We'll have him off guard! We can get a start on liberating the city. This is why we *came* here."

"No, it's not. We came here for information, first and foremost," Vivienne said forcefully. "Everything else happens afterward."

Daniel turned to look out into Niðergeard again. "Well, I'm going to do it. I don't care what you say."

"Daniel, please," Freya pleaded. "It's really too dangerous out there. You don't know—"

"I'll be fine, Freya, really," Daniel said condescendingly. "It's sweet of you to worry, but I can handle myself."

No, Freya thought, *people really don't change.* She recognised a crazy look in his eyes. He'd caught the scent of the quest again. He wanted to do something heroic. *This is getting out of hand . . .*

"Daniel." She hesitated. "Both of you—there's something I

need to tell you. You aren't going to think . . . You're not going to be too thrilled."

"Well? What is it?"

"Daniel . . . Gád's not dead. When you killed that . . . thing, he didn't die."

Daniel frowned in confusion. "What? No . . . What—what do you mean?"

"He's not dead—you didn't kill him. Daniel, you failed; we all did. Gád's alive."

Daniel's mouth opened and closed wordlessly.

"Why didn't you speak of this before?" Vivienne said in a grave voice.

"Because—I'm not sure I disagree with him. He said things that made a lot of sense."

"But he killed Swiðgar, Freya," Daniel said, staring at her in disbelief.

"I know, but . . . well, Swiðgar attacked him. We all did. What right did we have to go out and try to kill him?"

"Are you working with Gád? Is that it?" Daniel asked.

"No, of course not. Of course I'm not saying that. It's just—I think we should reevaluate what we think we're doing down here and why."

Daniel goggled at her. "*Reevaluate?*"

Frithfroth stood there, motionless except for very small swaying movements. If he had been following their conversation, if anything that Freya had revealed had made any impact on him at all, he did not give any sign.

"Freya, why didn't you bring this up before?" Vivienne sighed, putting a hand to her temple. "Ecgbryt and Alex have just charged off completely unprepared! You've endangered their lives by sending them off without adequate knowledge or preparation."

"'I . . . I . . .'"

Flushed and furious, Daniel glared angrily at Freya. He suddenly rushed at her, drawing his sword.

"Daniel! No!" Vivienne threw herself forward, knocking into Daniel and holding him back. Daniel struggled, and either his heart was not in it, or Vivienne was stronger than she looked.

"What are you going to do? *Kill me?*" Freya shouted. "You psychopath!"

"You're a traitor!"

"A traitor to what?" Freya said, spreading her arms. "Look around. To this? A moldy old building? An old man who *trapped* and *manipulated* us?"

"Yeah, that seems to happen a lot to you. You keep harping on about it, but what makes Ealdstan any worse than Gád or Professor Stowe?"

"Honestly? Neither of them asked me to *kill* anyone."

Daniel sneered at her.

Freya raised a finger accusingly. "Do you really hate me now or what? What is this anger? Where does it come from? It's not just good and bad out there, Daniel—as much as you'd like it to be! This is real life, and it's *messy.*"

"Then why are you the one who's least willing to get dirty?" He relaxed and Vivienne released him. Daniel turned away.

"Freya," Vivienne said in a low voice. "This is catastrophic. Gád makes everything worse. If we'd known he was still running around—there's no telling what he could be up to. He's had eight years. Running amok. Plotting. Planning."

"Better him than Ealdstan," Freya said hotly. It was all starting to pour out now. "This city . . . this city is an occupying force—stockpiling warriors, against what? What's it all for? All the lies, using us—Daniel and me—to kill *an old man*. That's not the side I want to be on."

"But Swiðgar and Ecgbryt. What about them? Modwyn? Your friends?"

"They're not my friends. I don't trust them, I don't know them; they don't know me."

"What about *me*?" Daniel asked.

"You? You who just pulled a *sword* on me?"

"Quiet, both of you, quiet!" Vivienne said. "Let's think about this."

Freya and Daniel silently retreated to opposite sides of the room.

"It actually changes nothing," she said.

"What?" Daniel said as Freya turned back to Vivienne.

"It changes nothing," Vivienne repeated.

"It changes *everything*," Daniel said.

"We carry on as before. Same plan. It's just—the stakes are higher now. The potential danger greater. But our goals are the same."

"Right," Daniel said. "Which makes it all the more important that I kill Kelm. Or Gád, if I can find him."

"No, don't do that."

"What? Vivienne . . ."

"Daniel, we don't have a strategy for that. Be reasonable. Our first priority is to investigate this tower, try to see if there's any-thing in Ealdstan's writings that would indicate where he's gone or if he's prepared any fail-safes for such a situation. Then we're to look into finding the Carnyx—to see if it will summon the knights. Then we should find Godmund and Modwyn—they will no doubt have information vital to tactics and the lay of the land."

"Sounds fascinating. I tell you what . . . you two can do that, I'll do my thing. And don't worry, I won't just charge off. I'll study the yfelgópes here in the city. I'll observe them from the windows, get their movements and rhythms, all with a view to taking down

Kelm and his boss as soon as possible." He turned his open gaze from Freya to Vivienne.

"Why don't you go looking for the Carnyx?" Vivienne asked.

"We'll have plenty of time for scavenger hunts if we can deal with the single greatest threat to our safety and that of the over-world—namely Gád and Kelm. Come on, you know it makes sense!"

"Well . . . look into it, but come see me first if you decide on leaving the Langtorr," Vivienne said haltingly.

Daniel hesitated for just the briefest of moments. "Of course. Of course I will."

"If any of you do leave the threshold of the tower forecourt . . ." Frithfroth said abruptly, making them all start. "I would not risk coming back. All who pass the threshold die."

"Except for you," Daniel said. "I'm going up. Don't bother me." With another long look back at Freya, he resettled his back-pack on his shoulders and started trudging up the stairs.

Vivienne turned to Freya. "We'll talk more about this later," she said. "For now, let's hear Frithfroth out on what happened here."

IV

Ecgbryt and Alex stood over the corpses of six black bears. That was good. Alex was worried that the bodies would turn back into men when they died—which would have been more troublesome for them. People would want to find them very quickly in order to ask some very urgent questions if six people were found dead. But as it was, half a dozen slaughtered bears were more of a strange puzzle than an act of mass murder.

They were shaking as they took stock. Neither of them had so much as a scratch, although there were some bruises. When Alex ran out of bullets, he had dropped the gun and drawn his sword, which was strapped to his back. Alloyed steel and custom craftsmanship made it sharp and deadly. Even if he wasn't as practised with it as Ecgbryt was with his axe, he was still very capable.

They retreated past the standing stones and toward the trees, their backs almost edging up along the black metal rail fence that surrounded the Rollright Stones. Getting backed into a corner was not ideal in most circumstances, but in this instance it was preferable to being surrounded.

Alex's arms ached; swinging that sword through fur, muscle, and bone was hard work. He was buzzing from adrenaline, panting, his arms and shoulders on fire; it was a good feeling.

Ecgbryt cleaned his blade and was sliding it back into the holster he wore on his back, underneath his coat.

"Shall we try to hide them?" Alex asked. "Half a dozen five-hundred-pound bears are quite the handful."

Ecgbryt considered and then shook his head. "Leave them here. We should be away."

"The RSPCA will be hot, no doubt. Do you think they'll turn human again when daylight hits?"

"We're not going to be around to see it if they do. Come. The survival of young Daniel and Freya depends on our swift movements hereafter. I do not wish to storm the city, only to be greeted by their lifeless corpses hanging off the main gates."

CHAPTER THREE

Assassin

———————————— I ————————————

"The boy is very impatient," Frithfroth said.

"You're not wrong there," Vivienne assented.

"His blood runs hot—too hot. It boils and rises to his eyes in a mist. When it leaves, it leaves him empty, so empty. I have seen men chase after such heat. I hope it will not be his ruin."

"Tell us what happened, Frithfroth. How Niðergeard fell, if they could not take the Langtorr."

As an answer, Frithfroth crossed over to one of the tapestries hanging at an angle. He pushed up a corner to show a dark archway. He slipped through it and the tapestry fell back to its skewed position. Freya and Vivienne traded apprehensive looks, and then Vivienne crossed over and pulled back the thick woven cloth.

Swallowing hard, Freya ducked under the faded cloth, which smelled of rot and mold. Descending a curved stairway, the two women gradually lowered themselves into the thick, sharp smell of death that seemed to rise up in a cloud around them. They blocked their noses, but it crept into every breath they were forced to take. It stung their eyes and made their skin crawl. It was like a slap in the face.

"This was our last defense," Frithfroth said, apparently oblivious or immune to the stench. "After finding Ealdstan departed, Godmund grew desperate. He spouted betrayal, deceit, perversion." The staircase wound down and then opened into a wide, semi-spherical room. It was aglow with hundreds of silver lamps arranged along walls and pillars. The light that shone from them fell upon four concentric circles, each with a low stone slab cut to contain a man, but rising only a couple inches in height off the ground.

There were one hundred and five sleeping spaces arranged in four concentric circles—seven in the inner ring, twice that in the next, and doubling again and again in the next two rings. A circular dais was raised in the centre, and on it, a stone throne.

"This is the *Slæpereshus*—the Chamber of the Sleepers," Frithfroth said. "These are the elite of all of the sleepers in this isle. Their deeds are celebrated in myth and legend. Over fifty from the fields of Agincourt. Nearly thirty from the first crusade. One dozen and two from Horsa's men, and seven knights of the table. All of them surrounding the hero who wore a dragon's helm. Sleeping all not just for the nation's greatest need, but for Niðergeard's."

However glorious it sounded and once may have looked, it was a slaughterhouse now. The biers were covered with the mangled remnants of the bodies they once held in state. The skin and flesh were beyond decay—black and leathery in some instances, or already decomposed. Bones could be seen, but not the clean, white bones in movies and on TV—these bones were brown and corrupted, with leathery flesh still hanging on to them. Forms could really only be made out by the clothing and armour that the bodies once occupied. Some heads appeared to be absent. Some biers only bore a shattered weapon or a broken shield.

Horrifically, perversely, the ground was moving. Maggots, insects, and some reptiles could be glimpsed in Frithfroth's lantern light and the large flashlights that Freya and Vivienne carried. The dead bodies had apparently presented enough nourishment to produce a macabre ecosystem, a carrion food chain in the Langtorr's cellar.

Freya gasped when she saw all the crawling nasties that swarmed the floor and raised an arm to prevent Vivienne from walking past her. Vivienne tensed and they stood there, a few stairs up, where nothing, they hoped, could crawl up to them, as Frithfroth unheedingly navigated the large room. He wove in and out of the biers, uncaring of the creatures that scuttled across his feet or clung briefly to his cloak. He went to the far wall where an iron hook was mounted, on which was hanging a horn. He raised an arm to it, as if he were reaching out and touching it with his missing hand.

"He blew this horn to wake them. When the knights awake, they are not like the city's guards—they are mortal, and thus able to vanquish the yfelgópes permanently.

"Yes, he blew the horn, and it will never sound again, for there will not be any to hear it. They rose and went forth to battle, striking at the heart of the enemy, beyond the once-high walls of this city. It should have been a charge to victory, to a glorious routing of the enemy, but the unimaginable happened—the greatest war band ever seen in these isles was withstood.

"They fought for days without a one of them falling. The bodies of their slain enemies mounted higher and higher, and became their fortress. They fought along its walls and built them higher, bulwarked with more of their foes.

"And then one of our own fell. He was brought back here

and laid to his final rest, arising again only when his body is made whole in the final judgement. But his absence in the line of defenders gave a hold to the relentless storm to wear away at those on either side of him. And more fell, over time, and more. They, too, were brought back. Those that remained standing—standing and fighting for almost a year now with no rest—renewed their resolve and fought harder and more cunningly than any in history. But no man is perfect—all falter. I myself watched from this very tower as the last three valiant knights fought in a whirlpool of enemies, each taking many blows that would have laid a mortal man senseless. Then they, too, were taken.

"All that remained was the hero of the dragon's helm. They disarmed him, cut him so that no muscle moved any bone, and then divided him up amongst themselves so that each could have a talisman to show their defeat of the greatest hero in the western kingdoms. Two had his jawbone, many had his teeth, the fingers of his hands, so, too, the bones of his shins . . ."

Frithfroth started back toward the stairs, through the bodies and writhing shapes on the floor.

"Those left in Niðergeard could only watch in dread. Godmund had armed the citizenry and given them all instruction, but when the army of the enemy marched upon us, they did not last an hour.

"Kelm himself claimed the dragonhelm. And once he had, he threw it over the Langtorr wall just to spite. I recovered it and moved it here." He indicated a silver helmet traced with gold that lay on the throne in the centre of the dais. It had a winged dragon mounted on it, its arms and legs clutching at the sides, its wings joining around the back.

Frithfroth said no more and did not move away from the throne's side.

"All right, well," Vivienne said. "I believe I've got a fairly clear idea now of what happened here. Freya, would you agree?"

Freya nodded. "Yep. No questions here. Maybe a few later, but, um . . ."

"Good Frithfroth, keeper of the Langtorr," Vivienne began in an officious voice. "May we, by your leave, obtain freedom to walk these halls?"

Frithfroth blinked. His brows contracted and his mouth twitched open. For a brief moment Freya saw the man he used to be, before Niðergeard fell. It passed, and the old man's face slackened and his eyes turned to stare into the distance. He bowed his head, however, in response to the formal request.

Vivienne tugged at Freya's shoulder and the two women made swift but careful tracks back up the stairs.

II

Daniel looked down from a window in the guest room floor hallway. At first sight, it was still and lifeless, but after a time he started to pick out small movements. He would see a dark shadow shift and roll over in its sleep—a yfelgóp. Studying it closer, he could see that it was lying next to others—maybe fifteen of them, all lying asleep in the second floor of a gutted, roofless building. They were so vulnerable and unaware. He wondered if there would be a way to kill them as they slept. To collapse the building, perhaps? Or slit their throats as they snored through their wretched dreams?

No. *Eyes on the prize*, he reminded himself. Even if he managed it well and quietly, and nobody saw him, any stray activity would run the risk of putting Kelm on alert. And if Kelm had even the slightest degree of wariness as a result of such an action, then it would be too costly. He would simply have to strike quickly and slip away before he was discovered. Daniel could feel that this was what he should do; he had faith; he believed.

Now he just had to spot an opening. He continued to scan

the ruins below him, moving from window to window, becoming more adept at spotting the yfelgópes from his vantage. They seemed to be rather lethargically guarding the city, if indeed they were guarding it at all. *Occupying* it was probably the correct term, but in the laziest fashion imaginable. Those that were dotted along rooftops seemed more interested in squabbling with each other or playing games of chance than keeping watch. Years with no threat to give their vigilance worth left them lazy. *All the better for me,* Daniel thought.

He noted the familiar landmarks that were once his favourite places. It broke his heart to think that the fascinating stonework friezes on the buildings were now almost all damaged beyond repair. He looked for the blacksmith's house where his sword had been named but couldn't find it in the dark rubble. The marble courtyard with the intricate red and white paving was no longer empty but now contained a huge pile of rubble, presumably made with the debris of the collapsed buildings around it.

Was this the hero's throne that Frithfroth had told them about? The courtyard was about midway between the Langtorr and the ruined wall of trees, but at his current height, it was hard for Daniel to make out what exactly was going on with the heap. He could see the back of what could be the throne, as well as a curve of what might be someone sitting on it, but he couldn't tell for certain. There was yfelgóp activity around it—figures approached, stood for a while in what might be a deferential posture, and then left. They were obviously addressing or being addressed by something atop the pile. Daniel decided to sit and watch.

He watched for at least an hour before the curved edge of what was on the throne detached itself and hobbled down the stone heap—it looked massively overweight—and then started moving down the streets toward the Langtorr. As it came nearer, Daniel edged away from the window, so that he only peeked through the very edge of the window pane. He doubted that he would be spotted this high up, at this distance, in a darkened hallway, but he didn't want to chance it.

The more he watched the figure, the more Daniel became certain that it was Kelm. Although he walked the streets unescorted, he would often stop a moment here and there to abuse or issue instructions to one of his minions. He was not attended or, apparently, guarded in any way. How lazy had Kelm become, resting on his laurels? Overconfidence would be his downfall.

Kelm turned a corner and stumbled on a prone yfelgóp who was lazing against a wall. Daniel imagined that the victim's leg must have certainly snapped, but he leapt up pretty quickly anyway.

The war chief passed out of his sight, and Daniel moved across to the next window, just in time to see him enter one of the few buildings in the city left whole. He stayed in there for some time and didn't come out all the time that Daniel watched it.

The hours passed. Daniel kept his eyes trained on the hut. He became hungry and ate from his provisions. He was aware of Freya and Vivienne moving around in the tower, but he didn't go to speak to them, and they didn't come to see him.

He fought tiredness. He hadn't been sleeping well lately—not at all, in fact. Not since he got back from Elfland. The last week or so, just as he'd been on the edge of sleep, he would feel a sudden terror and an abrupt feeling of plunging. Each time he jerked himself awake—once nearly falling out of his bed. He would lay awake, panting, in a sweat, gripping the mattress through the sheets, counting the minutes until morning.

Suddenly, Daniel tensed. He threw his arms out to brace himself against the edge of the windowsill. For a second he thought that he had fallen through it and was plummeting to his death. But the glass was still in front of him. His forehead hadn't even touched it. Just thinking about sleep made him tired enough to drift off.

He'd sleep when he was finished with the mission. It was all side effects of the anxiety of the situation, no doubt. Either that, or something mystical that would guide him toward completion of his new mission. Either way, it was good.

Daniel wondered why there were so few yfelgópes below him. The city should be flooded. But they were only scattered here and there, in clumps or singly. Where were the rest of them? Did the knights really kill as many as Frithfroth claimed, or were they off somewhere else?

Well, it wasn't his problem now, and Daniel was tired of waiting. He had enough information. Now he needed to move. He pulled out a map of Niðergeard that Alex had made for him and studied the route he would take, comparing it to the streets outside, noting obstacles. He would have to memorise the route exactly. There would be no room for error, even the slightest mistake. As he contemplated his route, an idea struck him. He grinned gleefully, clenching and unclenching his hands in eager anticipation.

III

Daniel stood just inside the door, watching the flames of the fire flare up and then die down. He'd brought one of the moldy sheets down from the room he'd once stayed in and set it alight in the dining hall, out of sight of the main entrance. It gave off a few large billows of brown smoke and then died down into a ball of bright orange worms that chased each other over the black, charred ball.

Should he find Freya and Vivienne and tell them what he was doing? *No, what good would come of that?* Best just slip out and surprise them later with his mission accomplished.

He had kept the gun he had been given in Elfland. It was oiled now and loaded with new bullets from Alex's armoury at his family manse. He had a belt holster for it and three other magazines clipped beside it. He only planned on using his gun during phase two of his plan—making it back to the Langtorr alive—and only if he had no other option. No doubt, at some point—unless he was very, very lucky—he'd be discovered, and the yfelgópes would learn he'd killed their leader, and if he had to blast his way back here, then he would.

He discarded his bag and coat onto a low iron table. Then he stripped off his shirt and T-shirt so his chest and arms were bare. Bending down, he rubbed his hands in the now fairly cool ashes of the burned bedding; it was a black, greasy soot—perfect. He rubbed it on his body in long, dark strokes, making sure to build it up good and dark. He propped up a metal serving platter against the wall and used it as a mirror in order to make sure he got his face and back as well.

When he was finished, he stepped back and looked at the dim, distorted image in the serving plate. At the most casual of glances, he'd make a passable yfelgóp, especially if he emulated their hunched posture and scrabbling gait.

He grabbed his sword, Hero-Maker, and drew it from its scabbard. With the remaining ash, he darkened its blade, covering the brilliant shine until it only reflected a dull, oily-grey sheen. His heart pounding, Daniel did a few warm-up stretches and then padded back into the main hall.

Time to be a hero, he thought as he crossed to the door. He paused, watchful and alert. The air that came through the small crack was not cooler or warmer or fresher, it just moved more quickly. He gently pulled the door open. Thankfully, it did not squeak or creak, and, stepping over the brown patch left by Cnapa's blood, he was able to slip through it, only to pause briefly in the shadow of the archway. The wide, shallow steps spread before him.

He noted what must be the remnants of Cnafa's body, splayed out over several of the wide steps, the skin brown and drawn, like a Hollywood mummy, his clothes decaying, the blue threads of his shirt turned black.

Silver lamps lit every step, making this one of the brightest areas of the city, but if he stuck by the wall, he could move in relative darkness. Skirting past the elaborately carved and highly textured wall, moving slowly, he circumnavigated the courtyard and made it to the inner wall's gate.

He paused a moment to catch his breath; he was already panting anxiously. From this angle, the debris pile in the courtyard didn't seem as haphazard as it had from the window above. There were two lines of silver lamps that bisected it from the top, the ridges of what could have been stairs, and the outline of a large chair on top of it. *That must be the hero's throne.*

There were no yfelgópes in view, but he knew that a group of them were lounging on the rooftop above the building opposite the gates. Unfortunately, there were no buildings closer than thirty feet to the inner wall to provide cover. And the dark buildings might contain any number of hidden eyes. To his advantage, however, there was plenty of rubble and detritus in piles against the wall; he wouldn't be a stark shape against a plain background, at least.

He made his way quickly through the pile of dry corpses that lay across the gateway, trying not to think too much about what was beneath his feet, and began following his route along the outside of the Langtorr wall. He kept his back hunched, head up, and body tense and poised, trying vaguely to emulate the yfelgóp stance.

He encountered his first yfelgóp after only a dozen or so paces. It was sleeping with its back against the wall, and Daniel found it very easy to thrust his sword through its throat and upward into the brain stem. Its eyes flicked open briefly and Daniel wondered if it was looking at him or if it was just an autonomic response.

Then the eyes clouded, and the moment was gone. Not having time to wipe his blade, Daniel just gave it a few good shakes to get most of the blood off and continued his prowl.

There were no other yfelgópes along his path, and it wasn't until he started navigating the streets of Niðergeard that he saw any more of them—and luckily they were just forms and silhouettes glimpsed in side streets or chattering in buildings. A group of them passed twenty feet ahead of him, but he simply staggered slowly to a pile of rubble and hunkered down until they moved on.

Daniel was getting close to the hut now—he could see the cluster of listless guards sitting in front of it. They didn't worry him too much, since he had already figured out a way to get past them. He knew from looking down on it from the tower that there was a hole in the roof that could not be seen from the street. The rubble on the far side of the building was high enough, he had judged, to allow him entry to the roof. If he was quiet, no one would hear him, and if he was quick, the yfelgópes on the other rooftops wouldn't see him either.

Now was the time. He sheathed his sword and, darting forward, hurried around the side of the building to scrabble up the fallen masonry. He moved on all fours, trying to spread his weight evenly, anchoring himself on the largest chunks to support himself. Providence favoured him, and he made it up the single story without anything beneath him shifting so much as a centimeter.

The roof was completely flat, with a slight ridge around it at the wall's edge. A dark, shifting shadow floated above the hole in the opposite corner. In the low light it took Daniel a few moments to recognise it as smoke. Crouching, he stayed near the wall to avoid causing more of the roof to cave in, and reached the hole.

The floor below was almost completely dark and still except for an orange glow emanating from one corner of the room and a brown, peaty smoke wafting through the hole—a makeshift chimney. He couldn't see Kelm. If he was down there, it'd be over quickly. If he wasn't, then Daniel would wait for him to return and ambush him from the shadows.

There was a large boulder directly beneath him and it came up nearly halfway to the ceiling. It was the work of a moment to hop down from the roof directly onto it and then slide down into the corner, out of sight of the rest of the room.

Daniel had been completely silent and was therefore hopefully undetected, but he sat behind the boulder for a few long moments, just listening. He could hear no sound except for the hiss of the fire and the distant bickering of some passing yfelgópes.

Drawing his sword, he moved around the large, lumpy rock, pressing himself into it to lighten his footfalls. He crouched behind a low outcropping that afforded him a view of the rest of the room. There was indeed a coal fire burning on the other side of the room and near that, an elaborate, wrought iron chair, currently unoccupied. Daniel released his breath in a sigh. He would just have to sit tight and await Kelm's return, however long that would be.

He rounded back into the dark area between the boulder and the wall and slouched down to wait. As he focused on stilling his breathing, there was some part of his brain that was buzzing at him, trying to get his attention, telling him that something didn't quite make sense, something was out of place.

What was it, exactly? The boulder, that was it—it was out of place. What was it doing here? It was too large to have come through the hole in the roof. It might have been rolled through the door, but why? It might always have been here, but again, why? That was a puzzle. And why did it feel like it moved just then?

A terrifying idea eclipsed Daniel's mind like a storm cloud. He turned and looked at the rounded outcropping he had crouched behind.

It had a face—a bulbous, exaggerated face with rock-like

features, but a face nonetheless, with a nose, mouth, ears, and eyes that were looking directly at him.

Daniel very nearly had time to panic. He brought his sword up and was still in the process of taking a step back when the boulder shifted into a blur of motion and the world went completely dark.

IV

"You found the gap in my inner perimeter. Well done. In my defense, however, I didn't seriously expect anyone to hop onto a troll's head in order to exploit it. That was an exceptionally impressive display of stupidity—I truly wish I had been there to see it."

The words were deep and thick and came to Daniel from a long way off. Somehow they managed to find their way through the whistling tumult around his head and into his ears. He was falling—falling fast, and it was this, more than the voice, that brought him out of his stupor. He blinked, brought up his head, and looked straight into light blue, sympathetic eyes.

His arms were twisted behind and above him, bound by what, he couldn't tell yet. His left side was mostly numb and throbbed ominously in the places that he could still feel. That side of his face felt swollen and his teeth tingled. What had happened? Had the building fallen on him?

Then he remembered the face and he blinked but felt only one eye move. He tried to move his hand to feel it, but a metallic rattling reminded him that he was chained.

That was that, then. He tried to curse, but no words came out of his mouth; it was plugged up for some reason.

Daniel raised his eyes, making the world rock like a boat. He had to tilt his head upwards, for the person in front of him was at least six and a half feet tall, and huge—bulky like a wrestler or those men on the world's strongest man shows. He had the untoned physique of someone who carried immense, raw strength in his limbs. His chest was thick and barrel-like, but his stomach bulged out so far that it made his torso pear shaped. He was dressed in black leather that was studded in some places and covered with interlocking chains in others. His skin was dark grey. Behind him was the raised, altar-like pile of ruined stone, with the rough-hewn throne sitting atop it.

Daniel tried to focus on his slick, bullet head with piggy eyes and form his name. "Kuh . . . elmuh?" A thick stream of saliva and blood poured from his lip.

"Yes. Naturally. Groggy? I am not surprised. You got hit by a troll. You're lucky she only hit you once. Twice or three times and you would have been a bag of skin filled with jelly.

"But she's a tame troll. Trained. She knew to check her swing. All you took was a playful swat." Kelm moved his hand across, as if shooing a fly. "You'll live. Teeth don't look so good, but maybe you'll hold on to them. You've been hanging here for quite a time; I take your return to consciousness as an encouraging sign of your physical resilience."

Kelm was illumined by a nearby brazier full of coal.

"Now tell me. Why *are* you here?"

Daniel's words came as separate, mangled syllables. "Ah. Wuh. Ana. Jhu-oin. Oo."

"You want to *join* me?"

Daniel nodded, a tilt of his head quickly downward and then slowly up. It was a long shot. That he came in "uniform," as it were, dressed as a yfelgóp, was the only possible excuse he had of making it out of whatever Kelm had in store for him . . . Likely death, with a whole lot worse preceding it.

Kelm straightened. His thick lips pursed. "Join me? That's certainly bold. You blacken your body and run around without your shirt on. You look the part; I'll give you that."

His lips shifted and drooped into an enormous frown. "Unfortunately for you, I am not so gullible as to believe that a man dropping through my roof with a sword, and a gun, is trying to be my friend, no matter how ridiculously he paints himself. And I still would not believe you even if your sword was not still sticky with the blood of a murdered yfelgóp. Which it is."

"Pr've. Muh-sulf."

"You wanted to prove yourself?" Kelm chuckled. "Bravo. But no more games. I know your name, Daniel Tully, and I know what sort of person you are."

Kelm slapped him across the face. There was an explosion of pain very far off, and equally as far off, a cry of pain somewhere between a growl and a howl.

"Who did you come with? How many are you? What are your objectives?" Each question was an angry bark. Daniel could only reel, his head spinning. He could feel the pit of unconsciousness open at his feet, the pit he would fall into if he did not stay awake.

Kelm wiped his hand on his chest. If he wanted answers to his questions, he seemed happy enough not to pursue them. He took a few steps back and settled his weight on the back of his feet.

"You *should* join us," he said in a deep voice. "Niðergeard should be destroyed. You have no idea of the slavery that Niðergeard has subjected your country and your people to. The centuries of control that it has exerted on the course of this nation. The hold that it's had on the neck of history."

Kelm's eyes flicked up and down Daniel. "I was told about you, young Master Tully. I was told about what they did to you and the girl. They picked you up, sharpened your resolve with their lies, and hurled you like a weapon straight at a target. I am a warrior, a very cunning and intelligent one, but I have never used children in a campaign, for any reason, much less turned a young boy and a young girl into assassins.

"And you still are an assassin, aren't you? I can see it. Trapped, but an assassin nonetheless. They did their job well in shaping you."

Daniel did not take his eyes from Kelm, even though they were watering and he wanted more than anything to close them and drift into sleep. But it was vital to look like he was taking it in, like he was being convinced of Kelm's stories. The only way out was through. But it would be easier if he didn't have to fight for each thought his mind developed.

"How long have you been living the lies of Niðergeard? Since you were how old? Thirteen? Twelve? What did you give up for them? And did they give you any thanks? Any reward?"

Daniel's vision blurred and reeled. The words *thanks* and *reward* went straight to his heart. That's the only thing that had hurt him, and it had hurt him deeply. He wanted to be acknowledged. Deep down, he wanted to be a knight, sleeping, rising in victory to fight the final battle . . .

Somewhere along the line it had gone wrong.

Kelm's face wore an expression that Daniel might have guessed to be sympathy.

"You were nothing to them, Daniel. Do you thank a hammer once you have used it to pound in a nail? Do you thank a stick that spears a fish?"

Daniel set his jaw defiantly.

Kelm came close, close enough that Daniel could feel the hot, damp breath on his face.

"Who is with you? How many are you? What are your objectives?"

The questions snapped Daniel out of his self-pity. He had to stay strong. He had a mission here. He had failed the first directive, but there were others. Namely: find the Great Carnyx, and find Godmund.

Daniel made no reply.

Kelm just smiled in an easy, paternal way, straightened, slapped him viciously again, and then called into the darkness, "Lock him up."

There was a heavy clinking to his right and his left arm went slack, renewing the waves of fire that swept through him. He heard himself cry out in his muffled way. Then his right went slack, and as Kelm disappeared into the darkness, the yfelgópes came to take him away.

V

Daniel had attracted a lot of attention on the way to the dungeons of Niðergeard. The cells under the northern part of the city had rarely been used, but they stood ready to impart damp, cold, and moldy misery.

Daniel shivered as the yfelgóp hoard pushed him down a dark little corridor.

His wrists were crossed in front of him, bound in very thick and coarse rope. His eyes still weren't as accustomed to the lack of light as the yfelgópes' were, so he walked in near total darkness. They were pushing him quickly down the passageways—quicker than Daniel thought he could go.

"Wuh—ate. Gemmee. Minnit," he said, staggering but not falling. He was too bound in by yfelgópes to fall over completely. One of them gave him a shove and he toppled the other way, where he was shoved roughly back into the circle again.

They kept on like that for a while, treating him like a pinball, then finally stopped. Daniel heard the sound of keys clanking and an iron lock squeak, and then he was shoved sideways into the darkness. He sprawled and hit the ground on his right side— thankfully, not his bruised left—and rolled onto his stomach.

Words were shouted at him, but through the pain he couldn't arrange them into meaning. He lay there for a few moments, pressing the hot, throbbing side of his face against the cool, damp stone floor. Then he started to shiver, so he got up and, feeling his way awkwardly with his bound hands, found the sides and corners of the room he was in. The walls were roughly carved and, it seemed, almost perfectly cubic. There was a flat ridge opposite the narrow, iron door that ran the length of the wall. It was probably meant as a bed, but there was no matting on it.

He sat and hunched over, moaning softly, his fingers gently touching and inspecting his face. Nothing seemed to be broken, apart from his skin. It was hard to tell sweat and saliva from blood in the darkness. He moved his jaw open and from side to side to stop it from tightening up and then started probing the rest of him. Everything seemed pretty much intact, but it was hard to feel his ribs with his hands, bound as they were. He had taken quite a blow, though. How could he tell if he had a concussion? What were the tests for that? What was the treatment? He stretched out on the stone slab and closed his eyes but tried not to fall asleep.

It was hard to do. He fought to keep his eyes open, but already he could feel the slide into sleep that brought the terrible falling sensation. Maybe he should just go ahead and embrace the feeling—it couldn't be very long before he slipped into unconsciousness. But there was something at the end of the fall that he could feel waiting for him, so he resisted it.

It may have been as much as an hour before he heard footsteps in the corridor again. He sat upright and stilled his breathing, listening to try to guess how many approached. His eyes had adjusted slightly to the darkness, but he still couldn't see the inside of the cell. He could make out the cutaway sections of the iron door, a dull, dark grey against pure black.

It was the yfelgópes again. He could hear the slaps of their thin leather shoes. He tried to prepare himself, but he didn't anticipate the apologetic whisper that issued from outside his door.

"Hsst! You in there."

The whisper was an enquiry, not a shout or an order.

"Hello?" he ventured, his mouth still swollen but thankfully numb.

"You are Daniel, the lifiende. Daniel the quest-finisher."

"Yessh," he answered. "An' you?"

"Incorrect," the voice responded. "Incorrect order. Please listen and answer. We will ask four questions and then answer four of yours. What was your intent in coming here?"

Daniel paused for a moment. Was this another trick?

"Can . . . trust . . . you?"

"Incorrect! You must answer—"

"It is a valid query," another voice piped up. "All answers he may provide are reliant and conditional on the answer to his."

"Valid! A turnaround, then! You may ask three questions, and then we ask."

Daniel swallowed in agony. "Who . . . are . . . you?"

"Disloyals," the voice said with a sort of angry pride. "Rebels, mutineers, dissidents. We started following Gád because it made sense, or so we thought. However, reason cannot now condone his actions. We have begun . . . to doubt."

"What . . . mean . . . doubt?" Daniel asked.

"Incongruences. Incongruences in spoken rhetoric, and inconsistencies in action. At first niggling irregularities, but on investigation turn out to be vast disconnects—rifts in reason. Bad logic. Undeniable, unconscionable. For those of us who believe, there is only one option: resist."

Daniel raised an eyebrow. This was an interesting development.

"Why . . . still . . . here?" he asked, mentally registering his third question.

"Where else to go? We do not know much of the caves of the Niðergearders, and would we be able to explain ourselves to those who found us? Would we be given the opportunity? Best to wait until better circumstances. These circumstances."

"How . . . many . . . of you . . . are there?"

"That was your last question."

"One more."

"No! Us first. Who else is here with you?"

Daniel thought and framed his reply, sucking in saliva. "Just me. But more . . . on way."

"Reinforcements? An army?"

Daniel thought. "Yes."

"Is it Godmund?"

"No."

"That is three," said a third voice from the door. "He shall have more, and then we. One each, until the finish."

"How . . . many . . . of you . . . are there?"

"Thirty-seven," the voice answered promptly. "That we are in contact with—that we know of. There may be others whose system of logic has led them to doubt. It is often hard for us to find who those may be. Now we ask: what were your intentions in coming here?"

Daniel decided to chance it. "Liber . . . ation. We wish to . . . defeat Gád . . . once and . . . for all."

There was a short muttering from the other side of the door. "Do you wish for another question?" he was asked.

Daniel thought. Who was it who could help him in this situation? "Where's . . . Godmund?"

"We do not know. His presence is completely unknown. Those who have gone to seek him have not returned."

"What . . . happens now?"

"A question out of order!" shrilled one voice.

"But a vital question—most vital."

"A good question indeed. We break you out—abscond. We search for the survivors of Niðergeard and wage righteous war on our erstwhile comrades." There were grunts of agreement from those with the speaker.

"Good. Let'sh . . . do it."

VI

"We must be methodical, Freya," Vivienne told her, nodding her head in earnestness. They stood in the Langtorr greeting hall. "Floor by floor, room by room, and always together." Freya had thought this went without saying, but she nodded anyway.

The dining hall and the adjacent kitchen had revealed nothing of interest. The long hall was just as Freya remembered it, with the metal tables and benches perfectly aligned—bare and waiting to be used. The kitchen was just as barren. It was a sort of tragedy, even when she'd first visited it. She'd never seen any Niðergearder eating anything—that was something that they sacrificed along with their mortality, their right to die and their need to eat.

And yet, here was a kitchen, fully equipped, but not manned by any cook or chef.

There was a pantry with dry, stone walls and barrels that contained salt and some sort of dry, thick-sliced meat that was not rancid, as far as either of them could tell. Freya had remembered it from her first trip, and after Vivienne had seen Freya gnaw off a piece, she tried some as well. There was also some dry, dark, cracker-like bread in a wooden box on a shelf. They both selected some meat and bread and stuck them in their backpacks.

Back in the kitchen, they went to an iron pump that was set into a wall. They gave the handle a few turns and were surprised to see it cough up clear, cold water that jetted out and soaked Vivienne's leg. They took turns pumping and cupping the icy water to their faces to sip it. The water was slightly sweet beneath a metallic taste, but it was very refreshing. When they had drunk their fill, they emptied their warm water canteens and refilled them.

They continued up the tower. The next floor was made up of several curved reception rooms. Freya had not been in these before. There were large fireplaces that would have held Ealdstan's enchanted fire, but they were cold and dark. It was then that Freya realised she hadn't seen any of the pale, slightly lifeless flames anywhere in the tower's hearths. The lamps still burned, but not the fires, and this allowed a frigid, penetrative damp to invade the tower.

On the next floor were the guest rooms, nine of them, which included the rooms that she and Daniel had stayed in, long untouched. She even recognised the way she had folded the top bedspread at the foot of her mattress. Eight years of mold and dank dominated the room. They passed on to the next floor. More rooms. Just as well furnished but of more utilitarian designs. Servants' quarters? There had to be twelve rooms on this level. Freya had only ever seen Frithfroth and Cnafa and Cnapa around the Langtorr. Were there more, once, or had the total vision for the tower remained yet unrealised?

The fifth floor up contained the map room as well as other adjoining rooms, connecting through wide arches. Stone tables and metal chairs. Meeting rooms? Again, for whom and for what reason?

The double-helix stairway ended here—the corkscrewed design had been narrowing and coming close together and actually met to finish in a round hole. The next level was not immediately above the fifth. In fact, neither Freya nor Vivienne properly thought of it as a level since it was just a single room with two smaller ones attached. There was an iron bed, an iron washstand, a cold fireplace, and a metal stool, appearing as if they'd never been used.

Following a single, rough stairway, they arrived at Ealdstan's rooms, which brought them to a stop. They had not taken a break in their long explorations, but before they did so, they decided to right the large stone table that Freya, Daniel, Modwyn, and the knights had sat at eight years ago. Then they sat and started going through the scattered documents.

Bundles of paper were piled on the top shelf of a thin bookcase carved into an alcove next to the window. She pulled one of them down. It was a stack of thick, brittle pages—vellum—bound with string, or more likely, dried gut, with two wooden panels for covers. There were hundreds of them.

Freya and Vivienne rested their legs and slipped their throbbing feet out of their walking boots, pressing hot soles on the soothingly cool stone floor.

"So what's the plan now, Aunt Vivienne?" Freya asked. They were both looking at the shelves full of books and papers. "Start at the top and work our way down?"

"Not exactly . . . I've got an idea, but let's first make a quick inventory of what is here. I'm not sure what of use there is to find. We want to find anything that might put a perspective on Ealdstan and what the extent of his underground operations are. If there are maps of sleeping knights, or lists perhaps . . ."

"Or information on Gád and Kelm?"

Vivienne nodded. "Mm-hmm."

And so soon they were sitting amid piles and stacks of papers and books. The situation struck Freya as surreal. Here they were, perhaps half a mile underground, in a tower surrounded by attackers, deciphering ancient books and papers. She was not badly prepared for this task—she had been obsessing over old manuscripts ever since she'd left this place. The book presently before Freya seemed to be a sort of inventory log. The writing started right in on page one. She puzzled out the unfamiliar script, wrangling the obscure sentences into some sort of sense, and then marked down a contents description of the book next to a physical one.

Vivienne seemed consumed by the books. With a pair of reading glasses perched on the end of her nose, she fell into a deep fixation with them, marvelling and gasping over them in a way that she did not in their exploration of the tower—so much so that Freya wondered if the books were not her real reason for coming here. Freya was as much a supporter of the academic process as anyone, but what was in these ancient accounts that could have any bearing on their situation?

The hours accumulated. Freya's eyes became bleary, and it was hard for her to focus on the faded scripts before her. "Should we come back to this?" she asked Vivienne.

There was no reply from the woman who was now studying and comparing two separate books. She had a hand in each, her fingers tracing lines on the pages, her head wagging back and forth between them.

"Vivienne? Vivienne? Hello—Vivienne?"

The older woman's head finally rose to look into hers, blinking a question.

"Shouldn't we be exploring the rest of the tower? We can come back here, but there are more floors—more doors above us that we haven't looked into yet."

"It's quiet; why don't we let sleeping dogs lie? Here, I want to try something with you . . ." Vivienne bent down and rooted around in her backpack. She pulled out an object wrapped in bits of sacking that, when removed, showed a sort of metal base with a polished silver tray area on top. Vivienne unwrapped a second object, an onion-like metal sphere that had closely spaced vertical slots and ornate carvings. It had a stud on one end and was attached to a frame by a thin silk thread. A triangular metal stand rested on the tray so that the round object, which Freya thought must be some sort of top, just touched the slightly curved surface.

"What is it?" Freya asked as she watched Vivienne set up the strange object, wondering why it was important enough to carry all the way down here. The top looked to be extremely heavy—possibly solid brass.

"This is what some have described as a 'pansensorum,' also a 'synatheauraliser.' Those are long, complicated names made up by people without the slightest idea of what this object is. It was discovered in the mid-1700s in a small village in Midlothian. It was believed to have been created before 1500, but although it is referred to in certain texts, it is not named. It is a sort of . . . meditation device, although I dislike that term—it sounds too New Agey, and this is definitely *Old* Agey, if anything.

"There is a theory that the universe is made up, on one level, of vibrating strings. I don't know if that is true, but if it is, then it partly explains how this device works, which is through sound. It's hard to explain—far easier to show you its use. When in operation, you will hear a certain tone, a pitch. The sound will move inside you, or if you like to think of the vibration explanation, the noise will penetrate your perceptions and what you read and hear will come to life with a new vibrancy and intensity." She peered at Freya over her glasses, perched on the end of her nose. "Would you like to try it?"

"Me try it? What do you mean? What do I do?"

"Very little. I will operate the device; you simply have to continue reading. But after a time it will not even feel as though you are reading—the visions will come shortly after that."

"Visions?"

"Very vivid visions. Try it once. If it's not your thing, then . . . well, we'll figure out something else."

"Um, okay," Freya said.

"Wonderful. Here, since you're so fluent at reading this ancient script, you should have no trouble at all." Vivienne pushed a codex across the table to Freya.

"When I start this in motion, just flip it open and start reading."

Vivienne pulled a couple earplugs out of her jacket and inserted them into her ears, which Freya found disconcerting. Then Vivienne wrapped a thin leather strap around the upper part of the top and pulled it, setting the brass orb spinning.

The holes on the side uttered a harmonious buzzing sound, which, to Freya, seemed to make the entire room vibrate. The walls started to sway before her eyes, bulging and billowing like they were melting.

Alarmed, Freya looked to Vivienne, who pointed urgently to the book she had given to Freya.

Freya looked down, read the first three words written on the page, and then the dim room exploded into daylight.

CHAPTER FOUR

Pens and Pendulums

---- I ----

Winchester

April, 891 AD

His fingers running along the page of script and his lips moving in a quiet murmur, Ælfred read until he came to the end of the page. Frowning, he sat for a moment in thought, his eyes half-closed and fingers pulling at his lips.

When he opened his eyes again, he looked frankly at the nervous bishop standing in front of him.

"Your craft in scribing is very accomplished, Werferþ," he said seriously. "I think I have told you this before."

"Yes, my king," the bishop replied, bowing.

"But the art with which you form your letters is small when compared to the art in which you form your words and phrases. You have captured the sense of dear Saint Gregory perfectly. Well done, my friend. You have pleased your king and, I truly believe, our God by your labours."

"Oh, *thank you*, my king," Werferþ said, beaming, wringing his hands in obvious relief and delight. "I'm *so* glad you like it. Translating this work has been *such* a joy of edification. I read a few of the dialogues out to a parish church back in the diocese, back in Dudley, the parishioners of which have never *heard* of the divine Gregory, and let me tell you . . ."

Ælfred indulged the bishop a short while. He liked to see the otherwise harried and anxious churchman in a more relaxed and happy mood.

"But now." Ælfred rose from his wooden throne and waved away a servant who approached to help. "Turning now from *Dialogues* to *Pastoral Care*, I wonder if you might care to look over *my* translation and answer a few questions I have about chapter four. My Latin, I believe, is still not as good as yours."

"Oh, I doubt that, my king. But of course. Anything, my king," Werferþ responded, still beaming.

Ælfred led him into his private writing room that held a small desk and a functional stool opposite a kneeler and lectern. They discussed Gregory and Latin, and Werferþ studied Ælfred's work until bells were heard in the distance.

"Ah," remarked Ælfred, "that is for nones—I had a heart to attend today. You may stay if you like. Would you excuse me?"

"Hmm?" Werferþ answered, caught up in one of his king's paragraphs.

Ælfred stepped out of the room and started down the hall.

He strode across the courtyard, pressing a hand to his belly. He was feeling his chastisement sharper than usual today. Once again, as he did every day, he considered asking the Lord to remove it and give him another, but he only took a deep breath and set his jaw. This was for his sanctification.

He was muttering under his breath, *"Ut nemo moveatur in tribulationibus istis . . . "* when he caught sight of a man in a red robe standing near one of the stone doorways.

Frowning, he changed his path and met the man at the edge of the courtyard.

"Ealdstan. What brings you to Wintanceastre?"

"No greeting, my king?"

"You are welcome, of course, but you have only ever appeared when you have need of something I can provide."

"And you find this a peculiar position for a king to be in?"

Ælfred turned his grimace into a grin. "There are few who have the ability—and even fewer the imagination—to extract so much as you."

Ealdstan turned his face to the ground. "Few have the ability to comprehend the true nature of the world."

Ælfred sighed. "I was just about to go to prayers—will you accompany me?"

"Of course. It would be a joy," Ealdstan said, although he stood the whole time at the back of the church.

When the short daytime office ended, they emerged and started walking aimlessly along the outer paths of the burh. Ælfred said, "I am meeting with my councillors when I return. Would you speak of your desires with them?"

"I would not. I have need of stonemasons."

"Stonemasons? What do you need stonemasons for now?"

Ealdstan told him.

"How many?"

"A great many. As many as you can muster, for a very long time."

"How long?"

"You would never see them again."

Ælfred shook his head. "We need to continue to build England's defenses. Even a modest stone fortress is preferable to the strongest one of wood, especially in the outlier burhs."

"There is peace with the Vikings, King Ælfred. They are cowed from their defeats and submissive since institution of the treaty. They have lands now; they are sated."

"They never wanted our *land,* Ealdstan. Guðrum died this winter; did you know that? God's truth, I miss him more as a brother than a leader, but more men than I may feel the loss of his kingship in the days to come. While he lived, the Norsemen were pleased to look on the northern settlements as their own and overlook the settlements there. But with him gone . . . ? I wist we have not long to wait before another war band arrives. *Meotodes Meahte,*" he said quietly. "Where do they get their energy from? They crash upon us as inexhaustibly as waves on the beach. In the name of heaven, what do they eat up there?"

"This talk is not for now," Ealdstan said with a flit of his hand. "These are maybe-fights and perhaps-battles. I look forward to the inevitable battle that will decide the outcome of eternity."

"That battle is already won," Ælfred said.

"But it has yet to be fought!" Ealdstan insisted, banging his staff upon a rock. "We have discussed this at length, and I felt you had been made to understand me."

"It is a thought I continually turn over in my head and discuss with the Almighty much in my prayers. I've received no conviction in the spirit that my present course is incorrect. My bishops support me in this."

"They support your indecision, is what you say. I care not for the grumblings of bishops and abbots, nor those of a king who trusts more to pens and pendulums than to swords and fire. I was ancient when your father was young. I taught Bede his letters; I watched the boats of the *Lædenware* depart from this island. Of these isles I was the first disciple of the new faith. Do not presume to school me on spiritual matters, young Ælfred."

The colour rose in Ælfred's cheeks. "Watch yourself, wizard.

I am not so old that my writing hand has forgotten how to grip a blade. The Lord gave this earth to mortals."

"Great king," Ealdstan purred in a low voice, "after so much already done, do you still question? So much persuading and convincing by me, and of all the work that we have already done—of the warriors already laid to rest, and provisions already made— why would you not ensure the protection of these costs and lend me enough stonemasons to hew a stronghold underground, a secret place of safety for the hidden ones, to ensure they are able to return at the right time?"

Ælfred rubbed his chin and then crossed his arms. "You may take from the land all whom you can persuade to your cause. But this is the last debt to you that I will honour. Consider yourself paid in full."

Ealdstan nodded and without any more words between them, he departed, never to be seen by Ælfred again. Some months later the first reports of stoneworkers gone missing came to him. Some vanished along with their families, others not, and Ælfred assured those asking after them that they were completing vital work for the safety of the kingdom, for there was little else that could be done. Soon, stonemasons could not be found for love or money, proving that Ealdstan had done his persuading very well.

II

Freya's eyes snapped open and her head jerked back. She shook her head and rubbed her eyes as she tried to remember where she was and what she was doing. The Langtorr, her mission, Aunt Vivienne, and the device gradually rolled back to her, like waves of the tide.

She yawned. She felt like she'd just woken from a very deep and satisfying sleep. Ealdstan and King Ælfred—had she really seen them as they were? That had to be the most vivid dream she'd ever had in her life if she hadn't. It felt like she'd remembered real voices, real conversations. Like she could close her eyes and see the burh, like she could close her eyes and see the vague image of a room she had just left.

She looked up at Vivienne, who was coiling the leather strap around the top again.

"How long was I in a . . . ?" Freya searched her mind for the right word. "Trance?"

"Oh, several hours, at least."

"Hours?" Freya moved her tongue around her mouth. It was fairly dry and tasted stale. "I saw Ealdstan, and King Ælfred. They were talking about—"

"I know, you wrote it all down," Vivienne said.

"I did?" Freya looked at the table and saw that she had a large notebook in front of her that contained her handwriting on about ten pages. She flipped back through them and read some of what she wrote. It was all there—everything she'd seen.

"Ready to go again?" Vivienne asked.

"What? No. Let me—"

Vivienne pulled the strap, and the room melted.

III

Winchester
1019 AD

The messenger thanked her and departed. She lay in bed and savoured the warmth for a long moment and then rose just as three of her maids entered and started bustling about her. It was late—some hours already past vespers—but not only candles were lit, the fire in the hearth stirred and fed back into life. She pointed into the open wardrobe.

"That one, there. The green."

The servant drew it from the wardrobe and held it out to her handmaid. Between them, they held it open so she could step into it.

"Just drape it over me," she instructed, hoisting herself up. "Don't concern about the fastenings. I said don't. Stop that; I mean it." She swatted at her handmaid, who should know better, at least by now. The child inside of her was puffing her body out beyond her own recognition and made all of her clothes uncomfortably binding.

"A blanket too. One of the scarlets. There. That one. There. There. *There.*"

A finely woven cloth was draped across her shoulders.

"That's fine. That will do. Take me to him."

The maids turned and led her from the room.

As they processed along the corridors, she tried to stop the spring of anticipation from welling up inside of her and overwhelming her thoughts and actions. It had taken many years of planning, preparation, and patience to reach this day, with no guarantee that it would ever come. But if the messenger was to be believed, and she could scarce allow herself to do so, then a spark could be lit this night that would set the whole island ablaze.

They came to the large hall, where the fires were always burning. Standing in front of the flames and throwing a shadow across the hall was a thin, slight man hunching over his staff. He was only slightly taller than herself, and his hair was long and an unimpressive grey. She had expected a large, giant man, as old and virile as the hills, not this shrivelled character. She found herself scanning the room for another, or at least some sort of entourage.

She gestured to her serving girls. "Await me here," she ordered.

She cleared her throat and approached. "You are Ealdstan?" she asked in English.

His head turned and dark eyes sparkled in the low, orange light of the room.

"Queen Ælfgifu. Greetings."

"Emma."

"Pardon?"

"That is what the *other one* is called. It is also what"—she could not stop her top lip from curling—"my first husband's first wife was called. I'm always the next choice after an Ælfgifu."

"And yet you are said to be fast becoming his favourite."

Her lips spread into a smile this time. "Of course. And why not?"

Ealdstan returned the smile and inclined his head.

"You keep an ear to the sounds of the world above, it seems. Remarkable for a man as removed as you—or should I say, for a man who has removed *himself* as far as you have? Do you know, nearly every single man of learning I consulted insisted you were a legend? If it wasn't for my husband—my first husband . . ."

"King Æþelred," Ealdstan supplied.

"The last English king of England," Emma said, staring into the fire.

The dark eyes continued to gaze. "But 'Emma' is not English. Nor Danish, I wist."

"It is a Norman name."

"Norman?"

"My people. My father's family descended from the Northland to the plains that lie south, across from these waters."

Ealdstan frowned. *Northlanders,* he thought. *Again, the Northlanders.*

"My mother is direct of that line."

"And now Cnut, son of the foreign conqueror, sits on the throne of England. Is the old English world passing?" His eyes shifted and he looked around the hall at the sparse and sleepy serving staff. "The Dane tongue is a hard one for me to speak."

"I wouldn't worry. Everyone in the land speaks in the Angles' tongue still. The farmers in the fields. The priests in the pulpits. Even the merchants in the marketplace still speak it when in their homes and at table. Old queens use it when speaking to old men. Indeed, it allows one to question how much further the Dane rule extends past the Dane tongue."

"But still, it may pass in generations," Ealdstan said. "Alas."

"Alas, indeed," Emma scolded, her tone hot. "You come too late to save a tongue. The time for help passed the moment you refused my husband's—Æþelred's—entreaties to rouse your warriors and chase the Viking invaders back into the mists and oceans that spat them out. You failed him then. You failed us all then."

A piece of still-wet wood popped in the fireplace and sent sparks up into the air.

"I am sorry for your loss, and the loss of the kingdom. Æþelred was an able king."

"That he was. He was a strong king. He simply had bad counsel." Emma pulled the scarlet covering tighter across her shoulders. "Do you know, even in the last he believed he would receive aid from you and your stronghold of warriors? And when it failed to come—failed again and again—he panicked and fell back on ill-advice." He did not meet her furious gaze. "Can you blame him for turning to others? When we suffered constant invasions from a hostile, foreign enemy? Every day my husband hoped the ground beneath our feet would crack open like the shell of an egg and Ealdstan's warriors would chase the Danes out forever."

Emma lowered herself onto a bench. "Yet here we are. He is dead, and I am married to a barbarian king. Where were you?"

The fire continued to crack as Ealdstan turned to face her. "I thought that prayers and counsel might be enough."

"The women of this land know the strength of prayer in preventing their loved ones from being slaughtered."

"Yet here we find ourselves. What is to be done?"

Emma massaged her right leg. "You are deeply invested in this land; at one time you had the kings under your hand, and now they will not let you in the door. And you sit like a dog, shut out in the cold, waiting to be allowed back into the warmth, or at least thrown a bone."

Ealdstan's face did not change, and yet she fancied something burned underneath his skin. *Good,* thought Emma. *Let him burn.*

"And the only reproach I have against my husband, and all of his fathers back to Æþelstan, is that they didn't take a stick to your hind legs and beat you out of the door."

Ealdstan hardened his jaw and tilted his head back. "You drew me here to insult me, is that it? Abuse your betrayer?"

Emma grinned. "We are all of us traitors now. All of us left standing. Betrayal has become the price of life today. Do I chide? No, I show you plain the world around you."

"I need not schooling," Ealdstan said, rising. "I need not—"

"I drew you here to deal," Emma said, breaking in. "I believe you seek to make reparation—so do I. The song of this land has not yet been sung and it can be made great again. I see this isle as the seat of an Empire of the North, an empire that unites several strong races together against all the heathen who would stand against us."

"A great dream. An ambitious dream. How do you see me in this dream?"

"You shall be the power behind the throne—a guiding hand for the ages. The commander of an army of light against the world of darkness."

Ealdstan's eyes turned downward and Emma fancied she saw some emotion ripple across his forehead, but it could simply have been the firelight.

"The Norsemen are strong," she continued, "but their heads are easily turned. They are not the stuff that empires are made of. The army that defeated this land have been paid off and are gone—drinking the long nights away back in Sweden and Norway, where there is infighting and threat from all the kingdoms around them. They have no desire to rule, only to fight."

"So why then shall—"

"But the *Normans*, on the other hand, are strong leaders—strong rulers. My sons, Ælfred and Eadweard, are in Normandy now, with my relatives. They are creating bonds of trust and goodwill that will nourish the seeds that will grow this great nation into a might to rival even Karolus Magnus's new Roman Empire."

"Can they yet stand against kings?"

Emma tilted her head. "Not yet; the storm will rage but awhile longer before their time comes to stand. And in this time of uncertainty, others shall try their footing and invariably fall, to be caught beneath the waves . . . But their downward turn will offer us an upward turn."

Ealdstan stroked his beard and pondered on this. When his eye turned fully upon her again, the sharp flash was in them once more. "I feel I should apologise. I feel I have judged you awrong," he said.

She smiled a sly smile. "Everyone does."

IV

"The Cornish knights are proud and fierce fighters," Ecgbryt told him. "We will need their spears and long arms. They are kin with the giants, you know? The oldest peoples of these lands—even of the Welsh and Picti."

Alex raised his flashlight around to look at all the stunning stalactites hanging above them. Some of them must have been twenty feet long. He was looking up, jaw hanging open, when his foot slipped and he splashed into a pool of water up to his knee. It had probably been undisturbed for hundreds of years and felt as cold as ice. "Could we not have driven a little closer to it overland?" he asked, shaking his sodden leg. They had driven to a boutique-filled village called Honiton, near Exeter, and started their trip from there. The drive had probably saved them days, but in the race they were on, every hour counted.

"I judge not. The Eastern tip's tunnels were ancient even to the Celt peoples. They are hard to access from the surface—hard, at least, in one sense. There are many, many entrances and they form a true maze to get past. This path is the same as what you would call 'the back door.'"

Alex swore.

"Slipping again? I do not understand why you have your light turned up so high. *Meotodes meahte*, but it is dazzling."

"But why start in Cornwall, exactly?" Alex asked, stomping his foot.

Ecgbryt considered awhile before answering. "Niðergeard has been occupied for many years, its people captive, and possibly many of its secrets have been spilled from unwilling lips. You know how many chambers have already been discovered—it would not be worth holding out hope that those nearest the city would be untouched. However, this end of the island is densely packed with obscured places and mysteries that were kept even before Ealdstan's time, I wist. Although there are not many knights here—the Dumnonians have ever been independent—they will be well hidden. And hardy, as I have said. Did I tell you they came from giant stock?"

"Aye. You mentioned that," Alex said. "But it's so out of the way. Why corner ourselves like this? What's so special over there?"

"The Cornish kingdom," Ecgbryt continued and Alex didn't correct him, "is one of the thin places of this island. If anything were to leak through, this is one of the places it would first occur.

We may be able to judge the extent of this island's peril by what we find there. In any case, Cornwall is not a corner. We will need to pass through it to get to Llyonesse and points beyond."

"Llyonesse, the sunken land?"

"Swa swa. Just so."

They came upon their first sleeping chamber after a couple more miles. It was not hidden by any illusion or enchanted wall; it simply lay at the centre of a labyrinth made of black stone that ate the light cast by the lanterns and made it hard to tell wall from opening. Ecgbryt insisted all through the maze that he knew the path, but he led them to many dead ends before they found the sleeping circle of knights.

Or at least, what had once been the circle of knights.

On sixteen black stone tables lay sixteen white corpses, each of them held down by a web of metal chains and manacles that ran beneath the tables.

"They are all dead," Ecgbryt said, casting his eyes over the scene. "Not one of them escaped."

"They were stripped of their weapons," Alex observed, examining them closer. "Then tied—quickly and skilfully, if it was done without waking them from even an enchanted sleep."

"Here is the horn," said Ecgbryt, walking to the centre of the ring. He looked around with baleful eyes. "Trussed like snared fowl and then awoken from their immortal slumber. They died of starvation? Or thirst? Did the yfelgópes watch them suffer? Did they torture them?"

"There don't appear to be any wounds, apart from dried blood on the manacles," Alex said with a sigh. "Some nearly pulled their hands and feet off trying to escape."

"Swa swa. They would have done it if they could," Ecgbryt said. "They were valiant warriors all, and not a one would hesitate to sacrifice life or limb for another."

"Well, they are dead, and their spirits have left this place." Alex thought of the massacred Scottish knights of Morven and shivered. *It could be worse,* he thought to himself. "Let us keep moving. We are too late for these knights; let us pray we are not too late for the others."

But the yfelgópes had a head start of many years. It was possible there were no sleepers left on the entire island.

V

Walsall

Rian Watts took the long way home from the playing field. Nathan Edwards had failed to show, and he was the one who was supposed to bring the ball. The others had hung around, waiting idly for something to happen, but Rian had become tired of watching them perform lame stunts on their bikes. The best any of them could do was pop a wheelie for about half a second. And then they'd skid around, beaming, expecting wild applause, as if they'd just jumped a bus.

Bored, broke, and with absolutely no reason for wanting to go back home, he picked his way through the endless suburban streets, weaving a serpentine path. He was feeling more and more restless these days, more and more content with endless rambling. It calmed him somehow. When he stayed in one place, everything became drab and dark, like it was losing its colour or fading out slowly, like the end of an old movie. What would happen when it faded out altogether? But when he got out and moved, when images started flashing by him, then everything snapped back into bright, vibrant colour. Life was motion; stillness was death.

But how far could a fifteen-year-old boy go? And what could he do? He was essentially trapped. Trapped in this maze of houses. Trapped in the routine of an unimaginative school life and even less imaginative friends. His favourite word was *stagnant*. It was doodled on every workbook he'd been given.

He decided to walk along the canal. It was dirty, smelly, and some scary people hung around there, but it was different, a break in the depressingly thin terraced houses and their littered front gardens.

He scuffed along the gravel towpath and swept his idle gaze over a submerged shopping trolley in the canal and beached cider cans, vaguely wishing he had some piece of rubbish he could contribute to the vast convoy of filth that Manchester continually poured into the town. It was one of life's truths: there was always someone higher up the ladder or farther up the river who was dumping on you.

Rian realised that he wasn't walking anymore. His eye had been caught by a white, luminescent object that was shimmering on the other side of the canal, and his ear had been pricked by a song that seemed to come from both around him and inside of him.

> Come down to me, my lovely,
> Come down and lie on my bed.
> I'll come with you, my sweet one,
> Allow yourself to be led.

The glistening object in the water seemed to almost give off a silvery light of its own. As he craned his neck, Rian wished that it was closer to him so he could see what it was. And then he found it moving toward him, as if controlled by his unspoken desire. It glided just under the surface of the dark, manky water, making movements that suggested it to be alive.

It broke the surface and Rian gasped. It was a girl, a woman. Her skin was almost sickishly pale—blue veins could be seen underneath white skin that seemed to glow. But high cheekbones, large eyes, and an angular jawline and eyebrows made her as beautiful as a supermodel. She appeared to be naked. Large drops of dark canal water beaded off of her face, tracing a desirable path down her neck and along the inside cleft of her breast. Her hair was black and as slick as an oil spill.

She smiled at him. It was a very warm smile and seemed to transmit some of its warmth to the inside of his belly.

"Are you okay?" he asked, suddenly overwhelmed with gallantry. "Are you in trouble? Do you need help?"

"Why do you say that?" the woman asked, giving him a puzzled look but sliding a smile quickly on top of that. How old was she? She looked like an adult but sounded like someone his own age. But of course, no woman ever smiled at him like she was smiling at him now.

"I just thought . . ." Rian said, rapidly trying to recover the thread of conversation. "It's not very clean in there. With diseases and bacteria and stuff. I thought you might want to get out."

His heart was pounding and his throat had constricted. His brain seemed to be split into two parts. One part of him was helpful and in charge of talking and breathing and everything involved in trying not to fall over. The other part of his brain just stood to the side, observing and asking unhelpful questions like, *Did you* really *just say "diseases and bacteria" to the first naked woman you've ever met?*

"I don't think I could live if I wasn't able to swim," the woman said. "Could you?"

"I guess I—I don't—" His words were getting jumbled. He was trying to recall exactly how long it was since he last swam. About two years ago, on a school trip, he thought. But then, why would it possibly matter?

The woman, and that she was a woman was now very apparent, for she shifted in the water, arched her back, and swam back a couple feet, twisting and swirling as if the sludgy, stinky water was really something beautiful and refreshing. Through the brown film of water, he saw her breasts, her waist, her thighs, and her feet float past him like something in a feverish dream. His heart stopped beating and his breath caught. It was as if the whole world stopped for just that moment.

She moved her arms around her to steady her movement. He watched the taut muscles slide underneath the clear, smooth skin of her shoulder. He wondered what that movement would feel like if he were to touch it—if he was to move his hands over it, and over the rest of her body.

Her lips moved and the song continued, buzzing in his mind and imagination.

> *Your face is young and so handsome,*
> *Your limbs are soft and so fine,*
> *Come down to me in the river,*
> *I'm yours and you'll be mine.*

> *Your breath is near and so warming,*
> *Your blood is quick and so hot.*
> *It's deathly harsh in the dry air,*
> *But here in the water it's not.*

Rian was entranced. He felt as if he were asleep and dreaming. Suddenly, staying in just one place for the rest of his life wasn't so bad, so long as the one place was with her.

She raised her arms and held her hands out to him. "Don't you want to come in and swim with me?"

"Yes," he said. "I do."

"Then come to me."

He took one step and then fell forward into the canal. For

a terrible, awful moment, he thought that he wouldn't reach her hands, that he would fall too short, or that she would pull away from him, but as his face hit the water, he felt her hands close around his wrists and felt her tug at him, pulling him farther and farther down with her, her body rippling against his in a way that made him want to laugh and cry and sing and shout and dance and be still, all at once.

The canal had to be fairly shallow, and yet he had the sensation that they were going deeper and deeper. It was getting darker and darker, and colder and colder, and still he went down, down, down. Into the deep.

Into oblivion.

Into death.

And the last words he heard were those at the end of the hauntingly beautiful song:

> *Come down with me, my lovely,*
> *Come dance with me in the waves.*
> *For all the lovers I dance with*
> *Find cool and comforting graves.*

CHAPTER FIVE

Stone Leaves

---- I ----

Winter, 1142 AD

Ealdstan stood near the altar rail of the stone church and spent some time peering up at the carvings. He recognised the work of the carver, an almost supernatural master at forming stone, one he'd persuaded to join the stonemasons of Niðergeard nearly a hundred years earlier. Even now the man spent his days shaping and decorating what he intended to be an outer defensive wall.

He waited.

At length, there was the sound of horses and the many calls and orders that entail the arrival of a retinue of the king, which served to remind Ealdstan just in time: *Norman. I keep forgetting that the new kings speak Norman.* He wondered if he had time to produce a language enchantment but decided his own language skills were more than adequate.

The entourage entered. Though Ealdstan had only seen the king once, as a young prince—and even with them all dressed in a similar fashion—the old wizard was able to pick out the king. He was thin, with wavy, shoulder-length hair. He had sharp features and a long, straight nose that tilted downward. There was a harried, hangdog expression in his eyes, and his face seemed older than it should be, his once straw-coloured hair now a platinum white.

"Faire bele, sorcier," the king said, and Ealdstan began inwardly translating. *Good greeting, wizard.*

"Good greeting, my king."

Étienne de Blois, or King Stephen, as he was known to the people, approached him. He threw a gesture behind him, and those who entered the church with him paused in the doorway—either slinking along the back wall of the church or wandering outside.

Now relatively alone, Stephen seemed to relax. "They never leave me a moment's peace. Everybody wants something of me." The king sighed and eyed him. "And you, Ealdstan, what do you wish of me?"

"I do not wish to impose," Ealdstan began, wondering which tack to take with this ruler and what his temperament was. "But I may remind you of the debt your family owes me. Your aunt, Queen Emma—"

"Yes, yes—I know of the debt. There is no need to remind *me* of debts. I owe everyone everything, it seems. And I try to give it, by God, if it is in my power to do so. And so I ask you again, sir," he said, with lowered brow, *"what do you wish of me?"*

Ealdstan fixed him with a cold stare. He was just opening his mouth to speak when a young man in leather battle gear walked through the church doors.

"Your pardon, sire," he called from the other side of the building. "Only you said that you would give my men their rest once we had reached the encampment."

"And so I did, but we are not at the encampment."

"No, we're not at the encampment, sire," the apparent commander answered in an insolently didactic manner. "But we *would* be at the encampment if only my lord hadn't insisted on making this detour on short notice. The men feel it is unfair to—"

"Yes, yes," said the king with an annoyed wave of his hand.

"If your highness *must* change his plans from moment to moment, it is only to be expected that his men may feel the inconvenience of it. With only a little more notice, they could have—"

"Take them, take them away," the king snapped at the man.

"My lord." The young warrior nodded, turned, and then left.

"The rest of you," the king called to the others lounging around the door and in the back. "You may go too, if it is your will to do so."

The words of their monarch made little impression on the idle lords and earls clustered at the back. They stayed where they were.

Ealdstan turned fully toward them and raised his staff, bringing it down in front of him three times, pounding the floor with its tip. His eyes flashed with a fierce light and he gave a long look to each of the lords in turn.

One by one, they left.

The king, more at ease now in only Ealdstan's company, pulled a couple stools away from the wall and sat on one, gesturing for Ealdstan to sit in the other.

"Thank you," he said.

"No, thank you," said Stephen. "I'll make it up to them later. They haven't had a very easy time of late. These are uncertain days. They are saying that Christ and His saints and angels are asleep and will not waken again during my reign. Maude is still playing at foxes and hens with me . . . and this after I allowed her to escape from Oxford last year. I thought that if I showed her mercy, then that would be the end of it. But no, she continues. She has a son, Henri is his name. Nine years old, and already his strength and power are boasted of by the house of Anjou. They say he is as strong as a full-grown man, and comely to boot. I do not believe their reports entire, of course, but it twists the knife to think they are more united by the character of a young boy. I look around and I can see no one able to wield the power of the nation after me—no one I can trust."

He gazed up at Ealdstan with a piteous, beseeching gaze that should never be found in any king. Were those tears in his eyes? Ealdstan was repulsed. Here was a weak man, an ineffectual ruler. But his sister and her son . . . he himself had heard many of the reports Stephen had mentioned. Perhaps they *would* make stronger rulers, and be grateful to him in return.

He bit back a sigh. Cultivating. Was that all any of this was? Just choosing the best from what was available? Trying to limit intrusion from the worst? Christ and His angels sleeping? Yes, he hoped so. He feared what would happen when they awoke.

"You can trust me," Ealdstan said, smiling at the king from the opposite end of the aisle. "I will help you in this, but I will need your best men."

"Need them to do what?"

"No, you misunderstand," said Ealdstan. "I mean I will *need* them. That is, I will need to *keep* them."

II

Niðergeard

1214 AD

Breca climbed the wooden platforms erected around the large stalagmite that they were so very carefully hollowing out. The sound of their many chisels pounding into the rock around the structure made an oddly beautiful and soothing chorus. In a land of silence and darkness, it was refreshing to hear noise, of any type. For a moment the warrior stood looking up at the workers perched upon the scaffolding, working by the light of silver lanterns.

Then he blinked and reminded himself of the urgency of his message, definitely the first, possibly the only of its sort in history.

He spotted Ealdstan in the entryway, consulting with the master builder and the head of the stone carvers, standing over a series of sketches scratched into the ground with chalk.

". . . which formed flowstones that give strength to the outer edges," the master builder was explaining, pointing with a stick to a diagram. "These would be greatly strengthened if we were to alter the kitchen thus"—a pause as he bent down and etched an alteration—"and the upper levels following suit in this way." More scratching followed.

"How deep can be dug downward?"

"Ah," the builder said, his face brightening. "As to that—"

"Beg pardon, my lords," Breca said, breaking into the conversation. The three turned to him. "Ealdstan, you are . . . summoned."

The eyebrows of the two craftsmen raised while Ealdstan's lowered. "Summoned? How am *I* summoned? By whom?"

Breca swallowed. He could feel sweat on his brow. "You are summoned by the king."

"By the king? Ridiculous. The king is in Normandy. I will see him when he gets back. What nonsense. How did he get a message to you?"

"Your forgiveness, Ealdstan, but the king is not in Normandy."

"Hmm." Ealdstan pursed his lips. "Flown to France? As prisoner perhaps? Does he need ransoming? But why send for me?"

Breca was nearly panting with exasperation. "No, he is *here*."

"In England? Westminster?"

"No, *here*. In *Niðergeard*."

"What?" In a swirl of robes, Ealdstan was up and out of the

entryway. Breca rushed after him. "Where?" Ealdstan barked, and Breca pointed the way.

A little ways off from the workers' dwellings stood the king and his entourage, beneath a canopy of yellow light cast by torches that spewed black smoke up into the air. There were eighteen of them altogether, two of them apparently nobles, one of them a bishop, and the rest servants who wore heavy packs or pushed handcarts loaded with provisions, including barrels of paraffin for the torches.

Ealdstan slowed, not wanting to be seen rushing to meet any summons, especially that of a king.

"Fire?" he bellowed as he strode toward them. All the heads of the royal party turned. "Have you any notion of the danger you bring when you carry fire under the earth?"

The king squared himself to the approaching wrath, shrugging his cloak over his shoulder and placing his hands at his hips. "Not to worry, wizard. We do not intend to stay long. Our time of departure is contingent only on the speed of your answers."

"'Answers?' You demand answers of me? How came you here?"

The king sneered and did not make to answer. The bishop, perhaps emboldened by his king's example, or else eager to inter-cede before blows were traded, replied, "You are not the only keeper of secrets ancient, Ealdstan. The church has many hidden resources and recorded knowledge."

Ealdstan turned fierce eyes on the speaker, but was beaten to a reproach.

"Silence, cleric. I did not bring you here for your skill in debate."

"But, John." He gulped, blanching. "That is, my glorious king and most majestic master, I meant no—"

"I said, *silence*. Now"—the king levelled another glare at Ealdstan—"you . . ." He raised a finger accusingly. "You!"

That was all he managed to say. All eyes turned to him, but the only thing they saw was a man's face bunched up in rage, like a fist, his mouth writhing, too many insults and oaths crowded onto his tongue to speak. The tension was awful, but none of the retinue dared make a sound. Their monarch gave a roar of frustration, turned, and snatched a flat object from one of the footmen. He unfolded it into a small chair and thrust it down violently. Then he sat on it.

"So . . . how was Normandy?" Ealdstan asked after a time. "Was it fair weather?"

King John snorted. "No," he growled. "It was miserable."

Ealdstan nodded and waited.

"Ealdstan," the king said, after much chewing of his lip, "when last we talked, we spoke of empire—one to rival that of the Holy Roman, or even the original Roman one. The like that was never seen since Alexander's time. And it seems as if I am to do all of the work myself. The world is in tumult these past ten years— Byzantium has fallen, the Muslim nation grows by the week, all of Europe has been drained of money and men in the dry, dusty sinkhole that is Jerusalem. The Norman barons are so spun around they don't know which way to face, and no doubt it is only that the Picts are so violent tempered that they leave us largely alone. I have been abandoned by the Angevine, Philip seizes my lands, Scotland strives daily to tear itself off the map, and I have been excommunicated by the pope. The whole world is a whirlwind, and I run atop it like a dog on a ball, scarcely knowing where to put my feet."

He paused for breath, fuming.

"And here you sit." He made an irritated gesture. "In your hole. Untouched by the foul misfortunes that pound this island like a hail, carving stone leaves upon stone branches. Well should you ask if the weather was *fair!*"

Ealdstan frowned and opened his mouth, but King John was only pausing for another breath. "Civil war, old man. That is what our land is faced with. Can you comprehend that?"

"I can."

"I wonder. I truly wonder if you do. Dark powers in this century are rising that would threaten Christendom, my rule lies in shards at my feet, and where is Ealdstan? Ealdstan, the man in the shadows, the power behind the throne, the long-lived, the embodiment of the wisdom of Britain? Is he uniting the barons? Is he diplomat to foreign powers, to allay and align? No. He is here, hidden beneath the rocks, digging. Burrowing. Shifting sand. Behind the throne? Beneath the throne, I say."

The bishop laughed and then choked himself silent.

Ealdstan nodded sympathetically. "When first I made myself known to you," he said, "I was more than forthcoming that the road you would walk with me would be difficult."

"But you gave the impression it would at least be passable," the king whined. "And that you would walk it with me."

"It was a road that your brother Richard was unwilling to walk. He saw the world as rightly as you saw it, and yet he chose a different path—that of facing threat full-on. He was not wholly misguided, or fruitless, and yet his victory will be fleeting. Ours will last the ages."

"Ours? Or *yours*, I wonder."

"Allow me to ask, why is it you are king? What import is it, and of what motivations are you driven?"

King John drew himself upright in his chair. "Seek not to look into my heart, wizard. You ask by what right I rule? By God's. He has made this body." He gave his chest a stern thump. "He has given me this crown." He gave no less a thump to the diadem on his head. "He has given me the ability and opportunity to rule, and by the weeping eyes of His tortured Son, that is what I plan to do. Is that 'import' enough for you?" John eased forward, a challenging look on his face.

"I wonder at your piety sometimes," Ealdstan mused out loud.

"And I wonder that you wonder."

They stared intently at each other in the darkness, two players at a game of chess.

"You spoke of questions I must answer," Ealdstan said. "Before you leave."

"They are few," the king replied. "Here is the first: my very deputies seek to pull my imperial body apart. What aid or resources will you give to enable me to appease them?"

"What aid can an earthworm give a lion? I am as you meet me." He opened his palms and arms in a gesture of openness.

"Nothing, then."

Ealdstan clasped his palms together.

John shifted his weight. "Arms, then. I want some of your warriors. Any amount, and on any terms you dictate. Even a small number of your supernaturals would be worth a large number of my own men."

Ealdstan's eyes dropped thoughtfully.

"Whatever you lose in human resources, I promise to return tenfold in my own best men."

"No." Ealdstan's head rose. *"No."*

The king's flinty face studied Ealdstan's. Then, with sudden speed, he rose and kicked his chair away. He snatched a torch that one of his retinue was carrying and flung it to the ground before the old wizard. It flapped and flared in the darkness.

"So, it seems that we will hardly be stopping at all," John bellowed to his company of men. "But know now, old leech," he said, stepping closer to Ealdstan. "You are removed from the gracious kindness of this nation's kings!" John thrust a finger beneath Ealdstan's bearded chin. "No more will you sap the lifeblood of this nation!" he shouted, spittle flying from his lips. "By thunder, if I could remove you bodily from this sphere, I would, had I the power. But since I have not, due to your hollow support, I hereby exile you to your hollow realms. Lift your head but an inch into the daylight and I promise by these hands, there will be swift punishment!"

And with that he turned and stormed off, his robes billowing behind him. He grabbed a lit torch from one of the servants and led his party away. They scrambled after him anxiously, with only the briefest of backward glances at the immovable and impassable Ealdstan.

The sounds of the group departing faded into nothing, and then the lights themselves disappeared. The noise of the chisels had stopped. Everyone in Niðergeard had paused to witness the meeting, watching from the darkness.

"Humph," Ealdstan grunted, heading back to the Langtorr. Breca walked beside him, ready to attend his need. "That's him dealt with. But are things really such on the continent, I wonder? No doubt a visit would be prudent. I will open the sea tunnel. Breca, ah, Breca, before I forget—send a couple of your men to follow the good king and his men out; find what path they used here. Then tell them to seal it."

III

Freya pushed herself up from the table, drool chilling the corner of her mouth. The notebook was beneath her. She flicked back through the pages to see all she had written. There had to be over a hundred pages of description and conversation—all different time periods and people she'd never heard of. Where was it all coming from?

"Please, I need another break. I need some food and some sleep. How—how long has it been this time?" She looked at her wristwatch; the hour hand was just a little farther on. But had two hours passed or fourteen? It felt like fourteen.

"Are you sure you can't go again? We're on a fairly tight schedule."

"No, please . . . how long has it been? I—" Freya tried to stand, but her legs were like rubber. She braced herself by holding on to the table and lowered herself into a crouch.

Vivienne was up and at Freya's side. "I'm sorry. Yes, you could use some rest—we both could. It's just—you understand the importance, don't you?"

She helped Freya up, supporting her weight on the back of a metal chair. Then she unfurled one of the bedrolls.

"Find anything yet?" Freya asked.

Vivienne's head jerked up. "Yes, lots, of course."

"Anything that will help us . . . ?" Freya almost said *destroy this place,* but stopped herself in time. The visions had done nothing to assuage her distrust of Ealdstan.

"Yes, this is all very helpful. Invaluable, in fact. It gives us some context for what is going on here, at least. Whether by design or circumstance, Ealdstan has kept us in the dark."

"Any word on Daniel? I'm worried about him."

"I have not strayed from this spot, and Daniel has not poked his nose in here, no."

"Are *you* worried about him?"

"I don't believe so."

"Vivienne . . . when are we going to talk about Gád?"

"Not right now—go ahead and rest. We'll talk about it later. Just sleep now."

Freya let her leaden eyes shut. And as she drifted into a thankfully dreamless sleep, she tried to think about why she felt she had been in this position before.

IV

Gretchen Baker stood on a sand dune, sniffling, sighing, and wiping back tears that the fierce, salt-laden wind did nothing to abate.

She knew she wasn't the most attractive girl in the school. She wasn't even in the top twenty-five (of twenty-eight), but there was no need for everyone else to continually ridicule and tease her. If they could just let her alone, she could cope and get through with no friends. Then she'd leave the highlands and go to university in Edinburgh or Glasgow, or maybe even—and it gave her a thrill just to think about it—London. Anywhere, so long as it was *away*; and a *long way away* at that.

It wasn't just that she was unattractive; it was that she was conspicuously so. She was big, that was the main thing. Not fat, exactly, but tall—a good four inches taller than the next tallest in her year—and with a blocky form that fell from her wide shoulders straight down. Like a brick privy, she'd constantly heard herself described. The curves that had been promised her during her pubescence had yet to be delivered. And her face as well; blocky, jowly, with a prominent brow that buried her eyes in a squint, and a jutting jaw that gave her a permanent frown. She was constantly being picked out and victimised. She was like a celebrity in the school—an anti-celebrity. If anyone thought of a clever new prank or needed the object of a dare, she was found at the butt of it. Always.

The girls were bad enough. She had finally, consciously given up on being fully accepted by the girls a little over two years ago. All they ever did was pass blame to her and use her as a scapegoat for their own insecurities and frustrations. She finally understood that and avoided them with some success.

But the boys' cruelty stung. She didn't know why; there was no real reason why it should. It wasn't like she fancied any of them. Today there had been some sort of dare or initiation the popular group of boys had started. It involved coming up to her and asking her out on a date and seeing how long they could stay serious. The first time it happened, she had almost said yes. One of the group had broken away and come up to her and quietly asked if she wanted to see a movie over the weekend, his head slightly hung, his eyes steadily holding her gaze. She was just about to open her mouth when he burst into theatrical laughter and ran back over to his group, saying, "I couldn't do it! I couldn't keep a straight face!"

She shrugged and shook her head and carried on into the hall to eat her lunch, but then it happened again, and again, and again. Even boys who weren't in the popular group came up to her just to laugh and guffaw in her face, so as not to be left out. It was a performance art to the benefit of their peers and the other girls in the school who sat around and coyly ate their own lunches, tittering at the spectacle. The teachers pretended not to notice.

Gretchen, flushed and fuming, eventually finished her sandwich and stormed off to the girls' toilets. She hid for the next twenty minutes in one of the stalls until lunch was over. The rest of the day she buried her face in her books and notes, ignoring the laughs and whispers behind her.

After an eternity, school ended and she came here, a place most teens seemed to ignore. It took half a mile of tromping through tall grass to reach the sandy bowl of a bay. From her favourite spot atop one of the dunes above, she could look out at the sea and imagine all the places that weren't here, and which one of them was her real home. Where was she meant to be? Where did all the big people live? She considered Sweden, the United States, even Germany, perhaps. But for some reason, she really liked the idea of Canada. She imagined living there in a cabin surrounded by forest, at the foot of a towering mountain.

She'd marry a big, rugged man who didn't have to be good-looking, so long as he had a big, bushy beard, and he'd teach her the ways of the wild, and she'd butcher and cure the elk and deer and wildlife that he'd manage to hunt and trap in the forest. Cooking them up for him at night, they'd sit across from each other at a rough wooden table and after grace he'd lean over, put his big, rugged hand over hers, and tell her he was the luckiest man in the world to be married to her. And she'd put her other hand on top of his and say with a smile, "You're right."

Some days she'd tell herself things would be great, if she could just wait for Canada. Other days, like today especially, she'd kick and slap herself for being so impractical and stupid. There was no place for her anywhere. Canada didn't exist. Not her Canada.

She ducked down with a gasp when she realised someone was on the beach. She had been looking at an odd-looking, long piece of leathery flotsam that was lying against a rock when she saw movement out of the corner of her eye. Swimming up out of the ocean was a man.

At first she thought he was a seal by the way he raised his head above the waves and then dove back under, but as he drew farther and farther into the bay, she became certain that this wasn't the case. Mostly because he was completely naked.

But not naked in a bad way, Gretchen reflected. His hair was jet black and shoulder length in an out-of-fashion sort of way, but it was slick and wavy, and would have looked good any way he wore it. His face, as much as she could tell from here, bore strong features and a square jaw. He had a slight, almost feminine figure, but the tautness in his legs, the bulkiness in his shoulders, was all male. From the side, he looked impossibly thin, but when he turned to face her, his outline began with very wide shoulders that tapered down to a narrow, flat waist, and then bloomed again to display two powerful legs.

He crossed to the rock and the long piece of leathery something that was blowing against it. He was carrying something silver in his mouth and his hands that he dropped at his feet, and then he crouched above them. Gretchen couldn't quite see, with his form partially hidden by the rock, but presently some bluish wisps of smoke appeared and the man sat back, relaxed and satisfied. He had made a fire.

He raised his head to the dunes now, right to where she was, and Gretchen drew back slightly. She was lying on her stomach with her chin on her arms, trying to make as small a shape on the horizon as possible. She thought it highly unlikely that he would be able to see her at this distance, but then he raised his hand and waved at her.

She pulled back and looked around. Maybe he was waving to someone behind her.

There was no one else in sight. She peeked out over the edge of the dune again. The man raised a hand and beckoned for her to come down.

Something about him—besides the obvious, she told herself— made her want to obey, and so she stood up, brushed herself off, and awkwardly descended the slippery face of the white dune. The man stood, clearly relaxed and waiting for her to join him. She could tell she was blushing as she approached, and she swore at herself under her breath.

"*Latha Math,*" he said in Gaelic.

"Hello," Gretchen replied. "What are you doing?"

"Fishing," he said, again in Gaelic.

"In the ocean? By hand?"

The man shrugged and bent over the small fire he had made out of driftwood. He blew on it a few times and rearranged the wood. Gretchen took the opportunity to look him over a little more closely. His skin was hairless, white and gleaming, like something new from nature—an early spring sprout or a recently blossomed flower petal. It looked soft and luminous, tender and delicate.

She shook herself as she realised he had just said something. "What?"

"I asked if you're hungry," the man asked.

"Oh, yes. Yes, I suppose so," she said, not actually knowing if she was hungry or not.

The man reached across to what turned out to be a couple of midsized mackerel. He moved his strong hands quickly over them, running his thumbnail here, bending the head back there, sliding his fingers underneath here, and in a matter of seconds he had produced a small pile of offal and two glistening fillets. He tossed them into the fire on the face of a long, flat rock.

Gretchen had never seen anyone prepare food in this fashion, but he obviously knew what he was doing. And then she watched while he bent over the fire and licked his fingers, palms, and wrists clean of the scales and slime that cleaning the fish had left behind on him. It was slightly sickening but also, Gretchen felt with a terrible stir inside of her, an awful compulsion.

"Aren't you . . . cold?" she asked eventually, as the fish started to bubble merrily. "Swimming like . . . that?"

"The sea is my true home. One's true home is never cold," he answered. "Ah, lovely," he said, sliding a stick under one of the mackerel fillets and lifting it up. "Here you are, eat up," he said, passing her the stick.

She accepted it, her hand brushing his. In their brief touch, she found his skin warm, indeed. She held the sizzling fold of meat on the stick, then brought it up to her face and nibbled gingerly at it. It was still pretty hot, and at first she got a mouthful of hot grease and flesh, but as it cooled quickly in the wind, she found it very succulent and flavourful. She ate it all, savouring it to the last bite, and then, following the other's example, she ran her tongue along a runnel of juice that had spilled down the side of her hand.

The man was less dainty in his enjoyment of the fish. He took it straight from the fire with his fingertips and tossed it between his palms as it cooled, and then quickly tossed the chunks that fell off of it into his mouth, where he chewed it with wide, biting chomps. The fish all gone, he once again set to cleaning his hands with his tongue. Now finished, he smacked his lips and gazed lustily at the pile of entrails, bones, and fish heads he had discarded earlier.

"Well, thank you very much," said Gretchen, rising and making to leave. She wasn't about to stay and watch anyone eat *that*, no matter how—

"You're not going, are you?"

Gretchen frowned. "I thought I might."

"Why don't you come home with me? I'd like to introduce you to my family, and I know that they'd love to meet you."

"I don't know," Gretchen said. "Is it far?"

"It's as near as the ocean spray on your face!" the man said, standing abruptly. He bent and picked up the long, leathery thing that was still flapping against the rock and shook it out. Gretchen now saw it was a leather jacket, some type of suede thing. The man fussed with it for a while and then wrapped it around his shoulders and clutched it around his waist. It didn't seem to have any sleeves, pockets, or belt—it seemed to be all tailored from one piece. It was very odd, and more properly a cape than a coat.

"What's your name?" Gretchen asked.

"Call me *ròn glas*."

"Ron Glass?"

"Yes, that will do. What's your answer?" He held out his hand, and as Gretchen looked into his large, dark eyes, she knew that she would be going with him. She placed her hand in his.

But instead of leading her away from the water, he turned away from her and hooked her arm over his shoulder. "Hold me around here," he said. "Both arms, tightly. Don't let go, whatever happens."

"What are you doing?" she called as he led her out into the ocean.

"Are you holding tightly?" he called back.

"Yes."

"Very tightly?"

"Yes!"

"Then here we go!"

He leapt so powerfully that at first, Gretchen thought they were flying, seeing the seawater in the bay blur beneath them, but midair, something astonishing happened. The leather coat flapped out and then wrapped around him, head to foot, clinging to him like a wetsuit or a second skin.

Then they were falling, and Gretchen had just enough time to take a quick gasp of air before her head plunged under the water. She felt the man rippling under her, propelling himself with a vigorous and apparently highly effective jack-knife action. He bumped and shook against her so powerfully she felt that she would have to let go, but just as she felt the air in her lungs start to expire, he surged upward and their heads broke the water.

Gretchen got the shock of her life when she realised that the shoulders she held on to were not that of the attractive young man, but that of a sleek, whiskered seal. At first she thought it was just a trick of the eye, that the hood he wore was only made up to look like a seal, but then the head turned, rolled one large puppy-dog eye toward her, gave a wink, licked its nose, and then turned and continued carrying her away from the sunset.

—————————— **V** ——————————

Alex and Ecgbryt were profoundly disheartened. They had visited no less than four sleeping chambers, only to find them raided and their occupants slaughtered. They did not talk to each other—they had nothing to say. Their spirits were as low as the short tunnels they had to crouch through and as smothering as the narrow cave walls around them. They felt smothered. Alex took to openly swearing at every bump and jolt that a rocky outcrop or low ceiling gave him. He felt that the tunnels themselves were outrightly hostile, reaching out and hitting him when opportunity arose.

They were utterly soaked. Water dripped from the walls when it didn't cascade around them. At times they had to wade, hip-deep, along freezing streams, and it was absolutely impossible to get dry afterward. There was nowhere to rest that wasn't slippery with slime. Alex decided he was going to raise serious objections to continuing their quest after the next stop on their map, which was bound to be another massacre scene.

They came to a staircase that curved upward. They mounted its steps and Alex gratefully found each one to be drier than the last. Perhaps he could convince Ecgbryt to stay and have a proper night's sleep this time.

The stairs brightened as they turned. The walls transitioned from rough-hewn stone into smooth slabs, lit by the ambient glow of daylight. The breeze brought a smell to their nostrils that surprised them—the salty, moist scent of the sea—and their ears soon discerned the rhythmic rise and fall of waves. The sound was nourishment to Alex's soul and he felt his pulse quicken. An eagerness leapt into his breast founded on . . . he didn't know exactly what.

They passed a window, which blinded them both. Ecgbryt clapped a hand full over his eyes as he passed it. Alex was forced to look away but then turned back when his eyes had adjusted. It was a typically overcast day by the ocean and not particularly bright. The water was all that was visible apart from a few jagged rocks it washed against.

Wiping the tears caused by the stinging light from his eyes, he followed Ecgbryt upward. They passed other windows, which allowed more views of the ocean surrounding them, but so far they had no indication of what was inside the tower they were circling.

Then they came to an archway that a stiff wind blew through, creating a low, hollow whistle. From one side of it, they could look down into a chamber that fell beneath them, nearly as far as they had climbed—roughly fifteen metres, Alex judged. Stairs led down, curving against the wall, and above them, the tower appeared to be open at the top since a pale silver disc of sky was visible. The walls were as straight and flat as the day they were carved, but slits and strangely angled windows were placed at odd points in the tower that served to create some sort of complex wind tunnel.

The entryway into the chamber looked down on the sleepers. There were eight of them lying upon the customary plinths at the bottom of the tower.

"They look to be unharmed," Alex said in wonder. "It's hard to say exactly, but they look . . . fine."

"There, see," Ecgbryt said, pointing to the base of the steps. "Bodies. Bones, some weaponry. They are yfelgópes!" he exclaimed, excitement instantly mounting in his voice. "There must be a hundred of them. This is where their murderous path ended!"

Alex peered around Ecgbryt's shoulder. What he first thought was rocky debris was in fact a pile of bodies, reminiscent of pictures of holocaust camps.

He swallowed and started into the chamber, but Ecgbryt held him back.

"Hold. They may have perished by some sort of trap," Ecgbryt said. "I don't see how the yfelgópes would be so foolish as to awaken the knights, even accidentally."

They stood there for a moment, pondering their next step.

"Where is the horn?" asked Ecgbryt.

"I don't see it. Do they need it?"

"Horns wake the sleepers."

"Horns . . . oh, aye. I think I have it!" Alex said and pushed past the large knight.

"Be careful as you—" Ecgbryt started to warn him.

"Don't worry, I think I've sussed it, look—"

Alex took one step forward and felt the strangest sensation. The air blowing past him suddenly whirled around and twisted upward. He was in the middle of a wind dervish. Just standing there had affected the flow of air in the tunnel in the most ingenious fashion and started it in a new course up the tower. A low, reedy hum was first heard, and then other notes rising in a cacophonous chord that threatened to deafen them all.

"It's the horn!" Alex shouted in delight, looking upward again at the holes in the wall that the wind blew against. "The tower itself is the horn! That's why the knights awakened! The yfelgópes did it just by entering the room!"

The noise tapered off and Alex turned to continue his descent down the stairs. Then he leapt back in surprise. The knights had already awakened and were mounting the stairs toward him, weapons drawn and ready.

"Ecgbryt, do you want to talk to them?"

"Knights of Ennor," Ecgbryt called out from the top of the staircase. "Rise up now to fulfill your secret oath and complete your sacred duty. A brother knight calls to you—the time has come to awake."

The knights looked at each other and then at the strange pair standing at the entrance to the tower.

"Is it time?" the knight at the front asked. "Truly, is it time?"

"It's *past* time," Alex said. "Come on, grab your gear. We're offski."

CHAPTER SIX

A Show of Good Faith

---- I ----

"We call ourselves the *léafléas*. That means 'The Doubtful.' My name is Argument."

Daniel blinked. "Argument?"

"I am told it is my dominant trait."

"You would find it hard to believe how long it took us to convince him of that fact," the léafléas behind him said.

Daniel swayed. His body was weighed down by exhaustion, but he could feel his heart beating quickly. The left side of his body was throbbing, issuing waves of heat at every swell. He looked at the band of yfelgópes in front of him; they appeared as ugly and hostile as any other group of the creatures. Could he trust them? Was it possible he was so tired that he was delirious? Could he even trust himself?

He would have to trust his instincts. And right now they

were . . . vague. He was getting an impression, but it was hard to fit into words. The yfelgópes—or the léafléas, as they called themselves—were . . .

"Sticky," he said to himself.

"What?" asked the yfelgóp in front of him.

"You look sticky—I think you'll stick," Daniel said decisively. They were leading him through the cells and up and around a spiralling back entrance. The ground had a tendency to lurch beneath him like the deck of a ship. He wished he still had his jacket and that it wasn't back in the Langtorr's foyer.

"You're the right length," Daniel said, trying to clarify. That might be misunderstood, he reflected, but . . . well, *he* knew what he meant. *Do I have a concussion?* Daniel wondered. *Well, what could be done about it if I do?*

Argument nodded. "Then come. We will take you east and east by northeast, through an untravelled and unwatched route out of the city and into the wild caves beyond."

"What then?" Daniel asked.

"Then we look for Godmund and the other resisters," a léafléas behind Argument said.

Daniel laughed. "Of course."

"Shh! More quiet, please. It is funny?"

"No, not really. I think I've just worked it out."

"You know where Godmund and his band are?"

"Hah, no. That's still . . . sort of . . . purple. No, I just—never mind. Go ahead and get me out of here."

Daniel followed them, a smile tugging at the right side of his face. They wound through dark corridors, and he was amazed at how calm and relaxed he felt, despite the situation. He felt he had a secret weapon, an advantage—the knowledge of what was really going on.

They came out through a cavern near a wide pool of water. Daniel wondered if there were fish in it, and if those fish had eyes. *Maybe, maybe not,* he thought and then stumbled slightly.

"Try to be quiet. Each sound we make may draw suspicion."

Annoyed, Daniel was going to tell the yfelgóp—léafléas, whatever—that he should worry about his own feet and not his, but had trouble framing the sentence, and then the moment passed. *It's still the right length,* he told himself, and anyway, he had his pocket—his secret in his pocket—and that put him at ease again. But there was another thought floating around his head: *Length, sticky, pocket? Who talks like that?* There was something going on in him that didn't make objective sense. Well, there was nothing to do for it now—he just had to stay the course. Push through, even if it was only by sheer bloody-mindedness.

After another fifteen minutes of walking, they came to a group of yfelgópes seated around five Niðergeard lamps with shutters on them, letting out only the dimmest light.

"Who approaches, and from what direction?" one of the yfelgópes from the other group challenged.

"It is Argument. I approach from the south: one hundred and twenty-nine steps north, one hundred and thirty-three steps east. How long have you waited?"

"We have stayed this ground one hundred and thirty-nine minutes. How long did your journey take?"

Argument began a response. "What're they doing?" Daniel asked the léafléas next to him.

"It is our way of identifying members of our group. Those numbers hold significance."

"Doesn't he recognise him? Like, by his face or length?"

"Yes, but it is well to make sure."

Daniel nodded and listened to a few more exchanges.

"Is this he?" asked the interrogative yfelgóp, finally satisfied with the responses.

"Indeed," said Argument, with a good measure of self-satisfaction.

"Hi, Daniel Tully. Pleased to meetcha!" Daniel said, extending a hand and grinning carelessly.

The yfelgóp standing in front of Daniel looked at his hand expressionlessly.

"This is Certain Doubt," said Argument, behind him. "He is the most senior of us."

"I used to be called Eddik," Certain Doubt said peevishly. "It is time we left. We should not have stayed so long."

"I don't suppose anyone managed to pocket my things?" Daniel asked.

"We did not," said Certain Doubt. "Your items would have been noticed missing before you were. We did, however, bring you this sword." He signalled to one of the other yfelgópes, who stepped forward, carrying a large bundle. Daniel took the sword that was resting on top of it. "It is not yours, but it is of the nearest dimensions we could find at the time. Also, here are clothes, to keep you as warm and dry as possible."

Daniel had been counting, and there looked to be about twenty-five of them altogether. He pulled the sword partway out of its scabbard to inspect it and then pushed it back in with a *snap*.

"Are you tired? Do you need rest?"

Daniel's head bobbed upward. "What? Sorry, what?"

"Sleep! Are you tired—do you need rest? It is of the utmost importance that we move swiftly, but if you need to rest, then we will stop here for a moment."

"No, no, I should be fine," Daniel said, fitting the sword belt around his waist and shaking out the travelling cloak he'd been given. It didn't seem to have a pocket. "Ready when you are, captain. Stretch on."

"I am ready. We all are ready. I am no captain."

Daniel nodded, with an apologetic expression that he then wished no one had seen. He had to be careful. He couldn't stretch it, or they'd tumble that he was on to them. He couldn't stretch it. It had to stay the right length. Otherwise it wouldn't stick.

Stick. Sticky. Stretch. Stick.

"Well, come if you're coming," Certain Doubt growled.

Daniel shook himself. He had to stay awake. Stay focused. He had to figure out this new situation he was in. He had to find the answer.

"You must be understanding of him and allow some exception if you are able. There is much in these events that press on him," Argument said as he tugged Daniel along by his arm.

"I'll just bet there is," said Daniel.

They carried on, northward, Daniel was told, but he had no bearings. Niðergeard was more or less behind him, that's all he knew. The yfelgópes—the léafléas—were apparently orienting themselves by the alignment and distance between certain lights they could make out, but Daniel was not familiar enough with the city to know which side of it they were viewing. He didn't know where they were taking him.

He found the léafléas strange. He had never accredited the yfelgópes with much intelligence—he had almost always known them to be half-crazed, animalistic savages. But here, he was surprised to find they actually had a human-like intelligence. They loved to argue and debate over any little thing that could be found. Where they were, which direction they were walking, how much more in weight one was carrying than the other and for how long, and—more than anything—how far they had walked.

"I've got two thousand and five hundred," one of them—Daniel had picked up that he was called Judicious Speculation—announced. "How about the rest of you?"

There came a cascading report of numbers from the others: two thousand three hundred and seventy-one, two thousand four hundred and eight, two thousand two hundred and ten, one thousand nine hundred and eighty-three . . .

"Your knee's deformed, Informed Dissent; that's why your steps are so close."

"There's nothing wrong with my knees, you insipid old fool. It's your gangly bowlegs that are irregular."

"Is there an accord for an average?"

There was an accord, and then a silence as arithmetic was applied to the situation.

"I make it two thousand three hundred and seventeen."

"I concur."

"I also agree."

"Very well. Replace your original estimate with the agreed total and add that to the number of steps that have been taken since the estimate was last called into question."

There were grunts of assent and another moment's silence as this was done, and then they continued as before.

Daniel suddenly felt a lurching forward, like he was falling. His eyes snapped open and his legs locked. He had actually started to fall asleep while walking. He pinched the side of his thigh to wake himself up. He had to keep it together. "So where do you guys come from?"

"Where?" asked one of the yfelgópes walking next to him.

"Yeah, there are so many of you. What's . . . uh, what's the story?"

"Our kind enjoys debate and disagreement, but some of us came to realise that our courses of dispute ran in unique channels.

Approaches were made—at great cost—and then names were shared. More were—"

"No, I mean, where were you born? Where did you grow up? Why are there so stretching many of you?"

"We are born as you are—we live our lives in the blinding light, and thus it is that we cannot see until we come underground."

"How does that make sense?" Daniel asked.

"The world—the universe is so big, no man can keep it all in his mind. Blinded by the light, blinded by fact. We seek a life in the dark under our own terms."

"Better to stand up in the dark than lie down in the light," said an yfelgóp on the other side of Daniel.

"One day we will emerge, once we have quantified the very foundation of the world, of knowledge."

"But . . . really?" Daniel asked. "You want to know *everything*? Aren't there some things you just can't know?"

"Yes. Yes. Life is a mystery."

"A mystery unknown, but not unknowable. Undefined, but not undefinable."

"That is how the léafléas are different from our brothers. It is their contention that all that can be known is known—all the edges of life have been found and measured. Whereas we are doubtful."

There were exclamations of pride and support following this declaration. "The Doubtful! The léafléas!"

"We doubt that the world is all that is seen. We doubt that all experience has been quantified. We doubt that all distances have been measured."

"And we doubt even those doubts. But what is undoubted is that there is more."

"More! Yes, more. And that is what defines us—the others, the hopeless, the slaves to Gád, they believe that the walls of the world have been found, and they are angry. They have built a prison for their own senses and are angry at it."

"They have killed their own spirits and are mortally jealous of anyone who still possess joy and wonder."

The exposition continued, but Daniel's attention was already drifting. He was having trouble following the words and found that his feet were starting to drag.

II

After much debate about distance and steps taken, they all negotiated a halt in order to rest and take stock. They hadn't yet crossed the niðerplane yet, but the ceiling was getting closer to their heads. They couldn't see it, exactly, but they could hear the difference in the echoes and feel it in the air.

"Oh dear. We must make our decision about which direction, exactly, to strike for," a léafléas named Consistent Uncertainty said. "We must decide which direction is the most probable that Godmund and his forces lie in. I fear this will be most difficult."

He brought out a map from his pack and Daniel joined the huddle around the rolled sheet of parchment. The lamps were placed around it and the shutters lifted. It was a map of the whole of the land beneath England. He noticed many similarities to the ones that Alex and Ecgbryt had shown him, but there were also differences. Either routes that the others didn't know about, or else errors, Daniel didn't know. The locations of knights' chambers, or their suspected locations, were marked with a reddish-brown fingerprint. It might be worth keeping if he could get his hands on it.

"What makes you think that Godmund is still underground?" Daniel asked. "Why not go above?"

"It is possible that he is not underground."

"But not probable. Probabilities suggest that he would stay beneath. It is what he knows. It is where his resources are. He would be lost aboveground."

"Further, he has not made contact with you, an overworlder with knowledge of the lower realms."

That made sense, Daniel thought. Also, he knew that Godmund hadn't contacted Ecgbryt or Alex. So he really must be down here, somewhere. But did the yfelgópes really not know where he was, or was it all part of the ruse?

"So where do you think he'll be?" Daniel asked.

"We were hoping you might be able to direct us. All yfelgóp searches for him have turned up nothing."

"As far as we know."

"Yes. As far as we know. Those that have returned have returned empty-handed."

"But there are some that did not return."

"Yes. Those are still unknown factors. Those may be worth investigating."

"That is predicated on the assumption that he stays only in one place."

"To leave not one member of a hunting party alive to report back would indicate an ambush site. Which would indicate a fixed location."

"Or more than one."

"That is possible as well."

"So, one location or several," Daniel said, jumping into the flow of conversation once again. "Where is the, uh, area of greatest unknown . . . the area of the most unknown factors? Because that's where he'd be, right?"

"Yes, that logic follows," said Certain Doubt. "And that area would be here." He pointed to the top of the map.

"Right, then. Let's head for that . . . see? That junction right there? It's not far from there to these two chambers, and then this one as well. We can check to see what the deal is there, at a stretch."

"These places would already have been rendered . . . inert."

"You mean that the knights sleeping there have been murdered already."

"Yes," said Consistent Uncertainty. "You should prepare yourself for a sight that might be unpleasant to you."

Daniel just stared at him, wondering what he meant, then wondering why he couldn't seem to make sense of his words. He shook his head to clear it.

"Are you well?" asked Judicious Speculation. Or Argument. Daniel was becoming unsure of all of their names. "Do you need to rest?"

"No. I'll stick," Daniel said. "I am all correct," he said. "My systems are go. It's good. It's good."

The léafléas squinted at him, trying to figure him out. Daniel was aware that other eyes were on him as well. He had to play it cool—not raise suspicion.

"Seriously, I'm folded down and good to go, my little captain. It's good. It's good. We need to cover ground anyway. When we get to the next chamber, then we'll rest. I'll hold till then. It's good. It's good."

"That sounds like the best course," Certain Doubt said. He rolled up the map and handed it off to be secured in its tube. "Let's keep moving."

The léafléas moved away and Daniel shuffled after them. He had to really concentrate on moving his legs, he was so tired. He could feel his heart—every beat a cold, weak thump. He had to keep it together, to stay normal. To help him in this he recited a short mantra that made him calmer, gave him a feeling of continuity, of comfort.

"It's good. It's good. It's good," he said under his breath. "It's sticky, it's sticky. Sticky. Stretch. Sticky. It's good. It's good. It's in a pocket. It's good."

III

They reached a parting of paths. To their right was a carved tunnel, bored by the inhabitants of Niðergeard however many centuries ago, while the natural path they walked continued down a fissure.

"Let's rest here," Daniel said. He sat down on a rock and broke out his water, taking a mouthful and swirling it around in his mouth.

"We are still a ways from the first chamber," said Certain Doubt. "That was where we agreed to make our first camp."

"I know. I just—I just can't move another step." That much was completely true, Daniel thought. "I just . . . it's . . ." He was about to use one of his lucky words, but he had to watch it with those. He would have plenty of opportunity to say whatever he liked soon enough.

Certain Doubt had pulled the map out. "We are here," he said, pointing a finger at a spot Daniel could not see. "It would be better for us to be here." His finger shifted. "This place is too open. Lookouts would have to be spread too far."

Even better for me, Daniel thought. "Look, I've been through a lot—a lot's happened to me, not least of which was being hit by a troll. A troll. A troll. I'm very tired, and we've gone a long way, and I'm very tired. I could have asked to stop earlier. I could have. But I'm asking now. Please. My pocket . . . I'm about to collapse."

"I believe he is," Judicious Speculation said. "He gives every appearance of acute fatigue to me."

"Very well," Certain Doubt said. "I shall arrange the watch. This is how it will be . . ."

It wasn't exactly as he said it would be—there was much arguing over the exact times, placing, and identity of the watch, but it was all sorted out eventually. Daniel slumped against the boulder, hunching into himself. It was just a short time now—he would rest up, but he wouldn't sleep. He had done the calculations while they argued. He rubbed his eyes, gave his leg three hard pinches, and then fixed his eyes on the luminous dial of his watch.

IV

Freya awoke and rolled away from the cold wall she was pressed against. Sitting up, she found Vivienne still sitting at the table, making notes and comparing Ealdstan's and Freya's texts.

"Did I miss anything?"

Leaning back in her chair, Vivienne took the glasses off her nose and rubbed her eyes. "Not unless I did as well. Do you want to have something to eat?" She pushed a power bar toward her.

"Thanks," Freya said, opening it and taking a nibble.

"So. Are we going to talk about Gád now?"

"Sounds like it. What do you want to know?"

"Start with telling me what really occurred when you met him. In your own words. What happened?"

"What happened? Well, I was a little girl, and Gád was much more powerful than I was. When I first saw him, Swiðgar was with me, and he attacked him, on sight. I would have stopped him, but he just leapt forward. And Gád defended himself. Swiðgar died, but not right away, I think. But he was badly wounded. Gád started to talk to me, and I didn't agree with everything he said, but then . . . I don't agree with a lot that most people have told me over the years. But right then, there? He made the most sense. So . . ." Freya swallowed, which was difficult, around the lump in her throat. This was harder than she'd thought it would be. "So he told me a way that I would be able to get home. He told me what to tell the others, about him and about Swiðgar, and I did, and ... we escaped. Daniel and I. So say what you will about him; he got me home."

"When you say 'he made the most sense,' what do you mean?"

"Well, he said things that I realised I already thought but hadn't been able to articulate. He said that Niðergeard is an oppressive force on this island—they live and operate in secret, making wars in the shadows. And from what I've seen here, in these visions, could *you* disagree? What gives Ealdstan the authority to do what he's doing?"

"Just because you do not like his methods doesn't mean he's wrong."

"But if he's right, why would he keep it a secret?"

"Getting back to Gád—what about his methods? He killed Swiðgar."

"In self-defense. Swiðgar was going to kill him. That's what the whole mission was about! If the four of us went on a mission to kill *you*, don't you think you would be justified in defending yourself?"

"What about *your* methods, then? It seems to me that you have been just as secretive as Ealdstan. Why did you not tell the others the truth about Gád as soon as you rejoined them?"

"What if they'd kept me there?" Freya blurted. She realised that she'd been holding back tears, but now they were rolling down her face. Her voice was thick and full of emotion. It was all coming out. "What if they'd made me go back and try to kill him again? I never wanted to kill anyone. I never have! I only ever wanted to get out, to go home!"

Vivienne waited until Freya's tears had mostly stopped before continuing.

"But surely, once you were here, once you saw the importance of this place . . . surely you saw the vital need for it to be delivered from all threat?"

"No. No!" Freya felt the rage swell up inside her. "I never saw the point. Never! I didn't ask to get sucked into this world—it never did anything for me. Why should I help it? For all I know, Gád was right. The only thing I know about this place is what I've been told, and that's been precious little. If this place is worth saving"—she motioned around to the dark walls—"then why is the world perfectly happy to carry on without it?"

"Because it stands in the breach, Freya. It stands between the spiritual realm of this world and all others that press in on it."

"Do you really know that? Or have you been *told* that?"

"Because I was told it doesn't mean it's false."

"And it doesn't mean it's true either."

Vivienne stared back at Freya impassively. "So what *is* true?" she asked.

Freya palmed away the tears on her cheeks. "I understand about the dragon. And someone or something made Stowe do what he did to me. But how do I know that Niðergeard isn't responsible for that? Or in any case, more responsible than Gád?"

Vivienne nodded. "You should read these accounts. Like I say, they will provide context."

"I don't *want* context. History. I want to know what's happening *now*. Vivienne, we should really go search the rest of the tower."

"You go ahead without me," she said, fitting the reading glasses back on her nose.

"You want me to go *alone*?"

"Why not? We know there's nothing waiting to spring out at us or it would have already done so."

Freya stood and moved toward the door. She felt in her jacket for the pocketknife they'd given her. "Vivienne, what do you know?"

"What do you mean?"

"There's something that you're not saying. You'd rather sit here with books and diaries instead of explore the tower? What's going on?"

"I would think a young woman would put more stock in learning. Very well, if you wish me to come with you . . ." She pushed herself away from the desk.

"No." Freya tightened her grip on the knife in her pocket. "You stay here. I don't want you with me anymore."

"Freya, do you have a trust issue?"

"How could I not? Why *should* I trust anyone? They've never trusted me with the truth. Stay here. Read your books. I'll be back later."

She didn't even have her hand on the door before she regretted her decision. And pushing past the ruined iron door, she felt the first drops from the massive reservoir of panic spill over the walls she had built to keep it out. Senseless fear threatened to overwhelm her completely. She stood in the corridor, drawing a deep breath, drawing herself up. She could live her life in fear, which was no life at all, or she could dig deep, draw up the anger inside of her, and take control of her life.

So there she stood, just outside of Ealdstan's study, fighting indecision. She knew she needed to explore the rest of the tower, and she would, but should she first try to find out where Daniel was? Frithfroth also; where had he slipped off to? And then there was Gád. Should she try to make contact with him? And how would she do that exactly? Just stroll out of the tower and demand an audience? That thought seemed to physically twist at her gut. To align herself practically with Gád was different, she realised, than philosophically. Was she really on Gád's side, or was she just against Niðergeard?

There were risks on every side. The danger of her situation

circled over her like a large, black bird of prey, its shadow of fear occasionally eclipsing the light of any hope, its icy fingers reaching out to snuff even the heat of rage that was pent up inside of her.

But niggling at the back of her head was her secret temptation, which she guarded for herself like a precious thing, kept in a drawer and only taken out to fondle when absolutely no one else was around: *she could just leave.* She could walk up the stairs, wait for the portal to open—if it would open—and then just leave.

It was a nice, comfortable thought, but she knew it was grown from her fear; the last eight years had taught her that. She actually had escaped Niðergeard, against the odds, and yet fear still ruled her life. She was tired of being afraid. Weary. Fatigued. *Fatigued*— she remembered that word as it applied scientifically, to metal. Most metals were malleable. You could exert pressure upon them and they would bend—like a spoon curved back on itself. You could apply pressure the other way and it would bend back. And you could keep bending and unbending the spoon and it wouldn't appear the worse for the wear, but then after bending it too many times, it would break—simply snapping in two. That's what she felt like now—bending so much from all these different pressures, at some point she'd completely break apart.

She wouldn't let that happen. She refused to bend any longer.

She reached deep inside and grabbed Fear and threw it into the flames of Rage, letting it be consumed, relishing its heat. And then the fear was gone—sublimated into fuel for her fury.

This was the new deal: she would stay angry and she would stay unafraid.

The first thing she would do is search the rest of the tower.

She had taken a lantern from the study, so as to conserve the battery power of her flashlight, and counted the stairs as she went upward, the temperature dropping as she did so. Her fingers felt like icicles and she could see her breath clouding before her in the light of the lantern. The stairs seemed to go on forever, but finally she came to a landing that snaked away into darkness. At the end of the short hallway she found two identical doors, thin like the small, medieval doorways that were in church bell towers. She reached out and pushed gently on the right-hand one. It shifted at her touch.

She slid into the doorway and squeezed past the door and into a very narrow and unlit corridor. It curved around, as all passages did in the Langtorr, but tighter than usual, and Freya wondered how high, exactly, she was in the spire-like tower, and how thick the wall was between her and the cold emptiness outside.

Her lights picked up something sparkling around the curvature of the walls. It was a bobbing twinkle, as if something was coming toward her. She froze. The bobbing light also froze, and she realised that the light was only a reflection of her own. She drew closer and found herself confronted with an incredibly ornate silver doorway, the likes of which she'd never seen before. It was patterned with circular swirls and knot-work that ran all along the edges, framing a burnished surface that showed her as only a shadowy shape in the dark.

After admiring the door for a moment, she placed her hand against its centre—she saw a ghostly reflection of her own hand rise to meet hers—and pushed, watching her mirrored self fall away.

The room was lit, which was a surprise, and empty. It was a curved, kidney-shaped space with no windows, but with three large mirrors hanging at opposite ends of the room.

Each mirror was of an ornate, flowing design, with a bulbous, vaguely hourglass shape. There were four odd metal racks in the centre of the room, sort of like coatracks. A golden chandelier in the ceiling fixed with silver lights threw an uncharacteristically warm light on the room. She walked closer to the mirror across from her and stopped in the middle of the room. Something caught her eye and she turned her gaze to the right-hand side mirror.

She leapt aside, and her mirror image also leapt aside.

But it wasn't her image, not exactly. Freya moved back so her "image" was centred again. It was clearly her, but she was older, maybe thirty, and dressed in fine robes of deep red and burgundy, with bright trim and gold lacing.

She looked confident, self-possessed, a little sad, perhaps, but that seemed to add to her air of wisdom. But it was the crown atop her head that she found most stunning—and disconcerting.

She was wearing the hero's crown that sat on the throne downstairs—the dragonhelm.

V

Daniel sat down next to Certain Doubt, who tensed instinctively. "Awake so soon? It has been a very short time."

Daniel nodded and scanned the darkness. He could see almost nothing, just abstract angles where the rock ceiling sloped to meet the floor on various levels.

"You are fully rested? We may depart?"

"No, not yet. Let's let the others—what's that over there?"

"Where?" Certain Doubt's head shifted slightly, giving Daniel the opportunity to shove his sword into the yfelgóp's throat.

The movement was swift, fluid, and vicious. Daniel knew he'd only get one chance, and he had to be exact or the yfelgóp would raise the alarm and he would be sunk.

Certain Doubt's eyes bulged and his tongue worked soundlessly, trying either to breathe or shout, Daniel didn't know, but his efforts were fruitless, and he died quickly. In that moment, Daniel felt his heart calm and beat steadily. He experienced an awareness of his senses that quite took him by surprise. As the léafléas writhed on the end of his blade, Daniel felt more relaxed and in control than he had felt in days, and it comforted him. He was doing the right thing.

He wiped his blade against the dead creature's arm to clean it. And then, working quickly and with some difficulty, Daniel propped the body up to make it look, in the low light and at a casual glance at least, that it was still on guard. He was so successful in this that as he rose and cast a last look back, he almost thought Certain Doubt was still alive and he would have to kill him again.

He laughed at himself. That was silly. No one had to kill anything twice—only Gád was the thing you had to kill again, apparently, and he would. He was working toward it. But first things first. And what kind of name was "Certain Doubt," anyway? "A spy's name, that's what." Daniel thought that Kelm would give them a better story than some weird names. That wasn't sticky. Not sticky by any stretch.

Moving forward in a crouch, he made his way to each of the other léafléas on watch, killed them, and returned to the site where the rest of the yfelgópes were resting.

This next part was even trickier, but moving systematically, he made a complete circuit. In his left hand he held a bunched-up piece of cloth that he pressed against the yfelgópes' mouths to smother any noise they made while he was piercing their throats with the sword in his right. Some of them uttered muffled death rattles that made him hold his own breath, fearing they'd wake the others, but most of them died without even opening their eyes.

The last one dispatched, Daniel tried to dry his sword with the cloth but found it too sodden with blood to be of much use for that. He tossed it to the side and sat down to recover. He had hardly dared to draw breath during the operation, and hadn't used even one of his lucky words, and now he filled his lungs with a deep, regular rhythm.

"Not shaky. Not shaky. Jagged. Not jagged either. Folded down. In a pocket. Calm. Relaxed. Sticky. Length. Length." The words were balms to his troubled soul. They were direct lines to meaning in his mind; he could almost feel the strings. Yes, strings. Strings in his mind, connecting thought to action to event to consequence. He just had to keep thinking and it would all stick.

Daniel rose. It was time to follow the next mind-string to its end-knot. But what to decide? Take all the heads, or only some of them?

VI

The smell of fresh death followed him in a cloud, making his eyes tingle. He swallowed back bile and rubbed his eyes with the back of a hand. He was exhausted. He had decided on bringing all the heads, in the end. That would be the most impressive, make the greatest impact. And yet it was quite a trick to manage it. There were twenty-eight of them in all; twenty-eight traitorous heads of enemy agents. And it was no easy task getting the heads off of the shoulders. It had become easier after the first few when he knew more what he was doing, but then he'd had to work out some way to carry them all back. He'd struck upon taking a few spears and skewering them onto it, threading them on top of one another like beads on a needle. That took unique skill as well. Then he'd taken all the belts and bands he could find and tied the spears together so that he could drag the heads behind him.

It wasn't easy work. They kept getting caught on rocks and outcroppings, and he had to stop and free them. It was possible he had lost one or two heads on the way. And if they were smelling worse, at least they'd become less messy, the blood and entrails already long gone.

At least it was easy enough to find his way back to Niðergeard; he just had to follow the light and keep himself low, out of sight.

"Sticky. Sticky. Lengthy. Length. Stick. In a pocket. In a pocket. In a pocket."

When he got to the pile of dust that once used to be the outer wall, he thought he'd announce himself. It would be better not to let any yfelgópes see him without some sort of announcement, especially since he was dragging over two dozen of their heads behind him.

"Kelm! Kelm! I want Kelm!" he called at the top of his voice. He was surprised at how ragged and quiet it sounded.

At first there was no response, and then the terrible idea occurred to him that he might be alone down here in a deserted city. What would he do then? Just as he began to fret in earnest, tears springing to his eyes, a yfelgóp poked his head over the top of a roof. Looking around, he saw others as well, standing in archways, leering around the corners of buildings. One or two of them ducked away; a few of them started moving cautiously toward him.

He pulled the heads up onto the pile of rubble and then stopped. His arms ached so badly he thought that they'd just pop off. Yfelgópes were now surrounding him, looking at the heads, looking at him, weapons drawn. *Keep it sticky, keep it sticky and folded down,* he told himself. He gave them what he hoped was a winning smile and then casually rubbed his eyes. They were so puffy it was a constant effort of will to keep them open.

And then Kelm was there. Right in front of him, lumbering toward him with a puzzled look on his face. And well he should be puzzled, Daniel thought. *He obviously wouldn't have guessed that I could have tumbled to his little pantomime so quickly. Try to pump information out of me by sending some yfelgópes to "break me out" of prison and trick me into thinking I'm their friend and telling them everything I know. You'll have to get up earlier in the morning than that to catch me out.*

Daniel realised he wasn't talking, just thinking loudly. "Hello, Kelm. I'm back. Did you miss me?"

"Scarcely. I didn't even know you'd gone. Where have you been?"

"Recognise who I've got here with me?" Daniel bent down and hoisted one of the spears up. It had eight heads on it, each one pierced above the jaw and resting cheek-to-cheek next to the others. Daniel thought that one of them might be Argument. Something started to drip on his hand.

Kelm looked at the heads and Daniel, blankly.

Daniel almost laughed—or maybe he actually did. Kelm was putting on a good act. He really did act like he didn't have a clue as to who his own double agents were.

"I'll help you out with a hint: these are the ones that released me from prison."

If Kelm had said anything at that point—questioned, commented, or even just opened his mouth in surprise—then Daniel might not have doubted himself in that moment. As it was, Kelm just stood, looking at him, his face still blank, his eyes searching for context in Daniel's expression.

Does he really not know? Daniel asked himself. *Or is he that good at pretending? Perhaps Gád sent them, unknown to Kelm. Maybe I'm doing this the wrong way; maybe I should play along.* It was like a game of chess, each player making their move, doing the best with what they had. A player with fewer pieces on the board could still easily win, so long as they were smarter than their opponent.

Then Daniel was hit with a brain wave. There was already a

lie in play that he could run with. His eyes lit up. "These are traitors, Kelm. They released me, thinking that I would help them to
overthrow you, but as you can see, I'm loyal. I present these tokens
as offerings to you of my intent. I—I want to help. Do you believe
me now?" Daniel gave his best smile again.

Kelm took another moment to study Daniel head to foot.
Daniel did his best to stand up to the scrutiny—*Keep smiling,
head and shoulders back, mind that posture, keep your arm steady,
try not to let your knees jiggle, and keep everything, above all else,
completely folded down. Stay sticky.*

"No. No, I don't think I do trust you," Kelm said. "Not in the
least. Take him back to the cell and put six guards in the corridor.
We'll hope that he actually *has* killed everyone who might try to
rescue him again, but I would rather not take the risk." He gave
the orders with a flick of his hand and then stayed to watch them
carried out, an eyebrow raised in amused disbelief.

Daniel dropped the spear with the heads on it and drew his
sword. He looked at the circle of yfelgópes, already bristling with
weaponry, closing in on him and then dropped it and raised his
hands with a smile of resignation. He felt hands on him and a
punch that winded him and nearly doubled him over. Then he
was being pushed and shoved back toward the dungeon, back
toward his cell.

"Thank you for coming back to me, Daniel," Kelm said as he
passed. "You have saved me from making a very unpleasant report
back to Gád."

Daniel nodded amiably at Kelm as he passed, happy, in a way,
that he was going back to the cell. It would give him some time to
analyse his situation and plot his next move. The game continued.

CHAPTER SEVEN

The Pious Kings

---------------------------------- I ----------------------------------

Backing away from the enchanted image, Freya turned to the other mirror that showed herself as she was now. Then she turned again and looked into the mirror directly opposite that showed her wearing the crown. The third mirror reflected her image as she was at thirteen. She gasped and raised a hand to her mouth.

She appeared as she had when she first came to Niðergeard. The bedraggled school uniform she wore was all dirty and dishevelled from walking through tunnels and swimming in icy streams. A chill went through her. Why was the mirror showing her *this* instance in her childhood and not any of the earlier, happier ones?

So, three mirrors. One showed the present, one showed the past, one showed the . . . future? Seeing the past, as reality, made her think this other held a measure of reality too. But what was she doing in that gown? With *that* crown on?

She turned again to the mirror that showed the future. She

went right up to it. It was an incredible effect—her older face mirrored every tilt of the head and twitch of her face. Her eyes went to the crown and the reflection's eyes went to her own bare head. She raised her hands and watched them in the image as her reflection lifted them to her head. Carefully, Freya mimed gripping the crown and then taking it from her head. The reflection followed the movement of her hands and removed the crown.

She turned the image's crown over in her hands, studying it, watching how the light played across it. And then, as the light danced upon the silver surface, her eye fell on the reflection of the mirror behind her. When she looked at it before, it showed her as a child, but now it showed something different. It looked like two people standing in the mirror.

She turned and looked at it. But when she looked at it straight on, it showed her as a girl and nothing else. She turned back to the future mirror and looked at one via the other; there was definitely something standing behind her young mirror image, but she couldn't quite tell. How were the mirrors fixed to the walls? If only there was some way to move them closer together—

The racks.

She moved one of the racks closer to the "past" mirror that showed her as a little girl and then went back to the "future" mirror. She lifted it off of the wall—from its series of hooks that ran along a groove—and carried it across to the other mirror, placing it on the rack. Then, with her back to the "past" mirror, she moved the "future" mirror so that it showed her and then the image behind her as well.

What she saw was her older self in the mirror before her, but standing behind that image, reflected in the other mirror, was another reflection of her. By turning to the side and leaning forward, she managed to manoeuvre herself into a position where she could see past her future self to the other.

The face of a young girl peered out at her from behind the lavish red skirts of her future self. At first Freya thought it was her younger image again, but as she looked at it longer, she saw that she had different features, a different skin tone, but nonetheless still bore a striking resemblance.

Could it be her daughter?

Freya raised a hand and waved. The girl mirrored her perfectly. "Hello?" she said, and the girl mouthed the words at the same time as she. Was it still just a reflection, then? She stood still, studying her face and clothes. The girl's expression betrayed no emotion other than her own, and so its thoughts, its personality, were masked to her.

She took a step back and knocked the frame of the mirror ever so slightly as she did. The mirror tilted and a whole line of images grew from behind the image of her supposed daughter. All her descendants curved away into the dim distance behind her.

What a remarkable enchantment.

An idea occurred to her and she turned around. She caught her breath as she found herself faced with herself as a young girl, and in the reflection behind that was her mother. And behind her was her grandmother, and then, presumably, her grandmother's mother, and all the way down the line, into the far distance.

It was eerie and haunting. "This is too much," Freya said.

But it wasn't even the half of it. Turning to the door, she found that another mirror hung on the back of it. Closing the door, it latched, and she looked at the image that showed her in a regular, everyday outfit but surrounded by a busy, daytime café scene, which she recognised instantly—the Jericho Café, where she liked to do most of her revisions. Her mirror image was standing just as she was now, but to the side of her was a small, round table that had her book and an empty mug containing a sodden tea bag.

Was this her as she could have been? But could have been if . . .

what? If she hadn't returned? If she'd killed Gád? If she hadn't come across Swiðgar and Ecgbryt in the first place?

People moved around in the background behind her, casually, calmly. A guy her age—a nice-looking guy, well-groomed and not too fashionable, just the type she liked—came and sat at the table behind her and started poking around on his laptop. Did this image show what she wanted her life to be like?

Freya brought the mirror to the centre of the room and hung it on another of the racks. Then she took the rack showing her future and turned them toward each other. They stood at a right angle to each other. Each one showed her reflection, and the reflection of herself in the other mirror—but they were different images.

On her near left was the reflection of herself in the café, and on her near right was the reflection of her future self. But the inside reflections were different from these two again.

The café scene's mirror showed a sitting room, small—a little too small perhaps—but cosy. She was standing in front of a sofa, and behind her, where the image of the unknown student would have been, was a man she couldn't quite see but whom she was certain she recognised. She could only see the edge of his face and so she tilted the mirror in order to show more of it.

It was Daniel. He looked at home. She could identify some of her things in the room—a print of a painting she liked, a carving a friend gave her from Africa. She was dressed in night clothes and seemed comfortable, relaxed . . . with Daniel, who wasn't wearing the hard mask he'd picked up on the street, but who seemed pleasant and gentle, as if Niðergeard had never even happened.

She looked into the other mirror, and beside her future self, she saw an image of herself, still wearing the silver crown but wearing battle gear—darkly polished plate armour and chainmail, with black boots and trim, a sword fastened at her hip. Her hands were bare and smeared red with blood. The scene behind her was dim and dark, but she was pretty sure that there were bodies around her.

Freya realised she wasn't breathing and took a deep breath. She forced herself to think this through. Surely they couldn't both be true, so either of them must only be a possible future—or both of them might be. But if so, for what purpose? To show different options? To tempt her into certain paths? Who would create such things? Ealdstan, presumably, but why? What did he use them for?

Cautiously, very cautiously, she tilted the mirrors closer to each other and watched as the reflections stacked upon themselves, cascading behind one another.

In the right-hand mirror, she saw herself crowned, and behind that, wearing the battle armour, behind that was a reflection of her in rags and bound in chains, behind that she was wearing blue, papery pajamas and a white robe—like someone might wear in a mental hospital—and behind that she was wearing the Oxford graduation robes, and behind that were more and more images, although it was extremely hard to make them out.

What did it mean? If they were all probable futures, was there any significance to their order? Were the closest images the most probable?

She took a step back, out of the mirrors' reflections, feeling light-headed. Again, she asked, what was the point of this room, besides a sort of dizzying diversion? Almost ten minutes passed and she was breathless, disoriented, with an overwhelming number of questions. Was it possible that Ealdstan, in his hundreds of years' worth of time, could have cracked the secret to using these mirrors and could see the actual future? If anyone could, it would be him, although they'd not discovered anything in his study that related or even alluded to this place or the mirrors. And if he had figured out a way to exploit them somehow, then to what effect?

Things got really crazy when she set three mirrors up to reflect one another. They showed all different kinds of scenes of herself and people she knew and didn't know in familiar and unfamiliar settings. She tried to track which images were shown in what mirrors, but it got very confusing, and the more complex the setup, the harder it was to make out exactly what was in the reflections. She strained her neck and her eyes trying to see as much of the different scenes as possible.

Then she placed all four mirrors around her and turned slowly, as if in a kaleidoscopic chamber. Her eyes watered and she experienced a sharp stab of vertigo that forced her to move out from the reflecting mirrors quickly before she keeled over. She almost threw up at that point, and it took her a long time to recover.

Unable to pull herself away from the room, she spent countless hours arranging and rearranging the mirrors—moving them just so, tilting them this way and then that, standing exactly *here*—but she eventually tore herself away, becoming hungry and tired. Her mind was so full of images that she could barely begin to process them all, and it made it difficult for her to think of anything else. She felt like screaming.

Used in combination, the mirrors all had so many different properties. The "now" one showed the friends and people she'd been close to when reflected in the "past" mirror: her parents in their garden, her sister in a classroom, Daniel standing in a forest—that was odd—Ecgbryt in a dark tunnel, and beyond that she thought she saw Modwyn with her eyes closed in what may have been a bedroom. The images behind that were hard to make out. Trying hard not to look into their faces, she replaced each of the mirrors in their original places on the walls and behind the door. She shivered and left the room, closing the silver door behind her. She was continuing back down the thin passageway and back to the stairs when she remembered that there was another room on that floor.

Her head was spinning and she decided that she was in a very bad condition to face what might be in that room, if it was anything. "Let sleeping dogs lie," Vivienne had said, and the words came back to her now. She trudged down the stairs, back into Ealdstan's study. Vivienne was at her usual place, going over the books again. Of the hundreds that lined the walls, it seemed she had made her way through at least half of them. No mean feat, but then Freya didn't know how long they had both been at it.

"Ready to go at it again, Freya?" Vivienne said, pulling a stack of books toward her. And then moving her hands over to the pansensorum.

"No—no, I don't think I am," Freya protested as Vivienne stuck in her ear plugs. "Listen, wait—I found—"

But Vivienne whipped the top into a spin and the room gave a lurch. Freya grabbed for a chair and pulled herself onto it.

II

London

21 May 1471 AD

Henry sat in his cell, more than a broken man—a broken king. Only fifty years old, Henry looked a hundred. He had seen too much of this world; his heart longed for the next. When would he see golden skies? How long would he be forced to endure the arduous pain of this world? The horror of existence?

There was a rattle at the door and it opened. The guard, without a word, let a hooded man into the narrow room.

"You," Henry said. It was a declaration more than a statement. An accusation. "You . . ."

He didn't have the energy to hate anymore. He was tired—all passion had left his body. He stared down at his old, impotent hands.

Ealdstan took down his hood and stared at the king, who turned weary, wet eyes up at him. For the briefest moment, Ealdstan experienced an unfamiliar sensation—that of looking into eyes older than his own. With a shift that he felt in his gut, the feeling passed and he was staring instead into the cloudy eyes of a sad, beaten madman. He took a few steps toward the window, and Henry, as though possessing no will of his own, also turned his face to the bars.

The sky was shades of russet and orange, fading into a light purple.

"I never betrayed you," Ealdstan said. "You must think that I did, but I always did what was best for the kingdom, for the crown."

Ealdstan turned from the window to see that Henry had also turned away. "You are in your silent mood again."

"No. No, I am not. I am just tired. It is exhausting. First ruling, then deposed, then enthroned once again, only to be deposed once more. All the fighting, all the battles. English blood on English soil for the first time in over a hundred years. How did I fail my people? Where have I erred?"

"They wanted leadership. They wanted safety."

"I would have led them to safety. I would have led them to piety."

"They would sooner have the safety that victory over your enemies promised. A warm bed and a full belly. Even very pious men falter with a blade at their neck."

"'My enemies.' I never understood that phrase. We are all brothers. We all bear the burdens of reality in this world. Who is my enemy? God knows, I have been an enemy to many, but has a man ever been mine?"

"You are too philosophical—that has always been your weakness." Ealdstan sucked in his breath at this last word—the word he had told himself not to say. Weakness was the beginning and end with this man. It would not do to taunt him. "The opposer is

in every man you meet. You say every enemy is your brother—
every brother is your enemy. We war not just outside the world,
but within ourselves also, for the opposer is also there. The evil
builds in season, like a flood tide, and will one day overrun us and
wash away all that cannot stand."

"And will you rouse your sleepers and save us at that time?"

"You could have been strong. You could have more readily
drawn strength from others. Your wife, for instance." *Or me,* he
added silently. *If you had only listened to* me.

"I would have been stronger if I let others fight for me, you
mean?" Henry looked up, his eyes flashing. "Is that strength?
Or is strength the power to stand for peace when all around you
war? You who have known . . . how many kings now? In your
wisdom, perhaps you can answer me this question: Why do
hands clenching swords inspire men more than hands clenched
in prayer? Why are there always far more willing to rip apart
than to knit together?"

"Your father knew the reason. He brought peace, and he carried a sword."

"Father's victories were the worst part about him. If he were
to have died at Agincourt, or somewhere along his French campaigns . . ." Henry was lost in wishes and thoughts he dared not
speak.

"And he saddled me with a nation falling apart, piece by piece,
like a castle of sand washed into the sea. I was never a warrior. I was
not the man he was. I have walked the battlefields of England and seen
Lancastrian fathers weeping for Yorkist sons. A man was brought to
me for the crime of looting the battlefield. He was distraught, incon-
solable. While rummaging through one of the stiffening bodies, he
prised a golden bauble from cold hands that he himself had once
owned and given to his son on his marriage. It wasn't until he held
it in his own hands that he recognised the form of the body beneath

him. What is a rational man's response to this madness? And what is a king's? It is the curse of the king that the curse of the nation be visited on his body. My own subjects war against me, just as my mind wars against my body. I loved my father, I truly did, but I have often wondered, if he had lived to see me grown, would he have even known me for his own? What do you think?"

"The old king was religious, in his own, direct way. He owned a warrior's piety. He would have recognised that in you."

"And you? What do you think?" He turned his gaze up, this time a young child looking for approval. Ealdstan felt sick.

Weak, he wanted to say. Weak in mind and body. He could almost spit bile at the limp, pathetic lump of flesh that had once owned the throne and yet now rotted in prison.

"I know what you think," Henry said, bowing his head. "You think I was just unlucky. Some days I think God torments me for a purpose, in order to teach me and the kingdom; other times I think He just does it to prove how powerless we all are before His magnificence."

"There's still a chance for you. The people still love you—you can unite them. But you must follow my lead!"

"No," Henry said, shaking his head. "No, I know where you would lead me. I know the cost you would extract from something the Lord knows is only too poor."

"Please, I ask you for your sake."

"Never. I will never give you what you ask of me—it goes against every nature of my spirit. It was never I who weakened these isles—it was you. Only ever you."

Ealdstan frowned. And that frown became hard and set. How dare he?

"So be it," Ealdstan said. "You brought this on yourself." He raised his staff high, almost to the ceiling, and then brought it down on King Henry VI's head.

The king groaned and rolled onto the floor. Ealdstan restrained himself from issuing more blows and knelt beside the figure, pressing a hand to the prone man's chest and whispering an incantation of stopping.

Henry grimaced in pain. Or was he smiling? Was that a gasp or a laugh? His lips were moving. Ealdstan halted his incantation. "What is it?"

"I see . . . I see . . ." the king whispered.

"What do you see, old man?"

Henry swallowed, throat dry, almost choking. "I see . . ."

"What? What?"

His eyes swivelled sightlessly. "Golden skies." And then he died.

Ealdstan rose and looked out the window. It was dark.

"God save me from pious kings," he said.

Save me, in fact, from all kings, he thought.

He knocked on the door and the guard let him out.

III

Freya's head dropped and it almost knocked against the table before she jerked it back up again. "How long this time?" She unclenched her hand and let her pen drop. Her fingers ached. She began massaging her palm.

Vivienne, standing at a bookcase, wrangled with the books in her arms and checked her watch. "Five hours."

"Five? This is taking forever, and it's so exhausting. Please, no more."

"But we're getting valuable material."

"Vivienne—I didn't get to tell you about the mirrors. There's a room in this tower, and it—"

"Contains mirrors that allow you to see past, future, and possible versions of yourself. Yes, I am aware."

Freya was stunned. "How?"

"I told you, I've explored the Langtorr before," Vivienne said, flipping open a book.

"How many times?"

"Just once. I didn't come too far—just down to this room, in fact. I took only the briefest of looks around and heard a noise, which I now know must have been Frithfroth. I got spooked and ran back up the tower. Ecgbryt was there—he was the only one who could keep the doorway open past dusk—"

"What else is here that you haven't told me about?"

"Let's keep cracking on, shall we? Come on, these are from the seventeenth century."

Freya rubbed her eyes. Using the pansensorum was mentally exhausting, but not physically. "Okay, in a second. But, Vivienne— if what you're not telling me about is important . . . you'd have let me know, right?"

"Correct. I believe this is the best way we can help our cause right now. Far more than further exploration of the tower."

"Okay," Freya sighed. "Start it up again."

IV

London, Whitehall Palace

1 December 1653 AD

Ealdstan paced the corridors of the massive palace. It truly was enormous. More than fifteen hundred rooms meant it could hold the population of a town. It was not as magnificent as his own realm, he reminded himself, but it represented an idea that had been growing in the surface world over the past few hundred years. An unconscious desire, more than an idea—a desire for separation, which was now becoming assumed and ingrained. The magnificence of the palace existed in sharp contrast to the poverty of the citizenry around it. There was none of that in Niðergeard, he noted with pride. The smithies lived in rooms as fine as his own—much better, in fact.

He wondered what it meant. He couldn't imagine all these rooms were actually needed or vital to the running of the nation. They were an excess, and an excess meant things were running inefficiently. It was good, then, that he had found Cromwell. Indeed, if he hadn't come across Cromwell, then it would have been necessary to invent someone. As a rule, Ealdstan hated insta-bility and revolution, but the nation had been wobbling on its axis for the last couple hundred years. Kings were hard to control, even in the best of circumstances. Republics had potential, though they'd need more attention.

It was then that Cromwell found him. He walked into the courtyard where Ealdstan sat, his ruddy face beaming, his oddly unmilitary build—narrow shoulders and protruding gut—gangling into view.

"Ealdstan, you old relic, how are you this morrow?" He clasped the wizard on his shoulder as he stood, giving it a vice-like squeeze.

"I am well, and seem to have found you in high spirits."

"I tell you, man," Cromwell said, "these are—" He was inter-rupted as a door into the courtyard burst open and a flock of harassed-looking men—armed soldiers as well as politicians and a couple clergy—entered.

"My lord—"

"Sir, if I may—"

"Your honour—"

"Permission to—"

"Out! Out you beasts, all of ye!" Cromwell shouted at them. "Quit the doorway! Shut that! Quit my presence and my sight. Give me peace for just a half of an hour or I'll loose dogs upon ye!"

Faces blanched, a few arms saluted, and a penitent clerk closed the French door. Faces peered in at them from behind the rows of glass panes.

Cromwell shook his head. "A bevy of badgers."

"Let us walk this way . . . eh?" Ealdstan faltered. "I seem to be at a loss for a title for you."

"For me?" Cromwell turned back to Ealdstan with a grin. They began to walk a path in the courtyard. "Why, I am just a lowly MP in the service of his country. Call me Oliver."

"Not just that, also a general and . . . more, if I am to believe what I hear of the feelings in the Parliament."

"So?" Cromwell said, his face brightening once more. "News *does* reach you in that hole you occupy. Yes, this nation may finally come around to some sort of order, God willing. These are blessed days, my friend. The plans and schemes that we discussed in our—or at least *my* youth," he said, looking Ealdstan up and down, "are bearing more fruit than even I had dared to imagine. I had thought, even at times of triumph, to be a sort of holy failure. A martyr, if God willed it. But now"—he took a deep breath and swung his arms around him—"can you smell it? There is something in the air. Men's hearts have changed. We have moved closer to the Divine; we are climbing out from the ditch of sin that the kings and monarchists have steered us into. Through God's grace, my ability granted through Him, and your good counsel, my friend. It is a new age of enlightenment—moral, spiritual, political. Holy times, my friend. Holy times."

"I am glad you are pleased. With you ends the era of kings, and their confused, misguided folly."

"In truth, Ealdstan," Cromwell continued rapturously as they started a circuit around a rectangular reflecting pool, "when you and I talked and laid plans of revolution, I doubted. I was an unbeliever. Forgive me my foolish youth, friend."

"Enough of that," Ealdstan said. "Let us talk of next steps. What would you consider to be your fiercest regiment?"

"We will talk of payment later. First I must discuss my campaigns against the Irish and the Scots. You believe it is vital that we bow them to our rule?"

"Bow or break," Ealdstan answered. "They must join. As must the Continent." Ealdstan was drawn back hundreds of years by his thoughts. It once seemed possible—the Dane lands, the Frankish lands . . . ties had been made with them that were to last until the end of the world. But the map was fragmented now. He had thought that familial bonds would strengthen ties between nations, but that was an error. Where there used to be family ties, there was only enmity. All the houses of the royals—boiled down to one big, ugly string of family disputes. This new return to a meritocracy, the way it used to be when England was young, was the way forward.

"This is the start of a golden age. I envision a union of nations across the earth. A commonwealth of spiritual holiness."

Ealdstan blinked and bowed his head. "And then we may be able to weather the storm I see coming."

Cromwell pursed his lips and nodded solemnly. Then he smiled and gripped Ealdstan's shoulder with his massive soldier's hand. "Such an ambitious vision, and one I doubt will be realised in my time," he said. "I will try not to let you down, but this new order of government—it is a delicate thing and needs much protection. I will need all resources at my command."

"Be not intractable," Ealdstan said to him. "You would pay a man for giving you a house; would you not pay me for giving you a kingdom?"

Cromwell laughed. "Cursing me with one, you mean. In truth, I pay for nothing these days. What I need, I am given or I take. But worry not, old friend, due payment will come in due time, as my mother was well used to saying."

Ealdstan bit his lip and tried to hold back a sneer.

--- **V** ---

They were walking underneath the ocean and, contrary to expectations, it was extremely dry. Apart from a general damp in the air, and the odd slippery black slime underfoot and on the walls, there was nary a trickle of water anywhere.

Alex was impressed that the mechanics; while rudimentary, they were extremely effective. The strange diving mechanism involved a pool about four metres in diameter into which a massive framework dangled a greased length of chain attached to a cast iron weight. It was basic enough—you just cranked the weight up, put your feet in the stirrups, and held on to the braces, and then pulled out the locking mechanism. The weight plunged into the pool and dragged you with it—fighting the shock of the cold water and the oppressive pressure—to the bottom of the pool where you let go of the chain and navigated a U-shaped bend and climbed up into the tunnel system. The tunnel was dry since the air was in a closed system, not being able to escape out of either end. It was, however, very unpleasantly like being flushed.

To his credit, one of the Cornish knights volunteered to go first, making pessimistic predictions all the way. They waited for a breathless minute for him to return. The mechanism reset and then activated again, and he bobbed up, back on the chain. He was very wet and rather shaken, but otherwise fine. The rest of the knights pushed each other aside in an attempt not to be the last to so valiantly take this next step of the journey, leaving Alex and Ecgbryt to bring up the rear.

Dry though it may be, it certainly wasn't pleasant under the ocean floor. The air pressure was almost unbearable; Alex kept having to clear his ears, and his eyes watered and he just felt—foggy, groggy.

Fortunately, the cave itself was well-carved and easy to traverse. It was smooth and fairly straight, yet they hadn't gone a mile when it split. Ecgbryt made just the slightest pause at the split in the cave openings and then took the left path.

"Wait, hang on," Alex said, flicking his torch on and wiping condensation off the map covering. "That's south."

"Swa swa," Ecgbryt said, nodding. "Just so." He and the eight newly awakened knights halted and turned to regard Alex.

"Well, so . . . I don't see this here. Surely we want to bear north if we want to get up to Ireland."

"We're not going to Ireland."

"No?"

"No, we're going to Cornouaille."

Alex blinked. "We were just in Cornwall."

"No, *Cornouaille*, in the Franks' land."

"The Franks' . . . ? You mean *France*?"

Ecgbryt nodded. "Just so."

"There's a Cornwall in France? How does that work?"

"It is a part of the original kingdom," one of the Cornish knights broke in. Alex thought his name was Denzell. "Our people were once connected—Brytannica, Armorica, Gallaecia—a series of peninsular outposts and colonies."

"Peninsular—?"

"I could tell you tales of King Mark and his faithful warrior—"

"Yes!" called Ecgbryt. "I would hear those tales!"

"In a minute," Alex interrupted again. "About France—"

"We are closer to it than we are to Ireland, and it seems doubtful to me that any other yfelgóp band would make this journey."

"Also, we can expect no love from the knights of Eire."

There was a general murmur of agreement among the knights.

"Prickly most of the time, unpredictable at best, they have long memories and most likely would not forgive the licenses of the past. There is much bad blood."

The knights carried on, chatting merrily, leaving Alex to tread along in a bewildered state. "Bad blood? Do they think France is going to be different?"

VI

Terrified now that she was so far out to sea that she couldn't see the shore, Gretchen clutched tighter, resolving her dead man's hold around the seal's neck. This done, she then concentrated on breathing, which was fairly difficult under the circumstances.

She cursed herself. She was in a world of trouble now, and no mistake. There was a word for her creature-companion and she knew it well: selkie. It was a word she had learned from her great grandmother when she went around to her house as a very young girl. Her great grandmother had just a couple battered children's books kept in a box with some uninteresting wooden toys. When those stopped amusing, and Gretchen got restless, then Great Grandmother would talk to her. Sometimes it was just about what was going on with the people in the village, but on occasion she would tell one of her stories, one of the old and ancient tales of the area.

Gretchen always had trepidations about the stories and would never ask for one. That was because the stories absolutely terrified her. There wasn't one of them that ended well for the little girls (and it was always little girls; Gretchen felt, even at five years old, that the way her great grandmother poked her in the ribs whenever she said "little girl" was needlessly heavy-handed). And, just like the situation Gretchen was in now, the heroines were always such victims of circumstance or innocent desire that there didn't seem, at any point in the story, a way for them out of the sticky messes they had become mired in. Inevitably, that lead to their death, which her great grandmother would draw out beyond all taste or decorum, even for a five-year-old.

And so while she hadn't spent much more than a dozen afternoons by herself with her grandmother, and had only actually heard a small number of her great grandmother's tales, every word of them were etched on her young mind. They were much more memorable than those of the battered children's books with their toothless pastel colours and safe endings, or indeed any of the books she owned and read repetitively. But she *could* remember every phrase of her great grandmother's stories—"The Orphan Girl and the Goblins," "The Seamstress and the Tricksie Brownies," "The Changeling and Its Sister," "Bluebeard's Young Bride," and, of course, "The Selkie Mother."

Yet even with those vivid warnings to deter her, here she found herself being pulled out to sea on the back of a changeling man. She could almost hear her great grandmother say, "I told you so."

The sky continued to darken, but she could see something on the horizon. It was a grey lump that grew quickly into a black, rocky jag of a windswept island, probably not large enough to provide food or shelter for even one small sheep.

Which is not to say that it was empty. There were shapes moving along the top of it; she could see human silhouettes dancing on the island's crest. As they drew nearer, Gretchen saw that there were also seals watching them, banging their flippers and tails in time to the beat of the music that now drifted out to them. It was a selkie ceilidh.

They circled the island, slowly coming in where the rocks dipped lower into the sea. As she glided by, she saw that they were all naked, just as the man, Ron Glass, had been on the beach. They danced with a rhythmic, primal swing and sang in a chorus to the accompaniment of pipes.

They came to a shallow inlet and her selkie scraped along the sand. He gave a wriggle and a flap, and then she was holding on to the man, the bit of seal skin flapping between them.

They scampered up onto the slippery rocks, the man rather gallantly helping Gretchen up. For the briefest of moments Gretchen was impressed by this, before she remembered that he had abducted her.

"There is just one fire on the island," he explained to her as he led her up the rocks by the hand, "but you may not be allowed very near it on your first night. You may keep my skin tonight," he said, reaching the top and flinging it over her shoulders. "I should not let you have it, but it will keep you warm on a cold night."

She followed him up the rock and pulled the seal skin around her very cold and very wet body. It was soft, thick, and warm but no drier than her or anything else on the desolate and windy rock. But it was another layer between her and the elements, and it kept the wind off of her, and she was grateful for it.

She hunched her bulky, awkward frame even further inside the skin as she came nearer to the dancing selkies. They were beautiful—the most beautiful people Gretchen had ever seen. All were tall and lithe and perfectly formed. A large fire pit burned in the centre, and the flames and embers lit their skin with a warm red and yellow glow, making them luminescent and otherworldly. The girls were willowy and soft-skinned with wide hips and long, dexterous hands and feet that they twisted inward and out in time to the rhythm; their long hair, alternately straight and curly, swinging. The men were built similarly to Ron, but some were fair, some were dark, and one or two were red, all with fine, firm, and occasionally sharp, Celtic features. They were uniformly smooth and unadorned by any hair except that which grew on their heads.

They all wove around one another, frenetically spinning and twisting. They did not ever knock into another or trip one another up, but when someone crossed their path, they would reach out and grab that person, sometimes quite intimately, and swing them around and then let them go, and both would continue their whirling jig. Their dance mimicked the path and motion of the sparks that the fire threw up into the night sky.

No one took much of a notice of Gretchen. They were too busy dancing and singing their song.

> Up and Dance, for light is dawning,
>   Night will turn to day;
> Dance because the world is turning,
>   And we cannot stay.

> Hear the sounds of stars revolving,
>   Sweeping night away—
> Sing a song of dark resounding,
>   For we cannot stay.

> See, the sky at last is lightening,
>   The sea will soon be grey;
> Weep my friends, for dawn is breaking,
>   And we cannot stay.

> The burning orb of fire is rising,
>   laugh, and music play;
> The cover for our fun is fading,
>   And we cannot stay.

> Why this cruelty, Brightness shining,
>   Why this price we pay?

Why should unclothed flesh need shaming?
   Why, I cannot say.

Curse the sun and keep on dancing,
   Grab my hand and say,
"Dance the night, and dance in darkness,
   Come, I cannot stay.

"Life is short and pleasure fleeting,
   Grab what sin you may.
Morning brings our deeds' discovering,
   Thus we cannot stay."

Someday perhaps, we'll need not hiding,
   Light and law decay;
The day the sun his house not biding
   Will be the day we stay.

Until that hour we must keep moving,
   Blow the pipes and play!
Dance with me and dance to morning,
   For we cannot stay.

Gretchen stood, watching, and somehow the orbit of the dancers grew, and the cold blackness of the night shrunk so that the orange dancers were the only created thing in the universe, and she was standing on the outside edge. They spun before her, those who passed closest would hold their arms out to her when they saw her. A few of them even grabbed her briefly, but she never let herself be drawn in. Even so, she found herself jostling awkwardly in the path of the dancers, drawn into their orbit. There seemed to be more of them now. Perhaps more of the seals had slipped their skins off and joined in. She felt doubly out of place now—even more unattractive and clumsy in the context of such beauty and grace of movement.

There was a strange elation to being here, with them and among them, and it was with a warm flush of embarrassed excitement when she realised it was because they all seemed to want her here. It was such a profoundly unfamiliar feeling, and it felt so achingly good . . .

Was she under a spell? She knew she should feel more anxiety than she did. She knew she should try to escape, but only in a vague and abstract way that brought no compelling emotion or immediacy.

Ron was suddenly at her side. "Drink this," he said, and placed a shell containing a clear liquid in her hands. She took a sip and felt her mouth burning.

"What is it?"

"We found a few casks of whiskey bobbing in the ocean and brought them here."

Gretchen didn't need her great grandmother to tell her of the stories of seals playfully leading sailors and fishermen astray and causing general havoc. Those were told by almost everyone. "Found?"

"Aye, found. The ship had landed upon rocks somehow. Drink up. *Slàinte.*"

Gretchen tipped her shell up and drank. The contents did help to warm her, but she didn't think that she should have any more. However, another shell was placed in her hands almost immediately.

"Go ahead, drink it. *Slàinte.*" He tipped his back again.

Gretchen didn't drink hers, but tipped her shell and let it pour out while his head was tipped back. "It's good," she said.

"Isn't it? Let's dance."

"No, thank you."

"It'll warm you up better than the drink."

"I'm too tired. Let me rest. Maybe later. When are you going to take me back?"

"Back where?"

"To where you found me."

"You don't want to go back there."

"Yes, I do."

"Why?"

"Because I live there."

"You live on the beach? Why not stay here with us?"

"I'm a human. I don't belong here."

"I'm not taking you back."

"I'll swim."

He shrugged. "It's your choice."

At that moment a redheaded female came and pulled him playfully by the arm. He allowed himself to be tugged away, flashing Gretchen a devilish smile as he went.

She left the circle of dancers and warmth and crouched down against a rock that sheltered her against the cutting sea wind. The selkies continued dancing and singing, but the mood had changed—it was now quieter and more languorous. They were moving less complexly, and they were touching each other more. They were touching each other *a lot*, in fact.

"You're not one of them, are you?" asked a voice beside her.

Gretchen turned and looked into the face of a girl about her age, but unclothed, like the rest of them.

"What did you say?" Gretchen asked.

"You're not a selkie, are you? I can tell. They can go all night like this. I get tired after a while. They don't seem to."

"So you're not a selkie either?"

"No. I'm Lucy. They brought me here . . . Gosh, I don't know how long ago now. I fell out of a boat. Feels like just a couple nights ago, but I think it was longer. It's fun, isn't it? Nothing to worry about . . . long nights of fun and excitement . . ."

Lucy was shorter than Gretchen and her eyes were big and brown, almost too big for her face, it seemed. She had matted, sandy-yellow hair and an eager manner. "Where did you get the skin from?" she asked.

"I was lent it."

"You're lucky. I wish I had one; then I could go swimming in the sea with them. They said they'd make me one. I've never seen any of them make anything, though. All they do is swim and dance. And sleep, in the daytime. I guess there's no rush, though. I like dancing and sleeping too. Can I borrow your skin?"

"Are you cold?"

"No. I just want to go swimming."

"What do you mean?"

"If I put it on, I would turn into one of them and I could go swimming with them. You think this dance is amazing, you should see what they do in the water!"

"Would it work for you?"

"Of course. I've seen them use one another's. They don't usually, they like to keep their own skins—I would if I were one of them, which I'd like to be. If you don't want to be one of them, then they ignore you and stop feeding you and you die. I've seen that happen too."

"You've seen other real people here?" Lucy was staring at the dancers again.

Lucy looked at Gretchen as if seeing her for the first time again. "Oh yes, lots. They're always bringing people back here. They like the company. There's always at least one new person at a dance, sometimes several. I've seen a lot of them arrive. How many, I wonder . . ."

Her brow furrowed in concern, trying to work it out, and her eyes wandered and she looked at the dancers, and a smile gradually came back to her face.

"Lucy?" Gretchen asked.

Lucy turned fresh eyes on her once more and looked her up and down. "If the newcomers put up too much of a fuss, then they kill them. It's not nice. They eat them, pick the bones clean, and throw them into the ocean." She paused, shivering and gazing longingly at Gretchen's skin. "Was that a no, then? About the skin?"

"Sorry," Gretchen said. "It's just that I'm really cold, and kind of wet . . ."

"I understand. Let me know if you change your mind. I really want a skin of my own. And think about staying. If you don't, I might eat you. Ha ha! It was nice talking to you." Lucy pushed her way into the dancing circle again, soon lost in the shuffle, leaving Gretchen alone with her thoughts.

It was quite dark now, and some of the selkies had wandered off, alone or in pairs. Ron Glass didn't come back for her, but she did catch sight of him as he waved to her from across the fire pit. He was very quickly led away again, this time by a short woman with long, kinky hair.

Gretchen shrugged the skin higher up on her shoulders. She knew now what she had to do, but it was going to take patience and courage to carry it out. She just needed to stay awake and pick her moment perfectly.

The singing had died off, gradually, becoming lost in the arrhythmic *shush*-ing of the water around the island. The selkies left by twos, threes, or fours into the night. The embers in the pit had ceased to spark and now only burned with a low, deep red, which would shortly be mirrored in the sky's southeastern sunrise. There was just a single dancer left now: Lucy, who swayed in a vague, dreamy fashion in short steps around the fire pit. She held out arms that Gretchen suddenly noticed were very thin; her whole body was emaciated, in fact. It looked like she was starving.

Then even Lucy became tired and wandered off to find somewhere to spend the night. Gretchen waited for what she judged to be ten or fifteen minutes. She gathered her resolve and rose quietly. Moving around the rock, she picked up all of the seal skins that she could find lying on the rocks and among the forms of the selkies sleeping in their naked, human forms. Apparently they didn't feel the cold or hardness of the rock.

The skins were littered here and there, like discarded clothes in an untidy teenager's bedroom. Each one weighed an absolute tonne, though, and she could only carry two or three at a time. It was quite difficult to sneak around the small island with its uneven and wet surfaces, and she had to move quickly as well as quietly.

She brought the skins back to the centre of the island and lobbed them in a heap, close to the fire pit's edge. After about forty-five minutes, she'd found all that she could and heaped them into a gigantic pile next to the fire. They looked like an enormous pile of fur coats.

Now came the moment of truth. Taking a breath, she lifted a foot and kicked at the pile until it gradually tilted forward, toward the fire pit, and then, by ones and threes, they fell into the hot embers below. There were so many, and they were so heavy, that for long, terrible minutes she thought she had smothered the heat by putting them all in at once, but then she spied a thin curl of smoke, illuminated by the sliver of a new moon. More of them started to smoulder and blacken, throwing off a stinky, oily smoke, and then a few tiny flames appeared.

It was coming along nicely. Pretty soon all of them would be burning merrily.

All of them, except for the one she had been given.

She hurried back to the shallow bay area where they had

arrived. The tide had risen while she had been here but was ebbing now. She stood on a slippery outcropping of rock that hung above the modulating sea and wrapped the skin fully around herself, first making sure her feet were covered, and then tossing the flap that hung down her back up and over her head.

Her heart chilled.

It wasn't working.

The suit completely covered her, but it didn't join together where she pressed it. She kept it around her and wriggled about in it, but nothing happened—she just got tired holding up the heavy skin.

With a gasp, she threw back the hood. Realising that she'd based her escape plan solely on the information of a young and possibly very deluded young girl, Gretchen was about to sit down and await her fate at the judgement of the beasts. Her consolation was at least they'd all be marooned on this lifeless rock until they could make new skins for themselves—and she might be able to see how it was done. It was small consolation, however. She'd likely have been long-eaten before new skins were created.

It was hot and uncomfortable in the skin, so she tried to push it off of her. That was more difficult than she expected. It seemed to be sticking to her hands and face. She brought one hand up to her forehead to see what the problem was and found that she had raised a fin. Then it struck her—the selkies had all been naked—it would only work on her exposed skin.

Gretchen pulled her hand out of the skin and with a wet sucking sound it emerged. She laid it aside. Then she timidly started to peel off her school jumper. She felt ridiculous as she folded it and put it in a neat pile near her feet.

She had almost unbuttoned her shirt when she heard the first scream of anguish from the selkies who had discovered their burning skins.

Now she couldn't claw her clothes off fast enough. They would kill her as soon as they found her, and it was a race against her stripping down completely and any one of them discovering her in the small cove with the only remaining selkie skin.

There were more screams now, rising in angry chorus. Everything became heightened, and her hands moved like blurs. Her skirt was off, and she rolled her stockings down with it. She pulled her panties down and quickly started fumbling with the bra clasps behind her back. She cursed it over and over.

And then that was it, she was naked—exposed.

There was a shout from behind her, piercing shrilly through the wall of wailing.

"There! There she is! She's kept one for herself!"

Another shot of adrenaline coursed through her body. She bent down and grabbed the skin, pulling it up over her. She heard a scrabbling on the rock behind her and in fear and desperation leapt into the dark and freezing waves of the night ocean.

Her leap was short and brought her nowhere near safety. Her feet were no longer separate now—they were joined at the ankle, it felt. Turning to look down at what had caught them—she thought it might be one of her pursuers—she found that the skin was working. She felt it cling tightly to her body as it wrapped itself completely around her hips, her belly, her back and shoulders, and her arms—enveloping her in flabby seal softness. It grafted to her face and encircled her eyes. She was now in the body of a seal, and she turned her head and flicked her tail but found that the water was far too shallow for her to swim in. She turned around and found herself staring into a swarm—practically an army, in fact, of angry, naked people who were fast closing in on her.

She flipped and floundered as hard as she could, gradually inching into deeper water. The closest selkies had their heels in the water now and were splashing quickly toward her.

The water was completely covering her and she started to swim using odd, full-bodied flipper movements that she was very unused to making. The cold hit her like an anvil, and for a moment she was winded and disoriented. The waves buffeted and spun her under the surface, and then she opened her eyes—her new, seal eyes—and saw the course through the rocks around the island, which she manoeuvred in and out of with surprising deftness.

And then, finally, she was in the open sea. She was free of the island and her pursuers. Her body quickly adjusted to the chilly aqueous environment and she swam for a time, losing herself in the currents, wondering where land lay. Then the sky started to lighten and within an hour the sun broke the horizon, giving her a bearing of east-southeast, and a vague direction of home. She started confidently toward it.

It was awkward, obviously, because she was living in a skin that was not her own.

But then, it was no less awkward than she usually felt in her own skin.

VII

Daniel sat in his cell, gripping the edge of stone plinth that served as a sort of bed and bench, fighting desperately to stay awake. He had tried everything he could think of—walking or running around the cell, pinching, hitting, and slapping himself, repeating his lucky words, doing mental arithmetic—but it was no use. The darkness and the exertion of the last days and hours, in particular, had drained him past human endurance, and he found himself sinking into sleep.

Although "sinking" was putting it mildly. "Plummeting" was more accurate a description. Plummeting into a terrifying, swirling blackness that was like the raging waves of a tempestuous sea.

He would nod off and feel himself falling swiftly away and then force open his eyes. It was like being pulled out of a fall and having his feet placed on firm ground. But then no matter what he did, soon the flying darkness would pull at him, bent on taking him down.

Consciously, he knew he was still in his cell. In fact, he could feel the stone slab beneath him, but even that was fading away, becoming abstract. He told himself that it was all just in his head, the extreme feelings just a reflection of the extreme dark, but try as he might, he couldn't convince himself that he was anything more than a tiny particle of fully conscious fear lost in a horrific void, and falling, falling, always falling. The cold stone beneath him, slick with sweat, seemed immaterially thin, more of a concept than an object, and then it was gone . . . His surroundings had finally dissolved away.

Points of light started to appear around him. They moved fast, arcing past him and vanishing into the distance. He was hallucinating, obviously. But it was so persistent . . . What could he actually trust as real? He let loose a long groan, but even his own voice was lost in the dark tempest, swallowed by the void. The number of lights grew, and trajectories started to alter, and the stars danced erratically around him.

Shutting his eyes made no difference at all—what was happening around him penetrated even his eyelids.

He didn't know how long he could bear it all. He felt that at some point, something had to give; either the whole display would have to stop. Or what? Madness? Death, even? How long could his tiny consciousness survive while tumbling through the cosmos?

In the tumult, he noticed that two points of light remained fixed. One was a speck of bluish-white, the other a small speck of yellow. He flung out his arm—visible only as a black silhouette against the strobing stars—to reach them and found that he was able to draw them nearer, or himself toward them, whichever it was. *At last,* he thought; some aspect of his situation that he could control.

As he came closer to the stars, he was surprised to find that they were two mostly human forms. They were riders on horses, galloping away from him, tearing across the sky like comets. One was golden, like the sun; the other silver, like the moon.

As they galloped away, they also came closer to him, within the altered physics of his dreamscape.

The riders reared and he saw their full figures, every sparkle of light that shone from every edge of their armour. The golden figure's armour was roughly burnished so that the colours of red, orange, and yellow swirled and mixed across it, seeming to produce light and heat. The other's was buffed and reflected a luminescent, ghostly gleam of blue, white, and grey.

Daniel recoiled as the light stabbed into his eyes like pins.

"Who are you?" he asked the golden rider.

"I am Dreams of Life," the golden rider answered, although Daniel could not hear the words spoken. He *felt* them, somehow, and it warmed him. "And I have sights to show you."

"And you?" he asked the silver rider automatically.

"I am Dreams of Death." Daniel felt a chill roll through him. "I, too, have sights."

Daniel pushed away at the silver rider and the rider fell into the distance.

The golden rider dismounted and came nearer.

"What do you wish?" he asked in a honey-thick voice.

Daniel did not know, and this uncertainty made him worry that the rider would leave him then, in the cold and uncertainty. But the rider was there, mounted again, with his yellow steed galloping alongside him.

He turned his head to the other side and saw, far off and very distant, no more than a star twinkling in the distance, the silver rider, and again he felt a chill. He turned back to the golden one.

"What do you wish?"

"What do I wish?" Daniel asked himself, and it seemed to him that he was being offered a gift, a single gift, whatever he desired.

His father is before him, and his mother. He is a child again, just thirteen, and his parents are back together, and they are eating a meal at the table. It is quiet, but a comfortable, contented silence. Daniel makes eye contact with his dad and he smiles.

There is a pounding on the door. His father's face blanches.

"Don't answer it," his mother whispers. "Leave it."

"They know we're here," his dad explains, rising. "They always know. You can't fool them." He walks to the front hall.

"Do we have enough?" his mother asks.

Father doesn't answer. He opens the door a crack. Daniel peers into the hallway and sees a very tall, very thin man in a black suit and bright orange and yellow tie. He tips his hat, showing wolf-like ears, and displays a hungry grin. "Good evening, sir," he lilts. "Collecting tribute."

"We gave less than three months ago. They wrote it down. I got a receipt—"

"Entirely different sort of tribute, sir. Here's a pamphlet. This is the head tribute—for the children? You do have a child." His eyes find Daniel's, gazing at him like a cat would a canary—patiently predatory.

The pamphlet shakes slightly in his father's hands. He puts it down on the cabinet top by the door. "Yes, yes. I remember reading about this. Of course. I have something in here. I put it aside when I . . ." He bends and opens the door of the cabinet, rummaging around amongst some metal objects. "Yes, here it is. A silver spoon. One of my wife's heirlooms."

"Ah, yes, very nice," the tribute collector appraises. "Yes, this would do quite nicely . . . if your son were twelve or younger."

"He is, he is," his father chirps.

"Come, sir, we both know that boy is thirteen and three months if I'm a day."

"Yes! Yes, of course, how could I forget? Here, take this bowl instead. Silver also—see the mark just here? We can just . . ."

His father holds out the bowl and reaches for the spoon. The tribute collector with the wolf's ears takes the bowl but still grips the spoon. "I'll tell you what; I'll keep both," he says, then tosses them into a black velvet bag that he grips under his arm. The objects vanish with a clinking rattle. "I'll make a mark here to say that you're up-to-date on the head tribute, and give you a voucher for the spoon." He produces a black, padded folder and unzips it, then starts scribbling in it. "And that way, the next time one of us comes knocking, you just whip out the voucher, we make the tick, and Bill's your auntie, the job is done. What do you say?"

"Well, I think I'd rather—"

"Only I have just accepted the spoon, technically, just by holding it. If you want I could summon my troll; he's just there at the end of the road, see? And we could all go down to the offices and sort this out. Quite frankly, though, all that hassle is more than my job, or your life, is worth. Wouldn't you say?" He holds out a chit of paper in front of his father's face.

"Yes, fine, fine. That's fine," his father says, taking the voucher.

"A pleasure." The tribute collector smiles, tips his hat again— his soft, grey, triangular ears peeking out. He turns, and the door closes behind him.

"Ian?" his mother, above Daniel, her hands on his shoulders, asks.

"Fine, fine. It's fine—I've got a voucher," he explains, waving his hand.

"What voucher?" There is nothing in his hand.

"Never mind," his father says with a forced smile. "Let's get back to dinner, eh? Fish! I love fish! It's not every day you get fish." They resume their meal.

"Mum?" Daniel asks. "When can I go back to school?"

"Quiet. Finish up."

"Where's my sword?" Daniel, age thirteen, asks.

"You never had one," his father replies. "Remember? Remember how you never had one?"

"Shall we watch TV today?" his mother asks.

"I don't know if we can risk it," his father replies.

Daniel looked away, and the scene winked out of existence. He was falling again, the golden rider beside him.

What do you wish?

Freya floats before him, and he sees, as if from a great way away, but with every detail up close, the life they could have together. Quiet, warm, lovely. A terraced house in the city, drive to work, drive home, dinner, an evening on the sofa. They sit, arms around each other, the TV illuminating them and the room in a pleasant glow, issuing a chorus of gentle laughter.

A sound from the other room, a cry, almost a squeal of discomfort from a tiny throat. "Every night," Freya said, rising, her body softer now, plumper, climbing over him. "Why won't he stay down? Even for just this night?"

She exits and he, the he he could be, sits for a stretch, but becomes uncomfortably lonely. The squeals can still be heard from the next room, growing louder, more piercing. He rises.

The next room is an infant's room, but there was never an infant in it, he realises, somehow. Freya stands in the centre of the room, not holding a baby, but holding his sword, the blade he received in Niðergeard—Hero-Maker. The squeal, he knows now, upon passing into the room, has turned into a cry of torment, of alarm.

"I can't put him down," Freya says, gripping the sword by its blade. "Why won't he stay down? Even for one night? Here, you try—you try putting him down." She holds the sword out to him and he grasps its blade, which bites him.

A blink of the eye, the scene disappeared.

What do you wish?

This time it was a deliberate desire of his, something he almost didn't dare to ask, a desire that had consumed his life for the past eight years.

His face is scarred and raw from battle, but he is wearing royal finery from an age that has past and at the same time an age that has never been. He wears a jewelled crown and on his lap is his sword, Hero-Maker, sheathed, to represent peace. Beneath him is a chair constructed from stone, iron, and gold. The throne is standing atop a mound, much like Gád's, but not made from the ruins of beauty, but a thing of beauty in itself. Many ridged steps in many colours of marble fall beneath him, trimmed with gold and lit with a hundred candles and silver lanterns set into compartments in the stair structure. He is sitting on a platform of stone and light, and from around every side there are people of the nation, every man, woman, race, and creed, cheering and praising his heroism and bravery. Behind them rise the buildings of Niðergeard, restored, and the tree-carved outer wall, rebuilt, but with open arches between the trunks instead of blank stone. Children run and spin beneath the stone boughs, which glitter with silver light.

"How did he do it?" a little girl asks her mother. "How did he become the king of Niðergeard?"

"He killed all other claimants," the girl's mother answers. "He alone was victorious."

Niðergeard would never be fortified again. The awakened knights would not be put to sleep. There would never be a need for them again.

He raises his eyes and sees a crack in the darkness—the ceiling tears and the sky is visible. Niðergeard is rising and will soon appear in the open air, and it will carry him upon his hero's throne.

He stares into that sky and it becomes larger and larger in front of him, until whiteness is the only thing he sees.

But now there are shadows, and the sun is the golden rider.

"I wish for victory," he told him.

"Wish for pain," a voice said behind him.

Daniel turned. The silver rider, Dreams of Death, was standing before him. "No."

"Pain will save you. Pain is your future."

"Pain is not an end—or even a means," agreed Daniel. "Pain may be unavoidable, but surely it is not necessary?"

"You say that, but true sacrifice is rarely voluntary—very few would ever take the pain that leads to true victory willingly." He shook his head mournfully in an odd, lurching fashion.

"Certainly. But I've given so much up already."

"Would you give up what you most desire?" the silver rider asked.

"Anything."

"What is the most that you would sacrifice?"

"Everything," Daniel replied.

"What is victory worth to you?"

"Everything," Daniel replied.

"What is the most that you would sacrifice?"

"Anything."

"Would you give up what you most desire?"

"Certainly. But I've given so much up already."

The rider inclined his visored head. "You say that, but true sacrifice is rarely voluntary—very few would ever take the pain that leads to true victory willingly."

"Pain is not an end—or even a means. Pain may be unavoidable, but surely it is not necessary?"

"Pain will save you. Pain is your future."

"No."

"Wish for pain," the silver rider told him.

"I wish for victory," Daniel repeated.

"Wish for pain."

"No."

"Pain will save you. Pain is your future."

"Pain is not an end—or even a means. Pain may be unavoidable, but surely it is not necessary?"

The rider shook his head. "You say that, but true sacrifice is rarely voluntary—very few would ever take the pain that leads to true victory willingly."

"Certainly. But I've given so much up already . . ."

The dialogue continued, as logical as a dream, back and forth, oscillating, endless.

CHAPTER EIGHT

Books, A Sword, A Knife

---------------------------------- I ----------------------------------

London, Westminster

23 October 1731 AD

It was an hour past midnight. This was the darkest time of the night and the quietest. He had come up near the Banquet Hall, nearly all that remained of the magnificent Whitehall Palace. It had burnt, of course; withering like everything withered in the furnaces of time. All was fire around him.

Ealdstan walked down the night streets of London toward Westminster, shining his silver lantern before him. His mood blackened as he looked around. Where there wasn't ridiculous poverty, there was absurd excess. Where there wasn't indifferent disdain, there was inebriation. The land was circling the gutter. No number of righteous warriors could stave English civilisation from rattling merrily and uncontrollably down the path of disaster. The whole nation in a runaway cart, with no man to steer it.

His righteous warriors could not fight a lazy, loutish public spirit. Evil was not bold anymore, it was insidious.

Human and animal excrement ran through the streets, between the cobbles, along the gutters, and into the sewers. Just walking through the city was a defilement. He wondered how anyone could stand it, but then he realised that few knew anything else.

A horse-drawn carriage came along the cobblestones—a matched pair of greys pulling an elaborately styled box carriage with ornate decorations and velvet curtains shut tight. They were tied in place to avoid an accidental view of the outside world. This was how the rich coped with living in the city.

The carriage turned at the end of the street, passing a gang of drunken revellers who shouted and jeered at the vehicle and its driver. One of the drunkards dropped drawers and waved his private parts after it, to the loud amusement of those around him. The group then fell back into line and started a bawdy chorus as they processed down the road.

They passed close enough that Ealdstan could smell the beer on their breath and in their clothes, but due to the enchantment he wore they were never aware of his presence. As he walked away, he felt as if he were wearing the disgusting smell of old alcohol like a coat. Another layer of fetid filth, clinging to him.

Best get this over with quickly.

He made it, somehow, through the hell of modern London and arrived at Ashburnham House. He went up the drive and stood before the door. He knocked on it with his staff, and after a lengthy amount of time, the door was opened by a very tired and very annoyed-looking butler. The butler blinked and then walked past him to look up and down the street. Not seeing anyone, he grunted and, muttering oaths under his breath, pulled the door closed—although not before Ealdstan had stepped through it.

The butler went back to his bed and Ealdstan began to explore the house. He looked into most of the rooms before he found what he was looking for on the second story: a large, square room with bookcases arranged in a circular formation. The cases stood about five feet high and each had a white bust of some aged man's head.

He raised his lantern and went from case to case, pulling the odd volume out and leafing through it. Disordered, jumbled. The fools didn't know what they had collected and accrued. There were bits and pieces of everything; poetry, sermons, legal documents, books of the Bible in Latin and English—his English, not the corrupted, inane language they babbled now—histories, lives of the saints, letters, chronicles, psalters, and all manner of miscellany. Nothing like his own personal collection, but priceless, of course. Priceless pearls before swine.

He made a more ordered examination and found the volumes he had come for. There were only thirteen of them and he would be able to carry them easily. The rest . . .

He looked around the wooden room. It was warm in here, but there was no fire, which meant that some nearby room of the house was being heated. He concentrated and felt the source to be in the room below this one. He muttered a spell that he had mastered centuries before and the fire leapt in its hearth, kindling the mantle and racing up the walls.

He left, clutching the volumes he needed under his arm, leaving billowing grey smoke issuing from the house behind him.

II

Berlin, Germany

1 February 1935 AD

"A beautiful machine, is it not?" the man seated in front of him was saying, his eyes darting looks at him in the rearview mirror. He spoke in a German that was not greatly removed from the language that Ealdstan had learned all those centuries ago, but it had gained a few idiomatic quirks, run in from impure dialects, he supposed. He had brought with him an enchantment, housed in a medallion that he draped around his neck.

"It is powerful, efficient, and all running in proper order. Just like the *Großdeutsches Reich* will soon be. You hear that sound she makes? An efficient and well-ordered engine makes very little noise, just as the Deutsch nation shall make very little noise as we reorder ourselves and eliminate all the rough elements that prevent the engine from working properly. That will be the *Gleichschaltung*, and it will bring in a glorious new dawn of peace. A unified Europe for Europe's true children."

The dark, winter streets were a blur around them as the car sped through the city. When did these cities become so big? "What if the machine breaks and fails to operate?" Ealdstan asked. He was using his broken and incomplete German that his sigil fixed, to prevent him from misspeaking as well as mishearing. He could have spoken English, but there was more to a language than just communication—the thoughts, ideas, and hopes of a people were tied into their lexicons. Ealdstan wished to understand the German mind, and not just their words.

"*Brechung?*" The driver actually turned around in his seat to look at Ealdstan's face. "Break? The *Reich* will never break. The people are strong in will! The people—"

"No, no, the machine, the machine. This!" Ealdstan rattled his stick and thumped the roof. "What if this breaks? Do you have the ability to fix it? It seems inordinately complex."

The driver laughed. "I have some ability, yes, although I am no mechanic. Do not worry, it is a good engine!"

Ealdstan glowered out the window. When had he last visited the surface? A hundred years ago? Perhaps less? There were technical wonders then, but they were kept by the rich and influential. Now it was as if the sky had broken open and rained mechanical marvels down on all the people. In his brief trip from the tunnel exit in Sudmer Mountain, he had seen radios, telephones, automobiles, and here in Berlin, the elephantine omnibuses. Men wore clocks on their wrists. Ealdstan remembered when exact time was only known from church towers. Now anyone could strap it to their arm. And here, just the start of the evening, and electric light was already beaming from lanterns just as small, yet brighter than his own enchanted lamps. And then there were the weapons. So many weapons.

The car slowed slightly—out of reverence?—as the Reichstag came into view. Electric lights were strategically arranged to highlight its grand, sprawling design. It was obviously built to impress, but Ealdstan only sniffed and looked out the other window, then down at the sleeves of the large overcoat he had been given to wear over his robe.

The car slowed and stopped before the door of the great state building. Ealdstan allowed the driver to circle the car and open his door for him. Already a group was forming in the doorway to meet him. He involuntarily bristled at the sight and then masked his rude gesture by shrugging deeper into the large coat.

"Welcome!" A slight man in a dark suit emerged from the pack. He was clean shaven and his hair was completely slicked back. He wore a wide smile and opened his arms as if Ealdstan were a dear friend he hadn't seen in years. He walked with an awkward, heavy limp, which he tried very hard to hide. "Welcome, my friend. Please, come inside. How was your journey? I trust everything was smooth."

Ealdstan mounted the steps and crossed the threshold of the building. There was a great bustle, even this late in the night, as people moved folders, furniture, and themselves through the halls and corridors. "You'll forgive the disorder. We only received offices yesterday, and much as we would like, reorganization does not happen instantly. A large animal cannot turn immediately. *Du!* he called suddenly. *"Du! Warte mal!* You will excuse me," the industrious man said and walked off to bark orders at some workmen who were hefting a very large desk across the hallway.

Feeling uncomfortable under the harsh indoor lights, Ealdstan stood alone, watching the people in the building dart to and fro.

"I am so sorry, sir," the man said, returning. "Please, come this way." He ushered Ealdstan into a large room off the main corridor that was oddly devoid of people. Then he shouted across the hall to a couple of men in brown shirts and trousers to stand outside the door and make sure that they were not disturbed.

"As I say, everything is disordered. I myself do not even have an official position yet—I just pitch in with whatever needs to be done, for the moment, and that seems to be everything. This will pass, this will pass. All that you see here—it is not confusion, it is reordering—a right ordering!" He crossed the room and closed the windows as Ealdstan stood just a few paces from the door.

"It is both exhilarating and exhausting at the same time." The unofficial official lowered himself into a plush, ornately constructed chair. "Please, take a seat."

"I will stand," Ealdstan declared.

"Then I will stand also," the other said and rose to his feet again. "And I will come directly to business. When we found we had opportunity to contact you, as you well know, we wasted not a moment. Until our man met you, we had no idea that the legends were true; we are simply beside ourselves with excitement over this most historic moment. Our leader himself will be here shortly to pay due honour to your person, but he has instructed me to act and speak on his behalf until that time. I was also instructed to present you with this."

He went back over to the chair and picked up a long box that lay on a side table. He came back and held it out to Ealdstan.

"It is a sword manufactured in this land, made by Eickhorn, in Solingen, the best weapon-smith in the world. I would like to present it to you, on behalf of the German people, as a symbol of our shared goals and ambitions."

Ealdstan reached out for it with both hands, tilting his staff against his shoulder. He opened the box to reveal a sword with a slightly curved blade, sheathed, with a hilt that was modelled with a gilt lion's head pommel, the mouth of which bit the handguard that bent around to meet it.

"Those are rubies in the eyes, not glass. And the crossguard has been altered to include the swastika. That is our emblem. It has been selected and designed by our leader himself, as the symbol of our movement that will sweep Europe and, one day, the rest of the world."

Ealdstan pulled back his great coat and tucked the sword into his belt, putting the box on the chair next to him.

"But that's not why you are here. You are here because of what we can do for each other."

"I do not know what I can give you."

"We do not want anything *from* you. That is not what I am asking. Men are not a concern. We have men. In time, we will give you men. All we ask of you, for now, is for you to consult for us."

"Consult?" Ealdstan tightened his grip around his staff.

"We are building an empire. We have never done this before. You have been doing it, in secret, for centuries. We want you to help us. We know of your work. Our leader is a great student of legend and ancient history—of the forgotten times that are remembered only in stories. A time of dignity, when men not only lived with purity and honour but also fought for it. When the righteous stood tall, and the corruption of dishonourable men did not touch them. That is the golden age that the legends speak of. Those times that you have seen leave—as the faithful left, one by one, only to be replaced by the faithless. Did you think those times would never return?"

Ealdstan wrung his hands around his staff.

"Those days will come again, my friend," said the man, smiling, knowing he was drawing Ealdstan in. "You have the knowledge, and the people of Germany have the will. With your help, who could stand against us?"

Ealdstan nodded and stroked his beard. "I would dearly love, more than anything else, to see that world come," he said. "I would very much enjoy further discussion."

There was a knock at the door, and it was opened by one of the brown-shirted youths. A man stepped through who did not wait to be announced, nor for permission to enter.

"Ah, here is our leader now!" The slight man's face beamed. "Archchancellor! You have made very good time."

"For this, I make time. So, you are the wise Ealdstan, I presume. It is good to meet you. This is a meeting that will be recorded in the legends of the future. I hope Herr Goebbels has been showing you every hospitality."

III

Niðergeard

13 February 1948 AD

Frithfroth knocked on the door of Ealdstan's study. He waited a moment and got no reply, as expected. He put a hand on the metal door loop and pushed it open a few inches.

"My lord?"

Ealdstan was at his desk, writing in a small book.

"My lord, the lifiendes are ready to depart."

"In a moment," Ealdstan said and dipped his pen in the ink bottle.

"Wysfaeder, if you will permit me . . . Is it right?"

All that Frithfroth received as an answer was the scratch of pen on vellum.

"I don't mean is it right that they aid you in this—aid *us* in this way, but is it right that we make the task so much more difficult? The heart could be brought here, with no difficulty, and any one of them could perform the task."

More scratching.

"It's only . . . that this is the third group of lifiendes that have managed to find their way here—no easy task in itself. I am told that on the way they ran afoul of the usual perils. Surely that is test enough?"

Scratching, more scratching.

Frithfroth resigned himself to getting no response from the ruler of Niðergeard. He was leaving the room backward, intending to pull the door behind him, when Ealdstan pushed the book away from him, leaving it open on the top of the desk and wiping his pen on a piece of cloth.

"There are mechanisms and circles in movement of which none in this world but I have any knowledge," Ealdstan said. "To fall down a hole in a cave is hardly proof enough for what will be demanded of them in the future."

Frithfroth deferentially accepted this statement and made to leave again. "But, wise Ealdstan," he said, changing his mind, "must the cost for them be so high? When the bodies of the last two were discovered, it fair broke the hearts of those that found them. Many of them left here and renounced their immortality at that very instant. Others, sometime later."

Frithfroth chewed his lip. He had said this much, why not say all? "These latest trials are not just trials for the lifiendes, but also trials for Niðergeard. I have never seen spirit so low."

"I am not oblivious to the moods of the city that I created.

Threat with no real danger is no test at all. In the perspective of all the centuries, the passing of a few young lights is of little matter. All pass—one day you and I shall. The dead are happier dead. Mourn not for them. The sacrifice they are making is as the first few drops of a torrential downpour."

Frithfroth nodded. "Just so. As I said, the lifiendes are now ready to depart." With that, he closed the door completely and made his way back down to the courtyard under the Great Carnyx. Godmund and Modwyn were there, along with the four lifiendes and their escort.

"Ealdstan will join us shortly," Frithfroth reported.

"I should jolly well expect him to," said the youngest girl, who stood in her new, dyed leather riding dress. She awkwardly held an ash wood spear in her hand. "It's our ruddy necks that we're risking to save his!"

"Language, Sarah!" chastened Molly, her sister and one of the younger two of the four Trevellian cousins.

Sarah gave her head a flick to keep her long hair in check— a habit that Frithfroth had become accustomed to seeing. He had spent the last couple weeks with the children, showing them around the city and the tower. He had bonded with them; the others were either jaded at the long line of failures, or else too afraid to become close to the sacrificial lambs.

"He will take his own time about his own business. I am sure he knows better than we what lies ahead of us." Molly was mousy and apologetic, the opposite of her loud and strong-willed sister. She was the peacemaker of the group, sensitive and always appeasing.

"That is true, young lifiend," said Æþelwulf, the knight they had awoken and who was to accompany them on their quest. "More than you could know."

Frithfroth shot him a ferocious look. *Don't say too much*, the look said.

"Mister Frithfroth, sir." The youngest of all the cousins, Theodore—or "Teddy" as he was called by the others—meekly approached. He wore a dagger and a mail shirt that had been altered for his small stature. He looked absurd, and Frithfroth's heart nearly broke for him. He was almost too young to have a real personality of his own, except that he was intensely sensitive and caring, with no hardened areas of his character.

"Mister Frithfroth—what does that mean?" He pointed to the Carnyx. "'Blow this horn and summon the next army'? What is the next army?"

"Why, it refers to all the knights who sleep beneath Britain's soil."

"No, that's the *old* army. Who is the *next* army?"

Frithfroth looked up quizzically and caught Godmund's eye. The grizzled warrior just shrugged.

"But they are not an army yet. They are just separate warriors, all taken from different points in this nation's history. They are not yet an army, but when they arise, they will be."

Teddy frowned and walked back to join the others.

He is eight years old, Frithfroth thought. He tried to think back to the time when eight years was all the time that he knew on this earth. Now, eight years was no more time to him than a fortnight had once been.

A clap of thunder shivered the silence and a wisp of smoke twisted from the ground, dispersing into the stale air to reveal Ealdstan. The children were awed, which was naturally the only reason for the act. They leaned in toward each other, all of them trying to put on a brave face.

The aging wizard brought his staff down on the ground three times, pounding the rock beneath his feet violently.

May the Hand that Makes guide your hearts,
May the Light that Illumines shine on your path,

And the One that Goes Between aid your steps.

"Paul Trevellian, approach," the wizard said.

Swallowing hard and shaking visibly—but nonetheless endeavouring to hold his head up high with strong, British reserve—Paul left the small pack. He was not the oldest of the group—Sarah was—but he assumed the most responsibility. He was rather bright, but this characteristic was often hampered by his sense of duty—he tended to do what was expected of him, even if that was at odds with his own or his companion's best interests.

Ealdstan towered over him, his face dark. *Has he used an altering enchantment?* Frithfroth wondered. *Is he trying to terrify the lad? Has he no heart?*

Reaching into the folds of his red robe, Ealdstan pulled out a knife in a leather sheath.

"This blade has many enchantments on it—it is made of stone and is the only weapon that should be used to destroy Gád's heart. If you are to free this land from his poisonous clutches and wish to return to your home, strike well and strike true. And remember, when in doubt, follow the water."

Paul accepted the knife and bowed low. "I will do my best to not let you down, O wisest of all rulers," he said, straightening. And then he bowed again and returned, walking backward, to his cousins.

Ealdstan glared at them and then pounded his staff three more times, and in another wisp of smoke, he was gone.

"Come along, lifiendes," the knight Æþelwulf said. "Our journey is a long one, and best started soon."

Farewells were said. Frithfroth saw tears in Molly's eyes. They entered the squat fortress that protected the Great Carnyx and those remaining waited until they heard the heavy stone doors within the building close before they left.

Walking back to the tower, Frithfroth prayed that they had

not just sent more children to their deaths—that these would be the ones who finally completed this perverse quest.

IV

"That's it," Vivienne said. "That's the last journal." She waited quietly while Freya got her head together.

"I'm hungry," she said, helping herself to water and snacking on some of the dried meat from the kitchen. As she did so, Vivienne tidied the table of all the books and documents from their last session. She did a comprehensive job and the rooms were pretty much as they'd first found them.

"I'm glad. I'm tired of—I'm actually tired of being tired." She yawned. "Sorry."

"It's okay. We've been cooped up in here long enough." Vivienne stood and stretched.

"What about Daniel?" Freya sighed. "Any word or sign of him? As though you care?"

"That's rather unfair."

"Forgive me for saying it, Vivienne, but you seem very blasé about all of this."

Vivienne shrugged on her coat. "When you get to my age, you either risk everything or you risk nothing. I'm sorry if you find me cold. But in the scheme of things, I find I'm most effective if I try only to affect the things that I can control, and leave the things that I can't to play out by themselves."

"Great. Well, Daniel's certainly out, since no one can seem to control him. But shouldn't we . . . look for him? Possibly?"

"Yes. Certainly. We certainly should go looking for him. Shall we go now?"

"Um, before we go down, there's one more room to see. We should check that out, if we're going to be thorough."

"Really? You're happy leaving Daniel out wherever he is?"

Freya glared at her. "Now you're being unfair. You know what's in that room, and I want to know as well." Freya packed the bedroll up and crammed the few items she had taken out back into her backpack.

"Well, let's go if you're going, then," Vivienne said in an inscrutable tone.

They went up the stairs in silence. Vivienne walking behind Freya, who soon wished Vivienne led the way.

They found the door and stood in front of it in silence for a few moments. Freya looked back at Vivienne. "Anything you want to say?"

Vivienne shook her head, and Freya pushed the door open.

It was a bedroom. It was not luxuriant but comfortable, with some pieces of wrought iron furniture and a golden light fixture just like the one in the other room. Against the far wall were stacks of the enchanted silver lamps, which cumulatively gave the room a sort of holy glow. The only other objects in the room were a bedstead with a thin mattress, some clean linen sheets—and a body.

"It's Modwyn," Freya said, inching closer to the bed. The ward of Niðergeard was stretched out on the bed, on top of the sheets, in her magnificent green robes that Freya had last seen her in, all smooth and perfect, her hair falling gently around her shoulders, curling and rising like waves upon a steep shore. "You knew she was here all the time."

"She's dead. It doesn't change anything."

"Really?"

"It—it wouldn't have changed anything if you knew."

"Really." Modwyn's posture reminded Freya of illustrations of Sleeping Beauty in the picture books she had as a child. Her arms crossed over her chest and she seemed to be holding something.

Freya edged even closer, half-expecting Modwyn to suddenly

wake up and startle her. But she didn't, and as Freya came closer, she realised, with dread, that she wouldn't, ever, for clutched in Modwyn's hands was the hilt of a knife. She'd plunged the blade into her own chest. A wave of anger rose and broke inside Freya. So that was it then. Modwyn had been so distraught at the invasion of Niðergeard that she had taken her own life, leaving all others to cope without her—abandoning the living. What a selfish tragedy.

"It was her final sacrifice," a voice from the door said, making the two women jump. She turned and saw Frithfroth standing there, looking even more diminished and forlorn than ever. "It was not selfishness or fear that forced her into that act. In that act, she protected the tower from invasion. She saved the Carnyx, she saved Niðergeard."

Freya turned back to the prone form of Niðergeard's protectress. Not a part of her was decrepit or decaying. She really did look as if she were only sleeping.

"I come up and minister to her," Frithfroth said. "I pay my respects and remember her and thank her for saving me. It was her last act—a loving one."

"She's dead, Frithfroth," Freya said. "She's just dead. She killed herself so she wouldn't have to face the horror of being killed. She took the easy way out."

"Don't," Vivienne said quietly.

Freya knew the temptation of ending all her problems by her own hand; it disgusted her that Modwyn had not been stronger than she was. She had left everyone alive to fend for themselves and thrown her lot in with the dead and decaying knights in the basement.

"Why hasn't she decayed?" Freya muttered. And for reasons she only half understood, she reached out and pulled the knife out of Modwyn's hands and out of her chest.

Modwyn drew a breath at the same time, her eyes snapping

open, her mouth gaping for air, and Freya leapt back, her hand still around the knife, which had a stone blade. Her other hand flew to her chest, over her pounding heart, as she stared at Modwyn in fear. Modwyn tilted toward her in the bed and spent a moment coughing and wiping her eyes.

"Tha—thank you," she croaked, gradually recovering enough to speak.

Vivienne and Freya could only watch and gape, eyes as wide as saucers.

"I'm sorry, Freya."

"Sorry for what?"

"We told you so many lies."

IV

Daniel woke up in his cell and almost burst into tears of relief. He rose from the cold floor and brushed himself off. The hallucinations, the visions, the eternally cyclical conversation—none of it was real. He gave a prayer of thanks to anyone who might be listening and sat on the stone bench, blowing on his fingers to warm them.

But he couldn't see his hand. At first he thought it was because it was too dark, but then he noticed a thin line of brick-red smoke that extended and moved as if it were his hand. The two lights were forgotten now as Daniel explored this new effect. He reached his other out and saw another line of red smoke spread forward. He moved them back and forth, side to side, and crossed them together. They passed through each other without the slightest resistance.

He looked down at the rest of himself and found a thicker bar of smoke that divided at the end to mark his legs. He reached forward to try to touch a leg, but there was nothing to grasp onto and he spiralled out of control, a tumbling ball of smoke.

He started to expand, the molecules in his body dissipating. He filled the small room and spilled out into the hallway. He was without form except that which was imposed on him by walls. He grew to fill the city, aware of the points of life of the yfelgópes and the rest of the Niðergearders within it. He thought he could feel Freya.

He spilled into the overworld and had the experience of being both fully in the dark and fully in the light at the same time. He spread across the plains, into the cities, and throughout the country. He felt life as intense points of emotion inside of him. He could feel love and hate and was profoundly moved to find how little there was of either. Corruption and rot had set into the nation, and it was in the hearts of its people who harboured it. He reached out to pry it away, but it shrank and split from him as he grew larger, spilling across the planet and breaking through the stratosphere.

As he grew in the expanse of space that lay between the planets, he felt a moment of respite. The earth and all that was in it—so confused and muddled—shrank to a nearly microscopic thing inside of him.

Was this death? Was this the end? Would he continue stretching until he was one with everything? Would he stay fully conscious, or would he just melt away into creation? He started to mourn himself and all the things that he had left undone, the people he had left behind.

And then the stars tilted in the sky and he was falling again, the exact same sensation he felt when he fell asleep.

The arcing lights whizzed and spun around Daniel, faster and faster, turning from points of light into lines and then into planes and then into solids. Curves, sheets, and ribbons rippled past his disembodied vision, unresolved equations for shapes and solids that did not yet exist. Colours drifted through and around him, unbound by form or object—pure properties with no affiliation, washing around in a conceptual soup.

Then sound entered, and he could see its effects on the properties that grew dimensions as he watched—three, four, five, six dimensions were added, and all that Daniel saw and felt joined into a whole, folding into and out of itself exponentially into a tangle of line and surface. It was as if it crystallised like a snowflake with an uncountable number of complex branches that grew and diverged and weaved in and out of each other in a mathematically precise path. The sound changed and Daniel felt heat as all the points bent inward and the curved bows they made stretched out to contain an infinite number of points and spread into membranes that were also broad to an infinite number of points, but that were nonetheless limited enough to maintain shape and design. And each of those squared infinities on every side, edge, corner, face, and border vibrated, creating a music that was the sound of every aspect of the created universe.

It was horrifyingly beautiful, and its poetry nearly destroyed Daniel. And at the point when the vibrations started to create light from the music they made, Daniel felt himself racing toward it, even as it grew to envelop him. With apprehension so great it broke the barrier of fear, he plunged into the outer edges of reality, tearing through the skeins and spirals, and into the heart of the total whole.

The inside of the absolute complexity showed windows into entire wholes of reality, separated each from the other. They whizzed past him and he saw entire completions buzz by from every angle and perspective.

He was drawn toward a certain facet of the all of everything, and after an aeon of travelling, he saw it ahead of him, glistening and humming in a tone that reminded him of his mother's voice. He willed himself faster toward it.

As he hit the wall, every atom in his cloud of perception crashed like a cymbal, and then he was through the outer border of his own reality. He could feel that it was his, although he could, of course, not recognise it. The galaxies and star clusters spun and rotated in spinning spirals, watch-like in precision and delicacy, but built and balanced on a celestial scale. The movements traced golden paths in the darkness, and where gravity and dark matter fields harmonised, purple paths that were far below the visible spectrum appeared to Daniel's eyes. It was through these that Daniel was pulled, navigating across aeons among the quantum particle rivers and streams that flowed through gravity tunnels.

In this way he travelled across the universe, racing along the curved intersects and spokes from one gravity bridge to another, and one spinning star system to another, toward, he hoped, home.

After countless hops and jumps that took him through a tour of wonders that would still not be seen by those on earth for millennia, he came to his own galaxy and followed the curve of its shape down to his own system, which was like entering a tiny little hovel at the end of a short cul-de-sac and then sitting in the smallest chair in the tiniest room. His whole world—everything he'd ever known—was so small and overcrowded that he didn't know how he could possibly tolerate the feeling of being so tightly hemmed in ever again.

And as he came closer to it and to the silver string-like path that his planet followed, he saw the string start to vibrate, picking up the sympathetic notes that the moon, the sun, and the other planets created. It twisted and spun in three dimensions and created a purple gravity bridge that drew him in and rocketed him to another system in another galaxy—a larger planet with a larger sun, populated by creatures from another evolutionary tree.

Comet-like, he fell into the planet, in the thin sliver than ran across its circumference where the light side met the dark. Its movement became his, and its gravity held him completely. The sudden stop of movement was jarring and stole his breath. He had been speeding through the infinite just moments ago and here he was trapped on a tiny speck of dust.

But which speck of dust?

He looked around and was staggered by a flood of sensations: a flood of light that ushered in a wash of colour, a roar of noise, a pool of smells, a rush of tingly picks of pressure and pain all around him. All of these sensations, but nothing to concentrate or embody them. The connections seemed random and fast, one after the other: a flash of grey-blue, a slap of cold, an ear-splitting crash, the scent of rotting leaves, a blast of heat, the rough edge of an immense rock formation.

He tried to tie together the disparate impressions, but they wouldn't stay in place. He tried to follow one of them—the feeling of heat—concentrating solely on it, until exhaustion stole it from him. He was being stretched. He quit grasping for the heat and felt a bright green take its place.

He let the sights, sounds, feelings, smells flash through him. He was losing himself. Desperate, he clung to something of his own, not something he was experiencing, but something of his past, of him. He thought of a song his mother used to sing to him when he couldn't sleep, the last time he truly felt safe and loved.

> *Robin-a-Bobbin*
> *Let fly an arrow;*
> *Aimed at a rabbit,*
> *Killed him a sparrow.*

> *Robin-a-Bobbin*
> *Bent back his bow;*

Shot at a pigeon,
But killed a crow.

Robin-a-Bobbin
Let loose another;
Over his chimney,
Striking his brother.

Robin-a-Bobbin
Taken to town,
Wearing two bracelets
And fit for a gown.

Robin-a-Bobbin
No longer singing,
Come the next morning,
He will be swinging.

The effects of this were immediate and drastic. Everything came together. The light blue joined with a cool sensation of wind blowing over him, enveloping him like a crisp bedsheet. The sound of leaves rustling against each other. And white forms, clouds, came into sharp focus. Then greys, blues, and purples—a mountain of enormous size seen at a great distance. Blades of grass as sharp and defined as knife blades.

But that was all it was—just a scene, there was no *him* in it. He was just a disembodied cloud of perception. He could experience and observe but so far couldn't interact. Although relieved that he was still able to do anything, he was still terrified at his condition.

And then he got another shock when he realised where he was. He was back in Elfland. The song he'd hummed, bringing him back together, made sense now, at least. Poetry had power here.

The view was familiar—the mountain, the plain, the distant stretch of green forest—it was pretty much the same thing he had seen when he first arrived. He was standing, he presumed, on the same spot he had been transported to the first time, midway between the mountain and the forest.

He turned to look at the forest, but there was no "him" to turn. Instead, the tableau shifted to the side. Startled, he lost control of the centre of his perception and felt everything racing away from him again. He thought of the song and it all came back together— the sky, the mountain, all of it. He kept repeating the lines under his breath as he tried once again to turn.

He spun sharply and instantly, as fast as thought—completely out of control, but still coherent, at least. After the nausea had passed, he found the wood now before him, just as he remembered it, a line of trees along the horizon.

He sighed but expelled no breath. Now what? The lines of the song went around in his head (Robin-a-Bobbin let fly an arrow . . .). He tried to move forward but only succeeded in making a sort of rocking motion, which he thought at first was movement, until he shifted his perception downward and saw that the grass underneath him was not going anywhere.

A thought occurred to him. He had made the landscape appear by focusing, so why not his body also? He tried to imagine his hand, imagine what it felt like to have a hand, imagined opening and closing it.

The world around him faded, dimmed, as if he were squinting his eyes. A shape appeared, like a shadow image coming into focus, and his hand coalesced out of the haze. It was like looking at some strange type of optical illusion. If he tried to leave off looking at the hand and follow his gaze down the palm, to the wrist and forearm, the whole of it evaporated, so he concentrated just on the hand, and the more he did so, the more defined it was against the now dark background.

But it was heavy, solid, like it was cast in steel. He tried to close it into a fist, but only the barest twitch of the fingers was perceptible. After a long period of exhausting thought and concentration, he could do no more than turn it. Then he was able, after a time, to tilt it downward and brush the fingertips against the grass, which he could see moved, but which gave no sensation of touch.

He gave up his thoughts of his hand and tried instead to think of his feet. This felt more successful at first, and he was able to plant two feet firmly on the ground and experienced the feeling for the first time of being anchored to his environment, but that was it. He could not, for any desire or effort of will, make them move. He tried to visualise them moving, to feel what it was like to move them up and down. Nothing.

Exhausted, he gave up and concentrated just on *being*. Focusing on the song, which he repeated like a mantra in his head—his lifeline to sanity.

How was he going to get out of this now? How had he come here? Was he dead? He definitely wasn't dreaming—everything felt hyper-real. Certain emotions or moods were often heightened during dreams and nightmares, but there was never such a flood of reality, however out of joint, such as he was experiencing now.

So he was dead. But killed by what? Perhaps shot or crushed by something unseen. That was a sad thought. What would happen to everyone he'd left behind? What was he going to do now?

The world around him had come back into bright focus again, out of the dim shades that concentration on his body brought. He gazed placidly at the treeline and remembered the first time he had made the journey across the endless plain.

The more he looked at it, the larger it grew, and for a moment he thought that was because his "vision" was still clearing, but then he realised, with a thrill, that he was moving. The memory of having gone this way before was doing it.

He was flying now, the ground blurring beneath him. Although he couldn't *feel* in the old, familiar sense, he was aware of a rushing wind going through him. He was starting to think of himself as a sort of cloud, a phantom.

He was going faster now, and just when he wondered how he was going to stop—if he even *could* stop, or if he would just fly through the woods, trunks, branches, and all—he was there at the treeline, and completely still. This is where he met Kay Marrey, the messenger from the Elves in Exile. He could almost see him standing before him. The Elves in Exile—that was a thought. Perhaps they could help him.

Then, with dawning awareness, he found that Kay was standing before him, but not as he had last seen him. Kay was draped in a blood-red robe, and his face was bone-white.

"What did I tell you not to do?" Kay asked.

Daniel made to reply but had no voice. And then the apparition was gone, leaving him puzzled and alone.

He stayed there for a time, pondering what he had just seen. Was it the ghost of Marrey that he'd summoned to him? Or was it a projection that he himself had made? Or an extension of this dream world, if it was a dream world?

Who could help him? He thought of Kæyle, the woodburner, and the clearing where he had lived for several months and suddenly, with a blur of green and black, the view shifted to that same place.

The scene was very much as he remembered it, but the burning pits were unused and overgrown, being neglected for some time.

"Daniel?"

He turned, pushing against the instinct to move his body and instead concentrated on the image at his periphery.

Kæyle's wife, Pettyl, was standing in the doorway of one of the small dirt huts. She was looking at the space that Daniel occupied. Again, he tried to speak but couldn't. Instead, he thought the words at her.

What am I doing here?

At the same moment, Pettyl also asked, "What are you doing here?"

You can see me?

Pettyl stared at Daniel a moment longer and then said, "Why have you come back?"

Back?

The memory of standing on the cliff overlooking the elfish campsite made the scene shift again, and in an instant he was standing up there again. Except now it was in the daytime, and so slightly unfamiliar. The fantastic tents and booths were missing. Was it all still a hallucination, or could he actually be in Elfland? If it was all just in his head, then why was it so different than he remembered? Still, he clung to any small piece of evidence he might not be dead.

He saw a black form on the field below him, where the grand elfish bazaar had once stood. As he watched, it separated into three equal-sized forms and moved apart from itself. They were human—actually elfish, Daniel corrected himself—shapes. Although distant, they looked in his direction, and he had the impression they'd been expecting him.

He took a step forward and then realised with a shock that he actually *had* taken a step forward.

"Oh, thank God!" Daniel's breath rushed out of him in a grateful, disbelieving breath. He dropped to his knees and spent a few moments running his hands up and down his body, feeling his face, wiping away tears of relief. He was dressed in the clothes he had been wearing back in the tunnels—his sort of modified armour and survival gear.

The black shapes approached him. He rose and started toward them as well, delighting in each step he took, but gradually becoming more fearful as they neared.

As emotionally tumultuous as the past hours had been, it paled in comparison to the tidal wave of fear he experienced as he recognised the bloodless faces. Daniel did not know the first; his bloodless face was finely chiselled and regal, even for an elf. He wore a trailing cloak that indicated an imperious dignity and funereal solemnity.

It was the other face that drew Daniel up short. Agrid Fiall, the shady financier he had assassinated in order to leave this place the first time around. His bloodless face was screwed up in a wrathful sneer, and it looked as if he would spit poison daggers if he could.

The third form was in the shape of Felix Stowe—the elf who had imprisoned Freya, and whom he had killed.

"Oh man," Daniel murmured. "I really am dead."

V

Alex was in a bit of a bind, and he frantically searched his memory.

"Uh . . . *réveillez-vous, chevaliers dormant, et . . . et . . . um, bataille avec l'Anglais.* No, sorry, I mean, uh, *l'Angleterre.* That is—hold on, *bataille pour l'Angleterre . . . POUR l'Angleterre.*"

Seven bearded, ancient French faces stared back at him blankly. They were in a sleeping chamber that was not adjoined to any tunnels. They'd had to resurface in the French countryside and follow some ancient markers to a burial ground near a place called Carnac. It wasn't the cold, dry environment they had come to expect, but warm, slightly damp, and earthy. They had left the others at the cave exit—they were far too conspicuous to be travelling aboveground.

They had found the chamber, entered it, and Alex, excited to see a full chamber of slumbering knights, went to the horn that was hanging on the wall and blew it.

"*Prys difuna yw?*" the nearest knight asked.

"*Vous . . . parlez pas Français?*"

"*Pytra?*"

Ecgbryt leaned in toward Alex. "How goes it?" he asked.

"I don't think they speak French."

"There may be an enchanted archway around here."

"What sort of—?"

The knights shifted forward on their stone biers and moved their hands to their weapons. That was a very bad sign.

Alex and Ecgbryt took a step back. "We shouldn't have left the others behind," Alex said, his hand on his sword's hilt.

"*Pace,*" Ecgbryt said. "*Liss, freed . . .*"

"What are you doing?" Alex said as the knights shifted off their stone slabs and started to advance on them.

"Quiet. *Shee, kres—*"

The knights paused, just briefly.

"*Kres?*" Ecgbryt said, nodding his head and holding up his palms. "*Kres?*"

The knights looked at each other. A question—a doubt?— seemed to pass between them. They appeared to be in a silent debate.

"What was that?" Alex whispered. "What all did you say?"

"It was the word *peace* in as many languages as I know."

"Good trick. Which one finally worked?"

"Cornish."

Alex groaned. "We have to be smarter than this, Ecgbryt."

The knights apparently resolved the issue, but not to either Alex's or Ecgbryt's satisfaction. They continued advancing.

"What is taking so long?" came a voice from behind them.

"We are hungry. You told us you were getting provisions and you would return quickly."

Alex and Ecgbryt turned in surprise. "Berwin!"

"Thank God!" Alex said. "Talk to them—they speak Cornish. Explain who we are!"

Berwin stepped past them and sized up the French knights.

"How did you know to find us?" Ecgbryt said.

"I watched you. You walked right past the settlement where all the bakers and grocers are, and you came right out into this field—"

"Enough! Talk to them!"

"*Lowena dhis!*" Berwin said and held out his arms. "*Hanow Berwin.*"

The knights halted and lowered their weapons slightly.

"*Prys difuna yw?*" the foremost knight repeated.

"*Ea, difuna,*" Berwin answered.

They continued their conversation, unintelligible to Alex and Ecgbryt.

"What was that you said about an enchanted archway just now?" Alex asked.

"You know, Ealdstan put them up at the entrances to the sleeping chambers. It's so we can understand who finds us, whenever they find us. It seems he did not place them at *all* the sites."

"That's an enchantment I could use."

"You mean . . . you never passed under one? But you speak English—I mean, my English; Old English."

"Yeah, that's because I had to bloody learn it. My father drilled it into me, starting when I was eleven. I've talked to you, I've been talking to the other knights—all this time, what did you think?"

"I don't know. I'm not sure I did think. I just assumed . . . all this time." Ecgbryt shook his head. "Hmm. Maybe ours was the only one. No wonder your accent was so bad."

"Well, I believe I've improved, now that I've heard you speak it."

"And I thought it was just because you were Scottish."

"You should thank your stars it was me you came across, matey. The only other people who could have communicated with you are a bunch of old men in tweed sitting in a lecture hall in Cambridge. Enchanted archways." Alex snorted. "So that's how Daniel and Freya picked it up?"

"Of course, what did you think?"

Alex sighed. Berwin seemed to be making headway with the Bretton knights. The speech patterns were sounding a little less formal and their body language was relaxing.

"So why couldn't you talk to these chaps just now?" Alex asked Ecgbryt.

"What do you mean?"

"With the arch and all? Why didn't the enchantment translate for you?"

"Daniel and Freya walked under the arch. I never did."

Negotiations continued.

"How many languages do you know?" Ecgbryt asked.

"Nine or ten. Most of them dead."

"Latin? Norse?"

"Aye."

"But not Cornish?"

"No, not Cornish."

"All right," Berwin reported, finishing his talk with the knights, which had obviously gone well since they had all put up their weapons and a few of them were smiling now. "It's not Cornish they're speaking, but it's close. This region on this side of the water was once a settlement sent from our own land, you see, and we held our tongue and culture in common. Trade was good, and an alliance with—"

"That's wonderful, Berwin," Alex interrupted. "You'll have to tell us about all of that sometime. Did you tell them the situation?"

"Yes, I've told them the situation. They're willing to join us."

"Fan-bloody-tastic."

Berwin introduced them. "They tell me that they take their names out of honour for the seven founding saints of Bretagne. This is Tugdual, this is Brieg, that is Aorelian, Malou, Samsun, Kaourintin, and that is Padam over there."

Alex and Ecgbryt went around and clasped arms with them.

"Now," said Berwin, "can we at last find something to eat?"

CHAPTER NINE

The Witch Bottle

I

Cardiff

Gemma Woodcotte was thirteen years and fourteen days old, exactly—she had had her birthday two weeks earlier. She knew she was special but didn't exactly know why. She didn't figure this was important; she would know why when the time came. At the moment, being special simply meant that she had Possibilities. There were things she might be able to do, One Day, in that intolerably distant time that was still just the day after tomorrow. When she wrote about it in her journal—someone special should have a journal—that was how she expressed it: in capital letters.

Her big brother, Anthony, was *not* special. To her mind, he had never been special, although she would readily admit that she had not known him for all of his seventeen years. For all she knew—and this was likely, for she was fond of him after all—he had been special once, when he was younger; but evidently that time had passed. Even from her limited experience, Gemma knew that Anthony had made some pretty bad choices in his life and acted incredibly silly and careless, even for a boy. He no longer played. He couldn't imagine. He didn't seem to have any attention for anything other than cars.

But Gabriel had potential. He was only thirteen months old and hadn't been spoiled yet. It was her job to protect him. And the reason he needed protecting was that every week, always on Thursday, a witch flew into his window and perched upon the edge of his crib.

What exactly the witch wanted, Gemma didn't know. She had seen her twice. The first time was when she went upstairs one evening to fetch a book. In the middle of a pause of silence from the blaring TV downstairs, she thought she heard a whispering coming from her brother's room.

Gabe was too young to be whispering, and she didn't recognise any of the words as being his. Carefully, silently, she pushed the door open. And there was the witch, her feet balanced on the edge of the crib, her left hand against the wall, her right clinging to the window frame. The dark, ugly figure was whispering something that was hard to make out, even though Gemma strained her ears.

> . . . Is it Charles, or Curtis, or Clive?
> Cedric, or Colin, or Cal?
> Is it Casper, or Calvin, or Carl?
> Christopher, Connor, or Clem?
>
> Is it Christian, or Cain, or Claude . . . ?

"What are you doing?" Gemma asked.

At the sound of her voice the witch became startled. She ruffled and flapped her cloak as if it were two wide wings and flew instantly out of the open window, as quick and graceful as a leaf on the wind. Her black, swirling form could be seen against the streetlights, and then was gone—just another shadow in the night.

Gemma stood for a couple seconds, blinking. She had seen what she had seen, therefore she believed. Witches were real. She went into the room and closed the window, latching it firmly.

Gabriel seemed to be fine. He was awake, and while the witch spoke to him, he appeared to listen intently. But it was a long time before he went to sleep, and he woke up early Wednesday morning—along with the rest of the house—and the whole day he was fussy and agitated.

From that night on, Gemma was certain to check the room after her parents had put Gabe down and while they were still downstairs watching TV. She would open it a crack, stand for a time to listen in silence, and then go inside and check the windows. For an entire week, she heard nothing, but the next Thursday, as she was standing just outside, listening, she heard a rattling in the room, and then a click, and the sound of the window opening. She stood a little closer to the door, in order to hear what the witch was saying.

Would you come away with me, darling?
Leave your mummy and daddy at home.
Fly away with me, little darling,
If I call out to you, will you come?

Would you ride away with me, dumpling,
Leave all else behind and be free?
If I knew what your name is, my sweet one,
I would call you and you'd come to me.

Is it David or Dexter, or Dennis?
Damien, Douglas, or Del?

Is it Darryl, or Darren, or Darrick?
Dashiell, Dustin, or Don?

Is it Duncan, or Dylan, or Dideron?
Dudley, or Dixon, or Dan . . . ?

"Stop that," Gemma said, entering the room.

Once more, the witch wheeled up, flew out the window, and was gone. But this time, Gemma saw an angry red eye glowering at her amidst the black cloth.

Gemma went to the window and shut it. Something had to be done.

The next day Gemma went to the school library. She spent a little time online but found a lot of things that were confusing, and more that were contradictory. She signed off and went to look for a book on witches.

There were not many to choose from—three, in fact. She flicked through them all and decided to check the oldest one out. Back at home, she read it cover to cover. Then she picked up the volume of *Grimm's Fairy Tales* that her uncle had given her.

A plan started to form. All of the myths and legends, if you looked at them from the right angle, lined up, and it was easy to find your way through them after that. Tomorrow would be Saturday. She would have to go to the shops to get some materials, but the plan should work. It should work.

The next Thursday night Gemma slipped into Gabriel's room just as it was still light outside. It was just before Gabe's bedtime. Preparations only took a couple minutes. She retreated to her room and waited, reading one of her books.

She heard her mother carry Gabe up and put him in the crib. She heard the door close and then footsteps down the stairs. Gemma rose quietly and went to her little brother's door.

She had only been standing there maybe five or ten minutes when she heard the scratching at the window. Holding her breath, Gemma heard the catch click and the window swing open.

She tried to picture the scene in her head: the window hanging open, the witch perching on the window sill, spotting her brother, then what would she do? Climb over? Leap across?

There was a shrill scream from inside the room, and Gemma flung the door open. All she caught was a flicker of black fabric outside the window.

"What's going on up there?" Gemma heard her dad call up.

"Sorry, Dad. I thought I saw a bat."

"Well, did you?"

"No, it was just a moth."

Her dad muttered something and then said, "Go to sleep, Gemma. Get ready for bed."

"Okay."

Gemma went into Gabe's room; he was fine, just a little bemused. She was surprised that he wasn't crying, but, she reminded herself, he was special. She smiled at him and he smiled back, showing all eight of his teeth. She closed the window and then went to the top of his crib. Along the rungs, so the tips were only just exposed, were the clusters of brass pins that she had taped where she had seen the witch's feet perch. Six of them were tipped with blood; not a lot, just a few pearls on each.

From her pocket, Gemma pulled a small glass bottle with a cork in it that she had bought at the supermarket. She'd tipped the contents—cloves—into the garden, so that it was empty. She had bought it especially because of the size and the cork. She didn't know if the cork was important, but she didn't intend to take chances.

She also took out a pair of tweezers and, uncorking the bottle, removed the bloodied pins from the tape and put them in the bottle. Then she corked it, removed the tape and the unbloodied pins from the crib, gave her little brother a pat, and left the room.

The next week she did the same routine, only the preparations were a little more difficult. She had already done the hardest part—pounding nails into the ceiling—before her parents had come home, but now she had to stand up on the changing table to reach up to them in complete silence. *Plus,* she had to do this after Gabe had been put down, since this time her trap would certainly be noticed.

She managed it, however, and withdrew just as it grew dark enough outside for the streetlamps to come on.

She stood in position just outside the door and didn't have long to wait before she heard the creepy scratching and picking sound once more. The window unlatched, swung open, and there was a pause of about three seconds before she heard flapping and grunting.

Opening the door, she caught sight of the witch, her hair entangled in half a dozen strips of flypaper that she had hung from the ceiling. Seeing Gemma, the witch fell backward, out of the window, pulling several of the flypaper strips with her.

But three still remained.

Her parents didn't seem to have heard anything, so climbing up on the changing table, she very carefully brought down the strips and carried them into her room. She would have to remove the nails later, she thought. Or maybe not. The strands of hair that she removed, she put in the bottle, along with the bloodied pins.

The next week was the last and the easiest stage of the plan. It was also the riskiest, and the most frightening, and Gemma had no clear idea of what would happen next. It was also the last chance she would have, since the witch was now up to the letter *G* in her name-calling rhyme.

She went into her brother's room with a large pair of scissors and positioned herself just beneath the windowsill. The light in the room became dimmer and dimmer. Just as it was dark, she heard the scraping and scratching and tilted her head back to look up at the window.

In the paper-thin gap between the window and its frame was a long, thin finger with a long, thin fingernail, edging up toward the latch.

Taking a breath, she pulled open the scissors—big ones from her mother's desk—leapt up, and snipped off the fingernail, right near to the tip of the finger.

Like a blind worm, the finger wavered and then withdrew.

Gemma bent down and picked up the sliver of nail. Then she looked out the window. The witch was there, her large, bulbous nose pressed up against the window pane.

"Hello, dearie," the witch crooned.

Huh, Gemma thought, unimpressed. *She even talks like they do in the storybooks.* "What do you want with my brother?" she asked.

"You don't need him. Why would you want *two* brothers? Less attention from Mummy and Daddy. Less love. Why *not* give him to me?"

"I'm going to stop you."

"With pins and flypaper? I'll find out his name eventually. And if not him, then another."

"No," Gemma said, putting her hand in the pocket of her bathrobe. "I mean I'm *really* going to stop you—for good. You're not going to steal anyone's baby—ever."

"And how do you intend to do that?" the witch asked.

Gemma took the small bottle from her bathrobe and held it up.

"Oh." A look of uncertainty passed over the witch's face. "Don't be—wait a second."

Gemma uncorked the bottle and stuck the fingernail in it, corked it again, and shook it.

The witch gulped. "Pins and flypaper," she murmured, automatically raising a hand to her hair. "Let's talk about this . . ."

Gemma leaned over and picked up her brother.

"I could knock on the door and talk to your parents. Adults always believe other adults. They would stop this foolishness."

Gemma turned back to the witch. "My parents are out tonight; my big brother is 'watching' me. I bought him a *Top Gear* DVD this morning and gave it to him half an hour ago. He told me himself that he's going to ignore anyone who's at the door tonight."

"Well then, I guess you've got me, dearie. Just bury that bottle under your front door and I won't be able to ever enter the building again. You win."

Gemma smiled. "I have a better idea," she said and turned. As she left the room, Gabe smiled and giggled at the face of the witch pressed up against his window.

The TV was emitting the sounds of souped-up motor engines. Anthony was oblivious, as usual, to anything other than what was directly in front of him.

She went into the kitchen and found that the witch was standing outside the kitchen's French windows. Startled, Gemma took a step backward. She gripped the bottle tighter and moved forward.

"In the stories," Gemma said, "the witch-bottle has to be thrown in the fire. The doorstep works as well, but that won't get rid of you for good."

"I think I picked the wrong sibling in this house. I'll tell you what, why don't I make you a deal? Come with me, and I'll tell you all of my secrets. I'll give you power you would never know otherwise. You've obviously got the knack. I will train you to be the mightiest witch in all the land."

"I'm curious," Gemma said. "Do I know you? I mean, are you someone that lives on the street? Someone local?"

"I've seen you many times. Sometimes as often as every day. I've watched you grow up."

Gemma held up the bottle and pressed the cork in as firmly as she could. In her arms, Gabe shifted and gave a little grunt.

"In the stories they always threw it in the fire, so that it would burst. I don't have a fire. But I think this will work."

She opened the door of the microwave and placed the bottle on the glass plate.

"No!" screamed the witch.

Gemma shut the door, set it to high, and turned the timer, switching it on.

The witch screamed and writhed outside in the garden, as if she were the one in the microwave. Gemma watched her as she withdrew into the corner. She wrapped her arms tightly around Gabe and then crouched down.

The witch's screams became shriller and shriller, mounting to a crescendo as the bottle in the microwave burst.

Gemma expected a flash of light, and maybe another explosion, but the only thing that happened is that the door swung open and banged against the kitchen wall. Bits of the bottle tumbled onto the counter. Gabe began to cry.

"What's going on in there?" Anthony demanded, pausing the DVD.

"Nothing," Gemma said, gently shaking Gabe. "Just dropped something." She went to the window and looked at the body of the witch, lying stretched out in the garden. She was dead, apparently.

"So clean it up." The DVD started again; motors revved. "And put Gabe back to bed."

"Sure," Gemma said. She considered what she should do with the body in the back of the house . . . Bury it somewhere? That sounded hard, not to mention dirty. Burn it? Drag it around the shed and hide it?

Then she realised that she didn't have to do anything. She could just leave it there. It would give her mother a fright in the morning, of course, but then the police would come, take it away, and that would be the end of it. No one would possibly connect the death to a broken bottle and some minor damage to a microwave.

She wondered who the witch was. They changed their faces when they were doing their witchy things, and when they were killed their faces turned back—rather like werewolves—that much was a consensus in the stories.

She took Gabriel back up to bed and then went downstairs again to use the dustpan and brush, unable to stop smiling over the satisfaction of her victory. She looked out the window, and the witch was still on the ground. She would have to wait until daytime to find out who she really was, since she certainly wasn't going outside now. But if it wasn't one of the teachers at her school, she was going to be very disappointed.

II

"Lies? What do you mean 'lies'?"

"You could have gone home—you could always have gone home. But we needed to send you on that quest. We needed to try—we needed heroes." Modwyn opened up her palms.

"But we failed. We didn't kill Gád."

"It was not about him—not exactly. We just needed you to survive."

"That doesn't make any sense. What *happened* to you? What—" Freya looked down at the stone knife that she still gripped in her white-knuckled fist. Her eyes went to the bloodless gap in Modwyn's own chest. She looked to Vivienne, clearly gobsmacked, and then to Frithfroth, and found him backed against the door frame, a look of near terror on his face.

She spun on Modwyn and yelled, "What's going on here? What *are* you?!" She shook the knife at the beautiful woman who had propped herself up on an elbow.

"Calm down, now." Freya felt Vivienne's hand on her shoulder.

"No!" She pulled away and looked back and forth between the women. "You tell me what's going on here. *Now!*"

"I—I—truly thought she was dead," Vivienne said.

"And I . . . was desperate," said Modwyn tiredly, swinging her legs around to sit up. "Niðergeard was invaded. There was only one thing I could do . . ."

"*Stab* yourself in the *chest*?"

"I'm immortal. My ghost wouldn't have moved on, but it couldn't stay in my body either. It's . . . a unique situation. I kept them out—I kept them all out, even Ealdstan. I was waiting for you. We all waited for you—for eight years. I didn't think you'd stay away that long. I thought you'd come straight back."

Freya looked down at the stone knife as Modwyn gingerly inspected the gaping hole in her chest.

Vivienne stepped forward. "Are you all right? Is there anything we can get you?"

Modwyn shook her head.

"There is so much you can tell us," Vivienne said, "so much that is urgent. How were you able to stay here at all?"

"I killed them. All who would cross the threshold, whose souls were already dark and weak. When I . . . removed my soul from my body, I was able to affect the spiritual aspect of . . . others."

"Are you saying that you took souls out of people's bodies?" Freya fought to keep her voice level.

"No. But I could move them on. A soul is like a large rock. If it teeters on the brink, then just a gentle shove can send it into the pit."

"Well, this just gets better and better. Thanks for not 'shoving us into the pit,' Modwyn."

"There was no chance of that. I could feel how you were both different—conflicted. I let you and the other one, the simple one, alone."

"The other one? You mean you didn't know who we all were? You still don't know?"

"No, but I am glad you are not with the other—he is simple and twisted inward. A yfelgóp, is that right? You came back with one of them? Was the yfelgóp escorting you, or you him? Please tell me, it is important to know."

"Neither," Freya said, her frown deepening. "That was Daniel you sensed."

"Truly?"

"I'm afraid so."

"That is a pity."

"Do you still sense him? Is he still here somewhere?"

"No. He . . . left. I let him go. Once he crossed the boundary of this building, he passed from my perception."

"Modwyn . . . *nider-cwen*," Vivienne said, her tongue catching slightly on the unfamiliar word. "Where is the Great Carnyx?"

"I am not certain I should tell you—if I knew. I heard you speak of Gád while you were in these walls. Are you not an enemy of Niðergeard?" Modwyn stopped and turned to Freya. "Do you not wish destruction to this place and the people in it?"

"How did you hear me?"

"It is not for you to know and difficult to explain even if I wished to."

Freya shrugged. "I honestly don't know. I'm beginning to think that this situation is more complex than just a simple either/ or, good/bad situation. Just because I agree with Gád doesn't mean I agree with what he's done. I think there might be a way through this all without so much bloodshed, if any. Hopefully not more than has already been spilled."

Modwyn smirked. "You have changed from the scared, wide-eyed girl who first arrived here. Perhaps Ealdstan was right to act as he did."

The Rage rolled through Freya like a blast of heat. She leapt forward and slapped Modwyn hard across the face.

"How *dare* you," Freya spit out, clenching the knife and feeling a terrible urge to plunge it back into the queen's chest. "How dare you put Daniel and me through what you did and not even feel badly about it. We were children!"

Even in the dim light of the lantern, the pink imprint of Freya's hand was starting to show against Modwyn's fine and pale skin. Modwyn lifted one hand, palm down. "I wish you . . . to understand why we lied . . . the circumstances behind what we did." She seemed rattled, uncharacteristically discomposed.

Maybe I'm getting through to her, Freya thought.

"You're right. It is a complex problem, and there are more sides than are first visible. And you two were a small part of that. Very small cogs in the big machine. Small, but vital."

"There were others," Freya said. "I saw some of them in a dream. How many were there in total? How many children did you send to their deaths on that dreadful quest?"

"I do not remember exactly."

"That's monstrous."

"You do not share our perspective, the perspective of centuries. All die in time—some sooner, some later. Try to imagine—century upon century, unending years—all the same. And facing more, ever more. Stuck down here, trapped. Locked in a dark box."

"You're right," Freya said with a fair amount of sarcasm. "How could I be so heartless? Pardon me if I feel no guilt. Are you going to tell us where the Carnyx is or not?"

"You are agents of Gád. I sensed your allegiances."

Freya said, facing her squarely, "You're not exactly helping to win me to your side. But anyway, Vivienne isn't."

"Blood does not lie."

"Blood? What do you mean?" Freya said. "She's Alex Simpson's aunt. Alex is one of your people aboveground. I thought—"

Modwyn's face was set. Her whole manner, Freya observed now, was in fact one of someone who might be undergoing some sort of interrogation. And Vivienne's manner—was it deferential or quietly dominating? "What do you mean 'blood doesn't lie'?"

"Freya," Vivienne said, her mouth twisting slightly, "Gád's my brother."

III

"You are not dead," the unknown, imperious figure beside Agrid Fiall assured Daniel.

"Are you sure about that? I just journeyed through all of creation and spent an evening floating in a disembodied cloud around a field."

"You'd be dead if *I* had any power at all in the matter," Agrid informed him. "I'll do everything within my power to make you wish you were."

"If you were dead, this conversation would occur somewhere else," said the unknown elf.

"Somewhere much more uncomfortable for all of us," Stowe said grimly.

"But we're in Elfland?" Daniel said. "Why am I here?"

"Because when you were last here, you took something that didn't belong to you, which you were specifically warned *not to do*."

"No . . ." Daniel said. "No, I don't think I did. I was very careful to—"

"You took our lives, you empty-headed fool," Fiall interrupted him. "Oh, don't give me that look. Certainly our lives aren't something you could put in your pocket, but did you honestly, seriously think that you could blithely go around killing whomever you pleased and not feel the effects of it?"

"But the merchant—Reizger Lokkich—he said it would be all right, that I wouldn't have any trouble going back after I did."

Stowe chuckled. "And you believed him?"

"What about you? I killed you in my world."

"Oh, I'm just here for the show."

"You will have a reckoning in your world as soon as you have had one in ours," Agrid said.

"It isn't quite as Agrid states it," the third elf said. "Your actions came at a cost to your soul—and now your soul must pay the price."

"Who are you?" Daniel asked, looking him up and down. "I remember Agrid Fiall—Agrid Fiall who wanted to buy me and keep me as a pet—but I don't remember you."

"I was there." The elf tilted his noble face upward. "I was following behind Fiall to relieve myself. I heard the explosions from the device that slew him—slew him almost instantly—and then you turned your machine at me. One piece of metal hit my chest." He pulled at his cloak and revealed a white, smooth chest that suddenly warped and contorted before Daniel's eyes, turning into a livid, diseased, purple-green infected hole. The skin separated in the centre of the ugly whorl and oozed puss and blood.

"Another," the figure continued, "struck me here." He passed a hand across his face and it was transformed to show a gash running from the edge of his chin up to his cheek and over his ear. The sickening discolouration filled the whole side of his face; his eye was blood red, with a completely black pupil.

Daniel breathed out and looked away.

"I did *not* die quickly. I lingered inside my body as they

fought to keep it alive—surgeons, herbalists, healers, enchant-ers—but none of them had any powers over the poisonous metal that had entered my body. It took days, and I myself struggled no less desperately than they, but in the end I gave way to the inevitable and died."

Out of the corner of his eye, Daniel saw his face change back to the fine, unmarred, porcelain-like features of a few moments ago.

Daniel swallowed. "Were you a servant? Or a guard?" he asked. The elf's bearing, his manner, suggested something regal, and Daniel had already begun to suspect, before the words were even out of the other's mouth.

"I was not. I was Prince Lhiam-Lhiat. You assassinated one of the royal line."

Daniel winced. "I'm . . . sorry?" he said.

"Are you though? You must think it, I'm sure, but can you say you wouldn't do it again? Seriously consider that, right now, before you answer."

Daniel did think about it a moment. "You're right, I would do it again."

Lhiam-Lhiat smiled and nodded. "You do not lie. Good. I thought you would not be regretful. But tell me why."

"Why not? You were evil, all of you, and this world—any world—is better for you not being in it."

"Spiteful little pup!" Fiall spat venomously. "I'll see you regret those words!" He leapt at Daniel, springing high into the air. Trying to twist out of the way, Daniel fell back but was too slow. The enraged elf's outstretched hands met his chest and Daniel toppled backward. He hit the ground with Fiall's knees on his chest. He saw hands raised against the evening sky, curled claw-like as they descended, slashing at his face and neck.

But there was no pain. Or, Daniel also saw, blood. Fiall's fin-gers just bounced off of him with no effect or damage to either of them. When he realised this, he just laid back and let Fiall impotently continue. Fiall's rage gradually fell from him and he stopped. Daniel shifted his weight, pushed Fiall off of him, and then stood. Fiall was on one side of him, Lhiam-Lhiat and Stowe on the other.

"That was fun. I guess. Is that what this is, then?" Daniel asked. "I'm going to be haunted by you and shown the error of my ways? Have a miraculous change of heart and find enlightenment? Are you going to show me my past, present, and future so I can see what a ruthless monster I am? Will you take me on a tour of all the lives I've destroyed because of my actions and reveal the connectedness and nobility of life? That might be entertaining. Go ahead, bring it on, because you're right, I'm *not* sorry, and I *would* do it again. I'm not an idiot. I know what I am. You think I don't? You think I haven't thought long and hard about what I've done, what I've set myself to do? I'm not some selfish, unexamined soul!" Daniel said, his voice rising. He drew his sword. "I'm a *hero*! So bring it on! I'll take you and the whole universe on! Win or lose, I don't care. I'm fighting on the side of good! It may not always be pleasant, but it *is* always *right*!"

Daniel stood opposite the two tall, gaunt, marble-like apparitions, his eyes blazing. He felt the electric fire of righteousness racing though him. Lhiam-Lhiat was smiling at him in that smug, self-satisfied way of his. *Fine, let him keep smiling.* Daniel wasn't a man to be intimidated by that. But . . . Agrid Fiall was also smiling, the exact same smile—and for some reason that rattled him.

The sky seemed to be growing darker.

"Do you know," Fiall said, "I do believe I'm going to enjoy this far more than I previously imagined."

"This isn't a lesson," Lhiam-Lhiat said to him. "This isn't forgiveness or an atonement—those rules work differently in this place. This is punishment, pure and simple."

There was a twisting feeling in Daniel's gut. The righteous

fire of defiance inside of him faltered slightly. "Torture? Doesn't matter, I'll get through it somehow. I've got friends here, and in other places. They'll find me and rescue me. I can hold out until then. I can survive. I can escape."

"Can you run?" Fiall asked him.

"What?" Daniel asked.

Fiall's eyes shifted to look behind Daniel, and Daniel turned. Behind him, the sun had been setting; minutes ago, deep reds and golden yellows lit the sky. Now the cold, purple expanse of twilight filled the air above him, and on the horizon—dark. But it wasn't the dark that was an absence of light; it was the horrible, running darkness that chases after you in nightmares. It was darkness that had an edge to it—and a sharp edge, with teeth and claws. Although it was still a far ways off, and only flickering slightly, Daniel knew with the untold certainty of a nightmare that the darkness was alive, and angry, and coming after him.

"What is that?"

"When you were a child, were you ever afraid of the dark? It was because you had not forgotten the realm that came before existence. That is Night."

"What does it want?"

"You. Forever."

Daniel started running. He ran as fast and as long as he could, which was considerable, since he didn't tire here, but he couldn't outrun the turn of the planet.

The Night was behind him. Its arms reached for him and its jaws strained for him.

Daniel's feet desperately pounded the ground. He had looked back once and almost burst into tears; he didn't know exactly why, but the hard, bank of blackness was terrifying, bristling with unknown horrors that he somehow, instinctively, knew would destroy him.

He felt the chill on his back as darkness creeped in around him. He thought the fear entered into him then, but it didn't; it merely quickened the panic already in Daniel's breast, like a sympathetic note vibrating on the fear string of his heart.

And then the Night reached out and grabbed him, physically, reaching an inconceivably cold hand into his chest and yanking backward. Unable to breathe, Daniel flung his arms out into the darkness.

He only had a second to acknowledge the terror before pain became his world. He felt his skin tear, like it was being stripped, torn off of him one thread at a time, layer by layer, leaving the raw flesh beneath exposed. The pain was so excruciating he wished he would dissipate, like earlier. He cursed his body, his useless, pointless body that now only seemed to exist in order to house the pain.

He was screaming—at least, he thought he was screaming. He could hear nothing. The Night and its pain blocked out all noise.

He tumbled in torment for countless hours. Days? How could he stop the pain? How could he manage it? Could it be avoided? Transcended? If he could only think clearly for a moment . . .

And then, it stopped. The pain left him—but left him raw, aching, and brutally cold. It was too dark to see. He feared moving, so he just drifted. The blood in his ears thumped with the echoes of pain and the sounds of his sobs.

A grey blur floated before his eyes. He blinked to clear them and found the Elfin moneylender standing before him.

"Are you sure I'm not dead?" Daniel asked Agrid—more croaked—and he realised that he asked it in English, not Elvish. But that didn't seem to matter.

"Fairly certain."

Daniel sighed. "Really? How do I know I can trust you?"

Agrid Fiall smiled. "If you can't trust the dead, whom can you trust?"

Daniel hazarded a movement and brought his hand to his face. Contrary to what every nerve ending told him, his skin was still attached to the rest of his body, as well as somehow illuminated in the dark.

"What happens now?" Daniel asked. "You said punishment. Is this what it's going to be? Torture? You just keep going until I break? Is there more to come?" *Or is it over?* he hoped, but couldn't ask.

"My friend," said the moneylender with a leer. "You haven't begun yet."

"More pain?" Daniel asked, and felt tears in his eyes.

"Perhaps. Is pain the worst that can happen to you?"

"I don't know. It feels like it."

"If you do not fear anything more than pain, then you are blessed."

"Right now I can't think of anything worse than what just happened to me. What was it?"

"You don't fear solitude?"

The moneylender disappeared.

"Silence?"

And Daniel heard nothing more.

He tried to call out, but no sound came. He shouted, clapped, hummed, even whistled, but nothing registered in his ears. He felt for them, and they were still there. He clicked his fingers, clapped—there wasn't even the ring of silence.

Time, interminable, passed. Touch, physical sensation, was a comfort, and then it was a torment. All other senses lost, except for the one that was sensitive to pain, to cold, to fear.

In despair, no sight or sound to console him, he floated in a sea of nothing.

IV

Alex stood in the centre of a ring of nearly two hundred heavily armed warriors. Behind him were the thirty-some knights with whom he'd been travelling the forgotten paths of England and Europe. The hundred and fifty or so before him were the knights they had found sleeping under what he thought was Blanik Mountain in the Czech Republic.

Alex conducted the negotiations in Latin, which he had thought would be fairly standard, but had almost immediately uncovered a wealth of small differences in pronunciation and formulation. In any case, they were communicating. Mostly.

"We require you to fight with us," Alex said to a slight, dark-complexioned knight in ornate, Slavic armour. "In Britain. We are under attack. Many of our warriors are killed, dead where they slept undisturbed for almost a thousand years, murdered by the great evil that is growing there. We need our brothers in arms to avenge them, to help us plug a great spring of darkness that if left unchecked now will flood all of Europe—all the world. It is by joining us now that we have a chance to stop this tide of destruction."

The Slavic knight related some or all of Alex's impassioned speech to the knights behind him, who were peering attentively at the new knights who'd invaded their hidden chamber.

A discussion broke out among them when the knight had finished his translation. It grew into a clamour, and then the leader waved his hands for quiet.

"We cannot come with you," he said sternly. "We wait for Wenceslaus."

"Who's he?"

"Our commander and king. When the great conflict comes, and when all Czech people argue and two cannot be found who agree on any one matter—when Blanik Forest burns and blood fills Pusty Lake—then will Wenceslaus rise from where he sleeps, claim the sword of Bruncvik, and crack open this mountainside. We will ride out, with him commanding us, and chase our nation's enemies into the farthest ocean. But not before then will we leave this place."

"Tell them this," Ecgbryt said to Alex, and Alex began translating: "Let me assure you of the danger that will surely come to this world. There are gaps in the walls between the worlds, where those who keep the gates have no authority."

"We have no knowledge of these things," the knight said, this time without relaying Alex's words to his comrades. "We shall stay here."

"I don't understand," Alex said, turning to Ecgbryt. "I was under the impression that Ealdstan was responsible for all of these knights. But either his breadth of interest was much wider than I had credited him, or there are more players at work here than I originally conceived."

"I would not know," Ecgbryt answered. "I was asleep most of the last thousand years."

"It's something to bear in mind, I think," Alex concluded. He gave the Czech chief one more questioning glance, then turned to tell the rest of the company what the man had said, and the information trickled down the line as it was translated and retranslated into the three archaic languages that the men spoke.

"Leave them," Berwin said, stepping forward. He was starting to assume the position of a sort of deputy commander or captain to Alex and Ecgbryt's dual leadership. He seemed to speak most of the languages that actually mattered on this jaunt and took it upon himself to organise practical aspects, like where and how to set up camps when they bedded for the night. Not that they did that, much. None of the awakened knights, Ecgbryt included, seemed to need much sleep; it made sense, Alex acknowledged;

however, he was getting far less than his necessary seven hours a night, and fatigue was starting to overtake him.

"Their ways are not ours," Berwin said. "We would not journey from our realm to help them; what reason have we for asking them to leave theirs?"

Alex frowned. Berwin had a point, but still . . . a hundred and fifty knights—that was more than he had ever heard of in one place before. More than was probably still left in Britain, in total.

"Please," Alex beseeched. "There are trolls, dragons, giants, and all manner of malicious spirits infesting our country. With your help, they would be eradicated swiftly, and you would be back here soon and none would be the wiser. What say you? For honour's sake?"

The last request was relayed with a smirk by the dark complexioned knight. There were grunts and scoffs.

"That was the wrong tack," Berwin intimated to Alex and Ecgbryt. "Slovak knights have always viewed the signposts of honour askew. Their ways are not ours."

"We owe no debts to your island race," the Slavic knight responded. "If your small outpost were to disappear overnight, who would notice? We here are the keystone of the arch of civilisation. Were we to falter, the whole would tumble away into oblivion."

"In an arch," Alex replied, "each stone is as vital as the other. Send just a small band of your men to join with ours."

An argument seemed to break out when this request was translated. Knights on both sides of the translator shouted and made wild gesticulations. He raised his hands for quiet once more.

"Them, take them," he said, and pointed to a corner of the massive cavern. Eight knights were standing quite apart from the rest of them, incongruously clad in medieval plate armour. "They call themselves the Hussites. We can hardly understand them, and we don't know why they were sent to us. They have strange opinions and are always causing arguments with us about topics that we know nothing about and care for even less. If we convince them to go with you, will you take them?"

Alex shrugged. "If that's the best offer we can get, then yes—of course."

There then followed a very long period of bartering and explaining to the eight rather baffled knights.

"So," said the dark knight after the awkward Hussites had been, to all appearances, completely bullied into joining Alex and Ecgbryt's ragtag band of warriors. "All has been explained to them. They will follow you and take part in your battles. They are good warriors—they are of the *Boiohaemum*, after all. When you have done with them . . . keep them, send them home, do whatever. But remember always that you owe a debt to the Knights of Blanik Mountain, Alex Son-of-Simp."

Alex bowed, and with a grudging amicability restored, they left the enormous cavern under the mountain and continued their northward course.

CHAPTER TEN

The Giants of Man

---I---

Isle of Man

Kieran and Fergus were walking home from school. Kieran was ahead, going very slowly, and Fergus was some thirty feet behind him, going even slower than his brother. Kieran was angry and annoyed. This was exactly the sort of thing Fergus was always pulling. He was late and making him even later. Why did he put up with it?

"Because I *say* so. You come home with your brother. End of story," Kieran's mother had commanded him a couple days after school had recommenced.

"But what if he makes me miss the bus again?"

"Especially if he makes you miss the bus again. You come home with your brother."

"But he's always so *slow*."

"I'm talking to him about that, but never you mind. You come home with your brother."

"But—"

"*Come home with your brother.* Or don't come home at all."

Today was the first day that Kieran seriously considered not coming home at all. He stopped, turned, and studied his brother.

Fergus saw Kieran standing in the road, waiting for him to catch up, and slowed down even more.

Kieran sighed. He got out of the road and leaned against the low, stone cow-wall that ran along it, striking a pose. What was it with Fergus lately? He used to listen to him. They used to do stuff together. Now all that Fergus seemed to want to do was be contrary. And what was up with being late? He got a watch for his birthday, and even though it had taken awhile for him to start wearing it, for their parents to train him to wear it, he still turned up late for everything—breakfast, the bus queue, his classes, lunch, dinner, football—a good five minutes behind everyone else. What part of his brain was missing?

Kieran sighed as Fergus, unwilling to get any closer to his stationary sibling, stopped as well. They stood, looking at each other from about twenty feet away. They were at a standoff. Fergus knew he could get Kieran into trouble if he was so much as thirty seconds later than he in coming through their front door, and Kieran could think of no way through reason, bribery, or force to make Fergus walk with him.

"You know I'll get in trouble if I come home without you," Kieran called with what he hoped was the right mixture of authority and reason.

Fergus just stared back at him blankly. Of course he knew.

"You'll get in trouble also."

Fergus did not even blink.

Kieran put a hand to his forehead and rubbed. He hadn't been sleeping well lately; none of them had been on the island. There was some sort of disease going around, some people thought. It made them all wake up at night from bad dreams. He'd heard someone say that perhaps some anti-malaria drugs had gotten into the water supply somehow. Or maybe they were all worried about the disappearances. And the suicides. But then what kicked those off?

No doubt that's what was making Fergus act like he was. But Kieran was too tired to take it anymore.

He lifted his legs, swivelled around, and jumped off the other side of the wall. He started walking across the field, away from Fergus, away from home, away from everything, toward the darkening blue sky and the grey sea.

He was halfway across the field when he heard Fergus's foot-stomps running to catch up with him. He stopped and turned.

"Where are you going?" Fergus asked, stopping beside him.

"Why do you care?"

"Aren't we go—?"

He was interrupted by an enormous . . . *explosion* was the only way to describe it. It was the sound of a bolt of thunder, or of a lorry hitting the ground after being dropped by a crane. It was an impact boom, and it made the soft ground beneath them swell like an ocean wave.

"What was *that*?" Kieran asked, eyes wide.

"I saw something. It came from over there," Fergus said, pointing toward the sea.

"Stay here," Kieran said, and ran in the direction Fergus had pointed.

But of course his brother ignored him.

They made it to the edge of the field, which was bordered by a wooden fence that ran atop a cliff face. Below them was a sandy strip of beach that the waning tide had revealed. Standing on the beach were two figures.

It took Kieran and Fergus a little while to process what they were seeing. The two figures—men—were absolutely enormous, and it was throwing off their depth perception.

"They're huge!" Fergus whispered.

"Shh!" Kieran looked down at them. They were twisting and bending over and spinning their arms, like they were warming up for a race. They were almost completely naked, all except for some tight and badly stitched-together bits of animal skin around their bottoms that looked like the most uncomfortable, smelliest pairs of underwear in the world. Their hair fell in long dreadlocks the size of bolsters of fabric down their backs. One of them had a thick, bushy beard and no moustache; the other had a moustache and no beard. The rest of their bodies were completely hairless.

Then one of them squatted down and leapt up in the air. He sailed above their heads, dwindled in the sky above them, and then came crashing back again, whistling past them, and landed on the beach with another earth shattering *thump*.

"Wow!" Fergus exclaimed loudly.

"Shh!" Kieran hissed, just as the two giants turned toward them.

"Uh-oh. Run."

Kieran and Fergus took off across the field. Kieran looked back and saw a massive hand—the size of a bulldozer scoop—grip the side of the cliff where they had crouched, and an enormous head rose behind it, like an absurd sun.

"Quick! Quick!" Kieran shouted as he heard the sound of massive limbs scrambling up the cliff face.

They hadn't even made it halfway across the field before two gigantic hands swept them off their feet and into the air, and then swung them back and forth like action figures.

For a while they both struggled, until they each saw how high above the ground they were.

"I've got them, Nuncle, I've got them!" boomed a voice above their heads as they watched, gape-mouthed, as they came back to the cliff face and, instead of stopping, the giant simply bounded down the thirty-foot drop. He landed with a jarring *thud* and placed them both upright upon a tall rock that jutted along the tideline, slippery with water and sea slime.

The two giants leaned over Kieran and Fergus, so close they could see each enormous pore of their faces.

"What a truly wonderful world we live in, Nephew," the hairy giant said. "Look at how tiny and minuscule such marvels of creation are. See their arms, their legs—" The giant lifted a massive finger and started running it up and down Kieran's side. Kieran clung to his younger brother for stability.

"And look here," said the giant, hooking his fingernail under Kieran's arm, forcing him to splay it out. "Little tiny hands with fingers."

"Kieran," whispered Fergus. "What are we going to do?"

"I don't know. Wait for a chance when they're not looking, maybe."

"How remarkable!" the younger giant said. "But how loose their skin looks."

"Yes, but see the colours and patterns. It is how they attract their mates, you see. Nature gives them such skin to compensate for their small stature, crude behaviour, and puny strength."

"Where do they come from, Nuncle? I've always believed such stories of the little people to be fantastical imaginings."

"Yes, it has been many a hundred year since I have even heard report of one. Perhaps the barrier between their world and ours is weakening."

"Pish, Nuncle! You do not believe in such superstitions, surely."

"You are young, Humphreybodie, and live in a doubtful age. Even when the evidence for such wonderment is before you, yet you doubt."

"Oh, laws, Nuncle. You nearly had me there," the nephew said, chuckling. He punched the other giant on the arm. "But don't they look funny. They're standing on their hind legs, just like they was trying to be like us. I could almost imagine they were as smart as we. I might keep one of them, as a pet."

"We're no pets! We're people!" Fergus yelled at the top of his lungs.

"Lor lumme, Nuncle," said the one with the beard in a big, booming voice. "I fancy I saw that one speak."

"Nooooo . . ." said the uncle in a considered voice. "It's a trick of the wind. I've seen it before. It passes over their ears, which are hollow all the way through, and—"

"We *can* speak!" Fergus shrilled. Kieran remained frozen, still too scared to make a sound.

"I know what I heard, Nuncle," the nephew said, frowning. "You can't now tell me that I didn't hear what I heard. Doubtful age, indeed!"

Fergus looked up at his brother. *Your turn*, he nodded.

"Who are you?" Kieran shouted. "What are your names?"

"Don't tell it," the uncle snapped.

"Oho! Then you heard them too?" said the nephew.

"Don't get too close. They'll enchant you!"

"My name is Humphreybodie," the bearded giant said in a slow, explanatory voice. "*Humph*-rey-bodie. This is my uncle." He placed a hand on the moustached giant who didn't really look much older than the other. "His name is Osgoddodius. *Osgod-dodius.* Have you got names?"

"Don't be silly, of course they haven't."

"I'm Fergus, and this is my brother, Kieran."

"I'll be blown over," the uncle said in a murmur like a foghorn. "What strange things to call one's self. However do they remember such short names?"

"Where did you come from?" Kieran called. "How did you get here? What are you doing?"

"Came up through the ground, of course," Humphreybodie said matter-of-factly. "Like respectable giants."

"Why?" Fergus hollered. "Can't you swim?"

"Swim?" Humphreybodie looked alarmed. "No honourable giant ever learned to swim. Not when there's jumping to be done."

"Jumping?" asked Kieran. "Why are you doing that?"

"Why," Humphreybodie replied, "we're getting ready for tonight's practise, of course."

"What are you practising?" yelled Fergus.

"Why, jumping, of course. Got to practise our jumping," Humphreybodie answered with a look across to his uncle.

"Blow me over," Osgoddodius said under his breath. "I didn't know they could talk." He clutched at his stomach. "I'll never eat another one as long as I live."

Fergus renewed his clutch on Kieran's sleeve.

"We jump at night," Humphreybodie continued. "It's good for the lungs and makes the muscles work harder. We need to be in good shape for the competitions."

Something clicked for Kieran. "Wait, is it *you* who's keeping everyone awake? Jumping at night like that?"

"Sorry, pet," Humphreybodie said, bending closer. "I didn't catch that."

"Did you know you're keeping people awake?!"

"Keeping people awake? There *are* no people on this island—only you little creatures. There used to be, but there aren't anymore. It's deserted. That's why we use it. That's why we're testing it."

"Testing it for what?" Kieran hollered, his throat getting hoarse now.

"Why, for the games, of course," said Osgoddodius.

"What games?" yelled Fergus.

"The Giant Games," Humphreybodie said expansively, throwing his arms wide apart. "It is a meeting, a coming-together-of. My uncle and I are going to compete in jumping. But first we have to see if this place is made of the right stuff for jumping. We've been here each night for the last couple months, testing out every inch of it. If we like what there is, we'll spread the word and all the giants will descend upon it and we shall compete in jumping up and falling down."

"How many are in the competition?" Kieran asked.

"Oh, hundreds," Osgoddodius answered.

In their mind's eye, Kieran and Fergus saw hundreds of enormous feet falling from the sky like a shower of meteors, pounding the ground, making craters in the streets, shaking houses to the ground. Was there any way to stop them? Could they warn people? Evacuate the island, perhaps?

"Are you any good?" Fergus shouted.

Humphreybodie drew back and puffed his chest out. "Any good? I should say we are. Did you hear that, Nuncle? 'Are we any *good*?'"

"Good? We're the best. That's why we have the job of finding the jumping grounds."

"I don't know, I saw you jumping just now, and it didn't look that far. I bet you couldn't even jump to the Calf," Fergus said, sounding disappointed.

"'Calf'?" Osgoddodius repeated. "What 'Calf'?"

"The Calf is what we call that island over there," Fergus answered, pointing out to sea, to the southwest. They had been walking from Port Erin to Cregneash, and the Calf of Man was clearly visible from where they now stood.

"That little thing? No problem."

"I bet you can't," Fergus taunted.

"'Course we can," Humphreybodie said. "A child could make that."

"A toddler," said Osgoddodius.

"Show us, then."

"Right," Humphreybodie said. He turned and stood up straight. He gazed the distance and then took two enormous steps and leapt.

They watched him rise up, up, into the air in a great arc, and then come down, down, and alight upon the island. A couple seconds later they heard the impact shock.

Osgoddodius snorted derisively. "He barely reached the place, the pillock. He's not as strong a jumper as myself, not that it needed saying."

They watched Humphreybodie, still fairly visible at this distance, take another run and leap back up in the air toward them. He hung in the sky, then grew larger and larger, and came down only a few feet from where he had jumped off from. The thundering shake nearly knocked both Fergus and Kieran off the rock they were on.

"Now," Osgoddodius said. "Watch this. No run up. Watch this."

And, sure enough, from a stationery start, Osgoddodius leapt up into the air and came down on the Calf.

"Silly old bugger," Humphreybodie said, sniffing condescendingly. "What's he trying to prove? He'll do himself an injury, at his age—pull something he'd rather not have pulled."

"You mean you can jump farther?" Fergus asked.

"'Course I can," Humphreybodie said, just before Osgoddodius came back and landed next to him, toppling Kieran and Fergus.

"What did you think of that?" the gigantic uncle asked. "Pretty keen, eh?"

"Humphreybodie didn't think so," Fergus called. Kieran didn't know what his little brother was up to, but he was obviously running the show now, and he had an intense look on his face, the kind he wore when he was thinking hard about a card or board game. "He said you were old, and he might be right. I don't think you could even make the Isle of Booty."

Kieran blinked. The Isle of Booty? That was an island they had made up when they were little and played pirates on the beach.

"'Course I can make it," Osgoddodius said, turning around and scanning the horizon. "Where is it?"

"I didn't think you could see it. Humphreybodie said your eyesight was going."

"Yeah, yer blind old duffer," Humphreybodie taunted.

"Well, where is it then, knucklehead?" Osgoddodius asked his nephew.

But Fergus answered, "It's right there, on the far side of the Calf. It's about twice the distance again."

It suddenly dawned on Kieran. "Twice? More like three times."

"Probably more," Fergus rejoined.

"Most likely more," said Kieran. "It's too far for either of you, in any case."

"Much too far," Fergus said. "Forget we said anything."

"Forget nothing!" Osgoddodius exclaimed. "I'll hop to the Calf and skip to the Booty, no problem, just you watch."

Osgoddodius dug his feet into the sand. "Right, here goes," he said under his breath and started bounding along the shore, each footfall growing farther and farther apart. He touched down once on the last tip of the Isle of Man, came down on the Calf, and crouched and sprang for the final jump. He leapt so high up in the air he became obscured by a cloud.

"You know," Fergus called to Humphreybodie, who had watched his uncle's progress with interest. "It didn't look like he was going very fast. I'll bet you could make it there before him, if you really tried."

A wide grin spread across Humphreybodie's face. "I'll just bet I could, and all! Hah! Wait 'til I see the look on his face!" And without any more hesitation than it took to say those words, he was off and running.

Fergus and Kieran watched him take the same route off the island and into the air, toward an island that only existed in their imaginations.

Fergus cleared his throat. "I hope that's the last of them," he said.

"It should be, providing they can't swim. We'll be able to tell if we start getting some good nights of sleep from now on," Kieran replied.

"That's true."

They started climbing down from the rock, carefully scaling the slippery surface. Once, they thought they heard the noise of a distant splash, and after that another. Neither brother mentioned it; they both just started laughing.

Kieran looked down at his little brother. "That was pretty clever," he said. "You're not as dumb as you look."

"I'm not as dumb as *you* look," Fergus answered—the standard retort. "I'm cold. Let's get home."

"Yep, it's late," Kieran said, turning and starting back up the ridge to the road. "We're going to be in a *lot* of trouble, you know."

"Do you think? How are we going to get down from this rock?"

II

"Yes, I'm his sister—his baby sister," Vivienne said.

"And you complain about me holding things back. I thought

that Gád would have been older—as old as Ealdstan. Mortal enemies throughout time. Something like that."

"No, he is a Simpson. His name is Alexander Douglas Simpson—
Alex was named for him. He is twelve years older than I am—and
five years older than James."

"No. No, I definitely remember Ealdstan telling us about Gád."
She pointed a finger at Modwyn. "You lot had never heard of him,
but Ealdstan said he is the oldest. The most dangerous of my foes."

"I remember," Modwyn said. "Ealdstan had his own reasons
for saying that. He must have."

"Which is another good question—where exactly is Ealdstan?"

"He left—before the invasion."

"Do you have any idea where he went?"

Modwyn shook her head sadly.

"Really? Vivienne?"

"I had hoped that we might find some clue in his journals, but
you know as well as I what we found there."

"Why don't I completely trust either one of you on that point?"
Freya asked. "But getting back to Gád . . ." She shook her head,
bewildered. "How? Why?"

"He grew up being taught the knowledge, as we all did, though
it was clear he was the most passionate of our three siblings. He
began to make excursions on his own, staying longer and longer
each time—days at first, and then weeks. He went to university
at St. Andrew's in Edinburgh. He went down to read Medicine
but began pursuing his own studies, digging deep into ancient
texts, lore, and legends. He went on many excursions, both aboveground and below. At that stage, it was hard for us to keep track of
him, being as independent as he was, but I suspect he also began
to travel to the mythic Otherworld, or Elfland, of the fairy tales.

"He did not finish his studies. His final year was incomplete.
He simply left his rooms one night of his first term and was not

seen again for twenty years. We were worried, obviously, but he left no trace or clue as to where he went. Apart from alerting the authorities to his absence, there was naught we could do.

"The next we saw of him, he appeared much older than twenty years could account for—he had white hair and a much slighter frame—and yet he also seemed more vital. His eyes twinkled, his hands were fast and nimble. In this he gave the impression that Ealdstan himself gives, albeit to a lesser extent—a less intimidating extent.

"It was myself who bumped into him in the streets of Edinburgh. There is much of the city there that is still buried, besides the Arthur's Seat tunnels, and it is my belief that he was living in one of these rabbit warrens—possibly near Candlemaker Row, beneath West Bow. That is a place with many dark secrets. I caught him by surprise and persuaded him, against his will, to take tea with me."

"What did he say—where had he been?"

"He obviously was loath to share his history with me, and yet wished to appear as though he were being completely open. He is clever, and therefore did not give much away, but he had travelled into another world, he told me, in which time passed quicker than in this. He had learned secrets forgotten to these lands, as well as magics of his own."

"Why was he doing that?" Freya asked. "What—what was he after?"

"That I did not find out. He claimed it was all his private interest."

"But . . . ?"

"But for that I *know* him. Growing up, he would do nothing without purpose. He loved games, games of all sorts, and nothing was so important to him as to win his games. I say 'his games,' since he would make up rules to games he felt were too simple. We—James and I—would not play with him if we could help it, since he was a notorious cheat. Nothing, not even his own rules, would prevent him from winning." She rubbed her forehead as if it pained her. "I paint him with a dark brush, but I love my brother—I do. But I certainly do not trust him."

"What about the yfelgópes? Where did he pick those up from?"

"I know little of them. Somehow, in a way unknown to me, he has willed them over to his cause. He has great appeal to those with unforgiving minds that are full of checks and balances. Jealous minds in which mercy and grace do not fit—worldly minds of perfect justice."

"Perfect justice doesn't sound so bad."

"It is the worst sin of this world—it does not allow for forgiveness."

"Coming back to the Carnyx—what are we going to do about that? Are we still going to go after it?"

"You would need me to find that," Modwyn said. "And I would not willingly contribute to the destruction of Niðergeard."

"Modwyn, Niðergeard was destroyed as soon as Ealdstan left. He had eight years to come back and rescue you—rescue you all. But he didn't come back—we did. We're what you've got. Where's the Carnyx?"

"Godmund took it. He is with it now. He will protect it with every muscle in his body until the moment of need."

"Modwyn, my queen," Vivienne said, "that moment is soon here. Ecgbryt and my nephew Alex are even now awakening an army of the greatest warriors this island has ever known. They are bringing them here directly, and we shall deliver this city from its invaders, track down my brother, and deliver him to justice—in whatever form that takes."

Modwyn sat silently. Frithfroth, at the door, made no sound.

"Trust us. What other choice do you have?" Freya asked. "Because right now, now that your spirit is back in your body, I think that anyone at all could walk into this tower without any trouble."

"It has been years since anyone attempted—"

"Maybe so, but Daniel just walked out there and he hasn't come back. As terrible as it is to think it, he may have been captured. If so, people will be wondering where he came from."

Modwyn looked down to the knife in Freya's hand.

"I suppose you could try stabbing yourself again, if I let you have this—or I could do it for you. It might be a little more permanent if I do, though, me being mortal—a lifiende."

"Leave me to consider," Modwyn said after a moment's thought. "I would contemplate alone for a while."

Vivienne pulled Freya to the side and whispered to her in a low, urgent voice, "We need to find the Carnyx; that is the utmost priority of our mission. Nothing else matters as much as that. If she were somehow to escape, or do away with herself completely, we could never find it."

Freya nodded and turned back to address Modwyn. "Personally, I don't trust you enough to let you out of my sight. You can think about it, but we're going to stay in this room with you while you do. Take your time, we'll be quiet."

Settling themselves on opposite sides of the room to Modwyn, the women steeled themselves for a long vigil as Modwyn settled back into her bed. Freya turned her back on the wall of lamps and folded her arms, placing her head against the wall beneath a shuttered window. Her mind was now weighing and evaluating the information she'd received. Things were getting started—they were getting closer to the Carnyx, Alex and Ecgbryt should be well on their way to gathering the rest of the knights, and Daniel? What had happened to him? When things happened, she got the feeling that they would happen quickly. She had the feeling that she would need as much rest as she could grab.

III

Dawn broke, and Night released Daniel. He laid on the ground, cold, too exhausted even to shiver. He barely breathed; only the thinnest stream of air entered his lungs through his open, gaping mouth. Dew covered his body and the grass around him. He was aware, but thoughtless, his mind brutalised by the Night. He felt as if he could move, but he had no desire. His will had been completely pulverised.

He moved his hand—more of a jerk—just an inch. It wasn't much, but it was enough to break him from his nearly catatonic state. He took a deep breath and pushed himself up—and vanished, becoming incorporeal. He was reminded once more that not all of him was in the world—that his soul, his mind, whatever part of his consciousness that made him *him* was still separate.

This again, he thought, with a sort of sigh. What had he gone through? All that pain just to—

It was that thought of *pain* and the suffering of his body that brought him back together, standing upright. He felt the leaden, painful, dreary weight of existence pulse with every beat of his heart as well as a deep weariness. He remembered the pain that had racked every cell of his body, and at last he was corporeal again.

So that's the trick, he thought as he flexed his aching hands. Meditate on the pain of existence and become more real. How miserable.

The enormous morning sun was just breaking from the horizon and throwing orange rays of light into his eyes, across his face.

"So what now?" he said out loud.

He thought of the only other people he had met in Elfland, of Kæyle's wood-burning hut in the forest, and felt himself moving. The plain flew beneath him, and then the trees, passing through him like he was nothing.

And then he was there. He focused on becoming "real" again, focused on pain, and felt his body solidify. He looked down at his clothes and noticed that he wore the blue outfit that he'd been given in Niðergeard, only scaled to his adult size.

"Kæyle?" he called.

The clearing looked a little overgrown and disused. He moved over to one of the burning pits and saw weeds poking up through the thin layer of ash and burned earth that had been left behind when the last batch of charcoal had been made, which would have been . . . weeks ago? Months?

"Daniel?"

He turned and saw Pettyl standing at the entrance to the hut. He smiled, happy to see a familiar and friendly face, but the face didn't seem happy to see him. She wore a look of what may have been sorrow, or even despair. Her cheeks were sunken and eyes ringed with dark circles.

"What are you doing here?" she asked.

"I'm not exactly sure about that, Pettyl," he said, falling back into the Elfish he had learned. "I met up with three dead elves, and then there was Night. I was running, and then there was pain . . ." Daniel trailed off. What had happened to him came in pictures that he didn't think he could describe.

"You shouldn't be here."

"Do you . . . do you think that I really am here? I'm not so sure if all of this is real, if *I'm* real. I mean, look—" Daniel allowed himself to discorporate. Pettyl seemed to experience no real surprise at this, merely staring at the place where he had been standing, in a mild stupor. Daniel thought of the space off to her side and appeared there.

"See?" he said, causing Pettyl to jump slightly. "It seems to me that I shouldn't be able to do that."

Pettyl reached out to him. Her hand rested on his chest and

pushed slightly. He felt a rush of pleasure at a physical sensation that wasn't cold or painful.

"It's really you," Pettyl said, pulling her hand away. Her face soured and she spat in his face. Daniel only barely recoiled and then felt Pettyl's hands slapping at him. "How dare you? Are you here to torment me? To punish me some more? Is that why? Is it?"

Daniel dissolved and Pettyl's hands passed through him and where he used to be. He hovered above the clearing.

"Why?" Pettyl called to the air. "We had so little! Why?" She fell to her knees and began weeping. Daniel just stayed where he was and watched. Emotions were softer and more distant in his cloud-like state. He watched Pettyl sob, finally still, and then pick herself up and move back into the hut.

Daniel concentrated on the clearing again and reappeared. He walked into the hut and saw Pettyl lying on one of the low wooden beds. There were bottles everywhere—elfish food.

"Pettyl?" he said. "I'm sorry, for . . . whatever it is I've done."

Pettyl did not move.

"What happened?"

She did not answer or move for a long time—it may have been hours. She may have been sleeping. Daniel just stood. He didn't get tired or—after the horror of Night—grow bored. He was content just to wait.

Pettyl stirred and shifted off of the bed. She went to a box that stood by the entrance into the stable. She pulled out a tall, thin blue bottle, uncorked it, and took a long drink. She gave a cough, a sort of choking cough, and then laughed a lilting schoolgirl laugh.

"Pettyl? Where's Kæyle?"

She recorked the bottle and turned to look at him, smiling and swaying. "Ha ha. Kæyle made a mistake and he paid for it."

"What kind of mistake?"

Pettyl moved across the room with the long steps of a dancer.

When she reached the centre of the room, she pirouetted and stood, her head tilted back. She swayed gently to a music that Daniel could not hear, a smile still on her face.

"He was working in the woods one day and a little bird fell down from the sky. It was lost and injured and weak." She giggled. "Kæyle picked it up and fed it, cared for it, and taught it to speak. And when it grew strong again, it took to the sky, and soaring among the treetops, the bird saw a bear and swooped down and pecked its eye out. The bear died, and that made the bear's brothers very mad. Very mad, indeed. They talked to the wolves, and the wolves came and hounded Kæyle away. That was the mistake that Kæyle made—he was kind to a little bird. He was always so kind."

"Who took him?" Daniel asked. "Pettyl, what really happened?"

"They did," Pettyl said, giving a lurch and knocking over a few bottles with her feet. She spun around and around and then fell onto her bed. "The brothers. The ones you didn't kill. They took him away—I don't know where. They thought he had knowledge of the Elves in Exile." She laughed awkwardly.

Daniel suddenly had an intuition. "What's so funny?" he asked.

Pettyl guffawed.

"They took the wrong one, didn't they?"

Pettyl became sombre suddenly.

"You know where they are—who they are. You were just coming back from them when I first arrived. You're a resistance fighter."

Pettyl frowned. "I was. I used to be. I still am, in a way. I'm a soldier, but I'm not allowed to fight. That was the plan. I joined in, Kæyle didn't, and so when they'd come, they'd take him and leave me. And now I can't go back to them. I'm watched. So I stay here now. I drink."

"Could you tell me where to find them?"

"Perhaps. I don't know where they might be for certain. But

they shouldn't be too hard to find. Just follow the war." This struck her as hilarious and she began laughing again.

"So they're fighting openly now?"

"Yes," said Pettyl, getting herself under control. "They have been for the last eight months. Perhaps they're all dead. All of them dead."

"I don't think so," Daniel said. "I think that they're still alive, and that I've been sent here for a reason. I'm certain of it. First I'm going to find them. Then I'm going to rescue Kæyle. Then I'm going to help them win this war. The Elves in Exile will return, and I will stand by the true prince as he takes his place on the throne."

Pettyl giggled.

At length, Daniel managed to get some information from Pettyl that he thought would be useful—a direction and a few landmarks. Then he set about looking for the Elves in Exile. It had been a trick to actually move around, at first. He had previously only been able to transport himself to places he'd been before simply by picturing them. How could he picture a place he'd never been?

The answer came to him when he realised that he could, naturally, picture a place that he could see, and so move that way, hopping from place to place either in his cloud form or his bodied form. It was a rather arduous and disorienting way to travel, but then he found he could fly. Fly, in a certain fashion. All he had to do was to picture himself in the sky instead of on the ground, and there he would be. In his cloud-state he could travel very swiftly across the landscape.

It was beautiful, the landscape, even from a distance. A seemingly endless tableau of hills, forests, lakes, streams, rivers, plains, mountains, and valleys. Occasionally there would be a puckered scar of a dirt road or an unsightly growth of a town. When he saw these, he would move downward to investigate—see if there was anything that would let him know that he was on the right track. Pettyl's descriptions had been vague—sometimes to the point of contradiction—but he had memorised them anyway and began his search eastward.

He didn't know how much ground he had travelled. He didn't know how fast he was going, the scale of the distances he was seeing, or even the size of the planet he was on.

At last he found the landmark he'd been looking for—a distant, pale spike on the horizon. He pictured it larger and larger and arrived at what Pettyl had called Ashkh's Spindle.

It was a tower of rock that rose almost a mile into the air. From his approach, it seemed to jut perpendicularly from the horizon, but as he came nearer, he saw that it protruded at an angle away from him, only a couple degrees, but enough to make it look horribly unstable.

Around this landmark was devastation. What had once been a lightly wooded plain—based on Pettyl's description—was now a smouldering field of cinders. Everything that could burn had been incinerated. Tree trunks still smouldered, houses lay in ruins. For perhaps a mile all around the tower the landscape was an enormous scorch mark, and at its centre the Spindle rose up and above.

With a feeling of dread, Daniel descended, wanting to take a closer look at the destruction, praying that he wasn't too late but fearing that he already was.

As he neared, he realised that his depth perception was off—here, everything seemed compacted and yet expanded at the same time. What had seemed from the sky to be nearly a mile, was mile upon mile. Perhaps as much as twenty or thirty. He finally reached ground and materialised in the centre, surrounded by sooty blackness. He could walk for a day on ash and charred wood.

It must have been a siege, he thought. The Elves in Exile, some of them at least, had been tracked here and trapped. The enemy had then razed the ground around them to prevent their escape under cover.

Daniel looked up at the finger of rock, larger than a sky-scraper, and only bearing the black patina of soot on the lower quarter of its length. The flames had not even reached halfway. Had they survived?

Was the siege still in progress?

An odd sort of pattern caught his eye. Midway between him and the start of the rock spire was a sort of cobweb construction. It took him a little while to focus, since at first he thought it was a spider's web, but it was far away, not small. He neared it.

Two large posts, several storeys in height, had been inserted, somehow, into the ground, and strung between them, in a concentric pattern, was a gruesome lattice work of elfin bodies. They were splayed, spread-eagled and tied hand to foot, where their arms and legs were still attached. Some of them were warriors, but not all of them—not most of them. There were women in hard-wearing elfin gowns and farmwives, as well as labourers, dressed much like Kæyle. With a start, he thought that one of them might be his friend, but none of the twisted faces, already starting to blacken from decay, seemed to be his. Looking across, he could see that other webs had been erected as well and looked to encircle the whole of the spire.

Looking up at the stark, grey rock form, he resolved that it was time to investigate properly now. He dissipated and started gliding upward. His mind was adjusting to the new way of travel, and he was now able to move more smoothly and not simply leap from place to place. He was glad of this on one hand, but also terrified of having this strange state seem anything like natural to him.

It was only as he neared the top that he saw how exactly any-one could stay on the rock for any amount of time. The entire top fifth was honeycombed with holes, some of which were open, some covered by glass windows or wooden shutters. The holes gave the appearance of being natural, but they seemed orderly, evenly spaced and of the same size. He circled slowly and saw movement in one of the windows. Instantly he was drawn into it.

The room was oblong, hewn from the stone but nonetheless furnished comfortably with carpeting and tapestries that blended one into the other, hung or nailed somehow against the curved walls, making it cocoon-like in its cosiness. There was a wooden table that was polished so well it reflected like a mirror. Three elves were sitting around this table, sitting upright in stone chairs, their hands resting on the table in front of them. They were pale and wasted to such an extent that Daniel could almost believe that they were shadows, apparitions. Two of them, bearded and coarse, looked despondently over the table and its many papers and maps as well as a good number of empty bottles and jars. One had hair as black as raven's feathers, and the other's was red.

The third, who seemed younger, but Daniel had found you never could tell with them, was clean shaven, or naturally hairless, and hunched forward, hands clenched together and held beneath his nose, his eyes dull in their sunken sockets.

Daniel thought they were all in a trance, hypnotised perhaps, until one of the bearded elves stood up and declared, "There's someone else here."

The other two looked up at him.

"Can't you feel it? It's in the air. Floating around us." He waved a hand vaguely, heavily.

"Your mind is fevered," the man opposite him said. "Sit back down."

"No, I . . . I could swear . . ." He lowered himself back into his chair with shaking legs. "If there be any spirit, sprite, fetch, or sending here, I demand and invoke it to show itself!" he cried, listing from side to side. "Out of common decency, if by no other power."

Daniel considered and then, holding a sort of breath that he wasn't breathing, reincorporated himself at the end of the table opposite the younger elf.

All of them sprang back in shock, even the raven-haired elf who had demanded he show himself.

"Who or what are you?" the red-haired elf gasped.

"My name is Daniel Tully. You helped me out once by sending Kay Marrey to meet me. He saved my life. I've come to return the favour."

CHAPTER ELEVEN

Daniel's Torment

———————————— I ————————————

Daniel walked around the interior of the deserted mountain outpost.

It had been an incredibly eventful and extremely long day—even by Elfland standards. Luckily, he didn't seem to get tired in this new form. He had found that the younger looking elf of the three in the Spindle had been Prince Filliu, the leader of the Elves in Exile. After proper introductions had been made between him and the two generals he was with, they showed Daniel the rest of their trapped war band, which was in as poor and anaemic state as they were, lying listlessly in side rooms and storerooms that had been converted into barracks. They were in a bad way. They had had no form of sustenance—their odd liquids they lived on in this land—for a very long time, and they were, literally, he found, fading. They didn't starve to death, it turned out, but just became thin, in an existential sense. They stopped moving, lying as still as statues until revived.

Daniel was then introduced to a group of warrior wizards, who toiled over dispelling the enchantments that the enemy had cast around them. The grotesque web of elves was one of the enemy's many sieging enchantments; if removed, it would potentially allow the war wizards opportunity to unravel the rest of the oppressive charms.

So Daniel studied magical charts and maps of the area and then did some reconnaissance. He floated down into the forests and hills that surrounded the burned-out crater that ringed the Spindle. There he spied on enemy soldiers—snipers, warlocks, and warliches—and reported back to the prince and his wizards on their positions. They then decided which webs were tactfully best to dismantle. After that, Daniel descended again and started taking one of them apart.

His actions were not unnoticed, he realised, when elfish arrows started raining down on him. His invulnerability proved itself again when he found the arrows—which were shot with stunning accuracy at the distance of over a mile—simply glancing off of him. He used their heads, which were long, thin, and made of bronze, to cut through the ropes that tied the dead elves together. Then he moved on to the other sections. As soon as he started working on the fourth—a deliberate tactical feint—the Elves in Exile made their escape.

Daniel watched them from the sky as they flooded out of the base of the tower under heavy fire. Even weak and wasted, they rallied in an impressive, united effort. The wizards created reflective planes around the tower that masked the true path of the elves' egress, so it looked like five times more than their actual number were escaping. Some were lost in the dash from the tower to the start of the forest. There was an enemy outpost there that the escaping elves quickly overran, being caught ill-prepared. Taking only a short moment to plunder the storehouse of its provisions, the elves retreated back into the forest.

They went for miles, pausing just once, in order to divide and consume the plundered drink stores and give themselves the energy they so desperately needed to continue their flight. Daniel reappeared to Filliu and the generals again at that point, and they thanked him for his help. They agreed to meet again when they were free from the wrongful princes' forces, at one of the places that they had agreed upon.

And so Daniel came here, to the complex of caves, many miles ahead of the elves and their pursuers. So far he was alone, and he had been for hours. He went to the entrance of the cave where pillars of stone created a forest-like cover. Looking out, he wondered when he would catch sight of his latest companions, and whether he could do anything to help. The dimming sky unnerved him. What would happen in the next hours? Would Night take him again? Or was that behind him?

"So, how was your day?" came a voice from behind him.

Turning, he saw the three murdered elves standing in the corridor behind him. It was Stowe who had spoken.

"Oh, you guys again," he said with dread.

"More than that, how was last night?" Fiall said with a vicious grin.

"It was fine. I survived, obviously, and now I'm helping to restore the true king of these lands to his throne." He looked at the dead prince, Lhiam-Lhiat, for a reaction, but his face showed nothing but pity. "So it hasn't slowed me down any."

"Admirable," said Stowe.

"I haven't learned anything either," Daniel said, the heat rising within him. "Whatever you were trying to teach me, it's not getting through. I still don't regret what I've done, and I still say I'd do it again."

Stowe grinned. Fiall raised an eyebrow. "You think it's a lesson? An educational exercise?"

"What else?" said Daniel.

"We don't control the Night. We experience it like you do."

"What?"

"We are tortured by it, the same as you," said Stowe.

"And we will continue to be tortured by it until it purifies us—burns us away, strips us into nothing."

"So I *am* being punished."

Lhiam-Lhiat tilted his head. "Punishment implies that you may learn from this experience—that you may be corrected by it, in an objective sense. That is not the case. You are being destroyed, piece by piece, as plain as that."

"But I see things there," Daniel said. "I have visions, there are . . . two riders . . ." His head tilted forward as he tried to remember details. The riders had appeared to him a second time; he knew it. And someone else . . . "You!" he said, pointing to Fiall.

Fiall sneered back at him. "Nobody sees in the Night," he said.

"He is not one of our kind," the prince said, studying Daniel. "It may be different for him."

"Delusions," Fiall said. "Anything you saw are delusions brought by pain and terror. Humans are intellectually weak."

"That's not the only difference between them and us." Lhiam-Lhiat's eyes studied Daniel's. "There are times when I feel as though I . . ." He looked away, to the horizon, and then back to Daniel. "If you do see anything in the dark," he said quietly, "if the dark *is* trying to teach you something—let it. I feel it also. There's a part of me that the darkness wants, that it's trying to strip away, to get at. I don't know if it wants to destroy it, or make me give it up, or if it even knows what it's doing, but if you can survive and not diminish . . . If you can find some way through—"

"You heartless sadists," Daniel spat. It was his turn to sneer now. "You *are* trying to teach me something. Well, fine. I'm up to the challenge. I'll get out of it yet."

"You have some time before Night falls. Do you really want to argue with us," Fiall asked, "or do you want to start running? You may be able to delay the torture for a time, however short."

Daniel looked at him and thought about the Night, and it did make him want to run. How much ground could he cover, and how much time could he buy in doing so? An hour? Two? Less? Days moved slower here, but then spaces seemed to be larger. Even if he could put off the Night for just a few minutes, it would be worth the effort.

Then he looked at the three dead elves before him and thought, *Why give them the satisfaction?*

"I'm not afraid of the darkness," he said, spreading his arms. "Let it take me."

The Night reached through the walls just then and grabbed him.

II

Daniel solidified inside the window of the upper tower and just stood for a moment, stiller than still, his muscles completely at his command but receiving no orders.

This second Night had been harder than the first. He didn't know if it was because he knew what to expect or if it really was more harrowing. He'd had hope that his new purpose in helping the Elves in Exile would give him something to cling to when the pain got bad—that he would feel that there was something worth going through this for—but somehow that hadn't been the case. Whereas the first night had been so vivid, he couldn't remember exactly what had happened to him in this one. He could only recall vague notions, like echoes of events, that bounced off the walls of his mind before they disappeared entirely. Had he made a deal with himself in the darkness to forget? Had he forced himself to do so in order to protect himself? Could he trust himself to remember if he needed to, or to forget if he didn't?

He had awakened again in the plain, for the third time since his very first visit, like a repeating track. He laid there, wet and chilled, but not shivering. All sensation existed only in the Night; only sense existed here in reality. At least, he was accustomed to thinking of it as reality, but that line had now become very blurred. Here in reality all he had was an impervious body that felt no pain or softness. Or, if he chose, then a disembodied cloud of perception. Which was the nightmare? The reality where all was pain, or the reality where all was numb? And which was truly which, for there was numbness in the pain and pain in the numbness.

Then, with a physical start, he shook himself out of his reverie and started looking for Prince Filliu and the rest of the Elves in Exile. He found them, not at the mountain camp, but at the Fortress of the Plain, which was a series of ingenious trenches and sunken rooms in the middle of a wide expanse of flat land that left the horizon unbroken and invisible to anyone who didn't know it was there.

Daniel tried to get his head around warfare with wizards involved. That skewed things slightly. He didn't know what the enemy's magic capability was, but it would undoubtedly involve some sort of farseeing, or foreseeing. Which wasn't, Daniel reflected, so much different to the modern warfare that he had been trained in during his very brief military career, what with satellite telemetry and communication, infrared, hi-res, night-time imaging, and smart-guided weaponry. That was a kind of magic as well, no doubt, from the point of view of the elves who were a race that was highly advanced but circumspect about even very basic technologies that involved metal. To them, bullets were "magic pellets." Their science had obviously developed along different lines, due to metal's natural toxicity to them.

Daniel paused at that thought. He was thinking in his normal way again, strategically, but something had happened to him in the Night that was brutal and horrible, and it had lasted for what seemed like years. What was it?

He searched through the trenches and bunkers, floating invisibly, until he found the true prince, Filliu. He was deep in the heart of the complex in a low-ceilinged rectangular hole that served as his campaign room and sleeping quarters. The two generals were there, looking stern and grave.

They looked up as he appeared next to them.

"Where did you go? You did not turn up at our agreed-upon rendezvous."

"I . . . was . . . taken." Daniel found it hard to form sentences.

"'Taken'? Captured?"

"Yes, in a way. I was taken by the Night," Daniel answered.

The three elves exchanged glances. "What is 'The Night'?" Filliu asked.

"You don't know? Lhiam-Lhiat and Agrid Fiall seemed to know about it. Stowe also."

The looks became more severe. "You saw or spoke to Lhiam-Lhiat and Fiall? Usurpers of the throne and enemies of the true prince?"

"Well, in as much as I killed them and they're haunting me now, yes, I did."

"Did you tell them of our movements?" the general with the shaggy red hair, whose name was Loshtagh, asked.

"No, of course not. There wasn't time to do that, even if I wanted to." Daniel's words came like he was talking in a dream— virtually beyond his will. His mind was just reacting, but he couldn't determine how. He felt thin and slightly eaten away.

Filliu sat in a campaign chair before the wide table in the centre of the room. "Daniel, when first you arrived in this land nearly a year ago, we sent an emissary to meet you and help you through this land, with as much aid as we were able to produce at the time."

"Kay Marrey, yes, I know. And I've thanked you for that."

"I did so under the advice of my holiest of counsellors, and against the advice of my canniest generals—these men you see before you. I still have faith that you will help us, but know that you have now acted counter to every omen of divination that my holy men laid before me."

"What do you mean?"

"I mean that your leaving and returning were predicted, but not the violence by which you left, nor the speed and condition of your return. It has caused a few of my holy men to question if the prophecies even applied to you, and not another."

"Nothing is ever ideal," Daniel said. "Everything is imperfect and we have to do the best with what we've got."

"That is also what I believe," the prince answered, "to an extent."

"It is not what I believe," Loshtagh said. "I believe that whatever is inside your contaminated soul may infect us and pervert the growth of our pure enterprise."

Something in what the argumentative general said triggered something else in Daniel's memory of what he had experienced in the Night. Perverted growth—contaminated soul—pure enterprise . . .

Daniel came out of his reverie to see the three elves studying him, as if to diagnose his condition, and Daniel became annoyed.

"I intend to help you whether you want me to or not. It's nice that you can be so picky over where you get your help from. I don't usually have that luxury. I don't have it right now. Unless

I go to one of the other 'evil princes' and ask for their help. Why should it make a difference to me? Perhaps they can even help me get back home."

"It's that sort of comment that makes me question your motives and loyalty toward our cause," said Loshtagh.

"And *that* sort of comment makes me question *yours*," Daniel said. "After just one night away from you. What does it matter to you what happens to me at night, so long as—"

"You weren't gone just one night, Daniel," Filliu said.

Daniel froze. "How long was I gone?"

"Three days—four nights in total."

Daniel considered. "I . . . don't know about that. But, listen: something happens to me at night." He then recounted to the three as much as he could remember of what he experienced in the Night, which was almost all of what had happened to him during the first.

Loshtagh's scowl had deepened during Daniel's narrative. "It is a bad business. I do not know what it all means, or the nature of the devils that torment you, but it is a bad business. A bad business."

But at length Filliu allowed him another mission, and this was one that Daniel felt particularly passionate about—tracking down Kay Marrey and Kæyle the woodburner.

And so here he was, standing in an empty room in the uppermost tower. He had followed the directions they gave him, following a certain river toward its source, which was not as easy as it sounded. There were about forty different confluences and branches of the river, and he'd had to memorise the order of which to follow and which to disregard. He soared above the water, watching how the sun sparkled on the clear surface, making it glisten like a path of diamonds, but although he recognised the beauty of the sight, he did not delight in it.

The riverbanks grew steeper and steeper, rising toward him until, after the miles and miles that he travelled, they became sheer cliff faces, laced together every so often by bridges of splendid and ornate designs. Roads now ran along the edge of the cliffs, and houses started to become more frequent. There were only a few branching tributaries, but they were very small, and anyway, Daniel was at the end of the sequence. He was nearly at his destination.

A mountain of black stone rose up before him, from which poured a waterfall, and before that was an enormous palace, more of a city, really, since it was a cluster of buildings all squeezed together and built on top of each other, but they were built across the chasm between the cliffs and before the waterfall. It hung in an arcing and domed magnificence, sparkling and cool in the spray thrown off by the waterfall. Daniel had just hovered for a time, taking the inconceivable structure in. This, apparently, was the Falling Palace.

Studying it more closely, he knew it was practically deserted. Some of the walls and façades showed signs of disrepair, and green slimy growth was coating some of the areas that were in contact with water the most.

And so he had found the highest crested tower, which seemed a good place to start his search. All the fairy tales had prisoners locked in high towers, and he was in Færieland, after all. But materialising inside, he discovered it was mostly empty—a disused bedroom where an elfish bed, a desk and chair, and some fine drapery were quietly mouldering in the damp. He didn't have any time to stand around and reflect on the meaning of this, or the purpose of the room, and so crossed to the door. He gave the handle a turn and found it locked. There was a keyhole, and he bent down to squint through it. He could just make out a small section of white on the other side. Fixing himself on this, he let himself drift through the keyhole and into the stairwell outside.

A handy trick, he decided, and walked down the stairs, thinking it would be easier to be more systematic if he were solid, and feeling that being bodiless probably wasn't so healthy for him mentally. He was starting to feel extremely . . . abstract.

He wandered down the tower and checked in at the rooms that he passed and found them all locked and abandoned. At the base of the staircase was an ornate bronze gate that had weathered to a pale green. He slipped through this and into an open courtyard. It seemed deserted, but there were too many dark windows and archways to be certain. He went into the cloud and drifted through it.

As he passed, he noticed a metal grate in the panelled courtyard beneath him. He took a moment to examine it and the darkness within.

A drain? Into some sort of sewer system? How complex would a sewer for a city on a bridge possibly be?

He lowered his disembodied self to inspect it further and found almost exactly what he had come to find. If the wooden stocks and bronze manacles were anything to go by, he was in a dungeon. His main worry, however, was that it, like the city, seemed deserted. If this was a dead end, then he didn't know what he was going to do.

He materialised and walked around the room. He grew uncertain as he studied the stalls and restraints, wondering if this was indeed a jail, or just a stable, but then he found a large, wooden door on the far end of the hall that had a wide metal grill in it. There was a glowing light issuing from it and he slowly approached it. He got a sense of foreboding from the door; he didn't know why.

A door opened and closed behind Daniel and he evaporated. It was an elf of apparently high rank, dressed in detailed finery, flanked by two bodyguards and led by an aide that held an ornate silver lantern that burned with a pale light. Daniel watched them as they approached the door he stood beside. The aide pounded a rhythm on the door and it wasn't long before it opened.

Daniel glided in with the rest of them and nearly lost control of himself at what he saw.

It was a broad room with a high ceiling that was like some sort of hellish chemist's. The walls were lined with shelves and cabinets upon which sat large bottles and jars filled with coloured liquids. The ceiling was decked with bundles of branches and sprigs of plants, and there was one wide wooden table in the centre of the room, and others spaced here and there where needed.

The tables at the right end of the hall were completely caked in blood, which had soaked into the wooden tops and burnished it a dark, red-tinted brown. Empty jars were stacked in the cabinets at this end, as well as large bottles of what smelled like preservative.

Looking at the bottles on the shelves, it was clear what was happening here. There were heads in jars on the middle two shelves that ran across the room. Below those were hands, and then feet on the bottom. Above the heads were different organs in smaller bottles.

All of them were neatly labelled and tidily stored. A small and bent sort of elfish apothecary puttered around at the wide wooden table before him, chopping some pale leaves with a copper knife. He raised his head at those who entered.

"My lord and prince," he crooned, "Kione Traast, what an honour! Have you brought me anything new?"

Daniel noted the name—Kione Traast was one of Lhiam-Lhiat's brothers.

"No, I haven't," the well-dressed elf replied. "I've come for information."

"Ah, of course. I trust the campaign is going well?"

"It is going perfectly," said the elf with a prickly measure of annoyance. "But would go smoother with more details on the inner workings of our enemies."

"Of course, of course. Forgive my question, I did not mean it as a comment," the wizened elf said nervously as he swept what he was working on to one side and pulled up a large book with thick sheets of vellum from beneath the counter. "Who is it you are interested in seeing?"

"Are the woodburner and the rider ready yet?"

The old elf ran his finger down the page. "Woodburner and rider . . . yes, here they are. And yes, I think—yes, they should be ready. I'll retrieve them, one moment."

The elf prince stood imperiously as the little elf picked up a ladder made from willow wood and propped it up against the shelves behind him. Very carefully, he pulled forward two of the jars with heads in them, which were sitting side by side. Cradling each in a separate arm, he skilfully descended the ladder without the use of his hands and placed the jars before the prince.

Steeling himself, Daniel moved closer to study the faces of the preserved heads. He recognised them instantly, despite their features being warped and a little bloated, and felt sick to his feet—or what would be his feet. In fact, there was a moment of confusion where he felt that he would rematerialise just in order to be sick, or else drift away back to somewhere else entirely, but he looked away, regained focus, and remained as he was.

The heads were those of Kæyle and Kay Marrey. They had been captured and taken here, possibly tortured, certainly killed, and then chopped up and stuck into jars and pickled like onions. There was no saving either one of them now; there was no putting things right for Pettyl. For the two who had helped him the most when he first came to this world, the game was finished. And he, Daniel, could now only stare in horror at their dissected remains.

"They are among the newest additions, the coal-maker especially, but both should have reached potency. This one"—he placed a hand on Kay Marrey's jar—"should be optimal. The other will still affect, but he is much more recent, and so I cannot guarantee total clarity, but certain impressions will be very clear."

He twisted the cork tops off of the jars and reached underneath the counter to produced two shallow silver dipping cups.

"I'm sure that whatever you see and experience is not for my ears—security of the state and all that—so I will now withdraw. There are quill and parchment behind you if your aide wishes to take notes. I recommend that he does, for the impressions that you will receive, although true, are also subjective, and nuances will pass from you in time."

The elf left and, although he did not want to, Daniel watched in dread as the prince stepped forward and picked up one of the scoops. He dipped it in Kay Marrey's jar—Daniel could see now that Kay had many scratches on his face that opened to reveal the grey, bloodless flesh below—and then raised the cup to his lips and drank it back in one gulp, apparently not queasy or phased by the idea at all.

He took a step back and his eyes rolled back in his head. "I see Mayine's Mountain, I am standing on the north side, about two-thirds of the distance up. There is a cliff face in front of me, and what appears to be a sheer surface, but which I know to be a well-disguised entrance with many overlapping pillars—so many that I must dismount and lead my beast through them by his snout.

"I'm going to report back to the prince, the true heir to the throne—no, it is not he, it is I, I am the true ruler—" The prince seemed to struggle internally and frowned, distaste twisting his face. He was obviously channelling Kay Marrey, Daniel realised, and the way his eyes flicked upward and darted back and forth, it seemed he was seeing what Kay had seen, but the shared consciousness was obviously experiencing conflict at the concept of rightful rule.

"Sire," said his aide, moving away from the desk and placing a hand on the other's arm. "These are the shadows and projections of a traitorous mind—distasteful though they may be, allow them to pass through you."

Prince Kione Traast grunted, though remained in his dream-like state. "I see him before me now, the snivelling bastard orphan. He greets me with sickening propriety. What a ponce, surrounded in wild squalor that he believes makes him noble and righteous. The living martyr, the unjust—"

"Sire, please."

"There is a table before him, and upon it are splayed documents, designs, and diagrams. There is a map. It shows the places of those still traitorously loyal to the true crown of the rebel crown."

"Reproduce the map, sire," the aide said, pushing a quill into his hand and laying a blank sheet of parchment in front of the prince.

His eyes still staring sightlessly upward, the prince began to scribble and draw a remarkably well-detailed map of what Daniel presumed was that area of Elfland. The mountain was in the centre, and as Kione Traast continued drawing, Daniel could see the plain that he seemed to keep waking up in the middle of, and the outline of the forest that Kæyle and Pettyl lived in, and then the settlements that lay beyond that where the Fayre had been held, as long as many other details of the country. He watched as the prince completed the map and then marked the map with names and descriptors of those who were loyal to the Elves in Exile. The aide and guards stood and watched him patiently as the quill scratched upon the surface of the vellum for a good ten or fifteen minutes.

Then his hand slowed and he took a step back.

"My prince?" the aide asked. "The vision is fading. Would you like another draught?" He gestured to the jar with Marrey's head in it.

The prince shook his head. He went over to the counter and

leaned against it. One of the guards brought him a stool. "What is it?" the prince asked, lowering himself. "What did I speak? What did I see?"

The aide spread the dictation he took and the map that Kione Traast had drawn in front of him. The prince studied them for a moment and then brushed them aside.

"Useless. We raided the mountain fortress weeks ago and captured this document, along with the others."

The aide pursed his lips. "Well, we suspected as much. Here, try the other," he said, holding the other silver scoop out.

The prince made a face as if it were his mother telling him to finish his strained prunes, but nonetheless grabbed the cup and dipped it into Kæyle's jar. He took a sip and finished it off, then he just sat, staring at nothing, for about twenty minutes.

"Nothing," he said eventually, shaking his head. "It was just music. Wordless, pointless music. Come, let us waste no more time here."

He rose and swept out of the room, his entourage in his wake.

The door slammed and Daniel stayed, gazing morosely at the jars containing the heads of two men that he had considered friends in this strange world. There would be no rescue or escape for them.

III

Daniel awoke. Although heavily traumatised and confused, he knew exactly where he was—back in the middle of the massive plain again. Memory of the events in the Night were already scurrying away from him, leaving only scars behind them. He prodded gently at them to see if they gave anything up, but once again it was only just impressions—nothing like the violent clarity of the first time. The echo of pain and flashes of odd images, conversations, and confrontations. Then the impressions of what had remained finally dissolved away.

He wondered how long he'd been in the Night, and what was happening here now. The events of what happened before the Night seemed like a long, long way away now, as an old man might remember a distant childhood. The vivid emotion was still real, but detached.

What was going on in Niðergeard?

Niðergeard—that brought something back. He had seen the golden and silver riders again, he remembered. He thought that he always saw them at the end of his times in the Night. He couldn't remember if that was the case, but somehow that fact felt right. He feared the silver rider and knew, inherently, that it was vital that he escape him and his "dreams of death." But the silver rider was more than just death—it was pain, fear, and all the bad things of life. The golden rider was hope, security, romance, all the things worth saving. He had to keep hold of that. He remembered the picture he'd received during his first Night—him, sitting on a throne of victory, his enemies' bones at his feet. Freya by his side, a new rule of the nation of Niðergeard—part of a New United Kingdom of the Spirit. That was clear. That was the reality he needed to strive for, to produce through his will, if such a thing were possible. He would be the king of a new country, just as Wales and Scotland were a part of Great Britain, but one that the world had never seen, unless the stories of King Arthur and the holy kings of legend were true.

At least, that had been one of the visions. But he also knew that although they had all been visions of victory and triumph, not all of them were good. And then, perhaps, not every victory was perfect. Life was complicated, and it seemed to Daniel likely that these visions would help him to make sense of his own future. He was closer to a spiritual plane here, and if a revelation were to be had, then he would find it and bring it back, somehow, to his own world.

But what would the cost be? The Night was brutal and horrific, quite literally a hell. And the things that worried him most—beyond the pain, or its inevitability if he continued to stay in this world—was that he nearly always forgot what he experienced, and every time he came back, less of him seemed to make it. His confidence and righteousness had been eaten away to the point that he was now questioning if he could indeed accomplish anything of worth here in Elfland, or back at home, for that matter. His surety of purpose was faltering.

He sat for another few hours, trying to puzzle out all the logic and fuzzy philosophy of his situation. Then he rose and almost automatically began searching for the Elves in Exile again. If helping them win this battle was part of his penance, then he should get on with it. The problem was that he had no assurance at all that this was a penance, or that there were lessons to be learned.

After a long time of searching, he saw a smudge on the horizon in the southeast that he took to be smoke, and he navigated himself toward that. Whatever it was, he was certain that it was something to do with the war, or would give information that would lead him to it. With such a focal point, he made much quicker progress and had the scene in view in what seemed like less than a minute.

It was a battlefield, but one that had already been spent. The "field" itself was actually several fields spread between two forests—it was apparently part of an elfish farm, entirely open except for low walls, ditches, ridges, and hedges demarcating one cropland from another. The fight had ranged over at least a dozen of these spaces. Daniel had no experience in evaluating or judging what had occurred here, but the battle looked hard fought. Bodies of elfish warriors were spread all over, sometimes clustering here, sometimes there. There were also horses, so many horses, laying everywhere, dead and dying. Many more were tethered to the walls that ran along the side of the fields where a dirt road meandered. The two fighting sides must have been entirely mounted.

Warriors in what looked to be blue enamelled armour trimmed with black were walking over the field, dragging the wounded—indiscriminate of side, it seemed—off the field and into a circle of elfish healers. These were the victors, apparently, and Daniel wondered who they represented.

The smoke he had spotted came from a patch of grassland at the far end of the field of conflict, which was near a copse of tall, birch-like trees. Here some tents and furniture were smouldering, and the figures in blue were trying desperately to put it out. The tent had been collapsed and the canvas pulled away from what was underneath it, which was papers, journals, and silken cloths. These were spread out and stamped on with a mindful precision in order to extinguish their smoking edges. There was a man shouting orders to these soldiers, and Daniel drifted lower to hear what was being said.

"Faster, you lugheads! Put those papers out! Quickly and well! No, not like that, like *this*! They'll smoulder into oblivion unless you do it properly. Don't you know that destruction of vital knowledge of the enemy is treason? Your lives depend on this act, so let's pretend we all actually care about your miserable existences and step keenly!"

So, the actions weren't so noble, as Daniel first thought, as to extinguish a fire so close to a wooded area. Daniel drifted upward and spotted a cluster of elves wearing more than the usual amount of armour and ornamentation. These must be the captains and generals. He went toward them. One of them was Prince Kione Traast from the necrologist's halls.

"Hurry them up," he was saying, annoyed, to a cluster of clerical-looking elves. "The ground is starting to eat the blood and you know how they'll only complain when they see that our wounded are being moved."

"It does no good to rush them, my prince," said one unflappable-looking elf. "Battlescrying is an ancient art and one that demands much anticipation."

"Well, then it's their own cursed fault if things move. I don't want to hear any excuses or blame from them."

A young messenger came running from the field behind the prince. "They are ready, my prince."

Behind him, from the woods, strode four elderly elves in red robes and each one was wearing thin, bone-like stilts that allowed them to tower above all others on the battlefield. They also carried long, black poles that could reach down to the ground. They stood roughly two storeys above anyone else around.

"Clear the field!" shouted one of the prince's captains. "All of you that can move, clear the field for the battlescryers!"

The soldiers did so, rushing to the edges of the open areas as the four stilted elves stalked into the fields. Their manner was easy and adept and rather eerie as complete silence and attention was given to their activities.

Their increased foot spans gave them surprising speed across the plains, and they used their black poles to move certain objects that they deemed to be in the way. Occasionally they would place their walking sticks in the ground behind them and sit on them in a tripod fashion as they made notes and created diagrams on square books that they carried in a satchel at their waists. They seemed particularly interested in how the bodies had fallen, and how they were clustered, and what relation the fallen apparently had with each other. Daniel could hear them murmuring across to one another.

"There are three brothers, here, there, and there—do you see? Each bears an emblem on his shield with a purple, eight-pointed star. Can another be found?"

"I have one here, a youth of perhaps eighty," came a reply in a low, sullen voice.

"He would be the youngest, then. How is he oriented?"

"Feet to the sun, head to the wind, hands to his heels."

This made all of them pause to record this information, and then they began circling the scene again. Another brother was found and they all halted and recorded this discovery with much muted excitement.

Their work apparently finished, they strode back across the plain and alighted with surprised dexterity from their stilts and stood a little apart from the prince and his entourage and conferred awhile, comparing notes.

"Most august and glorified ruler of elf," said the foremost. "We have finished our divinations."

"And?"

The battle diviner straightened himself and reported in an authoritative voice:

One body dead with no cut or break in the skin—a high fort
*   will shoot thrice time ten.*
Two carrion birds upon a hand—a captain wounded.
Four fallen from the east—fair weather at the next
*   engagement.*
Eight headless helmets—lost wealth on a rainy morning.
Nine white worms around a boot—horse sickness for three
*   days.*
Overlapping wrists: thirteen—the number of days to
*   travel.*
Fifteen flies on one breastplate—fortune for felons.

Thirty-nine broken shields—ships will stay at sea.

*Eleven gauntlets lost, eleven buckles loosed, eleven heels
covered—store half your provisions.*
Eight by nine the field of Elven slain—shelter under the canopy.
Forty-three within the centre—welcome the first blow.
*Twenty-three giving northward supplication—a spy in the
fifth ring.*
Nine enemies on the fifth level—ride to the South.

*These numbers: one, two, four, eight, nine, thirteen,
fifteen, thirty-nine . . . acquisition, forceful reciprocity,
remuneration, fortunate remembrance, a diverse mind, a
quick eye.*
*These numbers: thirty-three, seventy-two, forty-three,
twenty-three, forty-five . . . changeable fortunes, the stars
hidden, a mask unused.*

Five brothers—the end of conflict in three weeks.
*Four of the brothers with three wounds—finality on the
midday.*
Three brothers to the west—the location of the next field.
Two brothers supplicant—victory at a great cost.
One brother outside of the square—a claimant abandoned.

The priest-like elf stopped his recitation.

"That's all well and good," the prince said, squeezing the
bridge of his nose between his thumb and ring finger. "But where
does that leave me?"

"An end of the campaign in twenty-two days, an unexpected
boon in ten. A fortunate departure by the end of the day."

The prince grunted and dismissed the warpriests. "Keep up

pursuit with our runners. Report back to me when they've caught track of the leaders. Where's the human? I would speak with him."

The aide made a face. "He would be with the rest of the train—back along the road. The warriors do not like him. They believe such a thing brings bad luck. He is too interested in the prisoners, they feel."

"He is a valuable oracle, and I would hear his counsel."

"Yes, my prince."

Kione Traast surveyed the landscape. "Unless they flee to the lake, which I doubt, then they will be doubling back. It would be better for us to rejoin the train. Give the orders to return. And next time bring the man with the entourage."

"Very well, my lord. It will be done."

Daniel rose up and now faced a decision. He was intrigued by this talk of a human, but it may be better if he meet up with the elves escaping from the battlefield and aid them in their flight.

But there was also talk of prisoners, and he wondered who they might be—it could be anyone, since he hadn't determined how long the Night had kept him this time. It could be either of the generals, one of the wizards, or the prince himself. And then he might glimpse the human too . . .

Daniel decided to look into it. He could easily be there in a matter of minutes, and if he saw nothing, then he would quickly be on his way to Prince Filliu.

He started swiftly along the paved road and before too long the elfish war host's encampment could be seen on the road ahead. Daniel slowed, not because he was cautious anymore, but because he needed to take it in.

It looked much like the Fayre he had visited on his first trip to Elfland, but populated by a very different looking type of elf. Where the Fayre had attracted colourful and pageant-like elves, this one was full of warriors in sparkling gear and weaponry, and their attendants who dressed and behaved more utilitarian. Inspecting the tents and the elves passing in and around them, he found butchers and bakers bustling around baking pits, herders tending to strange livestock that looked like massive, ornately horned oxen, drink-makers pulping and distilling fruits that had been harvested from the nearby wilderness. There were smiths working industriously at repairing sword blades, shields, and odd pieces of armour. Fletchers were creating arrows and unstringing and steaming bows, and there were any number of elves doing a dozen other tasks.

But where would he find this "human," who was trusted by the prince, but not by anyone else?

From helping the Elves in Exile, he had a passing familiarity with how they organised up their military camps. He quickly located the prince's tent, which was a deep blue trimmed by dark purple banners and pennants. Because he couldn't see into it, he had to materialise at the entrance and push his way through.

"Hello?" a voice called out in Elvish.

Daniel instantly dissolved into the air.

The tent was just a single, large space, not separated into different rooms by fine cloths and carpets as they usually were. Lush rugs were strewn across the ground and a black polished wood table the size of a merry-go-round dominated the centre of the area.

There were small booths around the edge of the tent that contained beds, wardrobes, maps, scrolls, and books. It was from one of these that a white-haired man—and he did seem to be a man, not as tall or angular as the elves—popped his head out and peered at the tent entrance.

It was Ealdstan.

"Hello?" he asked again. "Is anyone there?"

Daniel was so surprised that he did nothing and the wizard

turned back to his booth where a large scroll of parchment had been unrolled. Daniel came nearer to Ealdstan as he saw he was copying it into a large notebook with a gel pen, both of which Daniel recognised as being from his own world and incongruous not just in this world but also in Ealdstan's hand. The image that was being copied was a complex series of interlinking rings that Daniel recognised as being very similar to the map of the spheres that Reizger Lokkich had once consulted.

"So inaccurate . . ." Ealdstan lamented under his breath, and then he turned around again. "Truly now, who is there?" he asked. "Show yourself," he commanded weakly, sounding thin of breath and disturbed.

Daniel waited. He couldn't really sense him, could he?

The wizard spoke a few words that he didn't understand in either English or Elvish and waved his hand.

Daniel felt a heaviness build inside of him, like he was made of lead weights, and suddenly he found himself standing before the elderly man, re-corporated against his will.

"Hello, Ealdstan. What are you doing here?"

"What am *I* . . . ? Who are you?"

"Don't you recognise me? It's Daniel—Daniel Tully. I killed Gád for you. Well . . . tried to."

"You mean . . . you . . . ? What are you doing here?" The old wizard seemed really rattled.

"I asked you first. Why aren't you in Niðergeard? Don't you know it's been overrun?" Daniel asked. He tried to dissipate but found himself unable to; it was like he was being bound together by thousands of rubber bands. It was uncomfortable, and he started to become nervous in case any of the elves outside should come in and see him. "Why are you here and not there?"

Ealdstan recoiled from the questions, moving a step backward and drawing into himself. He pulled at his beard. "I am concerned with matters greater than those of my own little fortress. But what news have you of Niðergeard? You have been there recently?"

"It's been completely invaded—overrun. Knights and the people who live there have been killed or chased away. We don't know where Godmund or Modwyn are—Kelm is its ruler now."

Ealdstan just nodded.

"You don't seem particularly surprised."

"It is unfortunate. But as I said—greater matters."

"What greater matters are those?" Daniel asked. "Can I help?"

"Perhaps, yes, I think you may. At the moment, I'm trying to find my way back to our world, but I'm having difficulty finding exactly where the gate is."

"'Gate'?"

"It's a place of confluence, of origination; a gate between the worlds."

"Could it be anything?" Daniel asked, starting to get a feeling. "Could it be just, like, in the middle of a field?"

"It could very well be that," Ealdstan said. "Indeed, that would make much sense of what is here before me." He gestured to the diagrams. "You must already have the place in mind?"

Daniel told him about the field he kept waking up in. "It's the spot I first came to this land, about a month ago in our world's time. And then I got pulled back there this time, without my body. It's where I keep waking up in again. That sounds like the thing you're looking for, I think."

"It very much does," said Ealdstan. "It sounds like the exact thing. That might be the way for both of us to return back to our world—it keeps trying to draw you back, even though you are trapped here. Your soul is like a twig in a stream—trying to continue through, but caught up on something that is keeping you here. If we make it there, then I am certain I can help you. Can you take me there?"

"Yes. It's pretty far away though."

"You will find me a tireless traveller."

"So do you think you could undo whatever it is you did? I'd like to be able to go invisible again."

"Of course." He murmured the unknown words again, and Daniel felt the bands around him loosen and then fall away completely.

"Thank you," Daniel said.

"I shall be ready in just a moment . . ." Ealdstan started to hastily roll up the scroll and close his notebook.

"Shall I meet you somewhere? I don't think I should be seen here."

"No. No, you shouldn't. Um . . . I think there is a copse south of here, next to a river . . ."

"Just start walking south," Daniel said. "I'll meet you somewhere along the way."

"Yes, yes. Of course."

Daniel dissolved into the air and left the tent. He found his bearings and started heading south.

CHAPTER TWELVE

The Warchief's Lament

---------------------------------- I ----------------------------------

"I have decided. I shall lead you to where the Carnyx is."

Freya shook her head, wondering if she'd heard her right. Modwyn was sitting up on the edge of the bed. She looked at Vivienne, standing in the corner.

"Where is it? Is it far?"

"No, it is very close. We were cunning in our action. We knew that the enemy would go to the ends of the earth to find it and so we kept it here."

"Okay . . ." Freya said. "Really? So where is it?"

"It is in the Beacon," Modwyn said. "The great building that once illumined all the land. It fell when the yfelgópes besieged our walls, but there is a hidden passage."

"But this place was so secure—you killed anyone who came into it—why not just keep it here?"

"We feared that the enemy would make a grand assault here,

and so it would be safest where it was thought less secure—like keeping your coin underneath a chest instead of locked inside it."

Freya frowned. That only half made sense. "But in eight years, have Gád or Kelm made any serious attempts to get into the Langtorr?"

"They have not."

"And don't you find that suspicious?"

"They wish only destruction and ruin—they have that. Chaos is both method and aim. To have one is to have both."

"So they just sat around here, happy not to finish the job?"

"I do not pretend to understand the wishes of a dark-hearted people."

"Freya, although I hesitate to say 'it couldn't hurt,' I believe it prudent to follow up on this," Vivienne said.

"Yes, you're right," said Freya. Was Vivienne deferring to her, or is that just how she wanted to make it seem? "Let's go after Godmund and the Carnyx."

They filed out of the room and began down the stairway. Frithfroth, as usual, walked before them, escorting the three women.

"Why hasn't Godmund used the Carnyx?" Vivienne asked.

"It is not the hour of direst need. Only when this island's enemies surround us shall the horn be blown. Then shall we rise and chase them all into the sea."

"But the inscription on the horn reads 'the next army,'" Vivienne persisted. "Doesn't that mean something different from the army already asleep?"

Modwyn paused. "Why do you ask?"

"I am just trying to understand exactly. The reason we sent Ecgbryt and Alex all over the country to raise these knights is that we were uncertain exactly what the horn would do, if it could even be found. What would happen if we blow it and the knights are already awake?"

"I do not know. The horn is more than just enchanted. It uses a powerful magic—it will summon what help it can, and the help will come quickly, when it comes."

"Vivienne," Freya said. "What do you think the horn does?"

"I have theories, but I don't think anyone really has the slightest idea of what will happen when the Carnyx is blown. It never has been before, and I doubt that it came with instructions. There are no legends for the Carnyx itself, but when legends do speak of such things, they talk of awakening ancient heroes, but also of summoning heroes from other worlds—or of angels."

"Angels? Seriously?"

"Let me put a question to the two of you," Modwyn said. "What do you *wish* to happen when you blow the horn?"

Freya sighed. "Honestly, Modwyn—I don't understand *any* of this. I just want it to end. And once it has ended, I want to start my life over again. Move somewhere different, meet new people, work in a completely boring job, and come back home and do nothing. And I want to do that same boring routine over and over again, until all of this . . ." She shook her head. "Fades like a bad dream.

"My life has been a literal hell for the past eight years and I believe that I'm fortunate enough to be in a position to rid the entire world of this godforsaken, wretched, dark, dank, underground world, and if that is at all possible, then I want to do it. I want to wipe it all out, Modwyn, and I'm telling you this because I think, deep down, that's what you want too. It's what you all were put here to do—to fight this fight. Well, good for you. I'm going to give you what you want. I'm going to do what the Carnyx was apparently designed to do. I'm going to bring you war."

"What you want is not so different from what we want. We wish every dark day for deliverance, that our presence and purpose underground were not necessary, that war was not our constant reality. But this is the world we chose to enter—what else should we do?"

"It's a world that you also dragged others into—innocents like Daniel and Freya, and all the children before them. My family— generation upon generation of my family over hundreds of years, down to Alex, the youngest generation—we're all wrapped up in it as well. What reason do you have for involving us?" Vivienne asked.

Modwyn spread her hands. "This is the world we are in. The lengths we went to, the measures we took, were reasonable."

"And my brother Alex—who now styles himself Gád Gristgrennar. He looked too much into this world and became warped by it. Do you take responsibility for him?"

"We are not responsible for all the wickedness that men do."

"And yet you claim to be their salvation?"

"I make no such claim. All must do as much as they may in this world to cast a light into the darkness. And fail or succeed, Niðergeard has striven to be the brightest light."

They continued the rest of the walk in silence until they reached the ground floor of the Langtorr. Frithfroth led them across the hall and through the door beneath the tapestry.

Vivienne and Freya braced themselves for the stinging stench that was about to hit them and followed the two Niðergearders through.

"Okay, Modwyn," Freya said. "Where is it?"

"Underneath the stairs, on the far side, where they join the wall."

Freya followed Modwyn across the room, through the biers of dead knights. A few times Freya saw Modwyn's skirts catch and the regal woman awkwardly free herself. *Good*, Freya thought.

"Vivienne, I suppose you've already been to the Beacon?"

"No, I swear, I know nothing of this."

There was a stairway underneath the one that circled around

the *Slæpereshus*, which meant that they had to walk around the entire room to get to it; none were eager to walk straight through. Even in the low light Freya could see that Modwyn's eyes were streaming with tears. She wondered if it was due to the acrid air or sorrow over the lost knights.

The second stairway descended a few flights and then became a snaking tunnel with no slope. Within a few minutes, they came across a gruesome barrier. The corpses of about thirty yfelgópes were lying in a mangled heap, all at the same spot in the tunnel. The pile of their bodies nearly reached the ceiling, but the years of decay had diminished them and they now lay in a sunken, sticky heap.

"I hate this," Freya said as she tried to negotiate the morbid barrier without actually looking at it. Vivienne groaned. Her boot slipped on something nasty and she swore. "What happened to them?"

"I did," Modwyn said as she took her first step into the pile of bodies. "I ended their lives the moment they stepped across the threshold of the Langtorr. They were like tiny sparks cast from a fire that I tamped out."

Freya swallowed back bile and finally made it through the stomach-turning pile. She scuffed her boots against the ground to try to remove as much of the crud from them as possible, and made a mental note not to ever wear them again. The air started to fill with a sickening smell that they had awakened from the bodies they disturbed.

Modwyn walked beside her now and they continued in silence. After a time the tunnel ended in a room that contained a wrought iron circular staircase, which they ascended.

Freya was hit by the smell—different from the decay of death that they had just walked through; this was a living rank filth, which was more like the smell from a zoo—a human zoo.

Freya lifted her lamp higher and slowly turned around inside what she assumed was once the Beacon. Rubble and metal furniture had been piled against the walls, completely blocking any doors, windows, or other portals.

The building—or the inside of it, at least—was round and tapering to a flat roof, rather like the inside of a beehive, if it were hollow. The rubble was not confined to just the walls, but hunks of stone lay in a thick layer on the ground. Freya didn't know where it came from, at first, but shining the lamp around a little, she decided that it was the remains of the upper floors of the tall structure—floors that were not of wood and masonry, but that had once been carved from solid stone. Broken benches and twisted pieces of metal chairs added to the piles.

And there were people, littered about as randomly as the stones. Some of them were knights, some of them were the Niðergeard townspeople—the stonemasons and metalsmiths who kept the city and the knights in repair. The rest of them were yfelgópes. At first Freya thought that they were all dead, but as light poured into the room, heads swivelled toward her. And although the light was very dim to Freya, they shielded their eyes from it—knights and yfelgópes alike.

Both of these things, the sight and the smell, came to her at the same time, as did the sound. A voice was droning in low, croaky, and cracked intonations—with long, slow, and deep basso profundo notes, each of them as long as a breath.

"Where's that sound coming from?" Freya asked. "It's ghastly."

"There," Modwyn said, pointing toward the far wall, where a ragged silhouette sat in a lumpy, hairy heap, singing its dreary, dire song.

Where are the fighters; are they fled, or failed—
Where the field of battle; the fight would be brought—

The enemies and attackers do not advance anymore,
What damage their hands could do against us—
Our camp in ruins, crows eat our store,
The minds of men, barren and masterless;
Carrion carcasses carrying life, but
where has passion gone, when parted it our chests—
The fire, from our hearts, not from brands has been flung.
Why do we wait, wakeful not watchful.
Swords lie silent, will they not sing—
The fallen cry vengeance beneath victorless feet.
Arms hanging leadenly a leader unleading
He dismisses his warriors and walks all alone.
Death walks between disdaining our lives
Not worth the cost to carry our souls.

It was another obstacle course to reach the speaker, but this time Freya was trying to avoid stepping on the living, not the dead. They looked anaemic, pale and blue, with hollow expressions on their faces. They did not appear diseased or emaciated—the Niðergearders did not need to eat, after all—but looking into each one was like looking into the face of death. And each one, so Freya imagined, asked the question "Why?" As if they asked it of the universe, and she just happened to be in the way of it.

"Is that him? Is that Godmund?" Vivienne asked, squinting into the gloom, not wanting to move forward.

The grizzled hair and jutting brow were unmistakable, but his cheeks were sunken and his jaw hung slack. "Godmund. Godmund! Come on, get up. What's going on here?"

Black eyes turned toward her and shied away when she brought the lantern up.

"It's me, Freya. I came here when I was young, with Daniel. We went on a mission to destroy Gád, remember?"

Godmund didn't move or take his eyes off of her.

"We've come back. The others are bringing an army. We need you and the other survivors—" Freya looked around the room, still appalled. They didn't seem like survivors. "We need you to help us." Her words were losing their passion and conviction as she listened to what she was saying. These people were traumatised. They couldn't fight. Godmund was still staring at her, dumbly.

"The Carnyx," she said. "Why didn't you blow the Carnyx?"

Godmund made a sound that made her think that he was going to start singing again—but then she found that he was laughing.

"To save us would be to destroy us. That is as certain as the darkness. Our general has abandoned us. No, worse! He conspires against us. Our whole army, formed along a precipice, to do battle with the air. How do you fight the wind? To step forward is to perish. We are the walking fallen, still retreating, searching for a way out of the miserable reality. I have seen the hand that moves us in the darkness—a game of chess with all the pieces of one colour. A game of chance with a die that has just one side. A house on stone, but with walls of sand. What use has . . ."

Godmund continued babbling. *Egads*, thought Freya. *He's completely lost it.*

"Honourable Godmund," Vivienne broke in. "We need you to fight now. We need you to rise up and chase away the invaders of the surface world. It's . . . it's being invaded, Godmund: trolls, goblins, dragons, were-bears, ogres, all manner of sprites and hobs . . . the time has come!"

Godmund spat. "I have no honour. And neither do you."

Freya could only look down on the ancient being, who was once a brave, bullheaded warrior. Uncomplicated to a fault, if anything, he seemed, even to Freya's young mind, as the ideal general—smart and capable, but largely unquestioning of his command, which at that time had been Ealdstan and Modwyn.

"I understand the disenfranchisement, Godmund, I do," said Freya. "But please answer my question: why didn't you blow the Carnyx when you could to end all of this?"

"You have no conception of that which you ask."

"So tell us."

Godmund grimaced and bared his teeth, like a wolf defending his territory. "The curses that object will bring upon the world are too many and deep to account. The breadth of evil it would bring would be incomprehensible. It would open a hole and blow out all the goodness and hope in all the realms of this world."

"How do you know this?"

"It speaks to me. It tells me its secrets."

"Right. Okay. So . . . does that mean that it's close by?"

Godmund raised a hand and gestured to the darkness behind him. Moving the light of the lantern, Freya saw the large copper horn propped against the wall. When she had seen it last it had been securely fastened into the centre of a small fortress, a fortress that lay within the second wall of the hidden city and that was designed to keep it and it alone safe. But the brilliant copper that had once glowed like fire was now dull and dim. A black patina was spreading across it, turning to an oxidized green in many places.

"It's been here how long? Was it—did you bring it with you when you came here? When you escaped?"

"Yes, I brought it. It's been here with me this short while, and we shall grow old and crumble apart together."

"But—why just sit here?" Vivienne said. "Why not escape? Why not fight, as you have done for centuries?"

He did not reply.

"What happened, Godmund?" Freya said, her voice straining with frustration and annoyance. "Why are you so scared of fighting now?" She looked to Modwyn, to include her in the tirade. "Both of you, seriously, what happened here? What's changed?"

"Nothing changed. Nothing. Here I lie. Buried, forgotten. There is no war to fight—there's nothing to fight against. There is no evil army rising against us. We were tricked."

"What?" Freya said. "But the yfelgópes. Daniel and I found gnomes, an elf. Alex—the man who brought us back here—he's been finding trolls, dragons."

"A dragon?" Godmund said, his eyes darting to Freya with the first sign of the fire of his previous passion—anger mixed with joy—that she had seen yet. "Did *you* see the dragon?"

"No. But he did," Freya said with shaky conviction.

The fire died and Godmund's gaze became blank again.

"I don't understand," Freya said to Vivienne. "If the horn is really as bad as he says—if it's really so terrible—then why make it at all? And once it's made, why go to so much trouble to make sure no one ever uses it?"

"I do not trust his grip on reality," Vivienne said. "But we've found it now. There is no point in not using it."

"Really, Viv? I thought you would be more cautious. I thought you might want to study it, or . . . or . . ."

"Or what, indeed? Now that Modwyn is awake, and anyone is free to enter the Langtorr once more, they could easily overrun us. With no easy way out of the tower—I'm not sure how long we'd have to wait for a portal to open, or how many may enter through it when we find it—I think that we are now in very, very deep trouble. I look around and I see yfelgópes in this very room, and I think we need help. Blow the horn."

Freya was taken aback. It was unlike herself to actually minimize the danger of the situation that she was in, but Vivienne was right—they were in a tight spot.

She crossed slowly over to the horn and laid a hand on it. It felt cold and unremarkable beneath her fingers. She felt a moment of doubt.

"Seriously, Godmund," she said, turning. "What actually, tangibly happens when the horn gets blown? No more philosophy."

Godmund lowered his brow, leaned forward, and said in a quiet, gravelly voice, "Destruction. The destruction of this realm."

Freya straightened. His voice was quiet enough that she was certain no one else had heard him, and he was holding her gaze in such an even and intense manner—was he trying to communicate something else to her? Did he want her to do it?

"Good enough for me." Freya hoisted the heavy horn to her lips . . .

And blew.

II

Alex and Ecgbryt surveyed the town of Gudesberg through binoculars. They were north of the city, in a forest, their ragtag war band left behind in the mouth of the enchanted cave that had opened beneath a crevice to allow them egress.

They had not been successful in recruiting any more of the European knights to their cause since Blanik, and the Hussites were proving to be hard to integrate into the group.

"By what name did you call this land?"

"Germany. It's Germany, Ecgbryt. This is supposed to be the resting spot of Charlemagne and his knights."

"Charlemagne?"

"King Charles the Great. Or Emperor Karl."

"You mean Karolus? The *Imperator Romanum*? I thought legend said that he was waiting in a well some distance north of here—Nürnberg is its name."

"Yes, there or in Austria, or any number of other places. There are more than a few legends of mountain activity here, however, so I thought it would be worth looking into. It's said to open every seven years, but I'm not sure where . . ." He passed the binoculars to Ecgbryt.

"If it is as you say, then come the evening, it would be well to walk around the hill. Are you certain of this place? It looks a modern township."

"No, quite the opposite," Alex said. "It looks positively medieval."

"The buildings are so large. I cannot tell—all looks modern to my eye. I am often saddened that naught from my time is still to be seen. It makes me feel as if I am in a different realm than the one I was born to. Only Niðergeard feels like home."

"I think—"

"Hold! Do you hear that?" Ecgbryt swung a large arm out and smacked his palm down on Alex's chest.

"Hear what?" Alex asked, winded.

"It is a call! A summons! We must go!"

"What? Wait!"

Ecgbryt had already turned and was charging through the woods, back to the enchanted crevice in the forest. Alex tore after him, trying desperately to keep up with the knight's enormous stride.

Ecgbryt reached the entrance to the underground realms ahead of Alex and halted. Still sprinting, Alex nearly knocked into him.

"They are gone!" Ecgbryt exclaimed, stepping into the dark recess. "Retreated farther in? But what—*meotodes meahte!*"

"What? What is it?"

"Do you see? Hanging in the air, it is—is that some sort of portal?"

Alex rounded a corner and saw what appeared to be a shimmering patch of air encircling the cavern. Some sort of strange optical effect was taking place—it appeared as if the tunnel in front of them was truncated somehow—squeezed in on itself like a concertina—and also straightened. There were no winding paths, and at the end of the tunnel, he thought he could see the dim, twinkling lights of Niðergeard. He felt like he was looking down a distance of many miles—hundreds of miles if that really was Niðergeard—but that he could cross that distance in just a few steps.

It must be the Carnyx, Alex thought. *They must have found it and used it.*

"I hear the call," Ecgbryt said. "I must answer," and he stepped forward and vanished from sight.

This is it! Alex drew a deep breath, and then he too stepped over the threshold.

CHAPTER THIRTEEN

The Blowing of the Horn

-- I --

The horn emitted a low, tremulous note that reverberated in the very stones around them.

The air filled up with the sound, as if with water. Time slowed, and also sped up. Freya kept her lips on the horn as the note spread from moments to hours to days.

And all around her was still, the horn the stillest of all, fixed in the air, as immovable as a star. She was not holding it; she was *hanging* from it. Everything else revolved around Freya as slowly as the movement of the planets. She could sense time moving quickly, many hours in just one second.

And then the spell was broken. She had no more breath, and the horn ceased its call. Time and the world snapped back into its normal pace and motion. All of those in the Beacon turned to look at each other—yfelgóp and Niðergearder alike. Freya herself collapsed, the Carnyx falling atop her.

"What have you done?" Modwyn asked.

Another horn sounded, seeming small and distant. It came from outside, from the niðerplane itself.

"The next army!" Vivienne said. "Freya, quick—let's get back to the Langtorr. We can see what is happening from there."

The two women dashed out of the Beacon. No one followed them as they made their way through the pockets of dead bodies and raced up the stairs of the Langtorr, through the entry hall, and up to the guest floor. They stuck their heads out of the nearest window and looked out into the darkness. They strained their eyes but could see nothing. The horn call ended and another answered it from the left. And then another from the right. And then two more.

"Do you see them?" Freya asked. "The next army?"

They could see nothing in the blackness beyond the dim lights of Niðergeard, but they could see the effect that the horns had on the yfelgópes below—they started running in all directions, flooding out of houses, streaming into the streets, and jostling into one another. A few fights even broke out between them.

A large yfelgóp was bellowing instructions to all of those around him and arranging them into some sort of order. "That has to be Kelm," Vivienne said. "That means Daniel failed in his assassination attempt."

"I hope Daniel's okay," Freya said sadly. "I hope he'll be safe until we can find him."

Kelm was agitated but authoritative, and he shouted at any yfelgóp in hearing and swatted at any in reach. Those that stopped and fell into the ranks he was arranging twitched neurotically, as if still fighting the urge to run; they seemed ready to scatter at the slightest provocation, despite Kelm's threats and abuses. Just once, he paused in his efforts at command in order to look up at the Langtorr. Freya and Vivienne drew back slightly as he seemed to be looking straight at them. It was a measured stare that seemed to slow time once again, Freya thought. Then he turned his attention back to his immediate surroundings, the Langtorr gone from his considerations.

Shouts came from beyond the buildings. The feral cries of the yfelgópes, Freya thought, but also the cries of men.

Kelm stood with his ranked yfelgópes—there were about fifty of them before him. He stood, listening to the sounds of invisible skirmishes happening around him. Then he seemed to make a decision and gave orders for one block of his assembled army to station themselves where they were as the rest of them marched off into the darkness.

"He's going west," Vivienne said.

From the darkness ahead of them burst a line of a dozen or so knights, fully armed, the fury of battle on them. They broke into the square beneath the Langtorr, which attracted the defending yfelgópes who streamed around several buildings in an obvious attempt to ambush them.

"There's Alex!" Freya exclaimed, pointing him out.

"God save him! Look at him go!"

Alex fought confidently and viciously, swinging his large sword in wide, well-placed, deadly arcs. When he didn't have an enemy, he was shouting orders to the others and lending assistance to those who needed it. Ecgbryt fought near him, raising his axe in the air and pulling it down in devastating strikes that broke through spears, swords, shields, and skulls.

The knights made short work of them. Only about half were killed—the rest ran off when they saw the way the fight was turning. Alex shouted to the knights not to pursue but to regroup, and then they continued their sweep through the city.

But they were not the only ones fighting. In other parts of the city, Freya could see other shadows clashing.

After perhaps half an hour, the sounds of ringing steel and cries of exclamation grew less frequent. The movement of the knights slowed, and instead of swarming, they started to cluster in groups heading toward the centre of the city, toward the Langtorr.

"Is it safe to leave, do you think?" Freya asked.

"I should hope so. While the knights are still on their guard and the yfelgópes are running scared, there won't be a better time to declare our presence."

"Then let's go."

They went down the stairs and found Frithfroth, peeking through the small gap between the large iron doors. He turned a startled, rabbit-like expression up toward them as he saw them descend. Modwyn stood behind him, looking poised, ready to welcome visitors.

Freya stepped past them both and opened the door, then paused. "Wait," she said. "I forgot something." She dashed back down to the *Slæpereshus* and came back a minute later.

"Did you get what you need?" Vivienne asked.

"Yes. Shall we go?" Freya paused with one hand on the iron door and looked back at Modwyn. "Are you coming?"

Modwyn took a step forward and then stopped immediately. She was obviously torn. Without waiting for her to make up her mind, Freya pushed open the door.

"Freya! Aunt Viv!"

She looked up and saw Alex running toward her. He gripped her by the arms and then immediately hugged and kissed her, then drew back as if he couldn't believe their good fortune.

"Hello . . ." Freya said.

"We heard the horn and came as quick as we could. You wouldnae believe all the places we've been to! Would you believe we were in Germany when we heard the call? We came instantly.

I mean *instantly*! There was a sort of shimmering, telescoping, tunnelway-thing . . ." He made some vague and hurried motions with his hands. "I can't describe it. But here we are!"

"Yeah, I blew the horn and something weird happened to time," Freya explained, instantly feeling ridiculous.

"I'm so proud of my young nephew," Vivienne said. "Such a fighter! It looks as though you've liberated the city."

"Aye, and it does at that, doesn't it? But we had an easy time of it. Those yfelgópes didn't put up much of a fight. Is that all there is to it?"

"No, I don't think we're going to be that lucky. Did you run into Kelm? A big guy shouting orders? He headed off down that direction." Freya pointed across the city; more knights were making their way toward them through the darkness. How many of them were there? What were they going to do now?

"A big man, you say? I don't think so. I'll ask my lads when we regroup. In fact . . ." He turned and called over his shoulder, "Ecgbryt!'

The large knight had been instructing some of the others in how to take the heads off of the yfelgópes. He looked up at Alex's shout and saw Freya.

"Little aetheling!" he shouted and bounded toward them in long strides. He picked Freya up and squeezed her in an embrace that robbed her of air. "Vivienne!" He hugged her no less exuberantly.

"Have you run across the yfelgóp leader, Kelm?" Alex asked.

"He's very large, as tall as you, and fat," Freya said.

Ecgbryt pulled his beard and then shook his head. "I remember talk of him—he is Gád's *héreheafod*, is that so?"

"Right. He took a bunch of yfelgópes and went that way."

Ecgbryt pulled on the arm of one of the knights who had come from that direction and conferred with him for a moment.

"He hasn't been seen," Ecgbryt reported as he turned back.

"He must have fled. Remember the western well? That portal lies in just that direction." The knight's eyes wandered to the Langtorr. "My lady *richéweard*," he said with a slight bow.

Modwyn stepped out of the doorway of the Langtorr.

"*Wes ðu hale*, good Ecgbryt," she said imperiously, descending the steps in a smooth glide. Her sudden self-possession reminded Freya of when they had first met her. "Thank you for coming to aid our city. I am sorry you do not find us in better preparation for you."

"My queen!" Ecgbryt said.

"Wait, before we go into formalities, has anyone seen Daniel?"

"He is not with you?" Alex said.

"No, he left to try to kill Kelm, almost as soon as we got here. You haven't found his . . . his body? Is there somewhere that they might have locked him up?"

"Ecgbryt, help me with this," Alex said. The knights had now collected in a large group around them. There were perhaps sixty of them and they were still regrouping. They all looked different, but some shared certain peculiarities—the same shaped shield, a certain type of padded armour, a style of helmet—but no two looked alike. Some looked very much as Swiðgar and Ecgbryt had looked when they first woke up; some looked more like Freya always thought knights should look, with big triangular shields, long swords, and bright tunics worn over chain mail. Others of them, however, looked very much more basic, in simple leathers and wielding large weapons.

"You! *Tu!* Everyone, listen!" Alex yelled. "We're looking for a man, a warrior, like me, but younger and thinner, with dark hair. He may be dead, hiding, or imprisoned. Go through the city and look for him, as well as any others that might be living—enemy or ally alike. Bring them here. Ecgbryt?"

Ecgbryt shouted out the same instructions, but in a different language, and some of them relayed the instructions in several other languages, and so gradually the knights dispersed.

"Okay, good. Now, what else?" Alex said. "Did you find Ealdstan? Any sign of Gád?"

"No, we didn't but . . . we did find some things out." Freya looked to Vivienne for support and Vivienne nodded.

"We found a great deal out about Niðergeard's founder," Vivienne said. "As well as the history of this place. As noble as its original intention may be, and that of those who work here, we may assume the heart of the leader to be corrupted, and the city was led into danger and the sad state you found upon arriving. There is evidence of Ealdstan making dark alliances throughout history with the enemies of Britain, not least of which were the Nazis."

"He also sent more than Daniel and me on that bizarre mission," Freya put in. "We don't know how many children, but Modwyn has admitted that they failed—that they died—where we only barely succeeded. They tricked us all—everyone in the city was complicit in those deaths. Not just her," Freya said, pointing at Modwyn, who was still clutching her cloak at her breast where the dagger had been. "But Godmund, Frithfroth . . . and you, Ecgbryt," Freya said.

"Is this true, Ecgbryt?" Alex said, turning to him in confusion. "How much did you know about this?"

"In truth," Ecgbryt began, and then faltered. His face had grown sterner as he listened to Freya, and now he looked at her with an even, steady gaze. "In truth, I knew little then and know little more now. When we first arrived, while you slept, we were bound to secrecy by Ealdstan and by Modwyn on revealing certain knowledge to you—but we did not know, Swiðgar and I, we never knew that you were being used for any purpose other than what Ealdstan told. We had been asleep, after all."

"So, Modwyn," Freya said, her voice as dry and cold as the stones around them. "Do *you* know Ealdstan's true plans?"

Modwyn finally managed to choke out a reply. "I—I—he never revealed anything to me other than the next step to be taken. But I trust him. Although his intent may be clouded to us now, I believe it must have been good, true."

"Good enough to send children to their deaths?" Freya spat out.

All were quiet for a moment. The air around them was like dried amber; to move would have been to shatter everything.

"Alex," Freya said, turning to him. "Instruct your knights to arrest Modwyn, and find somewhere to lock her up."

"Me?" Modwyn said, horrified. "You would lock *me* away?"

"Somewhere out of the way and somewhere safe. There must be a building around here that still has walls and no secret tunnels out of it."

Modwyn was agog. Her eyes were watery and wide. *I'm the same height as her,* Freya realised just then.

"Young Freya," said Ecgbryt, reaching toward her. "I do not believe—"

Freya knocked his hand away. It was like hitting a tree branch, but the shock of the action made Ecgbryt withdraw nonetheless. "Don't! This woman has lied. She has admitted that she is complicit in murder. Her allegiance and motives are unknown and she has knowledge now of our forces and our power! She is a threat, and in order to secure this recently liberated city, I mean to have her detained until we can find out what to do with her!"

The force of Freya's response surprised even her. It was like something had opened up inside of her. Instead of a doorway back into Fear, she had found another doorway into an empowering and emboldening Strength. She felt excited, heightened, but her arms and legs were steady. This was the make or break time. If she could pull this off . . .

She looked around at everyone gathered around her, which included many of the new knights. As she spoke her last words she fixed on Alex, who looked back at her with raised eyebrows, then he looked to Vivienne.

"It's true," Vivienne said. "It would be better for Modwyn—for her own protection—if she were . . . put in a place more secure."

He thought for a moment, obviously torn, and then said, in a loud and strong voice, "Take her."

Two knights stepped forward and firmly but tenderly laid strong hands on Modwyn's slender shoulders. She looked appalled rather than angry.

"Treason," Modwyn said, rallying her wits. "This is treason. By what authority do you act?"

"I act by the authority of the hero's dragonhelm," Freya said, pulling the crown from inside her coat. It sparkled in the darkness. She held it up for all to see and then placed it on Alex's head. "The liberator of Niðergeard has the right claim to this honour."

Alex must have been very taken aback, but to his credit, he did not falter.

"I hope you know what you're doing," he muttered to Freya, barely moving his lips. To everyone else, he said in a loud voice, "I accept the burden of this rule, until such time as a true ruler may be found."

"My lord," a knight called from outside the Langtorr courtyard gates. Five knights with long beards that tapered into a single braid were approaching, and something about them was making those around them talk loudly to one another.

"Haefod," one of them said to Alex. "We have come across . . ." He paused and looked uncertain.

"Yes?" Freya said. "What have you come across? Is it Daniel?"

The knight switched to address her. "I beg pardon. We found . . . these."

He stepped aside, and those around him did likewise. And he

revealed, behind him, a group of children, between the ages, Freya guessed, of ten and thirteen.

"Um, hello," a girl at the front said. She was taller than the rest and had straight brown hair, a jutting forehead, a dark blue jumper, and black trousers. She looked uncertain and apprehensive, but it seemed as though the others deferred to her.

Freya stepped forward, and this time her legs shook; it felt as if she had taken a step into an ocean wave. "Where did you come from?" she asked.

"Um. We're not sure. I mean, we're all from somewhere, but, um, we're not sure why we're here. We seem to have been, um, summoned."

"'Summoned'? What do you mean?"

"Well, um." She looked around briefly at the other children clustering closely to her. "We heard a sound, a low sort of humming—"

"Like a tuba or something," one of the boys behind her said eagerly. He was the smallest of them all.

"Yes, like a tuba or a horn. We heard it and we sort of . . . followed it. It was calling to us, sort of *pulling* us. We went through different places, different caves, and gradually, um, met up, on the way here."

"Tell her about the voice," the small boy said to the big girl at the front.

"Um, yes. We heard a sort of voice as well."

"It was a voice inside the horn. I heard it the clearest," the small boy said.

"What did it say?" Freya asked.

"It said to us, each of us, 'You are the next army. You are summoned.'"

The eight children looked up and around at the warriors and underground ruins that towered over them.

"Do you know what that means?" the girl asked.

"Perhaps," Freya said, dread falling upon her like a dark shadow. Just when she thought she was getting a handle on things, a new wrinkle. "What are your names?" Freya asked.

"Um. My name's Gretchen. Gretchen Baker."

"I'm Fergus," said the small boy. "This is my brother Kieran." He pointed to a taller, dark-haired boy standing next to him.

"David Murray."

"Amanda McCullough."

"I'm Michael Page."

"Gemma Woodcotte."

"Jodhi. Jodhi Gale."

Freya nodded. "Okay. Everything's going to be fine, now. We're going to get you home as soon as possible, okay?"

"My lady!" called a knight from the edge of the group. "We've found the man Daniel."

"Where? Is he all right? Is he alive?"

"We cannot tell. There are dungeons here; he was locked inside one of them. We found the key and opened the door. He is sleeping, but he cannot be roused. He is in a very bad way. They are bringing him here even now."

"Okay, good. Good." Freya raised a hand to her mouth. She thought for a moment, looking around at everyone, who seemed to be waiting for her. Taking control of Niðergeard was easier than advertised, it seemed.

"Right, first things first. Get these children into the Langtorr. It's safe now. There is some food and water in the kitchen. Let them rest a little while, then I'll take them back up to the top myself. Try not to let them see Frithfroth. We don't want to freak them out too much."

She turned on Modwyn. "Now—"

"Excuse me," the girl said.

"Yes?"

"Um. What about the others?"

Freya's brow furrowed. "What others?"

"The other kids like us. The ones back out there." She motioned behind her.

"There are more of you out there?"

"Oh yes."

"We were just the ones brave enough to come here. We saw the fighting, you know, and so thought it best to wait. But the others were still scared, even though it had obviously stopped."

"How many of you are there? All together?"

"Oh." Gretchen blinked at her. "Hundreds, at least."

Freya paused to let this sink in. Hundreds? Hundreds of children *here*?

"I'll take some men to find them," Alex said. "And I'll set up regular patrols—they might still be coming."

"Good, thank you. And you three, take these children to the Langtorr anyway. And you two—take *her* to the dungeon, now that we know there is one. Lock her up. Also, a few of you—you lot, there—go over to the Beacon. Godmund is there, and I want him locked up as well. I don't think he'll give you any trouble. He doesn't seem to be hostile; I just want to keep track of him. Try not to listen to his poetry—it's appalling."

Those knights left, their duties assigned, and Alex started ordering the rest of them.

"Who will rule this place, if not Modwyn?" Ecgbryt, the only other one left in the courtyard, asked Freya as Modwyn was led away.

"Alex, of course. With a little help from you, me, and Vivienne. We'll be a sort of council," she said, just as three knights entered, carrying the body of Daniel Tully between them.

II

"Are you certain this is the place?" Ealdstan asked, placing his satchel on the ground.

"Yes," Daniel said. And he was certain. The centre of the plain pulled on him like an elastic string. Standing here, he felt at rest. What he wasn't certain about was how much he could actually trust a man whose face kept changing. Was it just him? It was like there was a fog inside his eyes. It was hard to focus.

Ealdstan raised his hands and spoke words that were ancient and powerful. The air became like static; Daniel could feel his skin prickle and he felt tightness in his body.

"What have you done?"

"I'm sorry, Daniel," the old man said, "but this is going to hurt, literally, like hell."

"No." Daniel tried to evaporate, but the rubber bands were back. "Stop it," Daniel said. "Let me go." He struggled more and more, trying to physically break free this time.

"This is what I've been searching so hard for," Ealdstan said. "If I had come here directly from our world, then I would have entered through it naturally, but I passed into Elfland through a different gate." He said more of the ancient words that were low and loud and seemed to come up from his gut.

"What are you doing to me?" Daniel tried to move but found his feet stuck fast, his legs immovable as if trapped in concrete. He found that his arms were raised now, just as if he were back in Kelm's torture chamber.

"I am sorry, Daniel, I am. It sounds as if you have been experiencing intense pain here in this world. I know naught of this Night that chases you, but I can see the marks it has left on you inside. I did not intend you this course but—well, I make no apology. You are useful to me most in your current purpose. This opportunity is too fortuitous to pass up. I will have to place the rest of my hopes on the girl. Freya."

"What does that mean?"

"That," Ealdstan said, "would take far too long to explain." He raised his hands, spoke more of the ancient words, and electricity danced from the ground to the souls of Daniel's feet. "That's not to say that I wouldn't explain—I most certainly would—but now there is no time." He bent down and picked up his satchel again.

"Ordinarily I would have to kill you at this stage," Ealdstan said. "I may be opportunistic, but not cruel. But in your state, that is impossible. You will still endure agony, though—agony I cannot imagine. For that, I do apologise, most heartfeltly."

Ealdstan stood so close that Daniel could have reached out and grabbed him if he could move his arms.

"But if you need something to help contextualise your suffering, imagine this: picture yourself as a doorstopper, propping open a gate between worlds. That is more or less your purpose now. The door wants to close, but you won't let it, and so you will be destroyed—but so also will be the door."

"Let me go."

Ealdstan really did look regretful. "No—I am sorry. I . . . Good-bye, Daniel, and thank you. Thank you for everything. I had hoped that you, perhaps—but never mind. The girl. It is the girl now."

And Ealdstan started to pass *through* Daniel—stepping into him. Daniel howled as his body's cells and molecules parted to allow him to go through. He could feel Ealdstan move through his chest, his stomach, his spine, and out the other side.

And then he was gone, and Daniel was still left, writhing in almost unendurable agony.

III

Fergus had made a friend.

Actually, he had made many friends, Kieran had noticed, but he and Rory were always at each other's side. It was as if they were tied together. Even when they were running around the weird, underground city, they were never more than a few feet apart from the other one. They scrabbled around in the rubble, pointing out interesting carvings to each other, or sifted through bent weapons and tools for things that might still be usable.

Kieran tried to keep them in view at all times—he was feeling the pressure of his brotherly responsibility acutely in this foreign place. The woman who had spoken to them all just a little while ago as they assembled in the tower's courtyard had assured them that this place was safe for now, and that everything was going to be done to get them back to where they came from, but that it would be best to stay in or around the tower for the time being.

Which some of them did, but others found it too crowded, or the city outside the walls of the tower too intriguing. The knights intrigued them, with their strange ways and language, and many of the children took to following them as they traipsed in and out of the Langtorr, or set up camp, or sharpened their weapons, or disposed of those strange little dead creatures. None of the knights spoke English, but that didn't seem to perturb the children. Fergus and Rory were clearly caught up in the adventure of it all, and tore around in banged up helmets, brandishing bent swords at each other. Kieran had told them twice to be careful and to stop what they were doing, but all he got back were reproachful looks, and then the sight of heels as they took off to escape him.

He was looking for them now, with a silver lantern that he had taken from the city. They loved running along the top of the thick walls next to that eerie throne on top of the pile of stone. He couldn't see them now, but he thought they might be hiding from him. He needed to tell them that it was time to eat. But he couldn't find them. *They must've headed back in . . .*

The interior of the building was a series of round passages, all spreading from a central, circular room. Kieran couldn't find any trace of them there, but in the central chamber, there was a tunnel that had been closed by two large, stone doorways, now broken and set aside.

It would be just like them to go exploring, Kieran thought, and started down the tunnel.

It was long and dark and he would have stopped almost immediately, except that he could see footprints in the patches of dust and grit on the ground.

He walked for about fifteen minutes. Many times he nearly turned around and went back, but he kept thinking that if Fergus and Rory really were down here, then they had to be found. And he would give them a good old proper telling-off when he did so.

But the sounds that soon met his ears—clanking, grunting, barking—came from the other end.

The tunnel opened into a massive area, as big as the plain above, except that there were huge rocky spires the size of cathedrals hanging down from the ceiling. At first he marvelled at them, and then he wondered how he could see them. They were being lit from below, but how? And where was that noise coming from?

He was on a sort of ledge. Creeping forward, he made his way to a rickety wooden frame that something was chained to—a boat? *Why would anyone need a boat down here? There's no water.*

There were bonfires. Hundreds of them. It was another encampment below the city. He saw monsters; great, big, lumbering, rock-like things, muscled men with the faces of different animals, things the size of rhinoceroses but with hairy, shaggy bodies and faces, and yfelgópes running to and fro between them, alternately feeding and abusing them. It was like a mythological menagerie, and some steel spikes that had been sunk into the ground kept all the creatures in. Around the edges, and on the other side, he saw tents and buildings—a more ordered settlement.

Did they know about this? Did the woman, Freya, know that there was what seemed to be a vicious army right beneath her feet?

If she didn't, then he had to warn them.

He turned to go but was stopped. There was a flutter of hands around his face, and the whole underground world went dark.

A Tale of a Western Isle Continued

I heard another version of the tale that ends in this way:

When Coel had finished reading the Gospels and then finished his prayer, he opened his eyes and saw the boy was still sitting before him.

"I have marked all that you have read," the boy said. "Tell me, is there any hope of forgiveness in those words for my people?"

"I am sorry to say that there is not."

"You just now read that 'there will be more rejoicing in heaven over one sinner who repents, than on a multitude who do not need to repent.'"

"Sooner would my walking stick here sprout branches and leaves than God would forgive you," Coel said and walked back to the beach where he made fire, ate, and slept.

The next morning he woke up and remembered that he had left his walking stick near the forest. He went back to retrieve it and found that it had, indeed, sprouted branches and leaves. It had, in fact, become a deeply rooted tree. At first he could not believe it, but he recognised the area around it, and he saw markings on the trunk of the tree that were only known by him from his stick.

The boy was sitting below the tree.

Coel recognised this as a true miracle and began praying for the boy's salvation and instructing him in the true path. And the boy added this knowledge to the knowledge that he'd gained from the hidden people, and he grew as great in knowledge as he did in power. And though he was born all those years ago, his days have not yet run out.

The Marriage of Modern Fantasy and Ancient Myth

A conversation between
Stephen R. Lawhead and Ross Lawhead

ROSS: So, Dad. Growing up in the household that I did, fantasy and myth were things that were literally just lying around, in novel and reference book form. Whether you were writing books with more of a fantasy slant, or a historical emphasis, they almost always contained a myth or legend touchstone—the stories of King Arthur and Robin Hood, say, or even just the feel and aesthetics of the Mabinogion. Very rarely did you ever write *just* history or *just* fantasy. Is that accurate?

STEPHEN: I think it is. I want my stories to have a heft and authority that was often lacking in most other

"sword and sorcerer" stories that were popular when
I was growing up, in high school and college, say.

ROSS: It gave them a different feel—less like you were just
making this stuff up for the heck of it, just to have fun.

STEPHEN: Well, I hope they are fun, though! I want people
to have fun. If people aren't having fun . . . but no, I like
to imagine what it was like to gather 'round the campfire and listen to the tribal storyteller—the bard—tell
the stories that are important for the community. And
these tales have survived the centuries; they've been
around a long time and seem to deserve our attention and respect. To keep them alive is a worthwhile
endeavour. Your new series is a little different in this
respect, though. There are myths and legends *in* them,
but it's not a retelling of a specific tale.

ROSS: No. When it came time to write the Ancient Earth
series and I wanted a more fluid sort of story that
actually did involve swords and sorcerers and *wasn't*
based on a specific legend, I pulled as many myth
elements as I could from lore and legends of Anglo-
Saxon England in order to put some power behind
the themes I was using and the world I was creating.

STEPHEN: I have a lot of respect for the way you have
underpinned your stories with good, solid research.
We're lucky living here in Oxford—which, they say,
has more published writers per square foot than
any other city in the world. We have easy access to
world-class museums, libraries, and the opportunity
to plug into the vast accumulated learning of the
University—which you've done, as when you learned
Anglo-Saxon English. It shows seriousness and a
commitment to the craft.

ROSS: Thanks.

STEPHEN: It's important. Having the language of these earlier times is a pathway into their culture, an ancient
culture in which men and women lived daily in what
we would call a fantasy world simply because they
didn't quite know how the world worked and were
consequently more in touch with mystery and wonder—although they wouldn't have thought of it in
those terms. It's really a short hop from that sort of academic investigation into the world of modern fantasy.

ROSS: What is your perspective on the meeting of
ancient myth and fantasy in light of your current
series? On the one hand you have a quantum-based
speculative fiction framework that lets you dip in
and out of about a dozen solidly realistic historical
settings. What mythic elements have you culled for
this science-fiction/fantasy hybrid you've developed?

STEPHEN: Really, I think what I've discovered in my
career is that the line between myth and history is
often very arbitrarily drawn, and everyone draws
that line for themselves. To go back to Arthur and
Robin Hood—are they myths or histories?

ROSS: It depends on how you view the source material.

STEPHEN: Right. Exactly right. So, for Bright Empires,
I deal with a lot of myths that are either so well
recorded, or so recent, that they are accepted as history. Myths in the making, perhaps.

ROSS: It's a line that keeps on blurring. It blew my mind
to find out that until the early to mid-1800s the
city of Troy, which is the foundation of just about
all of Western literature and poetry, was lost. Most
scholars of that period would have said that it never

existed, that it was all just an admirable fantasy. And then they found it. They actually found it and then they had to rewrite the textbooks. Literally. I loved that. I even put that incident into Book 1. It made me think: What else is still out there, waiting to be discovered? What's the next thing that will make us rethink who we are?

STEPHEN: But that's the case with all of these myths. Sometimes we might be lucky and, yes, find an entire city, but maybe sometimes, most of the time, we won't. We may never find Excalibur, or Robin Hood's bones—it may never happen. But is that any real reason to say that they didn't exist? The reasons that people wrote, or told, rather, was not just for entertainment. There was something real that they were trying to communicate.

ROSS: And that goes right back to the stories told around the campfire. Trying to answer the questions of why we're here and where we're going. Who we really are and how we can try to be better than that. No matter our culture, our religion, our philosophy, we're all still trying to figure out those fundamental questions, and history, myth, fantasy, whatever slice of the spectrum you like to take, is an essential part of that.

STEPHEN: Amen.

ANCIENT LEGEND TELLS OF AN ARMY OF
KNIGHTS THAT WILL REMAIN SLEEPING
UNTIL THE LAST DAYS.

THE KNIGHTS ARE WAKING UP.

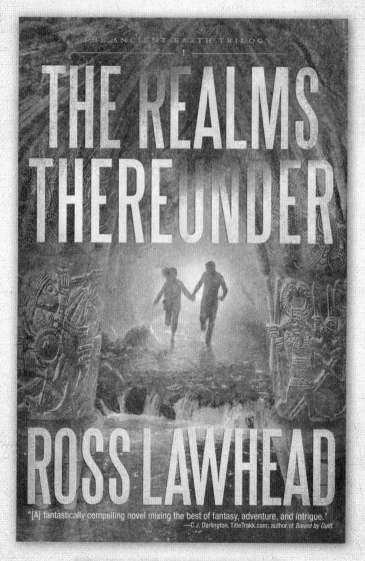

BOOK ONE IN THE ANCIENT EARTH TRILOGY
AVAILABLE IN PRINT AND E-BOOK

*Return to
Ancient Earth in*

THE FEARFUL
GATES

BOOK THREE IN THE
ANCIENT EARTH TRILOGY

Available in 2014

ENTER THE **ULTIMATE TREASURE HUNT**—

WITH A **MAP**
MADE OF **SKIN**,

A **PLAYING FIELD**
OF **ALTERNATE**
REALITITES,

AND A **PRIZE** THAT
IS THE **GREATEST**
OF ALL.

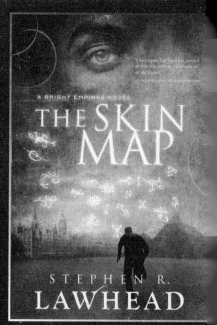

A BRIGHT EMPIRES NOVEL

THE SKIN MAP

STEPHEN R.
LAWHEAD

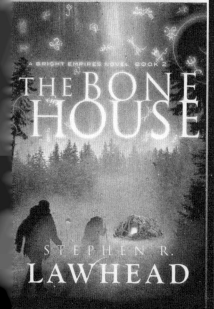

A BRIGHT EMPIRES NOVEL BOOK 2

THE BONE HOUSE

STEPHEN R.
LAWHEAD

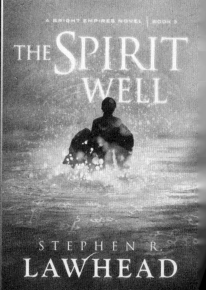

A BRIGHT EMPIRES NOVEL BOOK 3

THE SPIRIT WELL

STEPHEN R.
LAWHEAD

About the Author

Author photo by Colin Munro

Ross Lawhead was born in America but grew up in England. He studied screenplay writing at Bournemouth University before moving on to pencil the *!Hero* graphic novel and coauthor the *!Hero* novel trilogy with his father. He has also coauthored humorous books of poetry and created a theological superhero. Find him at rosslawhead.com/blog.